"I am absolutely wowe the story and craft in *Atomic Peril* and entertaining. The novel shines a bright light on the serious value of nuclear forensics. If I were still Director of the National Technical Nuclear Forensics Center, I would absolutely make this novel *mandatory* reading for every employee. I am simply blown away, and I can't wait to read Niemeyer's next book."

–**William Daitch, Director (2006-2015), National Technical Nuclear Forensics Center, Department of Homeland Security**

"A terrific nuclear thriller from a founding father of nuclear forensics. Readers who enjoyed Tom Clancy's *The Sum of All Fears* will love this book."

–**Rick Acker, bestselling suspense author**

Drawing upon his impressive and distinguished career in science and government, Sidney Niemeyer has created a fast-paced and intriguing techno-thriller. His masterful novel is a tour-de-force of nuclear forensic science that skillfully interweaves the "So what?" of what the science tells us with other key information. *Atomic Peril* gives readers an insightful peek at how decisions are made during a nuclear security event. It is a fascinating ride --- you will learn much and will not be able to put this book down!

–**Dr. Frank Wong, Former Director of Nuclear Defense Policy (2014 – 2016), National Security Council, The White House**

Sid Niemeyer is one of the pioneers of the U.S. nuclear forensics program. In *Atomic Peril*, he combines his scientifically profound insights and his long-standing experience in this field with a gripping story. The result is an exciting novel, a page-turner, that is frighteningly close to reality and a must read for fans of thoroughly researched thrillers.

–Dr. Klaus Mayer, Head of Nuclear Safeguards and Security Unit, European Commission-Joint Research Centre, Karlsruhe

Atomic Peril marries thrilling technical content with deeply personal characters. The fast-paced plot is paired with strong ties to each character and their personal journeys. The story provides stimulating insights into critical national security activities never before portrayed in popular media. The author's expertise is immediately apparent and will be greatly appreciated by any lifelong learner. This novel is a must-read!

–Stephen Hayes, Engineer, Lawrence Livermore National Laboratory

Sidney Niemeyer's novel is an accessible read on an underexposed national security topic. His characters are personable and well developed. The dialogue is believable and moves the story along at an exciting pace. This book is for the readers of Charles Cumming, Olen Steinhauer and Robert Littell, as well as anyone else looking for a good read. Excellent work, Dr. Niemeyer!

–Thomas H. Jourdan, PhD, FBI Supervisory Special Agent (Retired); now Professor of Chemistry and Professor of Forensic Science, University of Central Oklahoma

Sidney Niemeyer has created an exciting thriller that draws upon his experience working at the highest levels to develop nuclear forensics. The story breathes authenticity—from tensions between scientists and their federal sponsors to career pressures impacting personal lives. Just like actual cases, the plot unfolds step by step with each new finding. The book took me right back to the people, places, and events that my colleagues and I encountered in combating nuclear terrorism.

–David K. Smith, Senior Research Fellow, Centre for Science and Security Studies, King's College London, and former Nuclear Security Coordinator for Forensics at the International Atomic Energy Agency

ATOMIC PERIL

A NUCLEAR FORENSICS THRILLER

SIDNEY NIEMEYER

Quantum Publishing

Publisher, Copyright, and Additional Information

Atomic Peril by Sidney Niemeyer

Copyright © 2023 by Sidney Niemeyer

Quantum Publishing

This book is a work of fiction. Names, characters, places, incidents, and dialogue are products of the author's imagination or are used fictitiously and are not to be construed as real. Any resemblance to actual events or locales or persons, living or dead, is entirely coincidental.

ISBN:

979-8-9889843-0-6 *(Paperback)*
979-8-9889843-1-3 *(eBook)*
979-8-9889843-2-0 *(Audiobook)*

Cover design and interior design by CoverKitchen

ACRONYMS

AA: Alcoholics Anonymous

AG: Attorney General

aka: also known as

ASAP: As Soon As Possible

CBP: Customs and Border Protection

CIA: Central Intelligence Agency

DARPA: Defense Advanced Research Projects Agency

DC: District of Columbia

DHS: Department of Homeland Security

DNI: Director of National Intelligence

DOE: Department of Energy

FBI: Federal Bureau of Investigation

HEU: Highly Enriched Uranium

HRMU: Hazardous Materials Response Unit

IAEA: International Atomic Energy Agency

ICP-MS: Inductively Coupled Plasma Mass Spectrometer

ID: Identification Document

INMM: Institute of Nuclear Materials Management

ITWG: International Technical Working Group (Nuclear Forensics)

JAEIC: Joint Atomic Energy Intelligence Committee

JFK: John F. Kennedy International Airport

KGB: Komitet Gosudarstvennoy Bezopasnosti (Russian)

LLNL: Lawrence Livermore National Laboratory

MIT: Massachusetts Institute of Technology

NCTC: National Counterterrorism Center

NSA: National Security Agency

NSC: National Security Council

PAC-12: Pacific Athletic Conference

R&D: Research and Development

SCI: Sensitive Compartmented Information

SEM: Scanning Electron Microscope

SIGINT: Signals Intelligence

SIOC: Strategic Information & Operations Center (FBI)

SWAT: Special Weapons And Tactics

TRIGA: Training, Research, Isotopes, General Atomics (Reactor type)

PART 1: WHAT'S GOING ON?

CHAPTER 1

Livermore, California (December 12)

This morning Steven Carter arrived earlier than most of the thousands of scientists and engineers at Lawrence Livermore National Laboratory. It wasn't his usual pattern, but FBI Special Agent John Kittrick would soon arrive. Steven drove on autopilot through the winter fog into the mile-square site, passing by premier facilities where groundbreaking research took place. His mind was preoccupied with the intriguing case out of Moldova.

He parked the car and hurried to the Nuclear Chemistry Building. Little attention had been given to aesthetics in the building's design, with its simple concrete exterior and practical interior layout. For Steven, though, its superior functionality made it beautiful.

His pace quickened on the ramp leading to the back entrance as he recalled Kittrick's call two days ago. With palpable excitement, the agent had declared, "This is my most important case yet."

Steven went through the list of things to do before Kittrick arrived. As was true for most nuclear forensics investigations, the FBI was the lead agency. The FBI Laboratory lacked both the personnel and facilities to analyze nuclear materials, so the Bureau turned to the national laboratories for the needed nuclear expertise. Hence, Kittrick's visit. Though Steven's first love was research, a big part of the thrill of leading the best nuclear forensics team in the country was putting his knowledge to work on an actual investigation.

As he marched down the hallway to his office, he greeted people without slowing down. His first order of business was to get updates from his two "lieutenants." When he got to his office, a sticky note was affixed to his door. He smiled as he read it: *"In the basement—M."* As usual, Michelle Johnson had arrived before him, and often she was the last to leave the building. He dropped his briefcase next to his desk, threw his coat on the couch, and trotted down the four flights of stairs to the counting facility.

On the way, he congratulated himself once again for recruiting Michelle onto his nuclear forensics team. In a short time, she had become his trusted first lieutenant who kept his entire team operating at peak effectiveness. When he entered the radiation detector room, Michelle was talking to Chuck, the scientist responsible for the underground counting facility. She glanced at Steven, brushed back her shoulder-length hair, and smiled. "Be right with you."

She finished speaking with Chuck and then turned to Steven. "We're recalibrating the gamma detectors for the new case. Shall we find Ben now?"

She'd read Steven's mind. Ben Stefanek was Steven's second lieutenant. Michelle and Ben represented the two most essential disciplines on his nuclear forensics team. Michelle, a radiochemist, determined the abundances of radioactive isotopes, an older field with techniques similar to those used by Madame Curie a century ago to discover radium. Ben, a mass spectroscopist, represented a newer technique that measured stable and long-lived radioactive isotopes. Unfortunately, the contrast between their experimental specialties contributed to their frequent sparring.

"Is he here yet?" Steven asked.

"He promised to be in his office by now," she replied. "But I couldn't get him to pinkie swear."

Her sarcasm made Steven smile.

When they found Ben's office empty, they darted around the corner to the room that housed Ben's favorite mass spectrometer, the newest multi-collector instrument. They found Ben pulling a piece of equipment out of the electronics rack. Ben's frown deepened when he spotted them.

Michelle greeted Ben cheerfully as she walked over to him. Looking at his two lieutenants, Steven wondered if he could have picked two people who were more different. Ben was blond, blue-eyed, with an athletic build, whereas Michelle had dark hair with brown eyes and was rather petite. The contrast in personalities was also stark, and all in Michelle's favor.

"What's the problem?" Michelle asked.

Ben scowled. "The power supply for the inductively coupled plasma died."

Steven said, "If you can't get it fixed today, one of your other mass specs will do just fine."

"This one gives the best results. We better get it fixed."

Though Steven appreciated Ben's drive to produce the very best data, Ben's desire to always appear as the brightest star in the room was getting on his nerves. He sighed. "Any other problems?"

"Nothing else as far as the mass specs are concerned."

Steven turned to Michelle. "How about you?"

"The radiation detectors are good to go. The sample receival lab should be ready by the end of the day."

Steven nodded. "Everything sounds—"

Ben interrupted. "What do we know about the case?"

"Kittrick wants to give you the details himself."

As if on cue, Steven's cell phone buzzed. It was Brenda, his administrative assistant. "The Badge Office called. Kittrick's clearance documentation hasn't shown up yet, so he needs to be escorted in."

"I'll be right over to pick him up." As he dashed off, he told Michelle and Ben to meet him at his office in ten minutes.

While Steven drove to the Badge Office, he mused that this would be the first significant case he'd work with Kittrick. Earlier in the year, John became the FBI's lead investigator for nuclear forensics, at best a sideways move for him given the relatively low priority the FBI put on this new capability. He was still in his mid-forties, and like most special agents, he'd probably retire within the next decade. Steven suspected there was a backstory to Kittrick's career shift, but John seemed content with his lot. When he began his new role, he knew nothing about the science of nuclear forensics, but under Steven's tutelage, he'd made good progress up the learning curve.

John was sitting on a bench outside the Badge Office when Steven pulled up. The agent folded his slender body into the passenger seat and reached over to shake Steven's hand.

Steven said, "I'll have my admin work on getting a Lab badge for you."

John shrugged. "It's not the first time it's happened." They chatted amiably on the drive back to Nuclear Chemistry, but when they entered Steven's office and John saw the other two scientists, he snapped into FBI-agent mode.

"A week ago, the police in Cahul, Moldova, were called to a bar to break up a fight. They took three men down to the station for further questioning, but they were particularly interested in one of them: Vadim Grosu. They've long suspected he's part of a smuggling network but could never prove it, so they've kept a sharp eye on him. When they walked him into the station, one officer noticed something fall out of his pant leg. Turns out he was trying to get rid of it before they searched him."

"Not a smart move," Ben said.

Kittrick pulled a photo out of his portfolio and slapped it on the table. "This is the baggie he dropped. The police couldn't determine the nature of the black powder inside it, and Grosu refused to identify it, so the police sent it to a local university."

"Let me guess," Ben said. "It was enriched uranium."

John frowned and plowed ahead. "A geology professor identified it as uranium oxide. One of the physics professors analyzed its isotopic composition..." he paused and looked at Ben, "and determined it's highly enriched."

Ben smiled.

"To verify the results, they brought in a specialist in nuclear measurements. He determined the uranium is about eighty percent enriched, with an accuracy of ten percent." John ran his hand through his thinning hair. "Questions?"

Ben said, "So it's in the range of weapons-grade."

Michelle arched an eyebrow. "What kind of detector did the expert use?"

"High-purity germanium."

"That makes sense."

"How much uranium?" Steven asked. "Our receiving department will want to know."

"Just over one hundred grams," John replied. "The Moldova authorities will send us most of the material, but keep the baggie and about a tenth of the uranium."

Michelle tugged on her ear. "An interdiction of this much highly enriched uranium is significant but not unheard of. Why such a high priority on this case?"

"Moldova has a well-deserved reputation as a smuggling center for all kinds of goods, not just drugs. After a long interrogation, Grosu confessed he's part of a smuggling network. He claimed the network has enough of this uranium to make a nuclear bomb. According to Grosu, he took a small portion of it for a side hustle. That's why it was in a baggie. In exchange for immunity, he'll give the Moldovan authorities specific information that can lead them to the source."

"How did the U.S. get involved?" Steven asked.

John smiled. "Your efforts to promote nuclear forensics at the international level made a difference. When the Cahul police informed the Moldova federal government of their discovery, they asked our embassy for help."

Steven gave himself a virtual pat on the back. "Would you like us to do our usual suite of initial measurements? Even if we include age-dating, we'd only need to dissolve a couple grams of material."

"Moldova asked us to put a rush on our analyses. It will help them decide whether to accept Grasu's plea deal. How long will it take for the first results?"

Ben rubbed his hands together. "Within a day of getting the material, I can give you a very accurate determination of the enrichment level."

"Excellent. How much longer to complete the other initial measurements?"

Michelle said, "We should have preliminary age-dating results within a few days."

"One more thing," John said. "Even though Moldova wants quick results, make sure you follow all the standard FBI protocols."

"Got it," Steven said. The FBI put great emphasis on evidence standing up in a court of law, a part of their law-enforcement culture. This had been drilled into Steven repeatedly. In his personal opinion, he doubted evidence in court would be the top priority in a national emergency involving a nuclear weapon. But he'd learned long ago not to fight this particular battle. After all, the FBI was in charge of the investigation, and Steven had to follow their instructions.

John said, "I'll check on the status of the evidence shipment. Anything else?"

"That's all for now," Steven said. "John, you can use this meeting room as your temporary office."

At that moment, one of Michelle's fellow radiochemists rushed into the room. "Michelle, we've got a problem. I was cleaning up the sample receival lab and knocked over a bottle of acetone. A lot went down the floor drain, and the safety tech is threatening to shut down the room until a safety review is completed."

Michelle looked over at Kittrick. "Health and Safety tends to get in a dither about strong solvents."

John stopped arranging papers on the small conference table that had just become his desk. "Is this going to be a big problem?"

"We know how to deal with it," Steven said in his most assured tone. "We just need to expedite the bureaucratic review."

"Do I need a backup plan? Maybe I should call Los Alamos."

Panic caused Steven to open his mouth before he could think. "No!" he barked.

The moment the word left his mouth, Steven realized he'd come on too strong. But he couldn't let John's first important case go to his chief competitor. It could leave him out of the loop in the future. "I mean, no need to panic. We'll have everything ready when the material gets here tomorrow."

Agent Kittrick didn't look convinced. "I'll expect an update by this evening. Then I'll decide."

CHAPTER 2

Jihadist Training Camp, Afghanistan (December 14)

Malik Karimov took a deep breath of the cool nighttime desert air. He bounced sideways when his car hit a large rut in the dirt road, and the jolt brought to mind an image from that fateful night years ago. That evening began with dinner in his university apartment, prepared by his girlfriend at the time, Sina. A phone call from his hometown in Azerbaijan interrupted their meal. He recalled the feeling of dread that spread through him when his father's best friend greeted him and then said he had bad news. The next sentence was forever etched in Malik's memory.

"Malik, I'm sorry, your father was killed today, along with all your family."

Dumbfounded, hoping he was having a bad dream, he asked, "How?"

"An American drone strike where they live in Yemen."

"He should've never taken that job!" The rebuke erupted from a heart twisting in pain. His world turned surreal. Unlike his family, he was still alive, but in a more painful way, he too had died. It was like a bomb exploding in his heart. The life he had envisioned for himself—a good job, sending money back home, Sina by his side—was instantly changed.

He recalled slumping onto the floor and curling into the fetal position under the kitchen table. Sina dropped to the floor next to him and tried to comfort him. But one thought filled his mind. *The Americans need to pay.*

The seed of revenge that was planted that night was finally ready to blossom. When Malik topped a hill in this desolate corner of Afghanistan, the jihadist training camp came into view. His eyes lit up. After much sacrifice and years of plotting, tonight was the night he'd finally put his plan into motion.

Malik entered the tent of the camp's captain and gave him the letter from Raushan, Malik's powerful benefactor. The captain frowned as he read it and then looked up. "I can't imagine why you want to talk to Ahmad Abbasova, but I'll fetch him for you."

While Malik waited in an adjoining tent, he forced his breathing to slow. This step in his plan was critical, and he couldn't afford to get it wrong. He needed someone to run his operation while he kept his distance. He hoped Abbasova would prove up to the task.

A short and slight young man entered the room with a puzzled look on his face. Malik stayed seated but greeted him in flawless Azerbaijani. "I'm glad to meet you, Ahmad Abbasova."

Ahmad bowed slightly and placed his right hand over his heart.

Malik grunted and returned the gesture of respect. "What I say to you must stay in the strictest confidence. My understanding is that you are fluent in English. Is that correct?"

"Yes, my English is fairly good," Ahmad answered in careful English.

"Very good. For now, we'll talk in our native language, just in case anyone is listening." He waved his hand at a chair next to him. "I'm here to evaluate your ability to help me carry out a secret mission. Tell me about yourself."

The young jihadist began by sharing only rudimentary information about his upbringing on a farm in rural Azerbaijan. He became more animated when he talked about his university days in Azerbaijan's capital, Baku. His four years there had been the best of his unhappy life.

As Ahmad spoke, Malik's eyes locked on him. By the time Ahmad reached the end of his story, the young man was leaning back with his legs crossed. Then Malik asked him about the training camp.

Ahmad sat up straight. His eyes darted back and forth as if he suspected a trap. He first described his positive experiences at the training camp. Then he paused and cleared his throat. "My captain despises me because I'm physically weaker than the other recruits. He often ridicules me in front of the other men. Many of them laugh at me as well, or simply ignore me."

Malik pursed his lips, pleased with Ahmad's honesty. "Have you thought of quitting?"

"No way. During my university days, I became more aware of the outrageous ways the Western world has treated Muslim countries. The U.S. has been the worst. They are hypocrites who attempt to hide their imperialistic intentions behind high-sounding rhetoric. We've got to stop them."

Liking what he heard, Malik asked, "How committed are you to the cause of radical jihadism?"

"After graduating from university two years ago, I immersed myself in jihadist writings to further educate myself." Ahmad leaned forward in his chair. "I not only want to be a successful jihadist, I want to become a leader in the cause."

"If I decide you're the man for my job, I'll help you achieve your ambition."

"May I ask, why are you reaching out to me?"

Malik rubbed his forehead and shifted into a didactic tone. "I constructed a profile of the qualities I wanted. Then I drew upon my network of family and friends to identify candidates. You ended up on my short list. After investigating each person, you rose to the top."

Ahmad's jaw actually dropped. "What stood out?"

"You have many qualities that are important to me. At the top of the list, I need a trained chemist. Other aspects that stood out are your commitment to jihadism, the languages you speak, and some of your personal qualities."

The furrows in Ahmad's forehead deepened.

Malik answered the unspoken question. "Though your fellow radicals often treat you dismissively, they mistake your affability for weakness. From what I've seen so far, your drive, combined with your ability to deal with people, should enable you to recruit and lead the team you'll need to carry out my mission."

Happiness spread across Ahmad's face. "If Allah wills it!" he shouted. "When do we start? What's your plan?"

Malik moved his eyebrows up and down rapidly. He liked the young man's enthusiasm, but Ahmad's mettle was still an open question. He stared intently at Ahmad and then made up his mind. "Walk outside with me."

They left the camp and navigated by moonlight up a rocky slope. Fifty meters outside the camp's border, Malik stopped and spoke for the first time since they left the tent. "Before I give you my full approval, you must first successfully complete two tasks. Your team will build a bomb unlike any bomb jihadists have used before. I've already made arrangements through my financial sponsor to buy the key ingredient. One of your tasks will be to receive this ingredient and transport it to the place where you'll build the bomb."

"Okay. How do I contact the seller?"

"Not so fast. The other task comes first and will be more difficult. You must convince my sponsor you're the right person to lead my operational team."

"Who is he?"

"My benefactor is a very rich and powerful man. You must treat him with great respect, and above all, do not show curiosity about him. You will know him only by the code name Raushan, for he is indeed an exalted one in our fight against the imperialists."

A tremor passed through Ahmad. "How will Raushan evaluate me? It would help if I knew more about your plan."

"At the very moment the Americans commemorate the next anniversary of 9/11, I will cripple the imperialists' ability to meddle in Middle Eastern affairs."

Ahmad's eyes gleamed in the moonlight.

Malik wondered if his own passion had prompted him to say too much. His eyes closed to mere slits. "At this point, it's better for you to know nothing more."

He removed an envelope from his inner coat pocket. "This letter will authenticate you with Raushan. If you fail his test, because you know so little, he'll probably let you leave alive."

Ahmad shivered and stopped breathing for a moment. Then he took a deep breath. "What shall I call you? And how will we communicate?"

Snorting softly, Malik said, "You're full of questions, aren't you?"

Ahmad looked down. "I'm sorry."

"That will serve you well if you get to the operational phase. For now..." He extended his right hand toward Ahmad with his palm up, then bunched his fingertips together and moved them up and down. "Patience. You can call me Uncle, and I'll call you Nephew. If you gain Raushan's approval, I'll set up a meeting with you to lay out the plan."

Shuffling his feet in the dirt, Ahmad was silent.

Removing another envelope from his coat pocket, Malik said, "I've reserved a hotel room for you. Wait there until Raushan contacts you."

Ahmad squinted in the dim blue light of the moon as he attempted to read the name of the hotel inscribed on the envelope.

"And remember, Ahmad, don't show any curiosity about Raushan's identity. Have your wits about you, because he has rather strange ways of evaluating people."

CHAPTER 3

Berkeley, California (December 14)

Steven strode through the colorful array of characters spread across Sproul Plaza at the University of California campus in Berkeley. Students were chattering with friends, debating loudly, or taking in the sun on the steps of the administration building. Musicians competed for attention, and hangers-on from as far back as the 1970s mingled with the crowd. Going to Berkeley was like entering a different world, only forty-five minutes from the Lab. The *Nuclear Free Zone* signs posted at the city limits helped make the point.

As Steven approached the Social Sciences Building, he spotted Professor Robinson at the entrance. Months ago, the professor arranged for Steven to talk to his *Politics and Science* class about the difficulties in establishing a new program in the federal government. When the Moldova case came up, Steven thought he'd need to cancel. But the Moldovan authorities hadn't appreciated the complexities of shipping highly enriched uranium, and the evidence was delayed. Though disappointed at first, he welcomed the opportunity to engage with students.

Professor Robinson stepped forward and shook Steven's hand. "I should warn you that some of my students have strong feelings about a scientist who works at a nuclear weapons lab. Truth be told, I share their concern. It will be interesting to see if you can win us over."

Drawing himself up to his full six feet two inches, Steven said, "In the years I've promoted nuclear forensics in Washington, DC, I've experienced plenty of pushback."

The professor ushered Steven into his classroom and introduced him to the students in a positive, albeit perfunctory, manner. "Dr. Steven Carter received his doctorate in nuclear engineering at MIT. During his postdoc at Lawrence Livermore National Laboratory, he was introduced to the field of nuclear forensics. When he became a staff member at the Lab, he dedicated his career to developing the science of nuclear forensics. In time, he was also drawn into policy debates about the role of nuclear forensics within the broader framework of nuclear security. Today he is recognized nationally and internationally as one of the leaders in this field."

Professor Robinson paused to start a PowerPoint slideshow provided by Steven. Reading from the first slide, he said, "In cases involving illicit nuclear materials, nuclear forensics scientists make measurements on the material in order to answer such questions as: How was this material made? Where did it come from? When was it diverted from legitimate possession? The answers to those questions have political implications, especially when weapons-grade nuclear materials are involved."

Turning to Steven, the professor said, "Dr. Carter, the floor is all yours."

Steven scanned the audience as he stood at the front of the room. Some of the graduate students were leaning forward, but others were frowning, their arms crossed. He began by setting the historical context. "After the end of the Cold War, Lawrence Livermore was the first national lab to recognize the importance of a new threat. In contrast to thousands of nuclear bombs mounted on missiles raining down on our country, scientists at the Lab began to consider the threat of a single nuclear weapon covertly brought into our country and detonated on our soil. The impact on our society would be immense.

We developed nuclear forensics to determine the origin of a nuclear device and thereby help point the finger at the culprits."

A student uncrossed his arms and raised his hand. "Was that your only motivation? Or were you looking for a new program because your old weapons program was on the decline?"

Steven bobbed his head knowingly. "In the early days, many people in Washington made the same argument. It's a fair question. It's true the Lab at that time was looking for new applications for the capabilities it had developed during the Cold War. But the impetus for developing nuclear forensics was based on a genuine belief that it should play an important role in nuclear deterrence."

A quizzical look appeared on the professor's face. "It seems to me few policymakers share your view."

Steven snorted. "Frankly, the government sees nuclear forensics as a nice-to-have capability. Not a must-have."

"So why do you see it so differently?" the professor asked.

"From what I've observed in Washington, policymakers are slow to respond to new realities in the world."

A ripple of laughter swept the room. Steven was momentarily perplexed until he realized he'd lost the students' attention. Two interlopers stood just inside the room's doorway, holding up signs. One read *Outlaw All Nuclear Weapons* and the other said *MORE Health & Education—NOT MORE Bombs!*

The two protesters shouted the slogans on their signs. The professor gave a little wave and they left. Wondering if the professor had arranged the interruption to test his mettle, Steven regained his composure and said, "Every year on Good Friday, we have protesters at the Lab carrying similar signs. I appreciate their sincerity. But shouting slogans is easier than providing cogent responses to complex issues."

"Why not outlaw all nuclear weapons?" a young woman in the front row asked.

"Envision a world where that unlikely outcome has been achieved," Steven said. "In that case, it would be extremely advantageous for one nation to secretly develop just one nuclear weapon. Unfortunately, you can't put the nuclear genie back in the bottle."

Another student raised his hand. "Maybe a country could do that, but is it credible that a terrorist could build a nuclear weapon?"

"Good question. Without getting into the technical details, let me say it's fairly credible if a terrorist has a strong technical background. The principle of a gun-assembly device is widely known. In this design, two or more pieces of fissionable material are brought together very rapidly using conventional explosives to form what we call a critical mass. The critical mass is the amount of fissionable material that's needed to create a nuclear explosion. For technical reasons, this type of device uses highly enriched uranium, which is by far the most widely available type of fissionable material."

A woman in the back row raised her hand. "How do you get involved in cases?"

"I have to wait until somebody in the federal government gives us evidence to analyze. Most often it's the FBI. And that brings me to an important question. What if an interdiction of a small amount of fissionable material is the only clue that a dangerous nuclear threat is underway? I believe it's crucial to investigate every case of illicit nuclear materials until we are sure it doesn't point to a significant threat."

A different student raised his hand. Steven had noticed him following along closely, nodding when Steven made his points. "Could you describe for us just how damaging one nuclear bomb could be?" The student looked around at his classmates, a knowing smile on his face.

Steven guessed the student was one of the few majoring in science. "Let's consider the case of Hiroshima. That device had a yield of fifteen kilotons. Imagine a truck loaded with three tons of conventional explosives, similar to the one used in the Oklahoma City bombing that killed one-hundred-sixty-eight people and destroyed much of a federal building. Put five *thousand* of those trucks in one place in New York City and detonate them. That gives you some idea of the damage such a bomb would do."

Around the room, heads shook in disbelief. Steven understood the difficulty in wrapping their heads around such a staggering picture. Though he could readily calculate the yield of a nuclear weapon, it was merely a number that was hard to relate to everyday experience.

He waited while spinning minds grappled with the comparison. "Beyond the sheer magnitude of the explosive force of a nuclear detonation, there are other significant differences between a nuclear and conventional bomb. In a nuclear explosion, the causes of death are blast from the shock wave, thermal radiation, and nuclear radiation. The casualty data from Hiroshima and Nagasaki indicate that only about ten percent died from radiation. The extremely strong shock wave and very high temperature caused most of the deaths close to ground zero."

Steven grabbed the remote control and brought up the next slide. "On this map of New York City, I show two circles centered on Manhattan. The smaller circle has a radius of six-tenths of a mile, and in a nuclear detonation like Hiroshima, about eighty percent of the people within this circle will die. The larger circle extends to one-point-six miles, and about one-third of the people will die within this outer zone."

The students contemplated the diagram, imagining the extent of the carnage. A woman who had been doodling in her notebook raised her hand. "In your scenario, how many people would die?"

"Are you by any chance from New York?" Steven asked.

"Yeah, my accent gives me away."

"During working hours when the population density is highest, I estimate the total number of casualties would be well over two-hundred-thousand people."

The room became very quiet. Everyone's eyes were fixed on Steven. He let the silence linger.

The New York woman asked, "What about the radiation fallout?"

"The fallout would pose an enormous problem. Clean-up crews would be exposed to an enormous radiation dose. The area near ground zero would be uninhabitable for years. Just imagine if it detonated on Wall Street."

The professor spoke up again, his skepticism giving way to curiosity. "We'd like to hear what you actually do in a nuclear forensics investigation."

"I'll illustrate that by talking about an early case that became the best-known example of a nuclear forensics investigation." Steven brought up the first slide of a series that presented the results for a case involving a seizure of highly enriched uranium in Romania. He walked the students through the nuclear forensics investigation. Near the end, he mentioned that Russia was the most likely source of the HEU.

A voice with a thick accent interrupted. "Why you always blame Russia?"

"Are you from Russia?"

"No," the student replied, "former Soviet Union country, Belarus."

"We don't automatically assume illicit nuclear materials are from Russia. But here's the reality. Russia produced massive amounts of special nuclear materials. And Russia had minimal inventory control. Moreover, after the dissolution of the former Soviet Union, many facilities were poorly protected from theft. That's why illicit nuclear materials often come from the former Soviet Union."

"Do you interact with scientists from former Soviet Union?"

"Yes, quite a few through my work on the ITWG."

The student looked puzzled.

"I'm sorry," Steven said. "ITWG stands for the International Technical Working Group. It's an informal organization where scientists and law enforcement officers collaborate on the development and implementation of nuclear forensics."

The student who had asked the very first question raised his hand again. In contrast to his early pugnacity, his voice now hinted at admiration. "I liked the way you developed the clues for that Romania case. You're kind of a CSI for nukes."

Fighting to suppress a groan, Steven said, "Have you heard of the CSI syndrome? The CSI TV shows are wildly popular, but they paint an exaggerated and misleading picture regarding the precision and speed of forensic interpretation. This misleading portrayal has caused difficulties in real-world court cases because jurors expect a higher standard of forensic evidence than is usually possible. I've encountered the same difficulty in talking to policy people about nuclear forensics, because they assume it involves matching our measurements to a nuclear fingerprint. Sorry to get on my soapbox, but nuclear forensics is much more complex and difficult than the general public assumes."

An hour later, after a wide-ranging discussion, the seminar ended with the students giving Steven a round of applause. While saying goodbye to Professor Robinson, the professor said, "You strike me as a remarkably persistent man. Some might even call you stubborn."

Steven laughed. "That's what my wife says too. The stubborn part."

On the drive home, Steven replayed the seminar, taking note of where he could have done better. He smiled again, ruefully, when he recalled the professor's parting comment. Steven *was* stubborn. When he ran into a brick wall, he usually backed up and then ran at it a little harder. Unfortunately, the U.S. government still viewed nuclear forensics as a nice-to-have, but Steven was more convinced than ever it was a key to deterring nuclear terrorism.

His mind drifted to the only picture hanging on the wall of his lab office. A photograph of the horrific damage caused by the bomb dropped on Hiroshima. Only crumpled buildings and rubble are visible, but Steven knew that if the photographer had taken the picture immediately after the explosion, the picture would show thousands of bodies, incinerated beyond recognition. His goal was to help stop such a nuclear blast from ever happening again. The picture on his wall reminded him daily.

His phone pinged. He risked a glance and saw it was a text message from John. *Material due to arrive tomorrow.*

CHAPTER 4

The Lab (December 17)

On Thursday evening, the Moldova HEU arrived at the San Francisco airport, two days late. By that time, Steven had resolved the safety issue in the sample receival lab. Kittrick was happy, until the Lab's Shipping & Receiving Department claimed they couldn't finish processing the material by the weekend. Steven raised havoc up to the highest level of Shipping & Receiving. When that proved futile, he appealed to his Associate Director. Eventually, the added pressure worked, and Steven's team got their hands on the material by close-of-business Friday.

Frustrated by the additional delay, Steven ordered his team to work over the weekend. On Saturday morning, Michelle scooped out several grams of the uranium powder, while seven other scientists and John Kittrick watched. She shook her head as some of the powder flew off the metal spatula. "Darn electrostatic charging," she said. "We need to be careful handling the sample. It's very fine-grained."

Michelle thoroughly mixed the powder and then took a sub-sample for each experimental team. Two hours later, Steven and John headed down to the scanning electron microscope lab to examine the first experimental results. The SEM expert showed them her best image. The particles were no larger than one micron, and in the expert's opinion, most particles were actually clumps of smaller particles.

Steven asked, "Have you done any x-ray analysis yet?"

"So far, we've found only uranium oxide."

John said, "That confirms the finding of the Moldovan scientists."

"Once you finish analyzing this mount," Steven said, "I'd like you to do at least three more this weekend. And keep an eye out for anything unusual."

Over the rest of the day, Steven and John periodically visited the various scientists to track their progress. Of greatest interest to Steven was the mass spectrometry results, but the second time he stuck his head into Ben's lab, Ben irritably told him he'd call when he had something.

Late in the afternoon, Ben phoned. Steven rushed down to Ben's lab, John trailing behind. When Steven entered the room, the whir of the vacuum pumps provided a background noise that he found oddly comforting. He had spent many years in this same instrument lab.

Ben was perched in front of the computer that controlled the mass spectrometer. Its housing hid the mass spectrometer, except for the inlet system, where the sample solution was drawn up into a tube and injected into the inductively coupled plasma. The six-thousand-degree temperature of the plasma converted the solution into ions, which were then accelerated to eight-thousand volts and directed into the high-vacuum mass spectrometer.

Pointing to the computer screen, Ben said, "I'm only half an hour into this first analysis, but I've already got great data."

Steven peered at the output. The uranium-238 to uranium-235 ratio had already been determined with an accuracy of 0.1%.

Ben continued, "The enrichment level is 72.8%."

John gestured toward the instrument, which occupied a footprint of about eight feet by four feet. "How do you get such precise ratios so quickly?"

"It's pretty complicated," Steven said, "but the key is the multi-collector system. A separate Faraday cup collects the ion beam for each mass. We can move these cups to match the exact position of each ion beam. If you're here sometime when we have the machine apart, I'll show it to you."

"I'd like that. Now, about this Moldova sample, its enrichment is a lot lower than what the U.S. uses in its nuclear arsenal. Could you still make a functional device with it?"

"If you have enough of it, you could," Steven said. "But since the enrichment is much lower, the yield would also be lower."

John nodded and jotted down a note.

"Did you notice how high the uranium-236 is?" Ben said. "It's coming in at almost 12%." He glanced at John and added, "As you know, uranium-236 is a man-made isotope that's produced by uranium-235 capturing a neutron. The logical conclusion is that this uranium was irradiated in a nuclear reactor for quite a long time."

Ever since Ben announced the enrichment level, Steven's mind had been whirling. It was the same enrichment he'd measured years ago for the HEU seized in Romania. Before he could comment, Ben continued, "The isotopic composition reminds me of the Romanian sample."

John tapped his notepad with a pen, a quizzical look on his face.

Steven asked, "Do you have a question, John?"

"Not so much a question. More a concern. I've read up on the Romanian case. Originally, the Bureau was concerned that a significant quantity of this highly enriched uranium had been lost from legitimate control. Then several years later, HEU was interdicted in Nice, France, and it had virtually the same characteristics as the Romanian HEU. In this second case, the suspects claimed to have access to many kilograms of HEU. But nothing ever came of it."

Keeping a poker face, the muscles in Steven's neck tightened. Was John warning him that the FBI might take this case lightly? Even though the previous cases hadn't developed into something far more serious, it didn't mean that was true in this instance.

Steven sighed. "Let's get more data before we start interpreting. We've barely begun."

CHAPTER 5

The Lab (December 20)

Steven was proud of the progress his team had made in the past couple days. He hoped John would feel the same by the end of the upcoming review meeting. Originally, Steven had planned to invite all the scientists on his nuclear forensics team to this review. But he reconsidered and included only his two lieutenants. Ben might be less inclined to preen with a smaller audience, making for a more productive meeting.

Steven gathered the papers scattered across his desk and walked over to John's temporary office. Michelle was asking John about his Christmas plans, while Ben sat stone-faced, a coffee mug in his hand.

Steven said, "I brought in another Keurig from home. Okay if we set it up here, John?"

"Great idea," John said.

When the Keurig finished dispensing coffee, the agent took a tentative sip, offered an "mmm," and took a bigger swallow. "That hits the spot."

Ben put down his coffee mug. "I can get us started."

Steven resisted rolling his eyes. "I'd rather begin with Michelle. John hasn't seen any radiochemical data yet."

Grimacing, Ben replied, "If you insist."

Michelle handed out a packet of materials. "At this point, we've only completed about half of our radiochemical separations. The results for fifteen isotopes are shown on the first page. The first thing to notice is that the fission products are quite low. This implies that the chemical purification after the uranium was irradiated in the reactor was very effective. For example, using the cesium-137 abundance, we estimate an extraction factor of one million." She then commented on each of the other isotopes, including the hint of a small amount of plutonium.

"You got good results for thorium-230," Steven said. "What age did you get?" This was Steven's primary interest in the early radiochemical results. Time and again, age had proved to be a powerful clue in determining the origin of a nuclear material. In this case, the chemical purification step reset the radiometric clock.

Smiling, Michelle said, "Turn to the second page. We calculate a uranium-234 thorium-230 age of 11.5 years. With an uncertainty of about six months."

"In a couple days," Ben said, "I'll have my mass-spec results for thorium-230. My uncertainty should be about six times smaller."

Steven glared at Ben. Everybody in the room knew Ben's smaller uncertainties were due to the nature of the two techniques. Well, everybody except possibly John.

Before anyone else could comment, Steven said, "That means this Moldovan HEU was reprocessed six years after the Romanian material. So that's one clear difference between the two."

John said, "Usually you show results for more than one radiometric clock. How sure are you about this age?"

"You're right," Michelle said. "Whenever possible, we measure more than one clock in order to check whether the age-dating assumptions hold up for the sample. In a week or so, we'll have data for several clocks, and then I'll be more confident it's a true age."

Steven added, "In the past we've found the uranium-thorium clock is quite reliable for this type of material. Of course, as Michelle said, we'll confirm with additional clocks."

"Okay," Michelle said, "your turn, Ben."

Ben began by presenting the final results for the uranium isotopic composition. The values for the composition hadn't changed significantly compared to the earliest results, but the errors were smaller.

He then focused on comparing it to the Romania and Nice cases.

"Within the uncertainties, the uranium-235 enrichments for the three cases are identical. The other uranium isotopic abundances also agree within error, except for uranium-236. It's 0.4% lower for the Moldovan HEU. Given our small errors, that's another clear difference."

Michelle responded first. "How would you interpret that?"

"Most likely, they all came from the same type of reactor, but the uranium-236 abundances vary because the samples came from different production runs."

"Anything new from your direct reports?" Steven asked.

"The trace elements we've measured so far are fairly similar for the three samples, with one notable difference. The iron abundance in the Moldovan HEU is quite a bit higher. Right now, I don't know whether or not that's significant."

John asked, "In your opinion, what differences are significant?"

"I'll take a crack at that," Steven said. "As I already stated, six years separate the time of chemical purification. And as Ben just showed, the uranium-236 level is different. Both of those findings indicate these materials were not from the same batch of fuel."

"And don't ignore the obvious differences," Michelle added. "In both the Romanian and Nice interdictions, the uranium powder was in a glass vial and hidden inside a lead container. Quite different from HEU in a baggie. Plus, the baggie contained about ten times more material than in the previous two cases."

John nodded. "Okay, some differences, but mostly minor. Here's a question my management will probably ask me: Do you have evidence that large quantities of HEU are on the loose? How would you answer that question?"

Steven replied, "As we both know, technical data alone is unlikely to give evidence that a large amount of HEU has been diverted from legitimate control. I'd emphasize that once we know the source of the HEU, we can better assess the likelihood that a large amount was diverted. Here's another point to make—the interdiction of a small sample may be a tip-off that a larger amount is up for grabs."

John gave a closed-mouth growl, which came out as a muffled "huh." By now, Steven recognized it as John's signal that he was irritated or disappointed.

"Here's what I've heard from my boss," John said. "In the previous cases, you suggested the HEU in the glass vial was actually an archival sample taken for quality control. Such a sample would be relatively easy to steal. My boss bought that scenario. He also points out that in the Nice case, the suspect said he had access to much larger amounts of HEU, yet nothing ever came of it. My boss believes that the claim to have more HEU was false in the Nice case, and it's also a lie in this Moldova case."

"Perhaps," Steven said, "but here's an alternative. The facility with the archival samples also contains a stockpile of the same HEU material. We can reasonably infer this facility was not well-guarded, because a bunch of archival samples were diverted. So somebody with ongoing access to a large stockpile of HEU might have diverted kilograms of it."

"Perhaps, but here's a different scenario," John said drily, indicating he was deliberately mimicking Steven. "A potential buyer challenged this Moldova smuggler to prove he had access to a much larger amount of HEU. So, the smuggler emptied ten archival samples into a baggie. That would convince many buyers."

"Of course, I can't rule out that scenario." Steven took a deep breath. "Here's my plea. Even if it's not all that likely that tens of kilograms of HEU are on the black market, the potential consequences of such a large amount on the loose means we should keep investigating until we fully resolve the matter."

John's eyes narrowed. "Anything else?"

Steven noticed the set of the agent's jaw and figured the time for arguing was over. At least for today. He said, "Not at this time."

"One more thing," John said, running his hands through his hair. "The Director of the FBI Laboratory is pressing me for a report. Because you've made such excellent progress, I plan to get it to him no later than next week Friday."

Disappointment coursed through Steven. "That soon? We're just getting started."

"Tomorrow I head back to DC for Christmas. Next week, send me an update at close-of-business each day."

The request was disconcerting, but Steven said nothing.

When they left John's office, Steven motioned for his two lieutenants to follow him. He shut his office door and said, "How that meeting ended made me nervous."

Ben said, "Do you think the FBI will stop the investigation after they get the report next week?"

"The way John talked today, that's exactly what has me worried."

"We can't possibly finish everything by then," Michelle said.

Steven's lips tightened. "We'll do our best. Which means working throughout the Christmas break."

Ben said, "I expect you to remember this come pay raise time."

Michelle rolled her eyes.

Ignoring Ben's comment, Steven said, "But we'll take off Christmas Day."

CHAPTER 6

Kabul, Afghanistan (December 22)

Ahmad fretted in his hotel room for two days before Raushan's men picked him up. They put a hood over his head and drove to a secret location. Ahmad tried to strike up a conversation and received only a grunt in reply. Based on the fading sound of traffic in the early evening, Ahmad guessed they had come to the outskirts of Kabul. Eventually, the car stopped and one of the men pulled him out and led him forward. The slight echo of their footsteps suggested an empty room. In the silence, Ahmad's anxiety spiked even higher.

He heard the sound of fumbling, and then another door opened. A rush of warm air carried with it the scent of incense and a more subtle smell he couldn't place. His taciturn guide pushed him into the room and, without warning, jerked off his hood.

"Don't turn around," his guide said. "Stand here and wait." The man left through the same door they'd entered.

As Ahmad's eyes adjusted to the sudden light, he took in the richly decorated room. A tapestry of an Ottoman battle scene covered most of the wall in front of him. Paintings, all of them elaborately framed, covered another. His attention turned to another wall, bare except for an ornate desk made of exotic woods. He peered at two piles of paper on top of the desk. Why would they leave those papers out?

After several minutes passed, he wondered if Raushan would ever appear. Surely it wouldn't matter if he strolled by the desk and took a glance. He wouldn't touch the papers. He started to take a step toward the desk, but suddenly stopped. Uncle had warned that Raushan was very sensitive about his identity. "Show no curiosity" was Uncle's specific command.

Ahmad settled back into the stance he'd held since his escort yanked off his hood. He shifted his weight from one foot to the other on the tile floor, but otherwise remained stationary. His ragged breathing and the chirping of crickets outside marked the slow passing of time.

His head jerked involuntarily at the sound of a low chuckle emanating from behind the tapestry. A disembodied voice spoke. "You've passed the first part of your test."

Perplexed, Ahmad replayed the hidden man's declaration. Oh, he must be Raushan! Ahmad breathed a sigh of relief that Raushan couldn't read minds.

The deep voice said, "Let me welcome you with some tea."

Immediately, the door to Ahmad's right opened, and a large, heavily muscled man entered, carrying a teapot and two cups. As Ahmad drew in the rich aroma of the exquisite tea, he realized it was the source of the faint smell he'd previously detected but couldn't identify.

The man glided across the room and set the tea tray on the desk. He poured the steaming liquid into the two cups and took one to Raushan behind the tapestry. Ahmad surmised the tapestry hid the room's third door. Raushan must be sitting in an adjoining room, watching and evaluating.

The server brought the second cup over to Ahmad. The man stumbled just as he handed the cup to him. Scalding hot tea splashed onto Ahmad's chest and arm. Ahmad jerked away, stifling his gasp of pain. He flashed with anger at the man's clumsiness. In the next instant, he reconsidered. This hulking man would look more at home handling a machine gun than a teacup, but the graceful way he moved across the room did not suggest a clumsy person.

The tea server didn't seem flustered, nor did he try to help Ahmad. Then it hit Ahmad—this must be part of the test.

Ahmad mustered an impassive look on his face, despite his throbbing pain. He knelt to pick up the cup, which surprisingly was only chipped. He straightened up and looked inside the cup. Forcing a bemused look on his face, he lifted the cup to his lips and swallowed the spoonful of remaining tea. "Delicious! If I may be so bold, my kind host, may I have a second cup?"

Laughter erupted from behind the tapestry. "Very good, Ahmad. By all means, have a second cup." The deep voice continued. "As you've no doubt concluded, I am Raushan. I have only one question. It's not about your technical competency. I trust Uncle's judgment in that area. Your character is my concern. You appear to be a sincere Muslim. So this is my question. Is there anything in your past that would embarrass a good Muslim?"

Ahmad took a few moments to review his life. Better to err on the side of caution and bring up anything Raushan might deem embarrassing. He coughed and said, "I once got in trouble at school. One of the bigger boys wouldn't leave me alone. At first he called me names and taunted me. Then he began taking my lunch. When I didn't fight back, he became physical. Pushing and shoving escalated to beatings. One day I became so angry, I overcame my fear and set up a trap. I dug a hole in the ground, filled it with sheep dung, and then covered it up. The next day, I called the bully a name. When he chased me, I ran around my trap in a way that caused him to run right over it. He fell into the hole and began screaming. At first I thought it was funny, imagining him covered in dung. Then I realized he was screaming in pain. His leg was broken, a rather nasty fracture that required surgery."

Raushan said, "For a boy who would later aspire to be a radical jihadist, that doesn't seem so bad."

Encouraged by Raushan's comment, Ahmad added, "He was so mean, I was glad he suffered. In fact, I wished he would've broken both legs."

"Uncle told you he's made arrangements to buy the special ingredient you'll need. One person in the operation made a grave error. He tried to freelance and run a scam on the side. We cannot tolerate the security risk he poses. The final part of your test is to kill this man. Will you do that?"

Ahmad straightened, pulled back his shoulders, and raised himself to his full five feet six inches. "I will not fail you, Raushan."

Raushan grunted. "Failure is not an option."

A long silence ensued. Ahmad decided he should not be the one to break it.

The tenor of Raushan's voice shifted from interviewer to compatriot. "Here's the glorious mission that begins today for you."

Ahmad's nervousness turned into exhilaration. *I passed! At least so far.* Before he could stop himself, he blurted, "I can never thank you enough for this honor!" Drawing upon the meaning of Raushan's adopted name, Ahmad added, "I'm not worthy, oh exalted one."

"You're right to call me exalted." Raushan's voice rose in volume, shifting into the triumphant tone of a king's herald. "But there is another reason I am called Raushan. My name also means bright light. A bright light will appear in the sky over the heads of our enemies to announce the success of our mission. Seconds later, a giant cloud will take shape and rise into the heavens, marking the place of destruction and horror. You, Ahmad Abbasova, will lead the team that will build a nuclear bomb."

CHAPTER 7

Danville, California (December 22)

After Steven dropped his briefcase in his home office, his wife stuck her head out of their bedroom to tell him she needed fifteen more minutes. Carissa pointed to the family room and said, "Use the time to catch up with the boys."

Rounding the corner to the family room, Steven spotted his older son, Josh, playing a video game. He plopped down on the couch and asked, "How goes it?"

"Christmas break came just in time," Josh said. "My senioritis was getting bad."

"What did you do today?"

"Not much. Sure looking forward to skiing in Tahoe next week."

Steven's heart sank a little. Carissa needed to hear the bad news first, so he changed the subject. "Just imagine, a year from now, you'll have completed your first semester at college."

"And it'll be my first year sitting in the student section at Cal football games." His son was determined to go to Berkeley.

"After ten years of going to games together," Steven said, "it'll be strange cheering for the Bears without you sitting next to me." They commiserated about Cal's losing record this season and then analyzed the recruiting class for next year.

While they talked, his younger son, Jacob, watched TV on the other side of the room. Jacob didn't glance at Steven, not even once.

Steven found it much more difficult to relate to him. They had few common interests. Jacob didn't care for sports, nor did he have a scientific bent, gravitating instead to music and literature. And unlike his extroverted parents, he was extremely introverted.

Steven walked over to Jacob and sat in the nearest chair. Jacob continued to studiously watch his program. Finally, Steven said, "Hi, Jacob."

Jacob merely grunted and kept watching his show.

"What're you watching?" Steven said.

"Stuff."

"One of your favorites?"

"Does it matter?" Jacob kept his eyes on the TV.

"How did your day go?"

"You don't need to pretend to be interested."

Steven couldn't think of a response that wouldn't lead to an argument. *Oh, Jacob, I wish I knew how to reach you.*

Carissa rescued him by coming into the room. Her sweater top and tight jeans accentuated the curves of her well-toned body. She was a better athlete than him, and it showed.

"Let's go," she said.

After he started the car and backed down the driveway, Steven said, "I'm sorry it's taken me this long to go shopping." He had bought nothing yet for Carissa, so they were headed to the mall. During their first decade of marriage, they'd developed a rather odd approach to Christmas shopping that took into account his inability to pick out good gifts for her and her desire for an element of surprise. Together, they would visit her favorite stores and she would point out a half-dozen items that appealed to her. Then they'd go their separate ways so he could double-back and decide which ones to buy.

She laughed and said, "Better than last year. It's still a whole two days before Christmas Eve."

Halfway to the mall, he broached the subject he'd avoided the past couple days. "About this case I'm working on—"

"Uh-oh," she said. After twenty-four years of marriage, she'd learned to read him.

"Yesterday we went over our initial results with Kittrick. He's pleased with our progress and complimented us on our hard work. But he wants us—"

"I sensed a *but* was coming," she interjected.

Undeterred, Steven continued, "To provide a formal report by the end of next week."

"Don't tell me you're going to cancel our trip to Tahoe." Her voice carried an edge, heightening Steven's nervousness.

"Not exactly. I need to go back to work right after Christmas, even though it's a Sunday. And I'll probably need to work all next week." Out of the corner of his eye, he saw her shake her head. He hastened to add, "But I don't want the rest of you to miss skiing, so go ahead without me."

"Steven, don't you understand?" Frustration filled her voice. "It won't be the same without you. The boys are looking forward to spending time with *you*." She paused, and then in a softer voice added, "And so was I."

"Jacob won't miss me a bit."

Carissa began to twirl her hair with one hand, a habit she had developed when she was processing. "Know what I've noticed lately?"

Steven's stomach lurched a little. "I'm afraid to guess."

"You've fallen back into your workaholic pattern."

"This case I'm working on may be extremely important. If only I could tell you the details, then you might understand."

"Perhaps. But here's the issue." His hands tightened on the steering wheel as Carissa began to speak like the lawyer she was. "You always have a reason. Yet your reasons don't hold water when it happens over and over... and over. Admit it! You're a workaholic."

A spasm of irritation shot through him. "My job is demanding. And I want to be the best that I can be."

Carissa reached over and rested her hand on his leg. "I love that about you, your drive, your intensity. But—"

At that moment, Steven turned into the mall parking lot, and he seized the opportunity to change the subject. "Thanks for saying that, because I know my intensity sometimes drives you nuts." He assumed an upbeat tone. "So, where shall we eat?"

"Not quite yet."

He restrained a groan, parked the car, and turned to look at her.

She was stern yet calm. "Your intensity can't all be focused on your job. It's taking a toll on your family."

His stomach tightened. Whenever his wife brought up family issues, he felt an urge to withdraw. With the help of couples counseling several years ago, he knew it was an unhealthy response. He thought he'd gotten a little better since then, but apparently Carissa thought his "little better" was too little.

She wasn't finished. "Your children don't need less of you as they get older. They need you even more. Especially Jacob."

Guilt washed over him. The counseling had also made him painfully aware he'd been far too absent as a father. "I can't seem to connect with Jacob," he said. "I'm worried about him."

"Remember what you promised when I gave up my partner track at the San Francisco law firm and took a part-time job here in Danville?"

Steven gulped. "I wouldn't expect you to do all the heavy lifting with raising our children."

"And why did I ask you to make that promise?"

He felt like a reluctant witness at his own trial. He turned away from her and looked out the front window as he recalled their crucial conversation many years ago. "Because you gave up your career aspirations so we could have the bigger family I wanted."

His confession reminded him of the most painful experience of their marriage. When Carissa was pregnant with their third child, they were so excited it would be a girl. Late in the pregnancy, the doctor discovered Carissa's blood pressure had shot up. The doctor diagnosed it as preeclampsia, but it was too late to intervene. Carissa went into labor and their baby daughter was stillborn. Steven fought to suppress the still-painful memory of holding the cooling body of his baby girl.

He felt Carissa's hand on his shoulder. Reluctantly, he turned toward her again and tried to read her expression. To his surprise, he didn't see anger. Instead, in the dim lighting of the parking lot, he thought he detected deep concern tinged with fear.

"Steven," she said softly but with conviction. "I'm not only concerned for our *children*. There's a distance growing between the *two of us*. But you seem too preoccupied to notice."

His head snapped back. A fresh wave of guilt hit him, coupled with disbelief at her accusation. He wanted to open the car door and run, but instead, through clenched teeth, he said, "Don't you realize, Carissa, that I work so hard for you. And for the future of our boys."

"I sometimes wonder if you realize we have a growing distance between us, but you just don't care enough to do anything about it." She paused and her lip trembled. "I hope that's not true, because that'd be almost unbearable."

Steven was stumped. He didn't want to admit he was clueless about the distance she sensed. But it was even worse if she thought he didn't care. She was the love of his life. While he debated, she tilted her head and kept her eyes locked on him. As he reflected on her comment, he realized life *had* gotten in the way of giving her the attention she deserved.

He shook his head. "I do care. I guess I've been preoccupied." At the moment, his brain was too scrambled and his emotions too raw to say more.

Carissa seemed to recognize his confusion, because her hand slipped from his shoulder to take his hand. "Okay, we can talk about it more at a later time."

The December breeze flowing down the Dublin hills knifed through the thin jacket Steven wore as they walked toward the mall. He reached out and put his arm around his wife. Her auburn hair swirled in the wind as she turned her head to offer him a small smile. He wondered whether she'd get even more upset with his crazy work schedule after she went to Tahoe without him. More than anything, though, he was haunted by the questioning look on her face when she challenged him about the distance between them. He knew his response was pretty feeble, and he resolved to pay better attention to her... as soon as this case was done.

CHAPTER 8

The Lab (December 29)

Steven returned to his office after he made the rounds to thank each person individually for their hard work during the holidays and to tell them to enjoy an extra-long New Year's weekend. Michelle was waiting for him, holding two Starbucks cups. She handed one to him and said, "Happy New Year."

Steven took a sip. It was his favorite. He gave her a smile and said, "You're the best."

"Oh, before Ben gets here," Michelle said, "I want you to know I had a little talk with him yesterday."

"About what?"

"The usual, his attitude. I overheard him criticizing you a couple times this week. When I confronted him, he complained you cast a big shadow. He even suggested that if we continue to work as your assistants, it'll limit our careers."

Steven sighed. "What did you say?"

"I wanted to tell him he's an ungrateful jerk. Instead, I said we're lucky you're our leader. You've given both of us opportunities we never would have had otherwise."

"I've talked to him about this very issue before. After this case, I'll talk to him again."

At that moment, Ben knocked. Michelle surprised Steven by handing the second drink to Ben. "Here you go," she said.

Ben took a tentative sip. He looked puzzled. "How did you know what I like?"

"I've paid attention," she replied.

"Okay, guys," Steven said, "after we review all our data, we'll rough out the report. We need to finish it by close-of-business tomorrow."

For the next hour, they pored over the data, checking for errors and noting a few minor changes from their earlier results. Then Steven said, "In terms of the data, we're in good shape. I'm especially glad the two additional clocks agree with the first one, so we can say with certainty that this material was chemically purified eleven-and-a-half years ago. Now let's return to the discussion we had with Kittrick about the differences between this case and the previous ones in Romania and Nice."

"Don't you mean argument?" Ben said with a smirk.

Steven let Ben's comment pass. "We have three new differences we can point to. First, the amount of plutonium in the Moldova HEU is about a factor of two lower."

Michelle piped up. "But the uncertainty is quite large, so we should re-measure plutonium in a larger sample of the Moldova HEU. Then we—"

Ben interjected, "Will the FBI think less plutonium is significant?"

"As an isolated fact," Michelle said, "probably not."

"It might be more convincing," Ben said, "to compare the plutonium isotopics. In the prior cases, the compositions were rather strange."

Steven said, "Good point. Dissolve a large sample so we can get a good measurement of the plutonium isotopic composition."

Michelle said, "The level of volatile elements shows a second difference. Sulfur, chlorine, and bromine are two to three times lower in the Moldovan HEU compared to the Romanian sample. This could be a signature of the chemical purification process."

Steven said, "When Mark wrote up his trace element results, he suggested the HEU in these two cases came from the same reactor, but the reprocessing facility had improved its process by the time the Moldovan material was purified. The improved reprocessing step removed even more of these volatile elements. We should include his interpretation in our report."

"Which brings us," Steven continued, "to the third and most important difference—"

Ben broke in. "The glass shards."

Steven sighed. It would be nice if Ben would quit finishing other people's sentences.

Ben plowed on. "This week we examined all the Moldovan HEU powder under an optical microscope and did not find one glass shard. That's a pretty compelling difference."

Michelle squinted and closed one eye, a sign her mind was churning. She said, "In the two previous cases, the investigators cracked open the glass vials, so we assumed that's when the glass shards were created. Opening them was a bit tricky since the vials were originally sealed under vacuum by melting the open end with a torch. The FBI might argue that in this Moldova case, someone used a different way to open the ten vials that didn't create any glass shards. We should explore all the ways of opening a sealed glass vial to see if we can find one that doesn't create shards."

"Good idea," Steven said. "Why don't you work on that." He glanced at his watch. "Okay, let's wrap up now."

"What are the odds," Ben asked, "the FBI will agree it's too soon to conclude that this case is only a scam?"

Steven shrugged. That was the question he kept asking himself. "With our current data, all we can say definitively is that there are some clear differences between this case and the previous cases. We don't yet understand why we find these differences in such similar materials. Until we better understand, it's too early to conclude that this Moldova case does not point to a dangerous threat. We need to design the report to drive home this point."

"Good luck," Ben said skeptically.

Steven grimaced. Ben was always the pessimist, but in this instance, he was on target. Steven said, "We've got a lot to do, so let's get to it!"

Back in his office, Steven flexed his shoulders to relieve the tension. He was optimistic they could create a strong report. But would the FBI buy their conclusion?

CHAPTER 9

Danville (December 31)

The moment Carissa returned home from Tahoe with the boys, she told Steven they needed to talk before dinner. As they walked down their driveway and turned up the street, Steven reached out to massage her neck. Her unyielding knotted muscles deepened his concern. "What happened up at Tahoe?" he asked.

Carissa sighed. "Last night, while I was trying to get to sleep, I heard the boys arguing. Eventually it stopped, but when I still couldn't get to sleep, I went to check on them. The light was on in their bedroom, so I knocked. Josh answered and told me Jacob had left to sleep on the couch. I took it as an opportunity to have a heart-to-heart with Jacob."

Steven snorted good-naturedly. "That's the Carissa I know." When she pulled up her nose, he said, "Sorry, I was just trying to lighten the mood."

"Your timing is off," she said. "Getting back to my story, I didn't find Jacob on the couch, nor could I find him anywhere in the cabin. So I went out to the garage. When I opened the door, I heard, 'Oh crap!' I flicked on the light and saw Jacob picking up a bottle of beer he'd knocked over. His look of dismay crushed me. While he mopped up the beer, I just looked at him without saying a word."

"What did he say?"

Carissa mimicked her son's defiant tone. "'Are you checking up on me?' I explained I'd heard him arguing with Josh."

"And did you have that heart-to-heart?"

"Matter of fact, we did. When he saw I wasn't angry, he opened up. Last year he began drinking. When he started high school this fall, he found a group of guys to hang out with after school. Most days, they have some beer."

"How much is he drinking?"

"Usually just one beer, but he admitted that when he has a bad day, he drinks more."

He exhaled through pursed lips. "He's only fifteen and he has a beer almost every day."

"One of my girlfriends claims that if you have just one drink every day, you may already be an alcoholic."

Another couple was coming down the sidewalk toward them, so they walked in silent shared misery. Carissa shivered as the December sun went behind the clouds and she wrapped her arms around herself.

When the other couple was out of earshot, Steven took a deep breath and let it out slowly. He asked, "What should we do?"

Her lips tightened as she considered her answer. She stopped and turned to face him. "I'm not sure what *we* should do. But I'm sure about this—Jacob needs more from *you*!"

He gritted his teeth. "Jacob's an enigma to me. You have a much better chance of getting through to him than I do."

Her shoulders slumped. "I realize you have trouble relating to him, but that might be part of the problem." Then, in a spirit of conviction and challenge, she continued, "I wouldn't be surprised if Jacob's desire for alcohol comes at least in part from dealing with his emotional distance with you."

Steven jerked backward. Dumbstruck, he pointed at his chest. "You're blaming *me* for his drinking?" His anger flared. "Are you just trying to hurt me because you're mad about me not going to Tahoe?"

Carissa started to say something but then stopped. She tilted her head and stared at him.

He took a deep breath while he replayed their last exchange. His accusation was off the mark. It wasn't her way.

"I'm sorry I got mad. Your comment felt like a low blow."

"I have my own guilt about Jacob." She reached out to hold Steven's hands. "I certainly didn't mean to imply it was all up to you to address his drinking. He's *our* child. But I want, no, I *need* you as a fully engaged partner."

"I'll talk to Jacob," he said earnestly. "And I'll do some research on alcoholism." Carissa's plea reminded him of their difficult conversation a week earlier. He added, "I'll do my best to be more present with the family. Not only for Jacob, but also for the sake of our marriage."

As he spoke, Carissa scrutinized him. Apparently, she liked what she saw and heard, because she smiled. Not a derisive smile that said, *I'll believe it when I see it.* Rather an appreciative one that seemed to say, *Thank you, that gives me hope.*

She said, "We should get back to the kids. It's New Year's Eve, so let's try to have fun the rest of the evening."

On their walk home, she began to hum a tune. He chuckled and his eyes lit up when he recognized it as *Jingle Bells.* In their first year of marriage, after an especially invigorating hour of lovemaking, he had discovered Carissa in the bathroom, softly singing this song. But she had altered the words to suit her mood. With an impish look, she sang for him, "Jingle balls, jingle balls, jingle all the way." Since that day, Carissa sometimes communicated her amorous mood by humming the tune.

Later that night, as Carissa slept, his mind drifted back to work. He wondered how the FBI would respond to his report. He devised revisions he'd like to make. Then he thrashed through ideas for their next set of measurements. He imagined terrorists at that very moment using the Moldova HEU to build a nuclear device.

An hour later, he groaned. He couldn't turn his brain off. Would he really be able to change his work-life imbalance? When he assigned a number to the probability of success, he snorted in derision. *Don't be an idiot.*

He picked up his Kindle, but a minute into reading his book, an unbidden thought flashed into his mind. What if this Moldova case turned into a national security emergency? That would shoot his work-life balance to hell. How would Carissa handle that?

CHAPTER 10

Constanta, Romania (January 4)

Ahmad Abbasova held his breath while the rental car agent in Constanta checked his fake driver's license and credit card. He passed muster without a hint of a problem. He shouldn't have worried. After all, Raushan had provided the false IDs.

While he drove to the spot where he planned to kill Vadim Grosu, he reflected on how well his plan had progressed during the past two weeks. His original instructions from Raushan were minimal. The task needed to be completed promptly, and he could recruit one person to assist him.

The envelope containing the instructions included a photo, a cell phone, and a generous amount of cash. He had sucked in his breath when he pulled out Grosu's picture. Grosu dwarfed the other two men in the photo, and the menacing look on his face spoke trouble. The scar on his cheek suggested a man well-acquainted with danger. His instructions told him they would send a text when it was time for him to initiate contact with the smuggler. The rest of the plan was his to devise.

With time short, he reached out to Omar, one of his closest friends from his university days in Baku. Omar's skills as a mechanical engineer and his radical bent made him an ideal choice as his assistant and first recruit to his team. During the following week, they watched movies that included a variety of assassination strategies. Finally, Ahmad settled on a plan that offered an excellent chance of luring their target into their trap without raising the suspicions of the police. By that time, Ahmad was smoking almost three packs of cigarettes a day.

Five days ago, the anticipated text arrived. Through an intermediary, Raushan had paid Grosu's bail. Ahmad had only a few days before Grosu was slated to appear again in court. Immediately, Omar called the smuggler and enticed him by offering a one-man job that would be his biggest payday ever. The greed in Grosu couldn't resist, and he proposed meeting in Constanta, a Romanian city on the Black Sea coast.

Today, in just a few minutes, Ahmad would conclusively prove his worth to Raushan. He parked the car a block from the designated intersection. His fingers drummed on the steering wheel while he waited. He kept checking his phone. The blare of a horn from a passing car caused him to jerk upright and grab the wheel. After his breathing slowed, he checked his phone again. Still nothing from Omar. He started to worry—what if Omar's meeting with Grosu hadn't gone well?

Suddenly, his phone beeped. A text from Omar: *On my way.*

Ahmad's heart raced as he started the car, and he craned his neck to better see the intersection. A minute later, though it seemed much longer, he spotted Omar walking beside Grosu. Both men were smiling. *Good!*

When Omar and the target reached the intersection, Ahmad wiped his sweaty palms on his pants and put the car into gear. The two men entered the crosswalk. Ahmad waited until Omar maneuvered the target to face the opposite direction from which he was approaching, and then he eased the car away from the curb. Adrenaline coursed through his body, and he gripped the wheel tighter to keep from shaking.

He drove slowly as he waited for Omar to make his move. Timing was crucial. When the target reached the middle of the intersection,

Omar dropped the magazine he was carrying. Ahmad stomped on the throttle.

Omar stopped and knelt to pick up his magazine. The target halted two steps ahead of Omar and turned to check on him. Ahmad's heart hammered within his ribs as he accelerated. He needed to reach a speed that would ensure the target didn't survive. At the last moment, the target swiveled toward the approaching car. Too late!

The right side of the car's hood smashed into the smuggler. The sound of cracking bones was followed an instant later by the thud of the target's head and shoulders hitting the windshield. Ahmad slammed against his seat belt and almost lost control. With satisfaction, he spotted a bloody swatch of black hair plastered onto his windshield.

Straightening the car, he sped away as the target pin-wheeled through the air and hit the pavement. Breath exploded out of Ahmad's lungs and he gulped in fresh air. He made several quick turns to lose any pursuit. After about a kilometer, he was sure nobody was following.

He parked the rental car, his heartbeat still thumping in his ears. His instinct was to run, but he forced himself to casually walk away. Waiting to hear from Omar was excruciating. Three long blocks later, his phone finally rang. He ignored it. After the second ring, it stopped. Relief and joy coursed through him. Two rings was the victory signal. Grosu was dead.

He willed his pulse rate down to a moderate, steady beat. His clever plan had worked. *Raushan and Uncle will be so pleased!*

As Ahmad strolled back to the hotel where he would meet Omar, his smile grew wider and wider. People passing by probably thought he was the happiest man in the world. And they might be right. After all his worries, he had pulled it off. He was on his way to greatness.

CHAPTER 11

The Lab (January 5)

After the New Year's weekend, Steven's team focused on producing more results that might strengthen the argument that this latest case differed significantly from the Romanian and French cases. He walked over to the classified area of his building, arriving early so he could collect his thoughts before the upcoming crucial conversation with Kittrick. While he waited for the secure phone to ring, he reviewed the key points he wanted to make. At this juncture, he was positive the Moldova case indicated something more serious than a scam using archival samples.

The phone rang. Before it could ring again, he picked it up. "Hello?"

John said, "Good morning, Steven. And happy New Year."

"When are you going to brief the Director of the FBI Lab?" Steven asked. "Oh, and happy New Year."

"Later today. Thanks for the excellent report you sent last week. I'd like to talk about your latest results so I can add the most significant findings to my briefing."

"I'll focus on two new results that bolster the argument that the Moldova HEU differs in significant ways from the prior cases. First, we followed up on the hint that the Moldova HEU has less plutonium. Our latest results are definitive. It has four times less."

John said, "Okay, a clear difference. But what's the significance?"

"In the prior cases, we concluded plutonium was a contaminant that was introduced after the HEU was irradiated in the reactor."

"Okay."

"Our next step was to determine the isotopic composition of the plutonium. Not an easy task when there's less than one nanogram of plutonium per gram of uranium. This afternoon we got our first result. The plutonium isotopics are substantially different from the earlier cases. We believe the plutonium in the Moldova HEU is not a contaminant. Instead, it was produced during the reactor irradiation."

"Interesting," John said. "This new information should help to identify the reactor where the HEU was irradiated, right?"

"It can help to narrow down the possibilities." The way John was tracking encouraged Steven. "The second thing I want to highlight is our additional evidence that contradicts the hypothesis that a scammer simply emptied ten archival vials into the baggie to convince a buyer he had access to much more material."

"The no-shard argument in your report was interesting, but not entirely convincing."

Steven pressed his lips together. "After we confirmed there wasn't a single glass shard in the HEU powder, we tried every way we could imagine to open this type of glass vial without producing shards. We even brought over a glass-blowing expert from Berkeley to advise us."

With a note of impatience, John asked, "And you found...?"

"Glass shards in every case. Except one."

"Whoa," John said. "Doesn't that one exception undermine your argument?"

"It could have. The one experiment where we didn't find shards was when we opened a vial by using a torch to melt and remove the glass at one end. The glass expert suggested this method will produce some silicon vapor, so we used a scanning electron microscope to look at the uranium powder that was in the vial during this experiment. We found a thin film of silicon on many of the particles. However, when we examined the Moldova powder, we didn't find any silicon film."

"Okay," John said, sounding more receptive. "Your latest results expand the number of significant differences between the Moldova case and the prior cases. If my Lab Director asks whether we need to continue our investigation, what's my best argument?"

John's question aroused Steven's uneasiness. His tone became urgent. "The evidence is consistent with the hypothesis that someone, probably an insider, has access to an operational fuel production facility, and some HEU from that facility made its way into the hands of smugglers. If that hypothesis is true, the smugglers could have enough HEU to make a nuclear device."

"That sounds reasonable, but remember what I've told you before: Nobody in the FBI, other than me, understands the field of nuclear forensics. The evidence from nuclear forensics carries less weight than traditional types of evidence."

"Oh, I've had plenty of occasions to experience that reality." Steven put a hand behind his neck and gazed at the ceiling. "Let me ask you this, John. What's your opinion?"

"My opinion isn't the one that matters."

"It matters to me."

In the ensuing silence, Steven thought he heard John tapping his desk with the end of his pen. Then John cleared his throat. "It's too early to stop our investigation."

Steven pumped his fist.

John continued. "And too early to conclude this interdiction represents a serious threat."

"Fair enough. I have a gut instinct about this case, so just give me a chance to keep working on it. The stakes are too high to quit now."

After Steven hung up the phone, he sank back into his chair with a sigh of relief and mulled over their conversation. To his thinking, by the end of their call, John seemed more confident he could get his Director to green-light further investigation.

In his typical fashion, he assigned a probability that John would succeed. The odds were good. At least seventy-five percent.

...

Steven rushed back to the classified area later that day when Brenda, his admin assistant, informed him John wanted to talk to him again.

When he grabbed the secure phone, he asked, "What happened?" without bothering to say hello.

"The Lab Director was pleased with all the results you've produced, and he's sent your report to the embassy in Moldova."

John's neutral tone was disconcerting.

The agent paused. "From the outset, he fastened onto the similarities between this case and the two prior ones."

Steven closed his eyes as he struggled to control his apprehension. "What about all the differences?"

"I pushed hard on that argument, so my Lab Director consulted with his boss, the Director of the entire FBI. The FBI Director pointed out that nothing serious came from the Romanian and French cases. He believes the claim to have large amounts of HEU was simply a tactic to gain immunity. Both of them agree that the similarities between the three cases outweigh the significance of the differences."

A pit began to form in Steven's stomach. "Did they buy our argument that the Moldova HEU wasn't simply from ten glass vials?"

"Not really." John cleared his throat. "Here's the bottom line. The FBI Director decided we've done enough. If anything new about the case surfaces, he'll reconsider."

A surge of anger rose in Steven. "You've got to be kidding me! He's willing to take the risk that no bad guys have enough HEU to build a bomb?" With steel in his voice, born of conviction, Steven added, "It's way too early to stop the investigation. It's... it's a dangerous gamble."

"Watch it!" John said, now angry as well.

Steven struggled to gain some semblance of composure. "All I'm saying is, what if thousands upon thousands of people are killed because the FBI didn't do more to stop it? I wouldn't want to be in the Director's shoes then."

"That sounds like a threat," John replied. "I have my orders. And my orders are your orders. Immediately halt your investigation. Got it?"

In a pinched voice, Steven said, "Got it."

He hung up the phone and thought of the Hiroshima picture in his office. He couldn't let something like that happen again, not if he could do anything about it. But what more could he do?

CHAPTER 12

Castro Valley, CA (January 15)

Steven savored the crisp air as he and his friend Alan Yang sped down the short incline on Redwood Road and left the city of Castro Valley behind. They had become acquainted at the beginning of their Lab careers while they waited for their security clearances, but once they moved into different classified areas, their paths rarely crossed. Then, a decade ago, Alan convinced him to take up road biking, and their friendship blossomed.

During the three-mile climb to the highest point on Redwood Road, Steven's mind strayed to the Moldova case and then to Jacob, the two problems that kept him awake at night. "Stop it," he muttered to himself. His self-directed scolding worked about as well as it did during his restless nights.

Alan reached the summit a couple hundred yards ahead of him. By the time Steven dismounted, Alan was already breathing easily. "Glad you finally made it, big guy."

Huffing and puffing, Steven looked at his friend, envying his trim body. "Yeah," he said, "but with my superior weight, I'll beat you going downhill."

Alan was third-generation American Chinese. His brown eyes sparkled with merriment and his round, smooth face creased into a smile. Then he looked at Steven more closely. "You don't look so good," he said. "Is something wrong?"

"Chasing you up a hill usually leaves me looking pretty bad." He pulled out his Clif Bar and took a bite.

Alan's eyebrows twitched. "Want to tell me what's bothering you?"

Steven chewed as he pondered. Long ago, they agreed to avoid talking about work on their Saturday morning rides, and they rarely brought up family issues. But maybe his friend could give him some helpful perspective on Jacob.

"When Carissa came back from Tahoe with the kids, she had some bad news." As he told the story, Alan's look of concern grew into a deep frown.

When Steven finished, Alan was quiet at first. Then he said, "Did I ever tell you my brother is an alcoholic?"

"I think you mentioned it once in passing."

"It caused havoc in our family." Alan's face pinched. "How old is Jacob?"

"First year of high school."

"That's about the time my brother started drinking. My parents didn't help matters. They couldn't get on the same page on how to handle it."

Steven sighed. "Carissa's challenged me to step up."

"Did she say what she wanted?"

"You've known us long enough to know the answer. Of course she did. She asked me to talk to Jacob."

"Do yourself a favor and listen to her."

"I did, but it didn't go well." He was reluctant to dive further into his family problems. Time to change the subject. "Right now, that's not my biggest problem."

"The case we were working on?" It wasn't much of a guess by Alan since he'd helped Steven with it.

"Yeah," Steven replied, letting his breath out slowly.

"But it's out of your hands now."

"You're wrong there, literally wrong. I still have the material."

Alan fidgeted with his water bottle and took a swallow. He lowered his voice. "What do you have in mind?"

"I'm not sure," Steven said. "But I can't stop thinking about it, and I'm concerned about the possible consequences of doing nothing. I wonder if I should continue working the case. Without telling Kittrick."

Alan raised both eyebrows as high as they could go. "Whoa! That sounds like an enormous risk. If he finds out, it would probably be the end of your nuclear forensics career."

"I'm afraid time is slipping away. Answer this question for me. How long would it take a technically competent team to build a device?"

"I've run through those scenarios before," Alan said. "Depends on a lot of factors. About a year is a typical answer, but for a team with the right combination of experts, it could be as short as a few months."

"So...if I'm going to do anything, I better do it soon."

Frowning, Alan said, "Be careful."

A seed of an idea began to germinate in Steven's mind. "We better get going before we get any colder. Thanks, buddy, for the talk."

During the rest of the ride, Steven noodled on ways to continue analyzing the Moldova HEU without being discovered. Each option seemed quite risky. But it didn't sit well to just forget it, even though it was the FBI who shut down the case. This interdiction might be the only clue that a serious plot by America's enemies was underway. If he sat on his hands and thousands were slaughtered without warning, he'd never be able to forgive himself.

Near the end of their fifty-mile bike ride, he finally decided. He couldn't drop the case, even if it meant risking his career. He didn't know yet how he would keep investigating without Kittrick finding out, but he'd find a way.

CHAPTER 13

The Lab (January 17)

As the sun broke through the Monday morning fog, Steven Carter settled upon the way he'd secretly work on the Moldova case. His next step was to convince Michelle. He realized it would put her in a tough position, but he didn't see any other choice. When he got in his car, he turned off the radio, so while he drove he could imagine how their conversation might play out.

His nerves were jangling by the time he approached the Nuclear Chemistry Building. Rather than go to his office first, he took a detour to find Michelle. It didn't surprise him to find her already at her desk. Her work ethic was one of her many admirable qualities.

She glanced up when he knocked on her open door. He asked, "Do you have fifteen minutes or so? It's important."

Michelle pointed to the chair in front of her desk. "Good morning to you too. "

"Oh yeah, right, good morning."

She smiled. "What's up?"

After closing the door, he sat down. He crossed his legs, uncrossed them, and then crossed them again. He trusted Michelle, but would she trust him enough to go along with his plan? "I haven't been able to stop thinking about the FBI's decision. This morning I made a decision, but I won't act upon it unless you agree."

Michelle's cheery disposition suddenly became pensive. "Don't tell me you'll try to convince Kittrick to talk to his boss again."

"Even *I* am not that stupid. Case closed! I get it."

"What else can you do?"

"Sometimes, after a case is closed, we've done research using the leftover material. Why don't we continue analyzing the Moldovan HEU as part of an R&D project?"

She tilted her head. "You think Kittrick will go for that?"

He looked at her without speaking.

Frowning, she said, "You're not thinking about doing this without telling Kittrick, are you?"

"Actually, that's exactly what I plan to do."

She abruptly stood up, walked around her desk, and leaned against the front edge. She glared down at him. "I can't believe what I'm hearing. This isn't like you."

He spread out his hands. "I know. It wasn't an easy decision."

"Wow, Steven, that's a tremendous risk! If the FBI ever finds out, it would probably—"

"I know, they'd never work with me again."

"You could even lose your security clearance and your job."

"But I'm afraid it could be a huge mistake if we quit now."

She crossed her arms. "You think it's that important?"

Steven lifted his chin. "It could literally be a matter of life or death. For thousands of people." *Come on, Michelle, stick with me.*

Michelle's face softened, though only slightly. She walked back around her desk and sat. She closed her eyes, which Steven knew meant the wheels in her head were spinning furiously. "How do you propose to keep the FBI from finding out?"

Her question gave him cautious optimism. Like most national laboratories in the Department of Energy complex, LLNL had an internal research portfolio that was funded by an overhead charge. This portfolio gave the Lab freedom to conduct research of its own choosing. With assurance, he said, "We'll do it as an internal research project. And since the FBI usually relies upon us to store its nuclear material evidence, they'll probably never realize we used more of the HEU after they closed the case."

Michelle looked dubious. "But all that research money has been allocated for this fiscal year."

"Remember the project we stopped last summer because it wasn't panning out. Almost $100K is left in that account. The Lab agreed I could spend that money on any nuclear forensics research I choose. I'll use that money to continue working on this case."

Michelle shook her head. "But our team will recognize it's the Moldovan HEU, so word could still get back to Kittrick."

Steven pressed his lips together and audibly exhaled. "That's the weakest part of my plan. If Kittrick finds out in some way, I want the blame to fall on me and only me."

"And just how do you propose to do that?"

"We'll keep the team on this project small, and I'll tell them Kittrick implicitly gave me permission to go ahead."

Her eyebrows pinched together. "What does *that* mean?"

"I'll say that I broached the idea of a follow-on LLNL internal study to Kittrick, and he didn't reply. He didn't say no. And he didn't say yes. So I took that as implicit permission to go ahead, but keep him out of the loop."

Michelle's frown faded a little. "That's plausible." Then she shook her head again. Her hands clenched into fists and she put them on top of her desk. "But it's still a lie, Steven."

A tremor of shame shot through him. The importance of honesty had been deeply ingrained in him from an early age by his parents. When he became a scientist, the value of integrity was further embedded. It was fundamental to the practice of science.

His stomach twisted into a knot at the thought of end-running the FBI. Over the course of Steven's career, he'd had several significant objections to the FBI's implementation of nuclear forensics, but he always chose to challenge rather than evade. Circumventing the FBI in this way was tantamount to a lie. And as Michelle rightly pointed out, his plan called for him to explicitly lie to his team.

Anguish filled his voice as he responded to her accusation. "I hate the idea of hiding this from Kittrick and lying to my team. I've never done anything like this before. But I feel compelled to continue analyzing the evidence. This is the only option I've found that puts all the risk on me and protects the rest of you."

She bit her lip. "But I still know it's a lie."

The pain on her face and the doubt in her voice was like a fist to Steven's stomach. "If Kittrick ever finds out, I'll tell him I convinced you I had his implicit permission. That'll give you plausible deniability."

Michelle looked down at her clenched hands. She took a deep breath and then exhaled loudly. "I couldn't live with myself if a tragedy happens because we did nothing more." Her fists opened. "Okay, Steven. I'll go along with your decision."

A confusing mixture of relief and regret swept through him. "Thanks, Michelle."

"Two more questions," she said. "If we find more evidence that this case represents a serious threat, what then?"

He shifted into his I'm-the-boss mode. "All communications outside the team will be my responsibility, and mine alone. Make sure everyone on the team keeps everything in strict confidence. If the time comes to share our results with somebody in government, then I'll figure out who and how."

"Okay."

"What was your second question?"

"Will Ben be on the team?"

"He worries me too." Steven stroked his beard. "But if we keep him off this project, he'll probably find out sooner or later."

"Better to include him from the start." Michelle frowned. "But I'll keep an even closer eye on him."

"Good. And I think it's time for me to have another talk with him."

While Steven walked to his office, he wondered what kind of additional evidence would compel him to risk telling someone. And who would he tell?

CHAPTER 14

Kabul, Afghanistan (January 18)

Malik Karimov forced himself to control his excitement. Today he would launch the operational phase of his revenge mission. Dressed in business casual clothes and carrying a backpack, he strolled past the Kabul café he'd selected for his rendezvous. He glanced through the café window, then kept going without giving any indication he'd spotted Ahmad. After Raushan had verified Ahmad was not a suspect in the hit-and-run, he had delivered instructions to the young man on how to meet with Uncle.

Ahmad jumped to his feet and followed at a discreet distance. Malik zig-zagged through the city streets until he was sure nobody was following them. He entered a park and sat on the bench he'd selected for its isolated location. Placing the backpack on the bench, he gestured for Ahmad to sit next to it.

"Good morning, Nephew," Malik said. "You follow instructions well."

Ahmad flashed a smile. "Good morning, Uncle."

"Your mission begins today," Malik said. He patted the backpack. "The information you need to get started is in here. Your first job is to assemble your team and identify a location where you'll fabricate the weapon." Malik pulled a document out of the backpack. "This lists the kinds of experts you'll need on your team."

Ahmad asked questions until he understood the level of expertise required for each skill set. Malik suggested it would take at least six people to meet the requirements, and because some of the skills were quite specialized, Ahmad might need to recruit as many as a dozen.

Malik returned the document to the backpack. "Another document in here describes in great detail your base of operations." After they discussed specific aspects of the facility, he cleared his throat.

"Now we come to the most crucial step in my plan." He paused while he looked in all four directions. "I've already found someone who can supply enough highly enriched uranium."

This simple statement belied the effort it had required to overcome the most difficult hurdle in his entire plan. Malik's father had developed relationships with many influential Russian officials when Azerbaijan was part of the Soviet Union. After Malik graduated from the university, he fostered his own relationships with some of these officials, drawing upon the sympathy engendered by his father's untimely death. After several years of careful cultivation, he developed a network of contacts in the Russian nuclear complex. The rampant corruption among Russian officials, coupled with Raushan's ample provision of funds, enabled Malik to locate an asset with ongoing access to large amounts of HEU. The asset eagerly accepted Malik's offer of more money than he would make in ten years working at the nuclear facility.

Malik continued, "A smuggling network will pick up the uranium and deliver it to you. These smugglers have a proven track record with drugs, but they are open to all kinds of business." Malik pulled out a folded piece of paper from his wallet and handed it to Ahmad. "This tells you how to contact the smugglers. Arrange with them the time and place for delivery of the material."

Ahmad moved to put the folded paper in the backpack, but Malik put a hand up. In an emphatic tone, he said, "Security is extremely important. Not only to me, but also to the smugglers. Commit the information on the smugglers to memory and then destroy the paper."

"Okay, Uncle," Ahmad said as he put the folded paper in his pocket.

Ahmad fidgeted and looked at the backpack. "Have you picked a place where I should set up my base of operations?"

Malik rubbed his chin. Raushan wanted him to be hands-off for the rest of the mission, at least to the extent possible without risking failure. He replied, "I'm going to keep my distance from your operation. It's better for you to pick the exact location."

"Don't you even have a country to suggest?"

Malik gazed at him and rubbed his chin again. "This smuggling network often transports their contraband on the Black Sea. My suggestion is to set up your operation someplace in Turkey and take possession of the enriched uranium along its Black Sea coast."

"There are a couple of towns in Turkey where I have distant relatives. Communities with lots of Shiites."

"That could be helpful, but don't let anybody outside of your team know what you're doing."

"What if I have questions?" Ahmad asked.

"Of course, we'll need a way to communicate. Once you set up your shop, and you have the enriched uranium in hand, I'll send you instructions for processing the uranium and building the various parts of the bomb."

"How will you do that?"

Malik stared at Ahmad over the top of his glasses. "You'd do well to exercise a little more patience. We're going to use an old technology. I've kept a souvenir from my university years, an old set of DVDs of one of my favorite shows, *Quantum Leap*. Are you familiar with it?"

"Never heard of it."

"It's become a classic for sci-fi fans. When your facility is ready and your team in place, send me an email that you very much enjoyed the first season of *Quantum Leap* and would like the DVD with the second season. That DVD will contain a hidden file with instructions for the second phase."

"How will I access the hidden file?"

Sighing, Malik said, "I was about to tell you."

"Sorry."

"You'll need a password to open the file. I put a book in the backpack. Get it out and I'll show you how to use it to find your password."

Ten minutes later, Malik leaned over and put his hand on Ahmad's shoulder. "I think you're ready. Be careful and methodical in carrying out the plan. If you run into a problem you can't solve on your own, send me an email that the latest DVD did not arrive."

Ahmad pumped his fist. "I'm ready to take the quantum leap!"

Malik smiled. "I like your enthusiasm." His voice became stern again. "But be careful. Remember the old proverb: *Whoever keeps his secret, keeps his options open.*"

CHAPTER 15

The Lab (February 3)

Over the next few weeks, the small group of scientists working on the secret Moldova project made significant progress. Before they began, Steven spoke with Ben. He confronted Ben about his negative attitude, and to his surprise, Ben readily agreed he'd been off-base with some of his comments. He seemed sincere when he promised to do better in the future. To address Ben's angst about working in his shadow, Steven offered to jump-start him on an exciting new research project involving oxygen isotopes to geo-locate nuclear materials. By the end of their conversation, Steven felt he could trust Ben, so he brought him onto the Moldova project team.

Steven waited until today to hash out the implications of their new data. He hoped his meeting with Michelle and Ben would answer the question that had been swirling through his mind: *Is there enough evidence to show that the Moldova threat is real?*

When he entered the meeting room next to his office, his two lieutenants were already sitting at the table. "Thanks for clearing your calendars this afternoon," he said, as he pulled the Moldovan HEU analytical results out of his briefcase. "By the end of this meeting, I hope to reach consensus on an integrated interpretation of all our results."

"Let's dive in," Ben said.

"Here's the approach I'd like to take," Steven said. "We'll focus on the differences between the Moldova and Romania HEU cases. You two present our new results, and I'll play devil's advocate." In taking this role for himself, he hoped to inhibit Ben's penchant for assuming this adversarial role.

"Sounds good," Michelle said. "Want to go first, Ben?"

"Sure," he replied. "I'll start with the microscopy results. We've thoroughly examined the uranium powder on ten SEM mounts. Nothing new, with one very important exception. We found a silicate grain, a big one, about thirty microns. Once I knew it was there, I could see it with my naked eye."

Michelle pulled out a sheet with the data for this large grain. "It's a composite grain, primarily silica with a lesser amount of clay."

"We then examined it on the ion probe," Ben said, "and got some intriguing results."

For the next ten minutes, they examined the findings. In the contact between the silica and clay, they found small amounts of organic matter. They determined the oxygen isotopic composition of the silica and the carbon isotopic composition of the organic material, but the uncertainties were large because they used the ion probe to measure the isotopes.

Ben drew himself up. "Based on these results and my literature search, I'm confident this grain is an atmospheric particle from a dust storm in the Sahara."

Steven leaned into his self-appointed role. "You're probably right, but you can't rule out other sources. Not yet."

Ben grimaced, then nodded. "Okay. I'll keep working on it."

Michelle said, "Discovering this silicon grain prompted us to look for other extraneous materials. I ultrasonicated the uranium powder in water, then decanted the liquid. When I dried the liquid, I didn't really expect to see anything. To my surprise, I found pollen grains.

Ben took them to a botanist at Berkeley and she identified them as Betonia Bulgarica, commonly known as Bulgarian Betony."

Steven knew almost nothing about plant biology, so he asked, "Where might it come from, other than Bulgaria?"

"It's endemic to Bulgaria," Ben said. "Of course, nurseries in other countries sell this plant as well, but by far, it's most prevalent in Bulgaria."

Michelle tugged on her ear. "Could the pollen have fallen into the HEU powder when it was transferred into the baggie?"

"That seems reasonable," Ben said. "And the large silica grain probably fell into the powder at the same time."

Michelle said, "That's consistent with the fact that Saharan storms can transport dust grains hundreds of miles toward the Balkans."

Steven said, "Anything else from the SEM analyses?"

"No," Ben said, "but like we did in the Romania case, we followed up by analyzing the powder using the much higher resolution of the transmission electron microscope." Ben removed numerous photomicrographs from his stack of papers and spread them out on the table. "Many of the grains we saw in the SEM are actually clumps of smaller particles, similar to the Romanian material. But here's the important difference. The average size of the Moldovan HEU particles is five times larger."

Steven asked the obvious. "What do you make of that?"

Ben said, "In the Romanian case, we attributed the very fine grain size of the HEU to grinding it to produce a good archival sample. In contrast, I believe the Moldovan HEU represents the actual form of the HEU prior to making reactor fuel."

Michelle added, "And a typical fuel fabrication facility makes tons of HEU powder. It's reasonable to infer that whoever put the Moldovan HEU into the baggie also had access to a lot of it."

Steven felt his confidence growing that his instinct had been right. The FBI shouldn't have terminated the investigation. For a moment he dropped his devil's advocate posture. "That's about eight significant differences between the two cases—the material was reprocessed at different times, the uranium-236 is lower in the Moldovan HEU, the powder was found in different types of containers, the amount of interdicted HEU differed by an order of magnitude, the plutonium levels and isotopic compositions don't match, some volatile elements are lower in the Moldovan material, and, of course, the Moldova sample doesn't have any glass shards."

He had caught Michelle fidgeting several times during the meeting, without apparent cause. He recalled she had promised to finish reducing all of her latest data before today's meeting, and hoped she'd found something exciting. "Your turn, Michelle."

She dutifully presented additional data on trace elements and age-dating. Everything confirmed their previous results.

Then her voice went up in pitch and she spoke more quickly. "I decided to do a more thorough look at the residual fission products. We did radiochemical separations on larger samples and then counted them for a much longer time. What I first noticed, and it was quite a shock, was the clear presence of cerium-144. Its half-life is only 285 days."

Steven's head snapped back. His devil's advocate role vanished. "We didn't detect any cerium-144 in the Romanian sample."

"That's right, "Michelle said. "It's quite surprising, especially in light of the fact that when we analyzed each material, the Moldovan HEU was two times older."

Ben grabbed his copy of the radiochemical results and gave it close scrutiny. "Wow, Michelle! This is important. Too bad you didn't see it sooner."

Michelle didn't show even a flicker of annoyance. "The next thing I noticed was the cesium isotopes. The cesium-137 is about twice what we found for the Romanian HEU, but the shorter-lived cesium-134 is about ten times higher."

Realizing where Michelle was headed, Steven slapped his forehead. "Holy crap! The Moldovan HEU experienced a flux of neutrons very recently. Long after the chemical reprocessing step."

Michelle thrust her arms up into the air. "Exactly!" Her eyes wide and face flushed, she continued, "The most probable explanation is that—"

"We have some stupid smugglers," Ben interrupted. "They packed so much HEU close together that it started to generate enough neutrons to approach criticality."

Michelle pushed her hair out of her eyes. "It must mean the smugglers had many kilograms of HEU and the self-generated neutron flux probably began less than two years ago."

"Probably much more recently than two years," Ben said. He jumped up to the whiteboard. "We can estimate the time of this later neutron exposure by using the fact that there are so many similarities between the two HEU cases. We can calculate the cesium-134 to cesium-137 ratio at the time of reprocessing for the Romanian sample. Then we can model the time of the neutron exposure by assuming—"

This time, Steven interrupted. "Let's not get ahead of ourselves. We can model the details of the neutron exposure later. Here's what's important. We now have clear evidence that the interdicted Moldovan HEU was recently taken from a much larger source. Large enough to approach criticality!"

Ben added, "I'd say that's close to indisputable."

Michelle chimed in. "And the pollen indicates this larger source was probably somewhere in or near Bulgaria."

Steven leaned back in his chair, his mind whirling and stomach churning. His gut-instinct hadn't let him down.

As these thoughts flashed through his mind, Ben and Michelle kept quiet and watched him. Steven's feeling of vindication faded as he began to grapple with the terrifying implication. A large supply of

HEU was indeed on the loose. Somebody somewhere was trying to build a nuclear device!

As if she'd read his mind, Michelle said, "This is scary." She folded her arms and cleared her throat. "We can't sit on this."

Ben spoke more forcefully. "Got that right!"

Now that the moment of decision had arrived, Steven's stomach tightened and his jaw clenched. His secret research project could no longer stay hidden.

"You're going to tell Kittrick, right?" Ben said.

Steven narrowed his eyes as he looked back at Ben. "I'll sort through my options this evening. Meanwhile, don't say a word to anybody. Got it?"

Steven waited until each of them agreed.

After they left the room, he put his head in his hands. If he went to the FBI, they'd blow a gasket when they realized he had disregarded their order to stop. Most likely, they wouldn't even look at his new results.

So...where do I go?

CHAPTER 16

The Lab (February 4)

Steven settled on his next move the very next day. When he stepped out of his car at the Lab, a slight drizzle greeted him. He glanced up at the sky, hoping that forgetting his umbrella wouldn't invite a downpour. Despite the rain, he took his time walking over to Z-Division to meet with Alan Yang. He hunched his shoulders and turned his face away from the wind.

Z-Division was the Lab's primary conduit to the U.S. intelligence community. Few analysts in the intelligence community had nuclear expertise, so they relied upon scientists at the national laboratories for matters involving nuclear weapons. The entire Z-Division building met the higher security requirements for working with Sensitive Compartmented Information, commonly referred to as SCI.

Steven picked up his SCI badge in the Z-Division lobby, and after the attendant buzzed him into the inner sanctum, he navigated the maze to Alan's office. Alan's windowless space was its usual mess, with classified papers strewn all over his desk and piles of other documents sitting on the floor. The physical mess bore no reflection on Alan's work, for he was highly regarded for the readable, cogent analyses he produced.

Steven closed Alan's office door and sat in the chair Alan had positioned in front of his desk. "Thanks for meeting on such short notice."

Alan smiled good-naturedly. "Things are slow on a Friday. What's on your mind?"

"Remember our Redwood Road ride several weeks ago?"

"You mean the one where you wanted to gab more than ride?"

"Yeah, that one. I decided to keep working on the Moldova case."

Alan pursed his lips. "So you took the big risk."

Steven summarized his team's new results. When he neared the end, his cadence slowed as he described Michelle's startling discovery.

"Wow." Alan's eyes opened wide. "A recent neutron exposure!"

"The only plausible explanation is that the smugglers had lots of HEU."

"I agree. You have to run this one up the chain."

Steven seized upon Alan's segue. "This is where you come in—"

"Uh-oh. Did I just step in it?"

Steven put up his hands. "Just hear me out. If I go to Kittrick, he'd be so upset that I went behind his back, I doubt he'd even look at my evidence."

"You're probably right." Alan nodded sympathetically. "That's bureaucracy for you. Challenge someone's authority and they stop listening."

Steven couldn't blame his friend for his bitterness. "Yeah, I remember well your struggles when you worked in Weapons Design."

A flicker of anger crossed Alan's face. "It doesn't bother me anymore. My moron of a boss drove me nuts, but it pushed me to make the move to Z-Division. A great move for me, in hindsight."

Steven chose his next words carefully. "I considered going to Homeland Security, but if they took any action, they would probably involve the FBI. That would be terrible for me. Who do you think I should approach?"

Alan offered a wry smile. "I see where you're headed."

Steven held up his hands in mock surrender.

Alan continued. "The Department of Energy would also be likely to inform the FBI. There's one place where you can expect people to keep this type of information to themselves. The intelligence community."

His friend took a deep breath, held it, and then let it out. He doodled on his sticky notepad and finally asked, "Are you looking for my advice on who to approach?"

"With your years of supporting the CIA, you know a lot of people there." Steven decided it was time to make his big ask. "Here's what I really need. For you to approach a person at the CIA that you trust. A person who might act upon my findings. Ask him or her to send me an invitation to brief him."

Alan fidgeted with his pen. "That isn't the way the Agency works with us. We need to stay in our own lane. Your Moldova case has nothing to do with any of my Agency projects."

"But surely they'd want this intel," Steven insisted.

"I'd like to run this by my division leader first."

Steven hesitated. "Let's keep this between us. Your division leader would probably say 'no way.'"

Alan doodled again. He gave a deep sigh. "Let me think about it over the weekend."

Steven knew Alan struggled with fear of failure, and he felt a stab of regret. Mustering his most reassuring tone, he said, "I'm not asking for anything more than the invite. I'll take it from there."

"If my boss hears about this, my head will be on the chopping block."

Steven hated to plead, but he had to get through to someone who could make things happen. "I realize I'm asking an awful lot. But it's that important."

The deep frown on Alan's face worried him. Should he press even harder? His voice urgent, Steven added, "If something terrible happens, how would you feel?"

Alan's grip on his pen tightened until Steven wondered if it would snap. "I said I'll think about it."

To lessen the tension, Steven switched the topic to their bike ride the next morning. After finalizing their plan, Steven made his way back to his office. No way around it, he was using his friend. Did he go too far? During tomorrow's bike ride, he wouldn't even so much as allude to their conversation.

He expected an anxious weekend while he waited for Alan's decision. But he vowed to restrain himself from devising desperate alternative strategies in case Alan said no. Mentally, he assigned an eighty-five percent chance that Alan would say yes.

CHAPTER 17

The Lab (February 11)

One week after Steven asked Alan to arrange a meeting with the CIA, Alan was waiting for Carolyn K. to call. She had been his manager on a number of projects, and over time they developed a strong working relationship. When Alan emailed her with his request for a phone call, she agreed without knowing the subject beforehand. He flexed his shoulders to relieve his tension.

Before he agreed to help Steven, he had searched for any information he could find on the Moldova case. He was startled to discover the HEU smuggler was killed a month ago in a hit-and-run accident while free on bail. He doubted it was a coincidence, and it helped him make up his mind.

His phone rang, the secure one cleared up to Top Secret/SCI. He glanced over the bullet points he'd prepared and lifted the receiver.

Carolyn said, "I must say, Alan, you've piqued my curiosity. What's on your mind?"

Alan began with his rehearsed opening. "I've come across some alarming information. I've decided to let you judge whether it's important."

Carolyn stopped him. "Don't be nervous, Alan. Just tell me about it."

Alan proceeded with his prepared account of the Moldovan HEU interdiction and the key evidence the LLNL team had uncovered. By the end of his story, he felt more comfortable. Diving into technical details often did that for him.

Alan asked, "So, what do you think?"

"To be honest, I didn't follow all the technical arguments."

"Here's a non-technical argument that this case needs more attention. After the smuggler posted bail, he was killed in a hit-and-run."

"Interesting," she said. "But this nuclear forensics is new for me and that makes it hard to evaluate the strength of your case."

This was the opening Alan had hoped for. "Would you like our nuclear forensics leader to brief you?"

"Good idea. I expect you to come along too, but nobody else."

Alan winced. He'd rather not go with Steven, but he didn't dare push back. "When can we meet?"

"I'm leaving the country this weekend and won't be back at Langley until the week of February 28th."

"I can arrange to meet with others at Langley that week."

"Ah, a good cover story." Carolyn sounded amused. "How about March 1st?"

"Perfect."

"Before we hang up, I have one question. Why tell me?"

Alan's heart rate shot up. "Here's the dilemma. Carter doesn't feel he can go to the FBI with his new evidence, because they shut down the investigation a month ago. Carter responded by secretly doing further analyses as part of an internal R&D project."

"Hmmm," Carolyn offered. "This Carter has gone pretty far out on a limb."

"Yeah, and the branch under him is pretty small."

Alan looked down at his list and saw he had one more bullet point to cover. "I have one more favor to ask. Carter could use some cover too. Could you formally send him an invitation to brief you?"

"Not a problem," Carolyn said.

Alan got off the phone and rushed out of the building to tell Steven. Buoyed by the afterglow of success, he walked with the brisk gait of a confident man. He replayed the last part of the conversation, and his smile slipped away. Their desire for a cover story highlighted how far out on a limb Steven and he were putting themselves. What would happen if their ploy was exposed? Could Carolyn protect them? Would she even be willing to try?

CHAPTER 18

Northern Turkey (February 12)

Three weeks after he met with Uncle in Kabul, Ahmad Abbasova stood on a Black Sea beach as the early morning light crept over the hills. The salty tang in the air reminded him of a boyhood vacation by the Caspian Sea. His heart quickened when the sound of a motor came across the water. A few moments later, he spotted a large boat headed his way.

The boat stopped ten meters from shore, and an anchor splashed into the water. A large man jumped off the boat and waded toward him. The smuggler made no effort to hide the gun thrust under his belt. Without saying a word, he held out his hand. Ahmad handed him the authenticating document Uncle had provided.

The smuggler glanced at it and grunted. He waved back to the boat, and two other men loaded a box onto a small skiff and pushed it onto the beach. The smuggler cast an appraising look at Ahmad. "First time I carried this kind of cargo. You have impressive friends." The way he said it expressed doubt that Ahmad deserved the trust of his compatriots.

Ahmad looked at the box and asked, "Is that all of it?"

"You questioning me?" the smuggler snarled.

Ahmad's adrenaline spiked, and he quickly shook his head. "Not at all! Just surprised how small it is."

The two men dropped the box at Ahmad's feet. He didn't want to risk further insulting the smuggler by opening it, so he made a quick calculation. Yes, the box could hold the promised amount of uranium oxide. Trusting that the smugglers wouldn't dare cheat Raushan, he said, "I'll take it from here."

The smuggler grunted, and without another word, he headed back to his boat.

Once the boat was out to sea, Ahmad whistled. Omar appeared a moment later. Ahmad lifted one end of the box and motioned for Omar to help him carry it. The two of them carried the box the hundred yards to their van and, with a final burst of effort, heaved it into the back.

Still panting from his adrenaline rush and physical exertion, Ahmad said, "Let's take a look."

Omar pried off the cover. Ahmad peered inside and counted six plastic bags filled with black powder. He grabbed his gamma detector and verified it was enriched uranium. Smiling with relief, he opened one bag. He scooped up a handful, knowing it was safe to touch enriched uranium for a short time. His eyes glinted as the powder trickled through his fingers. "Black gold," he exclaimed. With his other hand, he gave Omar a high-five.

Omar said, "How about calling our operation Black Gold?"

Ahmad tilted his head and then grinned. "Not bad. But here's a better name. Operation Quantum Leap."

Later that day, when they reached their newly acquired shop, Ahmad typed a brief email. "*Dear Uncle. I've finished the first season of Quantum Leap. Please send the second season.*" After he hit send, he punched his arms into the air. He was ready to start building the bomb.

CHAPTER 19

Danville, CA (February 26)

With the temperature in the low 70s on this glorious Saturday afternoon, Steven suggested a walk at San Damiano, Carissa's new favorite place to unwind. They drove to the western edge of Danville and up to the retreat center nestled in the forest near the top of the rolling hills. As they climbed the short but steep trail to the very top, Steven decided it would be better to talk to Carissa about Jacob first. Then he would bring up his dilemma at work.

A week ago, Jacob had gotten into a fight at school. In the aftermath, the vice principal discovered a bottle of whiskey in his locker. The school suspended him for a week. Steven hit the roof and grounded him for a month. When he warned Jacob he was risking throwing away his future, his son challenged him, saying, "My future? Is that what you're really worried about? Or is it that I'm making you look bad?"

The accusation stopped Steven short. Where did his son get that idea?

Jacob then glared at him with disdain and said, "You don't really care about me."

The words hurt more than if Jacob had hit him over the head with a baseball bat. Later, when Steven talked to Carissa about it, he agreed it would have been better if he'd waited to cool down before talking with his son.

Nearing the top of the hill, he took Carissa's hand and said, "It seems to me Jacob has been in a better mood the past couple days. He's actually speaking in complete sentences instead of grunts. Maybe all the drama surrounding his suspension woke him up."

She began to twirl her hair. "Maybe. But something's off."

"Like what?"

"When I ask him how he's doing, he smiles and says fine. It's very different from the frank talk I had with him at Tahoe, and I don't think it adds up."

His optimism dissipated. "You think he's hiding something?"

She sighed. "That's my fear. Maybe he's turned to some other drug."

His heart sank. In his reading about addiction, he'd learned that many people who outwardly appear to have overcome their addiction have simply moved on to something else. He said, "I hope that's not it."

They reached the top of the hill. They surveyed their town below them, and Carissa pointed. "There's our home."

The sight did not give Steven his usual warm feeling. "I keep thinking about what Jacob said to me. Do you think he really believes I don't care about him?"

"I don't think so."

Regret welled up inside. "I wish he knew how much I love him." He closed his eyes and softly said, "No matter what happens, he'll always be my son."

Carissa took a deep breath. "It doesn't help that you're not home that much. And when you are, your mind is often elsewhere."

A spasm of guilt seized him. "I know I keep saying I'll do better, but it usually doesn't last long."

She bobbed her head in agreement, took his hand, and they resumed walking along the path.

He contemplated how to phrase his next sentence so it wouldn't sound like yet another excuse. "This case I'm working on is proving to be a very serious matter."

Looking puzzled, she said, "You told me the FBI shut it down."

"Yeah, I need to update you. Because I didn't stop working on it."

She turned toward him and raised one eyebrow. "Kittrick's okay with that?"

Within the limits imposed by classification restrictions, he did his best to explain his decision to go rogue and his even riskier step of going to the CIA.

She walked faster, and he pushed to keep up with her. "You're taking a huge risk!"

"This case screams for an aggressive investigation. I need to get somebody's attention."

Fear crept into her voice. "Even if it costs you your career?"

Deliberately, he said, "Even if it costs me my career."

"So, what's your next move?"

"Alan arranged for me to brief one of his contacts at Langley." He said it nonchalantly to mask the regret that surged again. He'd pushed his friend to the wall and Alan was very nervous about their upcoming trip.

She fixed her eyes on him. "Can I warn you about one thing?"

At that moment, something whacked Steven across his forehead. He staggered backward and his hand flew to his head. "Crap, what was that?"

Adjusting his glasses, he realized he'd walked straight into a low-lying tree branch. Carissa tried to stifle her laughter.

He rubbed his head. "Maybe I should wear a helmet next time."

She chuckled as she brushed leaf litter from his shirt. "I was sure that even you saw that branch right in front of you. Your focus drives me nuts, but sometimes it's just hilarious."

He smiled. "Glad you're laughing, even at my expense. So, what were you going to warn me about?"

The merriment in her eyes faded. "When you're sure you're right, you can come across as arrogant. I doubt that'll go down well at the CIA."

He started to protest, but she held up her hand. "Examine your motives. Are you taking this step just to prove you're right? Is it possible you've allowed yourself to be too readily convinced by your own evidence?"

Steven choked back his urge to argue and stayed silent for a long moment. Many times in the past, he'd regretted not listening more closely to his wife. "Maybe I do like to be right." He crossed his arms. "But that's not what's driving me in this case. Believe it or not, this is a national security emergency that nobody else sees coming."

On the way back to their car, they fell silent. Two and a half months had passed since the interdiction in Moldova. Time had to be running short. In Steven's worst nightmare, the HEU ended up in the hands of a well-trained scientist with nuclear know-how. At this very moment, the bad guys could be fashioning a nuclear device.

He glanced at Carissa. Her face drooped with sadness. Undoubtedly, she was thinking about Jacob, rather than the case that was constantly on his mind. Though she hadn't brought up the growing distance between the two of them, it probably still weighed on her too. He wondered just how much more pressure his marriage could withstand.

CHAPTER 20

Langley, Virginia (March 1)

Steven tried in vain to calm the thudding in his chest as Alan guided him through the maze of bland, indistinguishable hallways at the CIA headquarters. Though he felt well-prepared, he'd never faced higher stakes.

Alan stopped in front of an unmarked door. "Take a deep breath, buddy." After Alan followed his own advice, he pressed a call button. Moments later, the door opened, and a woman stepped into the hallway. In a formal voice, Alan said, "Carolyn, I'd like to introduce you to Steven Carter. Steven, this is Carolyn K."

Carolyn was rather short, probably not much over five feet. Her straight brown hair framed a nondescript face. When they shook hands, her grip was firm, and she looked directly into Steven's eyes with a penetrating gaze. Clearly, she was a person to be reckoned with.

She led them through a large room filled with a haphazard clutter of cubicles. A man signaled for her attention, and she stopped to answer his question. The deferential way he engaged with her impressed Steven.

Carolyn's office was large enough to accommodate a small conference table. She introduced the three men who were already sitting at the table. Two of them gave only an initial for their last name, as often was the case when CIA employees met with outsiders. But Steven promptly forgot their first names because of his dismay at discovering he already knew the third man. Dr. Frederick Bell was currently the chair of the Joint Atomic Energy Intelligence Committee, affectionately referred to as the Jake. He was on a temporary assignment from Los Alamos National Laboratory. Early in Steven's career, he had several run-ins with Fred, and they had developed a mutual dislike for one another. Of course, it made sense that Carolyn wanted the JAEIC chair to sit in on a technical brief related to nuclear weapons, but it was unfortunate that person happened to be Fred.

Carolyn sat at the head of the table and inclined her head toward Steven. "Thank you, Dr. Carter, for accepting my invitation to brief me today. I want this to be an informal discussion, so we'll interrupt with questions as we go."

Steven swallowed. "Thank you. I appreciate the opportunity to tell you what we've learned." He popped a mint in his mouth to restore some semblance of moisture. He glanced at Alan. His friend's nervous look was not reassuring.

Summoning his most confident voice, Steven took the group through his PowerPoint presentation. Fred interrupted with several minor questions, which Steven readily answered. The others followed the interactions intently without commenting. When he started talking about the large silicate particle, Fred interrupted yet again.

"Are you an expert on atmospheric dust?"

Steven tried to hide his annoyance. He was sure Fred already knew the answer. "No, but I have geochemists on my team."

"Are they experts on atmospheric dust?"

"They are competent to read the relevant literature and make credible interpretations."

When he described finding the pollen, Fred broke in again. "Have you ever used this method before to search for extraneous materials in uranium oxide powder?"

"No." He couldn't keep a hint of irritation out of his reply. The two of them debated the significance of the pollen finding until Carolyn intervened.

"Enough on this point! Please proceed, Dr. Carter."

Steven looked her way more often to gauge her reaction. Her face gave nothing away. Just what he'd expect from a spy.

He slowed his tempo when he reached his last piece of evidence, the short-lived fission products. It was critical for Carolyn to understand their significance.

Fred objected again. "Do you really think the smugglers were so sloppy that they almost started a chain reaction?"

At this point, Steven welcomed Fred's skepticism. "Frankly, that's the most likely explanation. And it means the smugglers had enough HEU to make a workable device."

Fred's long face grew pensive. "Hmm. You could be right." He drummed his slender fingers on the table. "I'd feel more confident in your finding if rigorous modeling produced this type of neutron flux for a given set of conditions."

It seemed the tide was turning in his favor. He'd already done some promising back-of-the- envelope calculations, but a full-up computer simulation would be better. "That's an excellent idea. Introducing moisture could be an important parameter."

Fred's drumming picked up pace. "And some type of container that reflects neutrons might play a role."

Carolyn held up her hand. "Okay, you two science nerds can go off later and work on your nuclear modeling. I've heard enough. Anyone else have further questions?"

Everyone around the table shook their heads.

"Thank you, Dr. Carter," Carolyn said, "for a very informative briefing. Alan, you can escort Steven out now. But I'd like the two of you to report back to me tomorrow."

Steven and Alan were quiet as they weaved their way back through the cubicles. After the door to the main corridor closed behind them, Steven couldn't restrain himself any longer. "How do you think the briefing went?"

"Pretty well."

A two-word evaluation wouldn't do for Steven. "I couldn't get a read on Carolyn."

"You don't get to her level in the CIA unless you can hold your cards close to the vest."

"I realize Fred doesn't like me, but he was more cantankerous than usual."

"Carolyn's no fool. I wouldn't be surprised if she encouraged him to give you grief."

Steven snorted. Maybe that was her plan, or just Fred being Fred, but in any case, Fred's initial skepticism helped make his case more convincing.

• • •

While Steven tossed and turned in bed that night, he replayed the meeting again and again. After only three hours of sleep, he awoke to a churning stomach. When Carolyn called to ask them to meet with her in an hour, he was relieved his wait to hear her verdict was almost over.

When they were ushered into Carolyn's office, she was at her desk. She gestured toward two chairs and finished jotting down a note. When she looked up, her face was unreadable. At last, she spoke. "Thank you, Alan, for suggesting I meet with Steven."

Steven's leg started to jiggle up and down.

She continued. "I talked to the Deputy Director for Operations this morning. At first, this case struck him as a wild goose chase."

Steven's stomach lurched.

In an even tone, she continued, "He agrees with me. We should investigate."

Waves of relief washed over Steven. Without thinking, he pumped his fist. Carolyn's eyes narrowed, and he dropped his hand back into his lap.

She pulled an old-fashioned cassette recorder out of her desk and placed it in front of him. "I need to know everything Kittrick told you about the interdiction." She hit the record button.

She peppered him relentlessly with questions. By the time they were done, he felt like he'd been through the Inquisition. He wondered what it would be like to face her as an adversary.

She finally stopped the recording. "I've got my work cut out for me. As for you two, if you identify where this HEU was produced, let me know."

"Will do," Steven said. "Will you update us what you learn on your end?"

"Only if you have a need-to-know."

Steven gulped. He might never know whether he was right about this case. For him, that would be torture.

CHAPTER 21

Peet's Coffee, Livermore (March 8)

Carissa Carter arrived early at Peet's Coffee in Livermore. After she secured a table in the corner, she ordered her friend's favorite latte and an iced Americano for herself. While she waited, she recalled with a smile the development of her friendship with Michelle Johnson. They first met six years ago at a social function when Michelle joined Steven's group at the Lab. What struck Carissa at the outset was Michelle's high emotional intelligence, a rarity among Lab scientists.

The first time the two of them met privately, they shared only basic information about their lives. As they became more comfortable with each other, their conversation veered into more vulnerable areas. Carissa talked about her pain when her parents divorced while she was in high school. Decades later, her parents still competed for her affection and often complained to her about the shortcomings of their ex.

In return, Michelle described how her mother died when she was in middle school. Grief overwhelmed her father, to the point that Michelle was pushed into taking adult responsibilities as a young teen. Her father was still single and emotionally dependent on her. From that time forward, Carissa and Michelle's relationship deepened until they became best friends.

Today's meeting came at Carissa's urging. She wondered if her marriage was in even more trouble than she realized, and she hoped to gain some clarity by sharing her concerns with Michelle.

When Michelle bustled into the shop, a little breathless, Carissa stood up and gave her a big hug. "Thanks so much for breaking away from work."

Michelle said, "From the way you spoke on the phone, I could tell it was important."

Carissa began by sharing her concerns about Jacob. Then, in a pinched voice, she said, "What's troubling me more than anything is Steven." She paused, wondering how much she should share.

Michelle said, "Whatever you tell me about Steven, it won't affect how I work with him."

Carissa took a deep breath and exhaled. "Steven has difficulty dealing with uncomfortable family issues."

She summarized their sporadic conversations regarding Jacob over the past several months. Her voice dropped to a whisper when she brought up the growing emotional distance between Steven and her. Michelle's face contorted in sympathy, mirroring the ache in Carissa's heart.

"I feel like I'm alone in all this," Carissa said. She wiped away the tear that trickled down her cheek. "I've started to worry, is Steven finding comfort somewhere else? Could he be having an affair?"

Michelle jerked upright so fast that her chair screeched across the floor. "Oh, no!" she said as she reached across the table and grabbed Carissa's hand. Looking directly into Carissa's eyes, she confidently said, "I'm sure that's not happening."

"How can you be sure?" Recalling her father's affair that broke up her parents' marriage, she said, "I think every man is susceptible to an affair."

"I'm around Steven practically all the time. I've learned to read the clues about how he's feeling. I'm sure if he was having an affair, I'd have sensed something was amiss."

Carissa felt indignant. Did her friend really think she was that clueless? Before she could get a grip on her anger, she fired back. "You think you're more likely than me to be able to tell if Steven is having an affair? How in the world can you think that?"

Michelle suddenly became still. She looked out the window for several seconds. Then she turned toward the wall. It seemed she was conducting an internal debate. When a look of compassion appeared on her face, Carissa grew even more alarmed.

Michelle said, "Maybe it's time to tell you this." She picked up her napkin and twisted it. "I hope ultimately it will be good for your marriage."

"You've got all kinds of crazy thoughts running through my mind. Just spit it out."

"Okay, a couple years ago, I noticed Steven seemed a bit off. Sometimes he'd come back from meetings with the Associate Director in a cheerful, almost jovial mood. Very uncharacteristic. Then, during a dry run for our directorate review, I noticed that after a woman finished her presentation, his eyes followed her back to her seat. When she looked over at him, he smiled. She smiled back, and then I would swear, she even blushed a little. That tipped me off."

A pit was growing in Carissa's stomach. "Oh no!"

"I asked him about it the next day." Michelle glanced at the table nearest them and lowered her voice. "At first he was evasive, but eventually he admitted to spending a lot of time with her and becoming emotionally attached. So I asked him outright, 'Are you sleeping with her?' He assured me he wasn't."

Carissa was stunned that she was hearing only now about her husband's unfaithfulness, two years later. She broke in with the demeanor of a prosecuting attorney. "And you bought that?"

"I convinced him his emotional affair was almost as serious as a sexual liaison. Then he assured me he'd immediately break it off. And I believe he did. He returned to being the same old Steven."

Gritting her teeth, Carissa said, "And why didn't you tell me earlier about this so-called emotional affair?"

By this time, Michelle had twisted her napkin into a pretzel. She gave it one final yank and laid it down. "I debated about it, but wasn't sure it'd be in your best interest. Especially when I was sure Steven ended it."

"I can't believe you kept this from me!"

Michelle's lips quivered.

Carissa's shock and anger began to give way to deep hurt and sadness. In a less accusing and more forlorn voice, she asked, "Why do you think he sought out this woman?"

"I didn't ask how it started because I didn't want to hear any more details. Then I had a thought. Frankly, this idea gave me more assurance he wouldn't relapse." Michelle shifted in her chair and began tearing tiny pieces off her tortured napkin. "When I tell you my idea, please don't think I'm accusing you of being in part responsible for his affair."

"I'm not sure I can feel much worse."

"His relationship with her began about the same time you got that big case. You did a great job, but it took a huge amount of your time. It was also the first year you were on the school board."

"Really? My busyness pushed him toward another woman?" Sarcasm crept into her voice, despite her effort to suppress it.

"I doubt that explains it entirely." Michelle paused for a heartbeat or two. "But I suspect it played a role."

Carissa reflected on that year. She sighed. "I did kind of lose my work-life balance that year. And since Steven relied upon me to hold down the fort at home, it threw him for a loop. It was the hardest year of our marriage."

"The two of you weathered that storm, so I hope you can weather this latest blow. Because I sense Steven needs you now more than ever." Michelle collected the remains of her napkin and put them in her empty latte cup. "I need to get back to the Lab, and you have lots to process."

A pang of regret surfaced through Carissa's pain. "Michelle, I'm sorry for how I spoke to you. I realize you were only trying to do what you thought best. For both me and Steven."

The two women embraced, discarded their empty coffee containers, and left. Michelle in a hurry. Carissa more slowly.

While Carissa drove home, she kept dabbing her eyes to keep her mascara from streaking down her face. As her shock ebbed, her anger with Steven grew. Instead of manning up and talking to her about his struggles in their marriage, he'd turned to another woman. Then he had kept it hidden from her. *Coward! Can I trust him again? Will I be able to forgive him?*

CHAPTER 22

Somewhere in Turkey (March 10)

Ahmad Abbasova opened the door to his shop, careful to hide his jitters. With a smile on his face, he ushered Uncle inside with a wave of his arm. "Welcome, Uncle, to Ahmad's Metal Works!"

"A good choice of location," Uncle said. "It fits in with the other shops in this industrial part of town."

Ahmad gave an inaudible sigh of relief. He was off to a good start.

He gave Uncle a quick tour of the front room where plows and other farm equipment were on display for the shop's occasional local customers. Near the back wall, two men were repairing a plow. The man at a milling machine checked the part he was shaping, while the other man tended a casting furnace. Ahmad introduced the two men and Uncle put his right hand on his chest as he thanked them for joining Ahmad's team.

Ahmad opened the door to the shop's back room, where three more members of his team waited. He asked his lead chemist to show Uncle how they had prepared the HEU feedstock for the melting and casting process. Uncle nodded politely as the chemist explained in detail the difficulties they'd encountered in reducing the uranium oxide to metal. They ended up using a solid-state reaction with carbon. For the trial runs, they used depleted uranium because it has the same chemical properties as enriched uranium but is readily available.

"We overcame every problem," Ahmad said. With an air of triumph, he opened a cabinet filled with grey tubs. "All our HEU is ready for casting."

Uncle nodded approvingly. "You have good reason to be proud."

Ahmad pulled back his shoulders and stood tall. It was the first time Uncle had expressed pride in him.

Uncle continued, "Now let's talk about the difficulties you've had with the casting."

Ahmad shuffled over to the vacuum induction furnace. He removed the top lid so they could access the cylindrical graphite crucible and copper heating coil inside the steel housing. "The furnace has worked well," he said, "but the metal ingots have voids. Based on the density of the metal product, we have way too many voids."

Uncle said, "The most important part of the casting operation, and probably the most difficult, is finding the parameters that reproducibly give solid uranium metal. I'm here to help with that."

Ahmad's neck muscles relaxed.

Uncle peered into the furnace. He pulled out a tape measure and determined the position of the copper induction coils. "Do you have drawings for this furnace?"

"Of course," Ahmad replied. He walked over to his desk and pulled out his annotated drawings.

Uncle spread out the sheets of paper and pulled a notebook from his briefcase. Mumbling to himself, he made notes. Ahmad pulled up a chair and quietly peered over Uncle's shoulder to follow his calculations.

After several minutes, Uncle turned to Ahmad. His voice and demeanor shifted to a professorial tone. "I did more research on casting uranium before I came. Now I understand better the importance of the temperature gradient over the mold."

Ahmad pursed his lips. "Do you think we need a greater temperature difference?"

"And why do you think that's important?"

Ahmad desperately tried to recall the papers he had read on metal casting. "We want the molten metal to solidify first at the bottom of the mold. Then the solidification front needs to move smoothly from the bottom of the ingot to the top at a rate that keeps voids from forming."

"Very good!" Uncle lightly punched Ahmad on the shoulder. "The more voids we can eliminate, the better our device will work."

For the next hour, they developed a plan for their experimental casting runs. Uncle's systematic approach to solving the problem impressed Ahmad. When Uncle included some of Ahmad's suggestions, a glow of acceptance enveloped him.

By the time they finished the plan, Ahmad felt like he had graduated beyond an assistant who simply followed orders. He had become more like Uncle's scientific collaborator. As a team, they would succeed in building this nuclear bomb!

"We'll start our experiments this afternoon," Uncle said as he stuffed his notes back in his briefcase. "Oh, that reminds me." He pulled a bottle out of his briefcase. "I brought some more yttria slurry. You can improve the way you line the graphite molds."

Ahmad held out his hands, palms up. "I'm a chemist, not a metallurgist."

Uncle frowned.

Recovering, Ahmad added, "With your help, I'll get it right."

CHAPTER 23

Istanbul, Turkey (March 14)

After several exhausting days of trial-and-error, Malik was confident he had found a technique that reliably produced good-quality uranium metal ingots. After reaching this milestone, he drove to Raushan's safe house in Istanbul. Upon his arrival, he was immediately ushered inside to meet with his benefactor.

Raushan said, "I hope you come bearing good news."

Smiling, Malik said, "We've solved the casting problem."

"Excellent. Can Ahmad carry on without you returning to the shop?"

Malik swallowed. "Probably. But I'd prefer to check on his work in person."

"To the extent possible, I want to hide your involvement."

During the drive to Istanbul, Malik had prepared for this moment. "The best way to do that would be to bring my assistant, Leila, onto our team."

"Explain."

"She's effectively become my executive assistant, and that includes setting up all my travel. If we include her in our plot, it will make things easier for me."

Raushan's eyes narrowed. "How close are you to this woman?"

"She's a friend, and I trust her." He kept his voice neutral to hide the fact that his professional friendship with Leila had deepened into something more.

"Is she sympathetic to the jihadist cause?"

"She's fervent about her Muslim faith." At Leila's urging, he sometimes went with her to the mosque. His old agnosticism was still firmly in place, but pretending to adopt the Muslim faith pleased her and also facilitated his relationships with other jihadists. His radicalism had nothing to do with religious faith. Instead, it was born out of his desire for revenge and his political ideology.

Hopeful, Malik added, "Let me explore whether she would support our cause."

Frowning, Raushan probed deeper. "Is this Leila more than a friend?"

This was the question Malik had hoped to avoid. Because romance had entered his relationship with Leila. "Actually, she's become my best friend."

"She's your best friend and yet you have no idea whether she is sympathetic to the jihadist cause?"

"I've been careful to hide my embrace of jihadism because that helps protect my role in our plan."

Raushan's eyes drilled into Malik. "It's too big a risk. Keep your relationship with Leila on a professional level, but close enough that you can use her to your advantage."

Malik struggled to not let his disappointment show. Leila had brought to life the part of him that had died years ago after his painful break-up with Sina, his girlfriend at the university. He had hoped to find a way his romance with Leila could blossom, but the look on Raushan's face foreclosed that possibility.

Malik said, "You're right."

"Among all my people, you are the only one who can plan and execute this kind of attack. After you succeed in this mission, I foresee future operations for you. We need to do everything we can so that no one will ever suspect you are the mastermind. That means after this trip, you don't return to Ahmad's shop unless it's absolutely necessary. I also want you to develop an additional measure that will further safeguard your role."

On the drive back to Ahmad's Metal Works, Malik devised various options to satisfy Raushan's demand, but he doubted any of them would satisfy his benefactor and de facto boss. When he arrived at the shop, he gave a generous amount of money to Ahmad's team and told them to go to dinner at their favorite restaurant in town. Once everyone left, he took Ahmad through the remaining steps. In addition to manufacturing the uranium metal pieces, Ahmad needed to build the steel gun that would house them. After he finished the gun, he would use more of the depleted uranium to test its ability to explosively propel the uranium metal parts to smash into one another to form the critical mass. If it passed the test, Ahmad would build another gun and ship it to the target destination. When they finished, he told Ahmad they'd pick up food and return to the empty shop to eat.

Ahmad looked puzzled. "Why are we coming back here?"

"There's a recent development I want to share with you."

Ahmad's eyes widened. "What is it?"

"Patience," Malik said. "We'll talk while we eat."

When they returned, after several sips of his tea, Malik said, "You're doing well, Ahmad. These past several days have given me even more confidence in your ability to complete the mission."

Ahmad still looked concerned and merely nodded.

"Raushan doesn't want me to come back to your shop." Truth be told, Malik also hoped he wouldn't need to return. Since he couldn't bring Leila into the loop, future trips to Ahmad's shop would cause her to raise more questions. He continued, "We'll handle issues using the *Quantum Leap* DVDs. It will take a genuine emergency for me to take the risk of returning."

"I don't feel quite so optimistic, but I appreciate your confidence in me." Ahmad stared at him intently. "Is that the extent of this development?"

Malik took another swallow of tea. "Before, I didn't care if someone could eventually trace the bomb back to me. Now Raushan wants me to change the plan so that no one will suspect my role in this mission."

"What kind of change?" Ahmad's voice betrayed his angst.

"I don't know yet."

"Let me get this straight. You won't return to help me execute the rest of the plan. Even though you're going to change the plan, but you don't know yet what will change." Ahmad pushed his plate away. "That sounds risky to me."

Malik abruptly stood up. The questioning by his protégé was outrageous! Without his intervention, Ahmad would still be in the jihadist training camp, enduring the insults of his captain. Malik stalked back and forth, hands clasped behind his back, letting Ahmad stew.

The silence stretched out until Ahmad meekly offered, "I'm sorry if I offended you."

Malik stopped and stood in front of Ahmad. He locked eyes with his assistant. "I recognize, *Nephew,*" he said, with stern emphasis on the code name, "that your impertinence arises from fear."

Ahmad bowed slightly, and his tone shifted to pleading. "But, Uncle, this is all such a shock."

Ignoring his half-eaten dinner, Malik buttoned his overcoat. "As I said, I will evaluate whether I need to return to help you. But come to think of it, don't cast the HEU until I send you the revised plan. Practice casting with depleted uranium and start building the gun."

He stalked out of the shop without giving Ahmad a chance for further protest.

CHAPTER 24

The Lab (March 15)

After Steven returned from briefing the CIA, Brenda demanded that he attend to the multitude of bureaucratic tasks he'd been ignoring. He took care of several every day, but the case remained his priority. He seized upon Carolyn's last instruction as his mandate. His team continued to analyze the Moldova HEU, while he and Alan pursued various avenues that might cast light on the HEU's origin. As the days passed, he became obsessed with one thought: What has Carolyn learned?

Finally, he couldn't take it anymore. Though Alan had begged him to not pester Carolyn, he called her. She was polite but terse. When she learned something he needed to know, she'd contact him.

Frustrated, he resolved to write an article that had been sitting on his back burner. It was time to publish the national security argument for thoroughly investigating every case involving illicit nuclear materials. Of course, he wouldn't specifically mention the Moldova case, but the FBI would get the point.

He pulled out the manila folder where he'd kept notes for the article. He opened a new Word document and was midway into the second paragraph when Michelle stomped into his office. Her face was flushed as she slammed the door behind her. "Did you see Ben's email?"

He had rarely seen Michelle this upset. "No. What's it about?"

"He's resigned."

Steven sputtered. "What? In an email?" He clicked his computer mouse and pulled up the email. It was short and to the point. Ben was leaving to take a job at the Los Alamos Lab. Effective immediately.

"I can't believe it! Six weeks ago I asked him directly whether he was thinking of leaving the Lab. He assured me he wasn't. But at that very moment, he must have been talking to Los Alamos."

Michelle mirrored his anger, her face scrunched with outrage. "If he walked in the room right now, I'd slap him across the face!"

He snorted as he imagined her reaching up to whack Ben, leaving her ruddy handprint on his arrogant face. "I wouldn't try to stop you."

She offered a hint of a smile.

Steven squeezed his chin. "I didn't see this coming. Especially after I promised to fund his oxygen isotope project."

"I should have known something was up," she said, calming down. "When you were at Langley two weeks ago, Ben complained you hadn't taken him along. I pointed out that the CIA asked for only two people. I was stunned by his reply. His exact words were, 'That's what *Steven* told us.' He went on a tirade, ranting that you keep both of us subservient. He used the same old line about you casting a shadow that limits our careers."

Steven rolled his eyes. "He's probably secured a promotion."

Michelle bobbed her head. "And he probably believes he's leaving a big hole in your team. It wouldn't surprise me if he tries to convince the FBI to start using the Los Alamos team instead of yours."

Scowling, Steven said, "That would be a shitty move. Right during the most important case of our time."

"Losing Ben will be a blow, at least scientifically," she said. "In the long run, though, we'll be better off without him. Frankly, I'm relieved I won't have to deal with his nonsense anymore."

After Michelle left, Steven slumped in his chair. It wasn't the first time somebody left his group, but after all he'd done for Ben, this felt very personal. And the timing couldn't be worse.

A pounding on the door interrupted him. What now? Before he could say, "Come in," the door opened. Alan stalked in, looking distraught.

"What's wrong?" Steven asked, hoping his phone call to Carolyn wasn't the reason for Alan's scowl.

Alan shut the door. "It hit the fan today! My division leader just read me the riot act for taking you to Langley."

Steven groaned. "How did he find out?"

"All he would say was that he was tipped off by someone at the Lab."

"Does your boss know I did an end-run on the FBI?"

"I don't think so."

Steven breathed a sigh of relief. "Is your boss threatening to punish you?"

"He might take me off all my current projects."

The panic on Alan's face hit Steven like a punch in the gut. Alan's hard-won reputation as an outstanding analyst was hanging in the balance.

"I doubt your division leader will make good on his threat." Steven summoned up a confident tone and added, "Your project managers at Langley won't put up with it."

"I hope you're right." Alan sounded doubtful.

Yet again, a wave of remorse swept over Steven. He'd pressured Alan, and now his friend was taking the hit. "A while back, you mentioned your boss encouraged you to take more risks. Tell him you took a risk because it was a critical national security issue."

"He doesn't appreciate his own words being used against him."

Steven's jaw tightened. "If we stop this Moldova threat, no way your boss can touch you."

Alan's face darkened even more. "And how likely is that?"

"I don't want to even hazard a guess." In a brighter tone, he added, "But we'll give it our very best shot."

After Alan left, Steven returned to his computer to work on his article. He paused with his hands poised above the keyboard. "Forget it," he muttered. "I'm going home before this day gets any worse."

On the walk to his car, it hit him. Ben must be the leak that got Alan in trouble. Few people knew he'd gone to the CIA, and Ben was the only one with a motive to spill the beans. Probably another part of Ben's plan to undermine him.

Steven threw his briefcase in the car and started the engine. He felt like he'd just gone two rounds in a heavyweight fight and taken a beating. He put his head on the steering wheel. Could this day get any worse?

CHAPTER 25

Danville (March 15)

Steven walked into his house well before dinnertime and headed to his home office. Carissa bustled out of the kitchen and followed him. Alarmed, she asked, "What happened?"

Though Steven had hoped to bury himself in his *Time* magazine, he seized upon her invitation to share about his day. First, he told her about Ben's betrayal and Michelle's reaction. Several times she interrupted to express in colorful language her opinion of Ben. When he described his conversation with Alan and his friend's panic, an even stronger wave of remorse hit him.

Sympathetically, she said, "You feel bad about your role in Alan's trouble, don't you?"

He chewed on his lower lip. "I wish I could have found another way to set up my CIA briefing."

"If there'd been another way, I'm sure you would've found it." She patted his arm. "Don't beat yourself up about it."

Steven appreciated the empathetic way in which his wife listened to him, and he realized he no longer felt quite so down.

Carissa began twirling her hair. "I don't blame you for being angry with Ben. But you need to forgive him."

"Forgive him? He's trying to sabotage me!"

"Yes, he's wronged you. You're hurting. That's where forgiveness comes in."

He threw up his hands. "Why should I let him off the hook?"

Carissa's voice became softer and her eyes moistened. "Forgiveness is more about letting yourself off the hook."

Frowning, he said, "That sounds like double-talk."

"I'm learning that when I hang onto my anger toward a person, it's like taking a drink of poison and expecting it'll kill the other person. My mom and dad still do that, even though they've been divorced for decades. It's so sad."

He gazed up at the ceiling. "You've never talked like this before."

"Lately, I've been reading a lot about forgiveness." She paused. "Because of you."

He sat up straight. "I realize I've been quite distracted at home, but this case has totally consumed me."

She narrowed her eyes and said, "I wish you'd said that without the but." Her lips pinched together and she added, "Jacob has been grounded for two weeks now. Have you had a serious talk with him yet about his drinking? Without yelling?"

"Without the yelling...no. I'll try again this weekend, I promise."

Carissa grimaced. "Do you realize you have a strange relationship with risk-taking?"

"Where did *that* come from?"

"When you're on your scientific turf, you take all kinds of risks. But in other areas of life, you play it safe."

He didn't like this turn in the conversation. He probably looked like the proverbial deer in the headlights. Forcing a light-hearted manner, he said, "I took a risk when I married you, didn't I?"

She grinned. "You wanted me so much, that wasn't you taking a risk at all."

He waggled his head. "You got me there."

The smile faded from Carissa's face. She sighed. "It's too much, all at the same time. Your problems at work and our problems at home."

Steven guessed at her underlying worry. "It's not helping us to feel any closer, is it?"

"Sometimes I worry we'll just continue to drift apart."

The melancholy in her voice tugged at his heart. Haltingly, he said, "Why don't just the two of us take a vacation in Hawaii this summer? And not only for fun. Let's use the time to work on our relationship."

Carissa looked more hopeful. "I like the second part of your suggestion, but I've got a better idea for where. Let's take the boys to visit your parents. Jacob has a wonderful relationship with them. Maybe they can get through to him. And we could take off on our own for several days."

"Good idea."

Later, while Carissa made dinner, Steven tried to read his magazine, but questions kept popping up in his mind. Was their marriage headed for the rocks? What was happening with Carolyn's investigation? Could they turn Jacob around?

Unbidden, a haunting vision arose. Jacob, standing on the edge of a cliff. When Steven reached out to grab him, his son looked at him with despair and fell to the rocks below.

CHAPTER 26

Malik's Work Office (March 17)

Malik Karimov called Leila into his office on the first day after he returned from Turkey. Smiling, she walked in and held out her arms. He remained seated and gestured toward the empty chair across from his desk. Her bewildered look of pain tugged at his heart.

Malik said, "My week in Ankara went well, but it's good to be back home. Did everything here go well?"

Leila shrugged. "Nothing I couldn't handle."

"I'm not surprised. That's why you're my most valued employee."

Her eyebrows arched. "I thought I was more than that to you."

"I still want us to be friends, but we need to keep our relationship on a professional level."

Hurt filled her voice as she said, "What does that mean?"

"For the sake of your career, we should be work-friends only. That means not getting together outside of the workplace unless it involves other employees."

"Did somebody complain?"

"I just think this is best for both of us."

Leila's face reddened, and she shook her head. "Really, just friends?"

"I'm sorry if I misled you." It pained him to pretend he hadn't also felt a romantic stirring, but he didn't dare cross Raushan. And after his conversation with Raushan, he realized romance had clouded his judgment and this step was best for the sake of his life's mission. He said, "I hope this won't affect our working relationship."

She turned back to him, her face still red. She forced a smile and said, "That won't change."

Later that morning, Malik found himself staring into space as he considered how he would meet Raushan's command to further safeguard his role in their plot. Frustrated, he decided to run at lunchtime. Maybe the fresh air would clear his muddled mind.

After he warmed up, he fell into his familiar loping gait and soon left his village behind. He took his favorite route through the forest, where the scent of the late winter air with hints of the coming spring brought back memories of another March, eight years earlier.

He had thrived in the stimulating academic environment of the American university, but at first he struggled socially. After meeting Sina, he began to adapt to American customs. He recalled one of the happiest days of his life, the day Sina said she loved him. Sina, his first love.

He bit his lip when he remembered the most painful day of his life, the day he heard the Americans had murdered his family. Sina was with him when the blow struck, but as a naturalized American citizen, she couldn't fully understand the fierce hatred of all things American that erupted in him that day. As she left, she turned to embrace him. With her head against his, she whispered into his ear, "I'm so sorry about your family. It's devastating. I hope you still believe that I love you."

He'd responded with a half-hearted hug. Though he'd often told her how much he loved her, and he was sure he would never love another woman as deeply, he couldn't reply in kind. The words "I love you too" formed in his mind, but didn't make it out of his mouth. All he could muster was a simple, "Thanks."

The promise of a bright future was shattered on that day. Secretly, he resolved to avenge his family. Knowing Sina would never be part of his revenge, he broke up with her. In the following years, his pain accumulated like layers of sediment in the ocean. Eventually, the pain hardened into a deep, though well-hidden, bitterness. Every time the hypocritical Americans declared that the accidental death of citizens was regrettable, yet somehow acceptable, his blood boiled. The stubborn American support for Israel and their meddling in foreign affairs, usually to the detriment of Muslim countries, constantly stoked his anger. Each new example of American hubris and injustice increased his resolve to punish American aggression.

The Americans destroyed his relationship with Sina. And eight years later, they took away his opportunity for love to blossom once again. Damn the Americans to hell!

The sound of a galloping horse interrupted his thoughts. He moved to the side of the narrow road and offered a distracted wave to a young man riding past on a magnificent black stallion. As he watched the horse and rider recede into the distance, it reminded him of a verse from the Quran that Leila had recently read to him. "And He created the horses, mules, and donkeys for you to ride and as adornment. And He created that which you do not know."

Yes, the stallion was a sign for him to ride fearlessly into the future. He recalled Ahmad's impertinent but relevant question, "*What kind of change?*" and Ahmad's angst about the risk of failure.

As the kilometers passed, Malik feverishly sought an answer to Ahmad's question that would satisfy Raushan. His breathing grew more ragged as he neared exhaustion. Abruptly, an idea popped into his mind.

He stopped to explore this new possibility from multiple angles. As its plausibility became clearer, his excitement mounted. With a shout of triumph, he raised his hands to the heavens. "I'm sure it will work! *Sag ol!* Thank you!"

CHAPTER 27

CIA Headquarters (March 22)

Carolyn's eyes opened wide as she read the classified email from Bill Yount, an old and trusted colleague currently stationed at the Azerbaijan embassy. Bill would call her soon with information regarding the alert she'd sent three weeks ago. Could this be her break?

She hadn't idly waited for the alert to do its work. The same day she received the Deputy Director's go-ahead, she tasked intelligence assets in Moldova to investigate Vadim Grosu, the smuggler who was killed after the Moldova police caught him with the HEU powder.

Her sources reported that Grosu was part of a smuggling ring, but to the best of their knowledge, this ring didn't deal in nuclear materials. They couldn't determine who had paid the hefty bail that allowed the smuggler to be released, only for him to be killed a week later in a hit-and-run. The Constanta police were thorough and concluded the dead man had been targeted. Eventually, they discovered the rental car used for the hit, but the driver had disappeared without a trace. She wondered who wanted Grosu dead? His fellow smugglers? Or a customer?

Her phone rang, and she saw it was the front desk. "Hi, Carolyn, Steven Carter is here."

Oh crap. She had promised to read Carter's draft of an *Arms Control Today* article. A week ago, Carter emailed it along with his classified report on the Moldova case, using Alan's secure JWICS account. He had asked to meet with her today since he'd be in town on other business. Even though she suspected Carter hoped to get an update on what she'd learned on her end, she agreed because their conversation might give her new insights.

She told the operator, "I'll send someone down to escort him." That would give her time to scan the article.

After she and Carter exchanged greetings, she pointed at her computer screen. "You're poking the FBI bear, aren't you?"

Carter spread out his hands and grinned. "You think?"

She scrolled down. "You say, and I quote, we should seek to establish a new international norm that puts far greater importance on conducting nuclear forensics investigations of interdicted nuclear materials. Such a norm will enhance the ability to detect the early warning signs of nuclear terrorist activity."

"Well, that is my opinion. One I held prior to this Moldova case."

"This will piss off the FBI, who will see it as bucking their decision."

Carter shrugged.

She was surprised by his nonchalance, given his precarious position with the FBI. But enough on the article, time to get to business. She pulled out her hard copy of Carter's classified report on the Moldova case. "You seem pretty sure the HEU came from Russia. But that's not too surprising, is it?"

"Granted. But with the additional evidence we've uncovered, we're close to pinpointing the actual facility."

"Take me through the details."

"We drew upon the database maintained by the U.S. government on nuclear materials around the world. In addition, we met with several scientists who've had extensive contacts with Russian scientists." For the next ten minutes, Carter explained the logic behind the report's findings. Then her desk phone rang.

To Carter she said, "Hold on a minute," while she swiveled to pick up her phone. The call desk informed her Bill Yount was on the line.

She turned back to Carter and said, "I need to take this call. Wait outside my office and I'll let you know when I'm done."

Carter looked disappointed, but he said, "No problem."

After she greeted Bill, he began his debrief. "Three days ago, I received a report from one of my more reliable sources. He's an asset in the drug trafficking world. A friend of a friend of this source heard somebody else brag about their involvement in something big. Something very big."

"If I counted right," Carolyn said, "this braggart has three degrees of separation from your source."

"Yeah, so I asked my source to meet with his friend again. I authorized him to offer significant payment for more specific information. That produced results. The braggart evidently is part of something called Quantum Leap."

"Quantum Leap," Carolyn said. "That's an old TV show. Not a phrase you expect to hear from a Middle Eastern lowlife." She drummed her fingers on the desk. "Would someone name a smuggling operation Quantum Leap?"

Bill said, "I wondered the same thing."

Her mind was spinning. "The *leap* part is consistent with something big. Calling it a *quantum leap* might be to highlight it's extremely big. Or it might be a subtle clue to the nature of the operation. Maybe this pertains to trafficking in nuclear materials."

"Not an unreasonable guess."

Her stomach tightened. "Quantum Leap might be the code name for a terrorist operation that's using the Moldovan HEU?"

"Or it could just be a whimsical name this braggart came up with."

"Any more information on him?"

"My source actually got us a name. Omar. But nothing more. Not his full name, or his nationality, or his location. And in Azerbaijan, Omar is like saying John Doe."

"For the time being, let's assume Quantum Leap and this Omar are connected in some way to the Moldovan HEU. Keep digging. And let me know as soon as you learn anything more."

After Carolyn hung up, she opened her door to find Carter leaning against the wall a discrete distance from her office. She said, "Something's come up. If I have more questions on your report, I'll call you."

Tentatively, Carter said, "Was it by any chance about the Moldova case?"

She took the measure of him. This Carter was one persistent scientist. At times, he could be cheeky. But it was these same qualities that enabled him to develop the evidence he'd brought her. He deserved a little encouragement before she sent him on his way.

She said, "I've got a new lead that might be linked to your case. Surprisingly, it came from Azerbaijan."

"At least you have another lead." He looked hopeful. "Thanks for letting me know, and now I'll get out of your hair."

After he left, Carolyn sat down at her classified computer to compose a new alert regarding the Moldova HEU. She copied her earlier cable that tasked agency assets to report any information that possibly was linked to the potential nuclear threat. Then she added, "*Pay special attention to any communication that includes the phrase 'Quantum Leap.' Immediately report any such communication directly to me and the Director of Operations.*"

She read through her alert to make sure it was clear and then sent it through the same channels she'd used for her first alert. As she shut down her computer, a sense of disquiet stopped her.

She reopened her computer. She needed to cast the net more widely. In half an hour, she pounded out a summary of the evidence she had so far. She wrote an email to a long-time friend at the National Security Agency, requesting him to put a high priority on flagging any communication intercept that included the name Quantum Leap.

After she attached her summary, she hit send and shut down her computer again.

Now it was a matter of waiting.

CHAPTER 28

The Lab (April 12)

Three weeks after Steven met with Carolyn at the CIA, he recalled Alan's estimate of how long it might take a terrorist group to build a nuclear device. The HEU was interdicted in Moldova more than four months ago, so if the bad guys had a capable team, they could have already built their bomb and at this very moment were transporting it toward their target. He desperately hoped the new lead from Azerbaijan would prove fruitful, but Carolyn was keeping mum.

Meanwhile, his team had continued their work and reached a new milestone: they identified, with a fair degree of confidence, the Russian facility where the Moldova HEU had been reprocessed and stored. It was quite an accomplishment, and he was excited to pass along the news to Carolyn. When he gave her the update, she cryptically told him that it might be helpful, but it wasn't her current concern.

Her response left him even more distraught. Time was running out. What more could he do? His stomach churned as he entertained possibilities. Maybe he could get some kind of help from other scientists at the upcoming ITWG meeting in Romania, which was right next door to Moldova. Maybe he should take a secret side trip to Moldova and do some investigating of his own. He shook his head. He should leave that kind of thing to the pros. After all, he wasn't Jack Ryan.

Brenda knocked on his door, interrupting his ruminations. "Your wife is on the phone."

"Got it."

He reached for his desk phone. "What's going on?" he asked.

"Jacob's been arrested," Carissa said breathlessly. She choked on the last word.

Stunned, Steven blurted, "Why? How? For what?"

"Drug possession." She started to sob. "And selling drugs to minors."

Incredulous, he said, "He's dealing drugs?"

"That's what the police say."

"What's Jacob say?"

"I haven't talked to him yet. I want you there with me."

He felt light-headed. His son, a drug dealer? "I'll pack up my briefcase and head home."

"Can't you leave your work at the office just one night?"

An old memory flashed into his mind. Early in their marriage, Carissa's frustration with him working on the weekends boiled over. She made her point by filling his briefcase with potting soil. "You're right. I'm leaving now."

He jumped on a Lab bike to get to his car quickly. His mind travelled in a thousand directions while he pedaled furiously. He took a sharp right turn into the parking lot, then spotted loose gravel on the road. Too late! The bike's back wheel slewed around and he lost control. The next thing he knew, he was lying on the ground, looking at the sky.

He heard a car stop. "Are you okay?"

"Don't know yet," he mumbled. His head hurt like hell. He rubbed it and came away with a bloody hand.

The driver of the car was now standing over him. "I'll help you up."

Gingerly, Steven extricated himself from the bike. When he stood up, he wobbled and then steadied himself. Blood seeped through the holes in his khakis, but other than that, his legs seemed okay. He kneaded his collarbone and flexed his shoulder and then breathed a sigh of relief. No bones seemed to be broken.

"That was impressive," the driver said, "keeping your hands on the handlebars."

"Too bad I wasn't wearing a helmet."

The man looked at his bleeding head. "You probably have a concussion. You better go to the emergency room."

Steven groaned. "My wife is going to kill me."

CHAPTER 29

The Lab (April 25)

The two weeks that followed were miserable for Steven. Fortunately, the bike crash hadn't given him a concussion, but unfortunately, the trip to the emergency room took so long that he never made it to the police station. Carissa was furious, which only made matters worse between the two of them. Their conversations often devolved into arguments. To top it off, his ulcer was acting up again.

Initially, Jacob had seemed chastened by his arrest. At the detention hearing a week later, the judge declined to dismiss the charges. Fortunately, the judge did agree to release him to his parents' custody until the adjudication hearing. When they got home, Steven ordered Jacob to sit down in the family room.

"You are in serious trouble," Steven said.

"Yeah, I heard the judge."

"Hearing is one thing. Listening is another."

"Whatever."

The dismissive tone in Jacob's voice set Steven's teeth on edge, but he tried to stay calm. "First things first, you need to stop drinking. And here's how we're going to help you with that. We are getting rid of all the alcohol in the house. And we're going to do random checks of your room to make sure you haven't snuck anything in."

Jacob's lower lip jutted out. "That's a violation of my privacy."

"In my house, you don't automatically have a right to privacy. And you just lost that privilege."

"That's not fair."

Steven snorted. "That's very fair. And I shouldn't even have to say this, but you can't afford even a hint of suspicion regarding drugs."

After this conversation, Jacob went into a sullen funk. Several days later, Steven caught Jacob sneaking back into the house with the smell of beer on his breath.

"What's the matter with you?" Steven asked, not bothering to keep his voice down. "Wasn't I clear about no more drinking?"

"I was just getting together with my friends."

"Are you telling me you had no idea they'd be drinking?"

"I wasn't sure."

"How many beers did you have?"

Jacob shrugged. "Maybe a couple."

"You're grounded once again. And you are going to start going to AA. Your mother will go with you to make sure you attend the meetings."

"That's bullshit"

"Don't talk to me that way."

After that, Jacob lashed out at the slightest provocation. When Steven asked Carissa about the AA meetings, she told him that Jacob sat through every one with his arms crossed, refusing to say anything.

During these same two weeks, work on the HEU case slowed to a crawl. Despite frantic digging by Alan and him, they gained little insight into the operations of the Russian facility they suspected. They were at a standstill. Making matters worse, Carolyn had gone radio silent. His anxiety over the Moldova case was becoming unbearable.

He stood up, wind-milled his arms to relieve the tightness in his neck and shoulders, and began to pace. He heard a sharp rap on his door and Alan stuck his head in.

"Carolyn would like to talk to you, "Alan said.

"That's funny. I've been thinking about calling her, even at the risk of pissing her off."

Alan put his finger to his lips. "No need. She's right here." He walked in, with Carolyn close behind. Dressed in jeans and a simple blouse, she could easily pass as a scientist at the Lab.

"Why didn't you tell me you were coming?" Steven asked as he shook her hand. He hoped she hadn't heard his comment. He hoped even more she came bearing good news.

She peered at the scab on the side of his head. Her eyes traveled down to the road rash on his arm. "Bike or motorcycle?"

Steven fingered his scab. "Bike. Going too fast around a corner and hit loose gravel."

"Tough break." She paused. "I want to give you an update on the Moldova case." She sat down and leaned forward. "And I wanted to tell you in person."

Steven shot a questioning glance at Alan. Alan gave a little shrug.

"I'll start with the bottom line," she said. "The CIA is pulling the plug on the Moldova case."

Steven reared back. "What the hell!" he blurted before he could stop himself. The air went out of him, literally and figuratively.

"I'm not happy about it either." She sighed. "To date, the Omar lead is a dead end. We haven't found a connection between the HEU in Moldova and Omar in Azerbaijan."

"You can't quit now." Pleading, he added, "The stakes are too high."

"That's not the way my boss sees it. Other priorities have emerged."

A sharp pain shot through Steven's stomach as his ulcer flared. "But you can't—"

Alan cut him off. "That's right, buddy, she can't." His friend stared daggers at him. "Carolyn's on our side. No point in arguing with her."

"So we do nothing and hope for the best?"

"SIGINT will still monitor for the code name Quantum Leap." Carolyn paused, put her fingertips together, and tapped her mouth. "You're going to Romania pretty soon, aren't you?"

"Next month for the ITWG meeting."

"My hands are tied. Yours aren't."

Steven's leg jiggled. "What are you suggesting?"

"I'm not suggesting anything." She hesitated. "Would you by any chance know a Dr. Tariq Nazari?"

Steven's leg stopped jiggling, and he sat up straight. "Yes, I first met him when I took a short sabbatical at MIT and Harvard. He distinguished himself in graduate school and I was surprised when he took a junior position at the Joint Romania-Moldova Nuclear Research Institute. It didn't surprise me when several years later I heard he became the director. Why do you ask?"

"We've learned that Nazari helped the police with some of the initial nuclear measurements on the HEU."

Alan asked Steven, "Will he be at the ITWG meeting?"

"He's been to a couple meetings before," Steven said, "so I doubt he'd miss this one."

Carolyn put her fingertips together and tapped her mouth. "Would it be unusual for the topic of the Moldova interdiction to come up in conversation at the meeting?"

"Not particularly, especially when I know the person already," Steven said.

Carolyn kept silent but smiled encouragingly.

Steven motored on. "I'll let Nazari know I led the nuclear forensics investigation here in the U.S. He might confide in me then. Maybe he made his own independent observations. He may even have ideas about where the HEU was headed."

Carolyn tapped her mouth again.

Steven snapped his fingers. "A while back, I had this crazy thought of trying to visit the police in Cahul." Carolyn's eyebrows went up, but she didn't comment. He continued, with mounting enthusiasm, "If Nazari introduced me, they might cooperate with me." He rubbed the stubble on his chin. "Have the Cahul police shared any of their conventional forensic evidence with the U.S?"

"Not to my knowledge," she said, "but don't quote me."

"At the very least, I'd like to get my hands on the baggie the powder was in."

"I assumed you had it." Carolyn sounded surprised.

"No, they repackaged the HEU. It's a long shot, but forensics on the baggie may tell us something more than we already know."

Alan broke in. "Seems like long shots are all we have left."

Carolyn looked at her watch. "Glad we could chat. Remember, I didn't suggest anything."

Steven grinned. "You were never here, right?"

She didn't smile back. "You're on your own now."

Alan stayed behind after Carolyn left. "Seems they tied her hands behind her back," he said. "She took a big risk talking to you."

The phrase *on your own now* reverberated in Steven's mind. Doubt intruded on his earlier enthusiasm. "And she's encouraging me to take a huge risk. If the Lab or FBI ever hears about my side trip to the Cahul police, I'll be in serious trouble."

"No bigger a risk than you've already taken." Alan's eyebrows arched. "So, are you going to do it?"

Steven took in a deep breath and then blew it out through pursed lips. "Not sure."

After Alan left, Steven weighed the risks and rewards. Willingness to take scientific risks was one of his strengths, but this course of action would be a whole different ball game. In fact, it would violate Department of Energy policy. DOE strictly prohibited Lab scientists from anything that smacked of an undercover role. If DOE or the Lab ever found out, he might even lose his job. And could he gain anything new that could help break open the case? Maybe. But probably not.

He put his hands behind his head and gazed at the ceiling. Did he dare do this without the backing of the government?

One risk outweighed all others. Terrorists were poised to do the unthinkable. But the FBI didn't believe it. Now, except for Carolyn, the CIA didn't believe it either. He stared at the Hiroshima photo on his wall as the flare in his stomach caught fire. He took a deep breath and let it out slowly between his clenched lips. *Dammit, it's a long shot, but I've got to give it a try.*

CHAPTER 30

Ahmad's Metal Shop (May 5)

Ahmad tightened the last bolt that attached the end cap to the gun barrel. Good, it fit perfectly. Tomorrow he'd pack the end cap with conventional explosive to prepare for testing the entire assembly with depleted uranium in a nearby secluded canyon. Uncle wanted to be sure the HEU parts in the bomb wouldn't jam when they fired into each other.

Omar was about to remove the mold pieces from the uranium rod they'd cast yesterday. Getting solid metal had proved to be a greater challenge for the geometry of this singular piece, and Ahmad hoped this latest effort would be a success. Omar grunted as he leaned into the effort. After the mold fell away, Ahmad determined the density and smiled when he realized they'd reduced the voids to an acceptable level. He was ahead of schedule. It wouldn't be a problem to detonate during the lead-up to America's 9/11 commemoration.

The man who usually worked in the front room stuck his head in the door. "You got something in the mail from your uncle," he said, handing a package to Ahmad.

Ahmad ripped the envelope open. He grimaced when he pulled out another *Quantum Leap* DVD. It was too soon, by at least a month.

The previous DVD had arrived several weeks earlier. Its hidden file described Uncle's change in the plan that would further hide his role in the plot. Though the change would make Ahmad's job more difficult and add weeks of extra work, it was an ingenious solution and well worth the effort. He was less enthused by Uncle's confidence they could still keep to the original schedule.

With a sense of apprehension, Ahmad opened the hidden file on the new DVD and read the first paragraph with growing dismay.

July 4th! The new target date!

Uncle wanted the Americans' national holiday, when they celebrated their freedom, to forever be linked to the greatest assault they'd ever experienced on their own soil. In comparison, it would make 9/11 look like a child's playground squabble.

His heart fluttered. Only two months from now. That was awfully soon.

Uncle instructed him to be ready for a call tonight when they'd settle on a new date for shipping. The rest of the file described the plan for transporting the device into the U.S. Ahmad was relieved to learn Raushan would handle the oceanic transport. Raushan operated many legitimate businesses, and he would include this very special product in one of his regular heavy equipment shipments to Mexico. The shortened time frame disconcerted Ahmad, but it gratified him to read that Uncle was counting on him to execute the last steps.

After a quick supper, he tossed an antacid in his mouth and paced back and forth in the empty shop while he memorized the code words they would use in their call.

His new burner phone rang. "Hello, Nephew. How are you this evening?" Uncle asked in an uncannily nonchalant tone.

Ahmad tried to match Uncle's tone. "Very well, Uncle."

"How many exhibition games do you need before your football team is ready to start the regular season?"

Ahmad double-checked his code word list. Yes, the number of exhibition games referred to how long it would take him to finish fabrication and be ready to ship. Each exhibition game represented two weeks of work. He made his most optimistic projection, so as not to disappoint Uncle. "It's gone well the past few weeks. Three more pre-season games should be enough."

"Really? That many?" Uncle's tone carried a dangerous edge.

Did Uncle expect him to work miracles? Ahmad ran through some options in his mind. His team had been doing well, and if he summoned up all his persuasive skills, he could get them to work longer days. "Maybe we can skip one exhibition game. But we need at least two."

"I talked to your league commissioner, and he changed the starting date of the regular season to May 27th."

Ahmad gulped. Finish everything in three weeks? He pushed back. "That will give us fewer practices. I'll need to shorten the playbook."

"What would you take out?"

Ahmad doubted the explosive test with the depleted uranium was necessary, and it would save a lot of time if he dropped it. He reached for his code word list, but his sleeve brushed it off the table. As it fluttered to the floor, he said, "I'd drop the set piece with..." Crouching on the floor, he grabbed the list and then added, "With the additional striker."

"Are you sure you won't need it?"

"It's the best move I can make to adjust to the new schedule."

"Okay, let me know if any injuries crop up."

Good. Uncle was offering to visit the shop again if any new problems proved too difficult for Ahmad to solve. "Of course, but I think my players are all in good condition."

Uncle shifted into his professorial tone. "I sent you my thoughts on your best strategy for the upcoming season. Do you have questions?"

Ahmad summoned up his most confident tone. "Your strategy for the season is clear."

"Once the season starts, you may need to make adjustments on the fly. Feel free to get back to me."

"Don't worry, I will."

After Ahmad hung up, he stretched to relieve the tension in his shoulders. In only three weeks, Raushan's men would show up to crate up their Independence Day gift to America and start it on its journey. Ahmad's team would need to work night and day. And despite the rush, he couldn't afford to make a mistake. Raushan's warning echoed in his mind—*Failure is not an option.*

CHAPTER 31

Bucharest, Romania (May 30)

The past month had been a succession of one anxiety-ridden day after another. Each passing day brought the prospect of nuclear Armageddon one day closer, while Steven stood helpless on the sidelines. When he finally boarded the plane to Bucharest, Romania, the weight of anxiety lifted slightly. At least he was doing something.

On the first day of the ITWG meeting, he scanned the gathering crowd and was relieved when he spotted Tariq Nazari. Steven made a point of greeting him before the opening session and invited him to dinner that evening. Nazari beamed and suggested his favorite downtown restaurant. At that moment, John Kittrick walked up. Nazari shook John's hand and invited him to join them for dinner. When John agreed, Steven groaned internally. John's presence would complicate his strategy for gaining Nazari's cooperation.

Steven's talk that day featured his results for the current ITWG collaborative exercise. From a research point of view, it had proved quite interesting, as it was the first ITWG exercise that analyzed uranium metal. He presented measurements for several radiometric clocks. The different apparent ages indicated this form of uranium would be difficult to date. He hypothesized that the casting process had not removed all of the radioactive decay products, violating one of the necessary conditions for obtaining valid ages. When he further suggested some decay products were more completely removed than others, leading to the wide spread in apparent ages, he was relieved to see heads nod in the audience.

Sure enough, when the session chair opened the floor to questions, other researchers shared they had found similar strange results. A hand went up in the back of the room, but Steven didn't recognize the person until he stood up. It was Alexander Stoyanov, a Bulgarian scientist who was attending his first ITWG meeting.

Stoyanov asked, "Is it reasonable to say that the shortest age is when the uranium metal was actually cast?"

Steven replied, "I don't have enough information to make that assertion. We don't even know the location of our sample relative to the entire cast of the metal. I suspect, though, that all the apparent ages are older than the actual age."

Then Nazari stood up, and after the chair recognized him, he asked, "Obviously, more research is needed to ascertain whether or not we can age-date uranium metal. What do you suggest as the next step?"

Steven smiled. He hadn't asked Nazari to pose this question, but he was happy to answer it. "The best approach would be to conduct a controlled experiment where we cast a uranium metal part. Then I'd section the metal along a vertical axis and analyze samples from along the entire length."

Nazari nodded knowingly. "That's an excellent suggestion. I hope you'll do it, and I'd be happy to collaborate with you."

Steven replied, "I'll let you know if I get funding for such an experiment."

Steven felt buoyed as he walked back to his seat. Though he wasn't surprised the age-dating results stumped everybody else, he was pleased that his explanation and impromptu proposal were so well received.

Later that evening, when Steven arrived at the restaurant, he discovered the party had grown to nine people. Nazari brought several Romanian scientists with him, and Kittrick had invited others as well. Not at all the intimate gathering Steven had hoped for. On second thought, though, the group's size could work to his benefit. As the group milled around the large round table, Steven gestured for Nazari to sit next to him. Unfortunately, John noticed and excused himself as he made his way around the table. When he sat on the other side of Nazari, Steven fought to keep from showing his disappointment.

Midway through dinner, and after he ordered a second round of beers, Steven waited until John turned away to talk to Alexander Stoyanov, who had come along with the Romanian scientists. Steven's legs tightened as he made his move. Quietly, he said to Nazari, "Did you hear about the incident in Moldova last December?"

Kittrick's head whipped around, and he frowned at Steven.

This time a groan did escape from Steven, though he doubted John heard it above the noise in the restaurant. But now that he'd asked the question, the die was cast.

Nazari replied, "The local newspaper reported it, and the police actually asked me for help with the case. Did they go to you too?"

"Yes, they asked the U.S. for assistance."

"They only asked me to determine the level of enrichment. I don't have your sophisticated mass-spec capability, but I was able to make a reasonably good measurement."

As they continued to discuss their results, their conversation became the focus of everyone at the table. Steven was careful to only reveal the results he'd previously reported to Kittrick, and he stayed away from offering interpretations. Then Nazari said, "Undoubtedly, you noticed the similarities with the earlier case in Romania. After all, you analyzed that sample too."

Steven raised an eyebrow. "That didn't escape my attention. What do you make of it?"

Stoyanov answered, "I heard that this Moldovan smuggler had access to much more of the same HEU."

For the first time, Kittrick engaged on the topic. "We were told he made that claim. Do you think that's credible?"

Stoyanov shrugged. "Hard to know what to make of it."

Kittrick looked around the table. "Does anybody have an idea where this material came from?"

Good, Steven thought. John just asked the most pertinent question.

One of the Romanian scientists said, "Probably somewhere in Russia. But that's usually the most obvious conclusion."

Heads around the table nodded, and the conversation turned to other topics.

Steven still wanted to talk to Nazari alone, hoping the privacy might prompt him to offer more information, but no opportunities arose that wouldn't draw Kittrick's attention. On the last day of the ITWG meeting, Steven saw John head toward the restroom during the morning break. He seized the opportunity and invited Nazari to join him for a brief walk outside.

Trying not to sound too desperate, Steven asked, "Can you tell me anything more about the Moldova case?"

Nazari pondered a few moments. "I can't think of anything else offhand."

Steven decided to risk getting more specific. "Have you, by any chance, ever visited the fuel fabrication facility in Novosibirsk?"

"No, why do you ask?"

"We'd like to learn more about it."

"One of my former employees once worked there. Come to think of it, I remember him mentioning their operation was sloppy at times. Employees sometimes brought souvenirs home."

"Souvenirs like archival ampoules?"

"I'd imagine," Nazari said.

This line of questioning wasn't yielding anything definitive, so Steven went in another direction. "Would you be willing to introduce me to the Moldovan police?"

Nazari's eyebrows went up. "What would you hope to learn that they haven't already told the FBI?"

Steven glanced around to make sure no one was within earshot. "The FBI kind of lost interest in the case. Which I think was a mistake."

Nazari tilted his head as he regarded Steven. Then he bobbed his head and said, "That reminds me of a talk you gave a few years ago. You were rather passionate about the importance of fully investigating every case until you could conclude it didn't represent a serious threat."

"Glad it made an impression on you."

Nazari gave a little snort. "You have that way about you." He paused. "Here's what I can do. I'll call the lead investigator and try to arrange a meeting for you."

"Thanks so much. And let's just keep this between the two of us."

A slight grin creased Nazari's mouth. "As you wish, I won't mention it to Kittrick."

...

Two days later, Steven entered the Cahul police station and found Captain Rosca waiting for him. The captain bowed slightly, and Steven said, "Thank you so much for agreeing to meet with me."

"To what do I owe the pleasure of your visit?" Rosca asked in halting English as he ushered Steven into his office.

For the umpteenth time, Steven wondered if he was crazy. But desperate times called for desperate measures. The captain's deferential manner was encouraging, but Steven needed to win his confidence. "As Dr. Nazari may have told you, I'm the American scientist who led the nuclear forensics examination of the highly enriched uranium that you interdicted. I was in Bucharest this week for a scientific meeting, and since you were nearby, I thought it would be good to talk with you in person. Do you have any questions about my findings?"

Indeed, the captain had questions. This new field of nuclear forensics fascinated him. Steven was always glad to talk about his craft with a person who was truly interested, so he patiently answered each question. Explaining the age-dating proved to be daunting, but

Rosca kept asking questions until he understood. Or pretended to understand.

Rather than making sure the policeman grasped the concept, which he might find insulting, Steven said, "You catch on fast."

Rosca settled back into his chair with a contented sigh. "You're a good teacher."

Steven asked, "What more can you tell me about this case?"

Rosca pursed his lips. "Did you know that while Grosu was out on bail, he was killed in a car accident?"

"I heard that."

"After that, I was told to drop the case."

Steven wanted to growl, but instead bit his lip. "Was it just a co-incidence he was killed right after he got out of jail?" He held out his hands to plead his case. "Doesn't that suggest this case is about more than a few grams of enriched uranium?"

Rosca snorted. "The smuggling network he belonged to is ruthless. They killed him for being stupid enough to get caught."

Steven went out on a limb as far as he dared to go. "I believe it's imperative to continue investigating this case. Can't you do anything more?"

Rosca shook his head. "I don't see what else I can do."

"Then I have one favor to ask."

"Is there something you aren't telling me?" Rosca asked.

Steven was tempted to allude to his additional evidence, in the faint hope it would prompt Rosca to reopen the case. Given the van-ishingly small likelihood that gambit would succeed, he held back. He replied, "More details will have to come from the U.S. government."

Rosca nodded.

Steven made one last request to keep his risky side trip from being a complete bust. "Could you at least let me analyze the baggie that contained the uranium?"

"I can't imagine how that would help. But why not? The case is closed."

When Steven shuffled out of the police station, he let out a loud breath and his shoulders slumped. He had taken yet another gamble, but it seemed he had netted little. Nazari had tried to be helpful, but his bit of insight on Novosibirsk just reinforced the FBI narrative. He doubted that Captain Rosca had withheld any information, yet all he had to show for his visit was the baggie. And like Alan had said, analyzing the baggie was a long shot. A very long long shot.

CHAPTER 32

Newport, Oregon (June 10)

Steven suggested to Carissa they postpone the family vacation to his parents' place, but she insisted they stick with the plan. She hoped Jacob's grandparents could break through his angry protective shell. It could make a big difference at Jacob's adjudication hearing in two weeks. Steven conceded the point, so three days after his return from Bucharest, the family piled into their minivan and headed north on I-5.

During the drive, to take his mind off his concern over Jacob, he kept going over the plan he'd developed with Michelle for analyzing the baggie. He snapped his fingers when a new idea popped into his head. They should examine the inner surface of the baggie using the scanning electron microscope. Perhaps electrostatic forces had caused some extraneous material to adhere. Not wanting to leave any stone unturned, not even a pebble, at the next rest stop he walked out of earshot and called Michelle with his suggestion.

On the second day at his parent's place, Steven asked his dad to take a walk. When the two of them reached the beach, Steven took off his sandals and inhaled deeply, relishing the salty tang of the sea breeze. The feeling of damp sand under his bare feet and the sound of waves thumping on the beach brought back fond memories as a boy vacationing on this same beach. He'd heartily approved of his parents' decision to make their Newport vacation house their permanent residence after Dad retired as a psychology professor at Oregon

State University. In Steven's opinion, this stretch of the Pacific Coast was the most beautiful of the entire U.S. West Coast. Maybe someday he'd retire here too.

Steven asked, "How did it go with Jacob this morning?"

"I talked to him about his addiction. He didn't open up much, but he did listen closely to what I had to say."

"How did you manage that?"

"I told him about my own struggle." In response to Steven's look of surprise, his father added, "I haven't told you this story before."

Steven shortened his stride to match his father's slower pace. Dad continued, "During my college years, I began drinking a lot, mostly on weekends. Then, during my early years as a non-tenured professor, I began drinking every evening to ease my stress. Your mother became alarmed, but I thought she was overreacting because her father was an alcoholic. Five years later, my first opportunity at tenure was denied—"

Steven interrupted. "You were denied?" Maybe this explained why his father seemed so distracted during Steven's early childhood.

Dad pursed his lips. "I don't like to talk about it because of what happened next. I went on a binge that lasted four days. When Monday rolled around, I was too hungover to teach my classes. When I asked your mother to call in sick for me, she put her foot down. Her exact words were, 'I'll be damned if I'll cover for you.' Then she gave me an ultimatum. Stop drinking or she was leaving."

Steven was stunned by this revelation. "What did you do?"

"At first, I resented the threat. Then I realized her ultimatum came from a place of love. So I stopped. And got help."

"How did Jacob react to your story?"

"His grandma's feistiness surprised him. But he tip-toed around the subject of his own addiction."

"Did he talk about his arrest?"

"He tried to convince me it was just a big misunderstanding."

"The case seems pretty strong."

"I think, deep down, Jacob's scared. But he's reluctant to talk about it."

To hide his disappointment, Steven picked up a piece of driftwood and flung it into the ocean. In silence, they watched the driftwood toss on the waves as it made its way back to the beach.

Dad turned to face him. "How're you doing, Steven? You seem more stressed than usual."

"Work has been tough." Steven sighed and launched into his tale of woe. He highlighted the career risk he took by going rogue and taking his evidence to the CIA. Dad nodded occasionally but didn't interrupt. When Steven neared the end of his story, the fear he tried to keep at bay welled up again. An image from an old movie came to mind. The good guy strapped to a table, a big buzzsaw slowly approaching. Steven felt like he was strapped to that table.

He shook his head, as if to wake up from a bad dream. "It's been three whole months since I brought my evidence to the CIA. Any day now I believe catastrophe will strike, but nobody's doing anything about it." His voice quavered. "It's tearing me apart. I was awake half of last night, running through various scenarios and beating my brains out trying to come up with something more I can do."

Dad's face screwed up in pain as Steven poured out his lament. "Could you have done anything different, son?"

"No. But I still feel like I've failed."

"The failure's not yours to own. You can't let it consume you."

Dad started walking down the beach again, with the waves occasionally sweeping in and lapping over their feet. "How's Carissa doing? Things seem a little off between the two of you."

Leave it to Dad to bring up relationship issues. But with the lid on Steven's emotions pried open, his usual reticence to talk about his marriage faded into thin air. "Carissa's not happy with me. A few months ago, she confronted me about a growing distance between us. I tried to respond, but if I'm honest, I haven't done very well. Then this case came up. Then the double whammy of Jacob's addiction and arrest. It's all too much for her." He paused. "For me too."

Dad was silent. Steven looked over and saw furrows of deep sadness etched into his father's face. Steven said, "Oh, Dad, we're not thinking about divorce."

His father seemed to summon up a resolve. "Something else happened early in my career. A year after I started at the university, my department added another young professor. A woman. Even though we were competitors, we shared the same pressures of teaching new classes, writing research proposals, and attracting graduate students. Our common challenges drew us to one another. As our relationship grew, we shared more personal aspects of our lives."

Steven's stomach clenched. "Oh no, Dad."

"I'll spare you the details. Today it's called an emotional affair. Though we didn't sleep together, my preoccupation with her pushed your mother to the periphery of my life."

"Did Mom find out?"

"I tried to hide it, but in time she got wind of it. I felt so ashamed when she confronted me."

Steven felt light-headed. Another shocker from Dad. A pit formed in his stomach as he recalled two years ago when Michelle accused him of an emotional affair. "Obviously, the two of you worked through it."

"It was painful and complicated. I'm telling you this so you don't go down the same road. The amount of stress you're under now probably feels unbearable. That's why it's more important than ever to keep your relationship with Carissa as your number one priority."

"Message received, Dad. Let's head back. Hey, how about that new quarterback of yours at Oregon State?"

Dad went along with the sudden shift of topic. On the way back to the house, they reviewed the prospects for the PAC-12 teams in the upcoming football season. But even a discussion about football couldn't distract Steven from his fears. The world was hurtling toward disaster. His family was marching toward a cliff. And he felt helpless to stop either one.

CHAPTER 33

Newport, Oregon (June 10)

When Steven and Carissa got ready for bed that evening, she asked about his talk with his father. He recounted his dad's battle with alcohol and Jacob's unwillingness to talk about his own struggle.

She looked up from removing her makeup. "Maybe with more time, Jacob will open up to his grandpa."

"Yeah, maybe." The tone of his voice betrayed his doubt.

"Did you know about your dad's drinking?"

"No. And I'm rather miffed he told Jacob before me."

Carissa put away her makeup paraphernalia. "Maybe he only tells people when he senses it might benefit them." She picked up her toiletry bag and headed toward the bathroom.

Steven stopped in the middle of hanging up his shirt. If only Dad had told him earlier about his emotional affair. He rushed over to intercept Carissa and put his arms around her. "Carissa, I love you so much. I want to apologize for neglecting you so often. My response to your warning about the distance between us has been haphazard. I'm sorry. Very sorry."

She pulled back to look directly into his eyes. "That means so much to me, Steven. Thank you."

"Dad had another surprise for me this afternoon. During those years he was drinking a lot, he had an affair." He felt her stiffen. "Actually, it was an emotional affair."

She pushed away from him, shaking her head. "That's hard for me to imagine."

He retold his father's cautionary tale. Carissa shuddered at the part about Dad becoming emotionally attached to the other woman. When he came to Dad's admission that he'd pushed his wife to the periphery of his life, she stared at the bedroom door as if she longed to bolt through it.

Finally, she said, "I'm not sure I want to hear any more."

Carissa's shock wasn't a surprise, but Steven was taken aback by the intensity of her emotion. He said, "I could tell Dad still feels a lot of remorse about the pain he caused Mom."

Carissa took a step toward the door. "I'll go brush my teeth now."

"Wait a minute," he said. Should he tell her about his emotional affair? Avoid Dad's mistake of not confessing? He'd come close to telling Carissa soon after he cut off the relationship with the other woman, but the fear that their marriage couldn't bear the weight stopped him. Could he tell her the truth now?

She kept looking at him, her head cocked at an angle.

He shook his head. "Never mind."

She was gone longer than usual. When she returned, she seemed more composed. Resolute, perhaps. She grabbed his hand. "We need to talk."

She pulled him over to the bed, sat down, and patted the bed next to her. Alarm bells went off in his head. She shifted to face him. "I've been waiting for the right time to tell you this. Steven, I know you had an affair with a woman at the Lab."

A grenade exploded in Steven's mind. *Damn my hesitation! And damn my lack of courage!*

When he started to explain he'd almost confessed a few minutes earlier, she shushed him. "Let me finish. When I first learned about it, it devastated me. I couldn't believe you'd do such a thing. After I absorbed the blow, here's what hurt the most. You didn't trust me with the truth."

Steven bowed his head. "I'm so ashamed." Tears trickled down his face. "I don't know if it makes any difference to you, but I never had sex with her."

"At least I don't need to deal with that image." Her voice stayed firm. "But it still feels like betrayal."

He lifted his head to look at Carissa, but stopped when he spotted her wedding ring. He'd broken his vow to her. And then hidden it. He had no excuse.

Still unable to look into her eyes, he opened his mouth, but the words stuck in his throat. He shuddered and finally said, "I am so sorry for the way I've hurt you. Can you ever forgive me?"

Gazing at her ring, he felt its reproach. Her diamond had become a symbol of his promise broken. The ring wobbled, and then her hand reached toward him. She lifted his chin until he looked into her eyes.

Steven was stunned. Where he had expected to see anger, he saw compassion. Her eyes glistened with tears. She shifted her hand to cradle his cheek. In a quiet voice, she said, "Steven, I've already forgiven you. It wasn't easy. When I first learned about your affair, I fantasized about ways to punish you. Make you feel some of my pain. My heart started to grow cold toward you. But that just made me more miserable."

He sobbed, overcome with remorse and gratitude. "How could you forgive me before we even talked?"

A small smile spread across her face. "A while back, I mentioned I've learned a lot about forgiveness. In this instance, I understood that our future rested on my being able to forgive you." She stood up and held out her arms.

He melted into her embrace and whispered, "I don't deserve you."

She gently pushed him away and then gripped his shoulders. "Though I've forgiven you, I don't feel like I can trust you again. Not yet, not the way I did before."

He marveled at his wife's forthrightness, compassion, and wisdom. He sensed the past half hour marked a profound turning point for their marriage. And for him. With fervor, he said, "I get it. And I'm going to earn your trust again."

She inclined her head and seemed to weigh his declaration. "I believe you're sincere, but old habits die hard. Like your dad said, we have a tough road ahead of us. So here's *my* promise. I'm going to fight for our marriage. When your work seems more important to you than me, I'm going to call you on it. Because I'll never stop loving you."

A short time later, Carissa was asleep while he lay awake, replaying the events of the day. As he drifted to sleep, Carissa's last statement echoed in his mind. *I'll never stop loving you.*

For far too long, he'd treated his work as more valuable than his wife and family. What a fool I've been.

CHAPTER 34

Nuevo Laredo, Mexico (June 11)

The bomb parts got to Mexico with no glitches, but that wasn't a surprise. Raushan's shipping company was well-positioned to execute that part of the plan. Ahmad and his team picked up the crates in the maritime port of Tampico and transported them to Nuevo Laredo. Uncle had chosen this port of entry because it was among the busiest along the Mexico-U.S. border. Omar was the first to cross into the U.S. with a crate, and Ahmad leaped into the air when he received Omar's text announcing success. As each subsequent entry proceeded without raising alarm, Ahmad's apprehension faded.

Ahmad stood on the walkway outside his second-story motel room, gazing at the port of entry into Laredo, Texas. He spotted Hamid walking into the parking lot. It was Hamid's turn to take a crate across the border, but Hamid was getting jumpy. Ahmad needed to calm him down so he wouldn't tip off the border agents.

They entered Ahmad's room, and he gestured for Hamid to take the only chair. He opened the struggling mini-fridge and grabbed two nearly cold bottles of Coca-Cola. Popping off the caps, he offered one to Hamid, and then sat on the bed. Ahmad took a big swallow and smacked his lips. "Okay, Hamid, let's go over the plan once more."

Hamid looked up at the ceiling. "I'll dress in business clothes and put all my paperwork in my briefcase."

Ahmad nodded. Raushan had provided all the business materials from a fictitious company owned by one of his many shell companies. "Don't forget to put your business cards in your wallet."

Hamid dipped his head. "I'll drive my rental car to meet the transport company's van at the storage site. After I confirm the driver's identity, I'll take my crate out of the storage unit and load it into his van."

"You don't need to worry about the driver asking questions," Ahmad assured him. "Raushan arranged for the transport company to include our crates among their legitimate equipment supplies."

Hamid seemed to relax. "I'll go first across the border. If everything seems normal, I'll text the van driver to go ahead."

"And if they bring the dogs out, don't worry. We've ensured the van has no drugs. Tell me, what does 'everything seems normal' look like?"

Hamid enumerated the warning signs he'd look for at the port of entry. Pleased with Hamid's thoroughness, Ahmad praised him. A tentative smile appeared on Hamid's face. "Thanks, boss. I'm ready now."

Ahmad gave him a thumbs-up. "Text me the all-clear when you arrive at your Laredo hotel."

Later that day, Ahmad walked down the street to eat a late lunch at a little taqueria he'd discovered. Their fish tacos were fantastic. Just as he sat down, his phone buzzed. Sure enough, a text from Hamid. Success. In celebration, he ordered a double portion of the tacos.

While he wolfed down the food, his mind drifted to his early days in the jihadist training camp. When he recalled the derision heaped upon him, his knuckles whitened as he gripped the edge of the table. If only they could see him now, on the verge of a monumental accomplishment. It will dwarf anything they could even imagine.

The desire to share his success seized him with unexpected intensity. He'd call his cousin, who had become his closest confidant. He'd already told him a lot about his grand adventure. Surely it wouldn't hurt to share this moment with him.

He checked his watch. Good, it was only 10:00 pm in Azerbaijan. He entered the phone number he knew by heart.

The phone rang several times before his cousin answered. "Who is this?"

"It's me, Ahmad." Moved by the voice of someone who loved him, he fought back his tears.

"What a surprise! You've never called me from this number. Where are you?"

"This is a burner phone."

"Are you okay?"

"I'm doing great!" Ahmad punctuated the last word by flinging out his arm.

"Wonderful." His cousin sounded relieved. "You haven't called in a long time, so I was beginning to worry."

"Sorry about that." His eyes flashed as he carefully worded his next statement. "I'm making excellent progress on my latest business venture."

His cousin picked up on his excitement. "Is it fair to say that you are moving forward by leaps and bounds?"

Smiling, Ahmad picked up on the allusion to the code name he'd whimsically given his operation. Looking around, he verified no one was listening. "You might even call it a quantum leap."

"Your name will go down in history as one of our greatest warriors."

His cousin's praise sparked joy in Ahmad's heart that raced outward until his fingers tingled. He grinned from ear to ear. "You have no idea how good that makes me feel."

Back in his room a little while later, Ahmad's head began to throb. His stomach felt queasy, and suddenly, he sprinted for the bathroom and threw up.

Wiping his mouth, he felt slightly less nauseous. But his headache was getting worse. An image of his lunchtime fish tacos floated into his mind.

He was supposed to take the last crate across the border the next morning. What should he do if he didn't feel better by then? Still try to make the border crossing? Or wait till later?

CHAPTER 35

Newport, Oregon (June 12)

Steven glanced at his vibrating phone as he took another big bite of the pancakes his sons had prepared for Sunday brunch. The 703 prefix was unfamiliar. He ignored it and gave his attention to the story Dad was telling Josh and Jacob. The lively conversation of the family around the breakfast table warmed him even more than the delicious food. It especially encouraged him to see Jacob join in, often smiling.

When he left the table, he remembered to check his phone. A new voicemail. He listened to it and almost dropped the phone when he heard John Kittrick's voice.

"Steven, this is John Kittrick. Call me ASAP at this number."

What could be so urgent on a Sunday? Probably not good news. Better to get it over with. When he got to his bedroom, he hit the call icon on the voice message.

Kittrick answered after the first ring. "You're unbelievable!"

Steven had never heard Kittrick so angry. He took a deep breath to prepare himself.

"Last night, the CIA informed us they intercepted a conversation that included coded language for a serious threat. The type of threat you warned us about. I did some digging and eventually discovered that three months ago you briefed the CIA on the Moldova case. Why is *this* the first I'm hearing about *that*?"

Steven's stomach lurched. *I'm in deep shit now.*

He paced back and forth. "I understand you're upset. But isn't the alert a bigger issue?"

"Are *you* telling *me*," Kittrick said, sarcasm dripping from every word, "what the FBI should be doing?"

"No, but I can't help wondering how credible the threat is."

John became indignant. "And you think we're not assessing it? The evidence seems somewhat weak, but we're by no means dismissing it."

Unsure how to respond, Steven held his tongue.

"You royally pissed off the Director," Kittrick continued. "He screamed at me about failing to control you."

Steven reached for the water bottle on his bedside table to moisten his suddenly dry mouth, only to find it empty. "I'm sorry, John. I realize I've put you in a tough spot."

Kittrick cleared his throat. "Frankly, Steven, I don't know if I can ever trust you again."

The words cut deep. Steven had always seen himself as a very trustworthy person. At least in his professional life. First Carissa, now Kittrick, expressing their doubts about trusting him.

He wanted John to understand the rationale behind his actions. "When the Director shut down the case, I got the sense you didn't agree. But of course you couldn't tell me that. So... I proceeded with an internal research project."

Kittrick became sarcastic again. "Cute move, but it doesn't change the fact that you disobeyed my direct order."

The bedroom door opened and Carissa breezed in. As soon as she saw Steven, the smile dropped from her face. In response to her quizzical look, he mouthed, "John Kittrick." She retreated and closed the door behind her.

Still trying to plead his case, Steven said, "Don't you at least want to hear about the additional evidence I've uncovered?"

"The CIA already sent us your briefing slides. And right now, I don't want to hear any more from you."

Steven couldn't let the call end without asking the question that kept buzzing in his mind throughout the call. "Did my brief to the CIA play a role in this intel warning?"

"Here's the reason I called," John said, ignoring Steven's question. "The Director scheduled a special meeting on Tuesday morning at 9:30 where you will account for your actions."

The threatening tone of Kittrick's voice unnerved him. "What? In only two days. I'm on vacation with my family in Oregon."

"Not my problem. Be there on Tuesday morning. Or else."

Steven gulped. "Or else what?"

"Just. Be. There." The steel in Kittrick's voice persuaded Steven that further argument would be futile.

In a resigned voice, Steven said, "I'll do my best."

"See you Tuesday morning." Kittrick hung up before Steven could say goodbye.

The bedroom door opened, and Carissa entered, looking puzzled and worried. "What's going on?"

"The FBI found out I went to the CIA. The FBI Director has ordered me to meet with him in DC. On Tuesday."

Carissa's shoulders drooped. "I was afraid something like this might happen."

The dread that had been growing in Steven leaked into his voice. "I'll bet the FBI has already made up its mind. They're going to fire me."

Carissa closed the door and walked toward him. She embraced him and whispered, "I'm so sorry."

"It's hard to imagine no longer working nuclear forensics cases." The words caught in his throat. "I just hope it ends up being worth it."

Carissa hugged him tighter. "You did what you thought was right."

He sighed. "Dammit, what a mess!"

His ulcer fired a warning shot. He had to face it—his career was headed to a place he'd never imagined. Sidelined. And forgotten.

PART 2: WHO?

CHAPTER 36

Laredo, Texas (June 12)

What a whirlwind the past twelve hours had been for Carolyn. She may have finally gotten the break she'd hoped for. The NSA intercepted a call that included the phrase *Quantum Leap,* originating from Nuevo Laredo, Mexico, right across the border from Laredo, Texas. She couldn't be certain it signaled a nuclear bomb was about to enter the U.S., but if she was a betting woman, that's where she'd place her chips.

She pumped her fist and then leaped into action. After running things by her boss, she dispensed with normal bureaucratic protocol and drew upon her extensive list of contacts to rally resources at the FBI, Department of Energy, and Homeland Security. Because she knew more about the case than anyone else, she packed her to-go bag and made it to her red-eye flight out of Dulles with minutes to spare.

When she reached the FBI Resident Agency in Laredo, a tall, dark-haired man dressed in a black suit was pacing in the lobby. "You must be Carolyn." His tone suggested she was not very welcome. Not a surprise. In her experience, FBI agents resented the CIA showing up.

She held out her hand. "And you must be Special Agent Cunningham from the San Antonio Field Office."

The agent hesitated and then extended his own hand. "You can call me Cunningham. Follow me."

He showed her to an office that contained only a desk, filing cabinet, and a bookshelf filled with notebooks and manuals. He gestured to the nearest chair and said, "Have a seat."

The scent of cranberry and orange drew her attention to a couple of scones in a box on his desk. Her stomach growled, prompting her to regret she hadn't picked up breakfast earlier at the San Antonio airport, but she resisted the urge to ask for a scone. "Where do things stand?"

The agent grunted and grabbed a bottle of water. "When I showed up at the Customs and Border Protection Office earlier this morning, Homeland Security had warned them I'd be coming. At first they were leery, but their attitude became, shall I say, a lot more cooperative when I explained we may have a nuclear weapon about to enter the U.S."

She chuckled as she imagined the scene. "Will it be evident at the border crossing that we are in an emergency?"

"Perhaps," he said. "But that might be good. It may deter the bad guys if they sense we've beefed up our inspection protocols."

"Let me ask you a question. Generally speaking, what's the likelihood of stopping a nuclear weapon from entering the U.S.?"

He squinted. "Given the amount of drugs that get through, not that great."

"Right. So why tip them off that we're looking for them? They'll either wait until we relax, or worse yet, move to another port of entry."

"Got it," he said ruefully. "Keep the operation as covert as possible. And since the bomb is nuclear, we have the advantage of spotting it using radiation detectors. We'll assign more people to monitor the permanently installed detectors. And I'll make sure all agents are carrying the FBI's small radiation detectors."

Carolyn let her skepticism show.

Cunningham frowned and added, "Even then, I'm guessing our chances aren't that good."

"I agree. That's why I asked DOE to send radiation experts from Sandia and Los Alamos National Labs. They're equipped with advanced portable equipment. It'll improve our chances significantly, but if the terrorists shield the device, it'll still be very tough to detect."

He grimaced. "You're not making me feel better."

She pulled her own bottle of water out of her purse and took a sip. "Given the location of the phone intercept, our best bet is to put all our resources on the Juarez-Lincoln port of entry. My guess is they'd pick it since it's the largest port of entry along the U.S.-Mexico border." She put her fingers together as she tapped her chin. "It'll take a least a van-sized vehicle to carry the entire package, so we should focus on larger vehicles. Agents should also be on alert for anything that suggests an attempt at shielding."

Special Agent-in-Charge Cunningham looked away from her. She kept quiet, realizing the FBI preferred handling matters in their own way, without the unwelcome input from the CIA. At long last, he spoke. "I have to admit, your suggestions sound reasonable. I'll give the orders to implement them."

"Just let me know how I can help."

"I'll go back to the CBP office and then to the Juarez-Lincoln POE. When the Lab guys get here, bring them to the port."

The agent stood up, and then held out the box of scones. "Help yourself."

She grinned as she took one. "Thanks. Did the rumbling of my stomach give me away?"

...

Four hours later, Carolyn was at the port of entry. She shook her head as she looked across the huge stream of vehicles passing through. Agent Cunningham had instructed the Sandia scientists, who showed up first, to focus on the larger vehicles. But the number of lanes outnumbered the experts by more than two-to-one. *The bomb could be passing through as I stand here.*

Her stomach fluttered when a Sandia man hurried over to the Lane Three booth. Cunningham ran out to the booth too. Minutes later, he returned, looking flustered. "It was just iodine-131. The Sandia guy told me it's used to treat thyroid disease."

"You drew attention, the way you ran out there."

"Yeah, I noticed. I need a better way to communicate with the Lab guys."

When the day faded into darkness, Cunningham invited her to join him for a working dinner in an office at the border station. While they waited for their food to arrive, the two of them brainstormed on clear but subtle ways the Lab scientists could communicate radiation hits.

An agent poked his head in and placed a large Whataburger bag on the table. Just as they unwrapped their burgers, Cunningham's phone rang. It was the FBI Director. While the agent gave his report, the volume on the other end of the line rose steadily.

Cunningham hung up and groaned. "I understand the anxiety back in Washington. Hell, every hour that goes by, my stomach is tied in more knots. But they should realize that their constant requests for information distract me from actually stopping the threat."

With genuine sympathy, she said, "Glad you're the operational lead, Cunningham."

"On the good news front, the Los Alamos team will get here later this evening. Then we'll have at least one expert on every lane." He grabbed his burger. "Let's eat before our food gets any colder. And by the way, you can call me Dick."

Before he took a bite, he asked, "What are the chances the bomb has already gone across?"

The fear that Carolyn kept suppressing bubbled up, but she kept her voice neutral. "I've wondered that too. No way to know."

"I can't think of anything else to do." He rapped the table with his fist. "So, we just keep at it."

CHAPTER 37

Laredo (June 13)

Carolyn massaged her neck and took a mid-morning break from watching the border station's array of monitors. Right after she went out into the hallway, her phone rang. Before it could ring again, she answered.

"This is Caro—"

An urgent voice broke in. "We just pinged on the Quantum Leap phone. It's in or near Lane Nine, approaching the inspection point."

She sprinted back to the monitor room. "Stay on the line," she ordered. Heart pounding, she burst into the room and yelled, "Dick! Lane Nine!"

Dick looked up at the monitor while he grabbed his phone.

She added, "Or possibly Lane Eight or Ten."

Dick looked down at the contact list he'd prepared. Then he dialed a number, presumably for the radiation expert on Lane Nine.

"Carolyn."

She looked around to find who wanted her attention. Then she realized the voice came from her phone. "We can't track the phone because it was turned off after fifteen seconds."

Her urge to run out to Lane Nine was overwhelming, but she needed to slow down and think. *What next?*

As a field agent, she'd developed a reputation as the queen of improvisation. An idea began to form. She ran toward the CBP supervisor, who was already moving in her direction with a look of alarm.

Without waiting for the supervisor to speak, she said, "We need to slow down Lanes Eight through Ten. Call the Lane Nine officer and tell him to pretend that a bee stung him and he's going into anaphylactic shock. He should run out of his booth, calling for help. Tell the officers in Lanes Eight and Ten to rush over to him."

The supervisor looked skeptical.

Carolyn said, "It's weak, but I can't think of anything else."

She looked at the monitor array again. The next several vehicles in Lane Nine were all SUVs or sedans. The first two had families. Shifting to the Lane Eight monitor, she spotted a white van three vehicles from the booth. Could that be it?

She grabbed the supervisor's sleeve. "One more thing. Tell the officers I'm coming out, pretending to bring medical assistance."

Without waiting for a response, she ran over to Dick and relayed her plan. Without looking up from his phone, he said, "I'll be out in another minute."

Taking that as agreement, Carolyn rushed out the door. Halfway to her destination, she heard a yell and saw a man run out of Booth Nine.

When she reached Lane Nine, the CBP officer was moaning on the ground, with the officers from Lanes Eight and Ten hovering over him. She knelt beside the presumably stricken man, took a ballpoint pen out of her pocket, and pretended to inject it into his arm.

She spoke in a low voice so only the three border officers could hear. "I'll help this officer get back into his booth." She pointed at the other two. "Quietly tell the Lab guys in these three lanes that the target is in a vehicle close to the inspection booths. Meanwhile, process the vehicles very slowly to give the radiation experts more time to screen each one."

Carolyn ducked into Booth Nine. Sweat poured down her face in greater amounts than warranted by the Laredo summer heat alone. Just then, she spotted Dick trotting toward her. Excellent!

When Dick neared Lane Nine, he spread his arms out and spoke loud enough to be heard by all the nearby vehicles. "We've had a slight medical emergency, but it's under control now. Our officers will soon resume processing."

Dick stepped into the booth and closed the door behind him. "We should just shut down all three lanes and do a physical inspection of each vehicle."

It was a reasonable tactic, but one Carolyn had already discarded. "That tactic relies upon one crucial assumption. That the terrorists are not under orders to detonate immediately if the device is about to be confiscated. Think about it. The terrorists would still have the propaganda victory of killing thousands of Americans with a nuclear weapon on U.S. soil."

He tilted his head as he processed Carolyn's logic. "It would also make it much harder to determine who was responsible."

Dick used his phone to move other Lab experts over to these three lanes. Minute by minute crept by with no sign of detection.

Her stomach tightened when a Los Alamos scientist in Lane Ten put his hand on his chin. When he removed his hand, she let out her breath. It was the signal he'd only detected a medical radioactive isotope.

She looked back at Lane Eight in time to spot a Sandia woman approaching the same white van she had noticed earlier. She nudged Dick. "My bet is on that white Transportes Grupo van in Lane Eight."

"I'll head over there. If he's our guy, it'll be easier for me to take him."

Several more minutes dragged by as the two experts surveyed the white van with their portable detectors. The Sandia woman placed her detector on the ground under the van and left it there, pointing upward.

"Smart woman," Carolyn muttered to herself. At a briefing yesterday, the experts agreed the radiation signal from a device would be strongest underneath a vehicle. Which suggested the screener should bend down in an uncomfortable position for an extended time while holding the detector. This Sandia woman had devised an easier approach.

The van driver's head swiveled from side to side, watching the two scientists. He kept at least one hand on the steering wheel at all times. As the minutes passed, the driver's movements became more agitated.

The car in front of the van started to move forward. Before the van could follow, the Sandia woman snatched the detector and looked at the readout. Shielding the screen from the sun, she studied the detector's gamma-ray output. She looked over at Dick. Dick had eyes on her. The Sandia woman put her hand on her chin. Deliberately, she extended her forefinger and placed it next to her nose.

Adrenaline surged through Carolyn. *We got him!*

Dick had positioned himself near the back of the van. As the van slowly edged forward, the driver focused on the inspection booth ahead, and Dick took three long, quick steps toward the driver's door. Magically, his gun appeared in his hand.

Dick yelled, "Stop! FBI!" He tapped the driver's window with his gun. The driver jammed on his brakes and jerked around, his face contorted with fear.

"Not another move!" Dick barked. "Keep your eyes on me. Slowly move both hands to the top of the wheel." Dick kept his gun pointed at the driver.

"Next, use your left hand to open your window. Slowly."

The driver complied.

Dick's handcuffs appeared in his other hand. "Give me your left hand." The cuffs snapped down on the extended wrist and moments later snapped around the other wrist. Dick reached inside the car, unlocked the door, and flung the driver onto the pavement.

Carolyn sprinted out of the booth, turned the van's engine off, and removed the keys. She unlocked the back doors. The van was packed with wooden crates. A CBP officer appeared at her side. He took in the full compartment and asked, "Shall we move the van to secondary inspection?"

"That would be easier, but it'd take longer. We need to confirm ASAP that we got the right vehicle."

By now, half a dozen agents and scientists were gathered around the van. Dick stood over the driver, advising him of his rights. Carolyn took charge. "I can't see any crates large enough to hold the weapon. Take some out, in case there's a bigger one hidden from view."

Two men were required to lift some crates. After they'd removed half-a-dozen containers, Carolyn realized nothing looked big enough to hold a nuclear weapon. Her stomach clenched. Was she wrong about the threat? Or did they simply miss it?

Her heart in her mouth, she asked the same Sandia woman to survey the cargo. The scientist ran the detector over the surfaces she could reach. "Okay," the woman said, and pointed at a box near the middle of the van's original load. "I think you should open that one." The box was labelled as farm equipment.

Carolyn was puzzled but hopeful. To preserve evidence and establish the chain-of-control, she said, "Dick, could you open this crate?"

Dick put on a pair of gloves. A CBP officer handed him a crowbar, and Dick pried off the top of the box. He reached into foam packing bits and pulled out what looked to be part of a plow. He glanced at Carolyn, and she tried to hide her tension.

After Dick placed the plow piece to the side, he reached into the foam bits again. He groped around, grunted with surprise, and pulled out a dark grey disk with a big, round hole in the center.

"Holy shit!" said the Sandia team leader.

"Keep your voice down," Dick said. "I think I know what this is, but you tell me."

Taking in the many fascinated eyes watching the spectacle, the team leader whispered, "It's part of a gun-barrel weapon."

Carolyn let out a big breath she hadn't realized she'd been holding. Ever since her boss shut down the Moldova investigation, she'd worried it was a mistake. The disk in Dick's hand proved beyond all doubt that the threat she'd feared was underway. A glow of satisfaction spread through her. Though the odds of stopping the bomb had not been in their favor, they'd done it! The thrill of success left her tingling.

Then her elation turned to dread. They had intercepted only one part. She knew enough about nuclear weapons to realize the complete weapon would include many such disks. Would interdicting only one disk be enough to stymie the terrorists? She had a bad feeling about the answer.

Dick said, "All hell is about to break loose. I'll call the FBI Director immediately. Carolyn, you tell your Director."

Carolyn looked at the anxious but excited half-dozen faces in their circle. "Word of this can't get out. This interdiction is classified."

Dick added, "Tell no one else unless you have permission from me or someone higher in your chain of command."

An hour later, after impounding the Transportes Grupo truck and conducting the initial interrogation of the suspect, Carolyn and Dick huddled before Carolyn left. She said, "I'll bet the other pieces of the weapon will come through this same port." She grimaced. "Or they've already gone through."

Dick said, "We'll interrogate the suspect until we get everything he knows." The fierce look on his face suggested it would not be a gentle interrogation. "And we'll keep searching at the border for other parts."

"What are you going to do with the HEU?" she asked, anticipating the answer.

"Send it to one of our nuclear forensics labs."

She recalled Carter's dogged persistence and all the risks he'd taken to get them to this point. "This interdiction would've never happened without the work of Steven Carter at Lawrence Livermore. I understand the FBI is quite unhappy with Dr. Carter, but if I may offer my opinion, it would be foolish to not call upon him."

"I'll mention that to the Director."

"We got lucky today." With a sense of urgency, Carolyn added, "We need to exploit *every* advantage we can get. Even then, we'll need more luck to stop these bastards."

CHAPTER 38

Alexandria, Virginia (June 13)

John Kittrick grabbed a package of hot dogs on his way to the back yard. It was the first day of summer vacation, so he took the day off. "I'm going to start grilling," he yelled.

His daughter grunted but didn't look up from her tablet. His eight-year-old son yelled back, "Great, cuz I'm starved."

"Me too!" John said.

While removing the hot dogs from the grill, his phone rang. He fumbled for it and dropped a dog on the ground.

He stabbed the answer button, and making no attempt to hide his irritation, said, "Who is it?"

"Dick Cunningham from the San Antonio Field Office. Is this John Kittrick?"

"Speaking. What's up?"

"The nuclear alert paid off."

John sucked in his breath. "Did you interdict something?"

"Get down to the Hoover Building and I'll call with the details. But first things first. Where should I send the evidence? The Director of National Intelligence has recommended Lawrence Livermore."

John growled. "Right now, Livermore is in deep shit with our Director."

"I know, I just talked to him. He'd like to say screw Livermore, but the White House pressed him to draw upon our premium capabilities. He's leaving the decision to you."

"I'm pissed off with Livermore too. Their lead nuclear forensics scientist went rogue on me."

"The way I heard it, if he hadn't, we'd be clueless. Is Carter's team the best you've got?"

John paused. Los Alamos was excellent too. After Ben Stefanek transferred to Los Alamos, he had dropped in on John at the FBI Lab. Stefanek sang the praises of the nuclear forensics team he'd just joined and made some pointed jabs about Carter. But, if John put aside his anger with Carter, the nod would go to Livermore.

"They are," he replied.

"That decides it, right? Fly the evidence to Livermore?"

"Okay. When will it get there?"

"By this evening."

"I'll call you back as soon as I get to headquarters."

In a daze, John hung up the phone. When he'd agreed to take on this unusual specialty, he thought he was destined to languish in obscurity. Nuclear forensics cases rarely made the headlines.

He hurried back into the house. His wife, Sue, looked up from the kitchen where she was setting out condiments. "What's going on, John?"

"Sorry, babe. An emergency has come up. I can't even stay for lunch."

"Really, John? It's that important?"

"More important than you can imagine. I've got to get to Livermore. Could you pack for me while I make some calls? I'll be gone at least a week."

Without waiting for a reply, he rushed to his office to call Carter. He hoped Steven wasn't already in the air on his way to DC. The phone rang once, twice. *Come on, Steven, pick up.* Third ring.

"Hi, John." Steven sounded harried and resigned. "I didn't expect to hear from you today."

"Where are you?"

"I just went through security at the Portland airport."

"Good. You need to get back to Livermore today."

"Say what?" Shock and confusion filled Steven's voice.

John imagined many questions were running through Steven's mind. "An emergency has come up. Both of us need to get to your Lab tonight. Then we can talk."

"Does this mean I'm off the hook?"

"That's tabled for the moment. The evidence should arrive by this evening. Put your team on alert so we can start working immediately."

"The receiving department will be closed by then. And they'll want lots of information before they'll process the shipment."

John remembered one investigation when he'd sat in his Livermore hotel room for two days while LLNL receiving dotted their Is and crossed their Ts. For the first time in his life, John said, "Screw the usual protocol." With greater urgency, John added, "Before you get on the plane back to the Bay Area, call your Lab Director. Tell him there's a national emergency. He'll be hearing soon from the FBI Director. Or if that's not good enough, we could arrange a call from the White House."

Steven chuckled. "This should be fun. It might take the White House, though, to break through the bureaucratic morass of a DOE Laboratory."

"You've proven you're quite adept at getting around the usual channels. So I expect you to figure it out."

CHAPTER 39

The Lab (June 13)

It took Steven several tries and one threat to get through to his Laboratory Director. At first, the Director wanted to simply expedite the normal protocol and send the massive amount of HEU to the Plutonium Building. Steven pleaded that it was a national emergency and pushed for sending the material directly to the Nuclear Chemistry Building. That would give the fastest and best results. The Director objected because the weight of the HEU vastly exceeded the building limit. Steven explained how it still could be done safely, and after a long deliberation, the Director agreed.

Steven sighed with relief. "I'll get to the Lab by late afternoon."

The Director said, "Let me know when the evidence arrives. I'll escort it from the Lab perimeter to Nuclear Chemistry."

Steven was impressed by the Director's willingness to get personally involved. And it didn't even take a call from the White House. "Thanks. That'll smooth the way."

It was dark when Steven met the Director at the Lab's entrance gate. Fifteen minutes later, Kittrick drove up in a government car. The agent motioned for Steven and the Director to get in the back seat, and when Steven hopped in, he saw a package resting on the front passenger seat. As they approached the Nuclear Chemistry building, the five scientists Steven had summoned for this initial examination were waiting in front. Kittrick carried the package containing the HEU disk to the special receiving lab the scientists had just set up.

Kittrick grunted when he pulled the evidence out of its package and laid it on a plastic sheet. Steven looked at the faces huddled around the HEU disk. The group throbbed with excitement, though tempered by the weight of their responsibility. Steven took a deep breath. The shape of the disk left no doubt. For months he had been sure someone had enough HEU to make a nuclear weapon, but now he was sure someone had actually built a gun-barrel device.

What a surreal day! This morning he thought the FBI was done with him, and tonight he was the key scientist in the most important nuclear forensics case ever. The stakes were high. The value of nuclear forensics was about to be tested like never before. His team needed to quickly determine where the HEU came from, how the disk was manufactured, and discover other clues that could point them to the identity of the culprits.

They skipped the usual first step of developing a thorough written plan, because Washington expected their first results by tomorrow morning. Kittrick directed Michelle to document each step as they formulated and executed it. Steven was still smarting from the past couple days and concerned about Kittrick's "it's tabled for now." He decided he would hold back on his own ideas and speak up only when necessary.

Kittrick first gave an update on the forensics done in the field prior to shipping. "We know this disk is highly enriched uranium because the Sandia reading in the field gave an enrichment of about 80%. But that number has a large uncertainty, so our next step is to get a more precise measurement. The disk was wrapped in plastic when we interdicted it. The FBI dusted the exterior for fingerprints and also collected trace evidence. I suggest we start as we usually do, with high-resolution gamma counting before we open the package."

Steven bit his tongue. Thankfully, Michelle cleared her throat and shook her head slightly. Kittrick glanced at her and said, "On second thought, let's take off the plastic first. After we complete our initial examination, we'll gamma count."

Following Kittrick's instructions, a scientist from the Lab's Forensic Science Center cut away the plastic and placed the plastic pieces in evidentiary bags for later forensic processing. He then brushed the exterior of the HEU disk to collect any adhering materials. Next, he began the laborious process of photographing every surface of the disk. Though Steven knew photo documentation was important, he chafed at the need to wait before starting the analytical work.

An hour later, Kittrick asked Michelle to set up the gamma counting. Michelle tugged on her ear, and Steven knew she was about to push back. "How long should we count?" she asked. "Even if we count for several hours, our level of uncertainty will still be on the order of 20%."

Steven internally applauded. *Good for you, Michelle.*

Kittrick tilted his head as he looked at Michelle. "Hmm, we need a more precise value by morning." He looked at his watch. "At 3:00 am our time, I'll start getting calls from Washington. What do you suggest?"

"Because time is of the essence," Michelle said, "we should next remove a tiny amount of material for mass-spec analysis."

John looked intrigued. "How much would you remove?"

"The fastest way to get a small sample, say a milligram, would be to use a file. That's far more than we need. Right, David?"

David had taken Ben's place as the new leader of the mass-spec group. He hesitated and looked at Steven. Steven nodded, and David answered, "A hundred times less would be enough. I'll use the multi-collector ICP-MS, so we don't need to do any chemical separations. If all goes well, two hours after you give me the filings, you'll have the uranium isotopic composition."

Kittrick glanced at Steven, and Steven nodded his assent. John said, "What kind of accuracy do you expect?"

Sounding more confident, David said, "For the 238 to 235 ratio, about a tenth of a percent."

Kittrick gave a thumbs-up. "Let's do it then."

CHAPTER 40

The Lab (June 14)

Steven returned to his office at 3:00 am and found Kittrick on the couch. The FBI agent swung his legs down and stood up. "Wish I had a couch in my office. These three hours of shut-eye should get me through another long day." He popped a Sumatra pod into Steven's Keurig. "Does David have a result yet?"

With pride, Steven said, "He sure does." He paused for dramatic effect. "The enrichment is 81.2%, with an uncertainty of 0.2%."

A puzzled look crept over Kittrick's face. "That's a very different enrichment than the Moldova HEU powder, so that rules it out as the source. It's also not as highly enriched as the HEU in weapon-states nuclear arsenals. What do you make of it?"

"I'm surprised too. The enrichment is somewhat unusual, which might be an advantage in narrowing down its origin."

The Keurig sputtered as it finished dispensing Kittrick's coffee. The agent grabbed the cup and took a sip while eyeing Steven. "You've been reticent in offering your opinion. That's not like you." Kittrick's lips tightened as he leaned toward Steven. "We should talk about our phone call two days ago. Because you went behind my back, I wasn't in a position to argue on your behalf with the Director. I don't apologize for that. Or for anything I said during our call. But for the sake of the country, we can't let that affect the way we work together. Can I count on you?"

Steven was glad for the chance to clear the air. He looked directly into Kittrick's eyes. "You can count on me." Remembering the agent saying he no longer trusted him, he added, "Without a doubt."

"Good." John scratched his head. "It's ironic that the alert based on your analysis of the Moldova HEU led to the interdiction in Laredo."

Of course, that irony hadn't escaped Steven. "It's hard for me to believe they're not connected in some way. Maybe the original deal fell through and the terrorists found another source. We're now fairly sure the Moldova HEU was fuel for a particular Russian research reactor. The 81% enrichment for the Laredo HEU may point to a different research reactor."

"We should have somebody look into Russian research reactors while we do our experimental work."

"Funny you should say that. I have a friend in Z-Division who's an expert. Shall I bring him over?"

John offered a rueful smile. "I think I've been set up." He looked at his watch. "The Director will call any minute. Can I tell him the Laredo HEU is definitely not from the U.S.?"

Steven hesitated. It was too early for such a definitive statement. "Phrase it this way—the enrichment level is lower than what the U.S. uses in its nuclear weapons."

"Okay." John ran his hand through his hair. "Let's develop an experimental plan for the next couple days. Who should we include in our discussion?"

"For the first draft, I'd just bring in Michelle. Later, we can bounce it off the whole team."

"Find out how soon she can join us." John's forehead furrowed. "By the way, Ben's departure leaves quite a hole in your team, doesn't it?"

"That was my first reaction. Ben's a brilliant scientist, so it was a sock in the gut for me. But it's ended up a blessing in disguise."

"How's that?"

"One of the brightest scientists in our division is Sven Hutcheson, a cosmochemist. I've found that the mindset of cosmochemists and geochemists is well-suited to nuclear forensics. When Ben quit, I talked to Sven. He's agreed to spend up to a quarter of his time on nuclear forensics."

"That's not much."

"Almost everybody on my team is part-time on nuclear forensics. I'm sure Sven will make a big impact."

"Coming from you, Steven, that's high praise indeed."

John's phone rang. "Just as I predicted, it's the Director." He scooted his chair next to Steven and angled his phone toward him.

"Good morning, Kittrick." The Director's voice was loud enough that Steven figured he could have heard him from the other side of the room. "What can I tell the President?"

After John gave the Director a summary of what they'd learned so far, the Director asked, "So I can say the HEU is definitely *not* from the U.S., right?"

Steven drew a finger across his throat. John replied to the Director, "We can't yet rule out a U.S. source of enriched uranium, but it's definitely not U.S. weapons-grade."

"How long will it take you to finish all your nuclear forensics measurements?"

"Weeks to complete all of them."

"Weeks?!" exploded out of the phone. "That's unacceptable."

"Of course, we'll prioritize the analyses."

"When will you have enough of a nuclear fingerprint to match to your databases?"

Steven barely suppressed a groan. The popular idea of a nuclear fingerprint had taken root outside the nuclear forensics community, and unfortunately, it conveyed a level of specificity that rarely could be achieved. Thankfully, John had often encountered this mistaken notion among non-scientists, so he was well aware of the problems it caused. Unruffled, he replied, "It's more complicated than that, sir."

"Complicated is not what the White House likes to hear."

John rolled his eyes. "Yes, sir."

"You better have a lot more to report by tomorrow. Our working assumption is that a terrorist group has infiltrated the U.S., along with the other parts of the bomb. We need to track them down and fast."

"We'll do our best."

The Director hung up without saying goodbye.

John scowled. "We couldn't get high-level officials to participate in nuclear forensics exercises before this, so now I have to educate them on the fly."

Steven commiserated. "Well, better you than me."

CHAPTER 41

The Lab (7:30 pm, June 14)

Steven awoke with a start. The strange appearance of his surroundings momentarily confused him. Then he remembered. He was still at the Lab.

He glanced at the clock on his wall. Only four hours of sleep in the past thirty-six hours.

He scooted over to John's temporary office, where he found the agent with his head in his hands. John jerked upright.

"What's the problem?" Steven asked.

"The calls from DC are driving me nuts. Seems like everybody who knows about the case has my phone number. I tell them to contact the FBI SIOC at headquarters, but many of them want to hear the latest directly from me." John walked over to the Keurig. "When I took this job, I thought I'd have less stress, not more."

"Is that why you got into nuclear forensics?"

A pained expression flitted across John's face. "Not exactly." He stared out the window without seeming to see anything. "You know, I was an excellent investigator in the criminal division, one of the best, I was told. One day I... well, let's just say I made a big mistake. It put a lot of people at risk, including me."

"Everybody makes a mistake from time to time."

"It turned my supervisor against me. When I heard the nuclear forensics position was opening up at the FBI Lab, I jumped at the chance."

"You seem to have embraced your new role."

"It's proved to be the right move for me." He pushed the brew button on the Keurig. "How about checking with everybody before the night shift takes over?"

"Good idea. After I make myself a cup."

The aroma of freshly brewed coffee shortly after waking made Steven feel like he was starting a new day, even though the sun was going down instead of coming up. "Can I ask what had your knickers in a knot on that last call?"

John sighed. "Your Secretary of Energy was a pain in the ass. When he heard the interdicted HEU didn't go to the Plutonium Building, he threatened to shut down the operation."

"Don't tell me the HEU was moved there?"

"No, they finally settled the issue during this last call. It included the Attorney General and the Director of National Intelligence. Your Lab Director convinced everybody that keeping the evidence here was justified."

"Good for him." Steven grabbed his cup of coffee as they left the room, and on his first sip, managed to burn his tongue.

When they entered the receiving lab, a technician from the Plutonium Building was tending a circular saw. An FBI examiner, who had flown in earlier that day, was monitoring the progress.

John said, "How's it going?"

"Slower than I'd hoped," the technician said. "It took us quite a while to set up and find the best cutting parameters. We just started the second cut across the disk."

The FBI examiner chimed in. "Before we did any sawing, we used a drill to obtain gram-sized samples from both the top and bottom surfaces."

John peered at the hole on top of the disk. "It doesn't take a very big hole to get one gram of uranium metal, does it?"

The FBI examiner said, "Actually, the original hole was shallower. Michelle asked us to drill deeper so we could compare the interior of the disk with the near surface. I gave the okay since you were on the phone at the time."

"Seems reasonable enough," John said. "When do you expect to finish the second cut?"

The technician looked up. "In about an hour."

"Good, then we'll select the areas to cut out of the slab and prepare them for surface analyses."

The FBI examiner asked, "Did you see the email from Oak Ridge?"

"My phone keeps ringing," John said, "so I haven't checked my email for a couple hours."

"Their top uranium metallurgist will get here tomorrow."

"Excellent." John turned back to Steven. "Let's check in with Michelle next."

They found Michelle in her chemistry lab. As they walked in, a wisp of hair escaped from her ponytail, and she blew it out of the way as she dispensed a sample solution onto the top of an ion-exchange column.

"We don't want to disrupt you," John said.

Michelle smiled. "Not a problem. I can take a five-minute break."

"How did the sample dissolutions go?" Steven asked.

She sat down on a stool and took off her gloves. "For each sample, we dissolved enough material to create one big pot solution for all the mass spec, radiochemical, and trace element analyses. After an hour in nitric acid, the samples had some residue left. So we heated them in nitric acid under pressure in a Parr bomb for a couple hours. That dissolved about half the residue. We reserved the remaining residues for possible later examination."

"Good idea," Steven said, mostly for John's benefit.

John gestured toward the columns in the fume hood. "What chemical separations are you doing?"

"I'm separating the thorium and protactinium daughter products from the uranium. That'll give us two clocks."

Steven said, "Based on our results for uranium metal in the international exercise, we expect the uranium-thorium age from the bottom sample to be closest to the true age."

John peered inside the hood, a concerned look on his face. "You're running six columns. Are those for six different samples?"

"I'm doing replicate samples for the original drillings on top and bottom. Plus one sample from each of the interior drillings. By doing them in parallel, it takes very little extra time. And we have enough detectors to count the six samples in parallel too."

"Are you taking a risk of cross-contamination?"

Michelle's eyebrows arched as she tugged on her ear. Steven fought to suppress a grin. If John knew Michelle well, he'd know better than to ask that question.

In an even but emphatic voice, Michelle said, "Not in my lab." She stretched her arms in the air and then massaged her shoulders. "I'm beat. My replacement will be here soon, and then I'm going home to get a decent night of sleep." She looked at John with concern, and then at Steven. "From the looks of you two, you should do the same."

John grunted and yawned. "Steven, let's check in on the mass spec, trace element, and SEM labs, and then go home. Or in my case, my hotel."

Steven said, "If any questions come up, day or night, my team will call me at home."

"Sounds good." John took a step toward the exit and then stopped. "Michelle, when will you have the first result for an age?"

"By sometime tomorrow, we'll have our first preliminary results. But at that point, we won't be in a good position to assess its validity."

John ran his hands through his hair. "Why does it take so long?" Somewhat apologetically he added, "Washington is pressuring me."

"The chemical separations take quite a while, and—"

Steven interrupted. "We have ideas on how to speed it up, but our proposals haven't been funded."

Michelle continued, "And to get reasonable statistics, we need to count some samples for a long time."

John looked annoyed. "I've got to report significant new results by no later than tomorrow afternoon."

A wave of alarm passed through Steven. He had been burned in the past when he communicated technical results to higher levels of government. Though he always attached the important caveats to his results, all too often the caveats got dropped when someone summarized his report and passed it up the chain. Sometimes, that caused political authorities to unwittingly misinterpret the technical information. In a few infuriating instances, some people deliberately misrepresented his results to serve their own political interests.

Steven reared back slightly and his jaw jutted forward. "Like you told the Director, we'll do our best. And that's all I can promise." In a more conciliatory tone, he added, "Let's talk to Alan tomorrow morning about possible Russian research reactors as the source."

"How about we get together at 8:00 am?" The tenor of John's voice made it clear he wasn't asking a question. "And bring along your latest data."

Internally, Steven groaned. To be well prepared, he would need to get to the Lab two hours before the meeting. Suddenly, he felt wobbly. But he slapped on the most sanguine look he could muster and in a bright voice said, "Not a problem."

CHAPTER 42

The Lab (June 15)

The morning meeting didn't go well. Alan asked for more time to compile his research on Russian reactors and didn't show up. Steven did his best to cover for Alan by updating John on the new isotopic and trace element results they'd gained overnight and showing him lots of pictures from the scanning electron microscope. At this early juncture, however, he wasn't able to offer the type of leads the FBI Director wanted. John scheduled another meeting for late afternoon and insisted Steven produce something by then that would allay the Director's unrelenting pressure. Steven bit his tongue and refrained from sarcastically asking whether the Director wanted fast answers or the right answers.

The team worked feverishly throughout the day. An hour before the afternoon meeting, Alan called, sounding worried. He didn't have anything definitive yet and wanted to skip again. Steven told him, in no uncertain terms, that further delay wasn't an option. Instead, he suggested a revised approach for Alan's brief that should prove palatable to John.

Just before the meeting was due to start, Steven waited for Alan outside the conference room. When Alan appeared, he asked, "You doing okay?"

"Better than this morning."

When they entered the room, everybody else was already sitting at the conference table: John at the head, Michelle across from him, with David, Sven, Mark, and Danny, the Oak Ridge metallurgist, scattered around it. The chair next to John was left open for Steven, and Alan took the last seat at the foot of the table.

"Okay, let's get started," John said. "Danny, what can you tell us about how the HEU disk was made?"

The grizzled metallurgist cleared his throat. "The appearance of the disk suggests it was formed by melting the uranium in a vacuum induction furnace and collecting the liquid in a mold. Not surprising. That's how I'd do it. We found quite a few carbide inclusions in the SEM images, consistent with using a graphite mold. Mark found a high level of yttrium, which suggests they used yttria to coat the mold."

John held up his hand. "How significant is the use of yttria?"

"It's a distinguishing feature, because other common coatings are erbium or zirconium oxides. Mark also found a fairly high level of zirconium, but not nearly as high as yttrium. So, most likely they used yttria-coated molds."

"Anything else?"

Danny held out his hands. "What I found most striking is the high quality of the casting."

John looked intrigued. "Explain."

"A common problem in casting uranium metal is the formation of voids. If the terrorists know what they're doing, they'd aim for high-density metal. Which means limiting the voids. Though this disk wouldn't meet our standards at Oak Ridge, the quality is quite good. Either the terrorist group has a person with prior experience in casting uranium metal, or they have smart technical people who experimented until they achieved a good result."

John said, "That's a subjective inference, but given your experience, it's a valuable insight." He looked around the table. "Michelle, give us the latest from radiochemistry."

"Okay." She tucked her hair behind her ears. "I'll highlight the three most significant things I've found. First, the fission products are quite high. For example, the non-volatile fission products are ten to twenty times higher than for the Moldova HEU. That tells us that this uranium was previously in a reactor and subsequently reprocessed, but the degree of purification in the reprocessing step was rather poor."

"That could be a useful clue," John said.

Michelle continued. "Second, the bottom sample gave a much younger apparent uranium-thorium age than the top sample, which we expected from the results in the international exercise. Here's the data for both samples—"

John interrupted. "Just give me the bottom line my Director will understand."

"The nominal age is 0.4 years. But that's an upper limit, because we suspect the casting process did not entirely remove the thorium daughter product. The bottom line—I'm quite confident the uranium part was produced within the past five months."

David raised his hand, and when John nodded his way, he said, "Our mass-spec age data agree with Michelle's. I suggest we analyze samples along a transect from bottom to top to develop a better estimate of the time of casting."

Steven jumped in before John could comment. "That's a good idea, but it will be quite time-consuming. We'll do it later." He turned to Michelle and said, "Please continue."

Michelle chimed back in. "Third, uranium-232 is clearly present. That confirms the prior conclusion that this uranium has been in a nuclear reactor. Potentially, it can also give us another radioactive clock."

"Very good," John said. "Who's next?"

David raised his hand again. "I've got more mass-spec results." John nodded and David proceeded. "We've completed duplicate uranium isotopic analyses for both the top and bottom samples. They all agree within error. Uranium-236 is present at a high level, consistent with reactor irradiation, but it's about two-thirds the level of our most recent case, the Moldova sample. We also detected uranium-233. These high precision isotopic results should prove pivotal in identifying the source of uranium."

Silently, Steven applauded. Short and to the point.

John said, "Please send me your best values based on all your measurements, and include the two-sigma errors."

David pulled out a sheet of paper and passed it to John. "Here you go."

John mimicked doffing his hat as he took the paper. Steven grinned.

"Now let's hear from Alan," John said.

Steven shot a glance over at Alan. Alan wiped his forehead and then withdrew several notecards from his shirt pocket and laid them on the table.

John's phone rang. He looked at it, cleared his throat, and accepted the call.

"What do you have for me, Kittrick?" Steven recognized the FBI Director's voice.

John motioned for Steven to step outside the room with him. "I'm in the middle of a meeting, sir, where I'm getting all the latest results. If I call you back when we finish, I'll have lots more to tell you."

"Well, good," the Director boomed, "because progress on our end is slow. The driver of the Transportes Grupo van seems to be a dead end. He claims another man, a stranger to him, gave him the crate. He was told by his employer to cross the border a few cars behind the stranger and then give the crate back. When we told him he transported a part for a nuclear bomb, he was horrified. We're confident he had no clue."

John said, "Too bad."

"We need more from your scientists. When you determine where the HEU came from, or where the part was made, we can follow the trail from that end."

"Yes, sir."

"Whip those scientists into shape and give me something I can work with."

CHAPTER 43

The Lab (4:45 pm, June 15)

After Steven and John returned to the conference room, John apologized for the interruption and asked Alan to begin.

Alan began with a brief history on the development of Russian research reactors. "Up until the late 70s, the most common fuel was 90% enriched uranium, with a few reactors in the 80-90% range. Then in the late 70s, the Russians began converting some research reactors to 36% enriched uranium to address proliferation concerns. Yet, many of the old reactors continued operating with the more highly enriched fuel."

Steven noticed John shift in his seat, so he motioned to Alan to speed up. Alan nodded and said, "Here's the key point I want to make. The high level of uranium-236 in the Laredo HEU indicates it experienced a lot of burn-up in a reactor. That means the uranium fuel before the irradiation had a much higher level of enrichment than what we measure now. In order to identify the reactor in which this uranium was irradiated, we have to rely upon calculations. We pick a variety of compositions for the initial uranium and select different operating conditions for various types of reactors. After we do the calculations, we compare the modeled results for the uranium isotopic composition to what we've measured."

John ran a hand through his hair. "I wouldn't want to explain that to my Director. I think you're saying you don't have a table of Russian

HEU compositions for various reactors that you can simply compare to our measurements. Instead, you have to do a bunch of calculations."

Alan looked relieved. "That's right."

John thought for a moment, tapping his pen against the tablet on which he'd been taking notes. "How accurate are these calculations?"

"It depends on how much we know about the reactors and the conditions under which they operated."

"How long will the calculations take?"

"Longer than I'd like. It'd help if I could draw upon experts across the laboratory complex, but your non-disclosure form doesn't let me."

Exasperation crept across John's face. Everyone around the table heard his all-too-familiar harrumph. "Who do you want?"

"I'll get you a list within an hour."

"Good. Anybody else have something significant to report?"

Mark, their trace-element expert, spoke up. "The trace elements gave one puzzling result. We found an unusually high level of copper, 255 parts per million."

Steven's head jerked back. "Isn't that orders of magnitude higher than we've ever seen in a HEU sample before?"

"About ten times higher."

John sat up in his chair, eyes wide open. "That's strange."

Around the table, heads were shaking. It reminded Steven that in many examinations of nuclear materials, they found at least one weird result that went unexplained because they didn't have funding to investigate further. He wondered if this weird result was significant.

John turned to Danny. "Can you think of an explanation?"

"Off the top of my head, no."

So far Sven hadn't said a word, but he spoke up now. In a calm voice, the grey-haired scientist said, "I just started analyzing my first specimen on the ion microprobe. I'm looking at chemical variations on the micron scale."

John leaned back. "What do you hope to learn from that?"

"I'm not sure." In a confident tone, Sven added, "But I've often found it provides unexpected insights."

John shrugged. "Okay, as long as it's not keeping you from something more important." John looked over the two pages of notes he'd taken. "I've got a lot of new information to give the Director. It should help him with the White House. Thanks for all your hard work."

Steven had a gnawing sense they could do more with Danny's metallurgical insights, but he couldn't put his finger on it. But as people got out of their chairs, it suddenly hit him. "I have a question for Danny. How common are the induction furnaces the terrorists might have used?"

Danny perked up. "Quite a few companies make lab-sized vacuum induction furnaces."

Steven said, "We know the metal was cast quite recently, so most likely their reactor furnace was delivered within the past year or so. That should help to narrow down the list of possible delivery locations."

With a tremor of excitement, John broke in, "I should've thought of that. Danny, can you come up with a list of global furnace suppliers?"

"I'll have it to you later today."

"Okay, let's all get back to work."

John followed Steven to his office.

"I have a question to run by you," John said.

"Okay, come on in."

John closed the door and stood in front of Steven's desk. "Washington has asked me several times, 'Could there be a second bomb?' How would you answer?"

"That's a tough question. Until we know where the uranium came from, or have a lead on the perpetrators, we can't really answer that question."

"That's similar to my response."

"I imagine Washington doesn't like that answer. Remind them that the biggest barrier for a terrorist who wants to build a nuclear weapon is acquiring enough highly enriched uranium or plutonium. Most likely, a terrorist won't have enough material for more than one bomb."

"But I shouldn't assure Washington there isn't a second one?"

"That's right." Steven pressed his lips together. "I just hope these terrorists aren't being assisted by a nuclear state. Because then a second device would be quite feasible."

John harrumphed and said, "I'll keep that thought to myself."

CHAPTER 44

Malik's apartment (June 15)

"What the hell happened?" Malik Karimov demanded. Yesterday Ahmad Abbasova had texted him the bad news that the U.S. intercepted one crate at the border crossing. The purpose of today's phone call was to discuss the setback on new burner phones.

Defensively, Ahmad said, "Maybe they noticed the unusual number of crossings by the same company in such a short time."

Ahmad's response sounded rehearsed. Malik said, "Raushan shut down the transport company to cover his tracks. He's upset and wonders whether you tipped off the Americans in some way."

In a querulous voice, Ahmad said, "Maybe I just got unlucky."

"Maybe. Just don't get unlucky again."

"What's the new plan?"

"We need to take additional measures to keep the Americans from tracking you. I've sent new identification materials for all of you. Stay in Laredo until you receive them tomorrow. Then, turn in your rental cars and take taxis to San Antonio. Only two men in each taxi, so you don't draw attention. Pay with cash. Rent two new cars in San Antonio and continue to the target."

"Will the bomb still work with one less piece of HEU?" Ahmad's voice betrayed his anxiety.

"I've come up with a solution," Malik said. "It requires fabricating a new steel part. Raushan will take care of that, and in less than two weeks it will arrive at the assembly site he already leased through one of his shell companies."

"Are you going to send instructions on how to install it?"

"It's too complicated for you to handle on your own." Malik grimaced and his voice became stern. "I need to come myself."

Malik heard Ahmad take a sharp breath. Ahmad said, "I'm sorry, Uncle. I know you wanted to keep your distance." His apology sounded sincere, but his relief was evident.

"Repeat back to me your instructions." When Malik was satisfied, he ended the call with a warning. "No more screw-ups. If anybody gets out of line or draws attention, get rid of them. Permanently."

When he hung up, he was confident he'd instilled the fear of Allah in Ahmad. The young man would be extra careful.

He brought up the flight schedules again on his computer. How could he travel to the U.S. on such short notice without raising questions? Leila would probably wonder because he usually made plans for foreign travel far in advance. An idea began to form. He opened Google and started searching.

CHAPTER 45

The Lab (June 18)

Steven's team churned out lots of new data in the next couple of days, but they seemed no closer to identifying the source of the HEU. This morning, right after Steven got to the Lab, John walked into his office for an impromptu meeting. John's mood seemed to have shifted. Yesterday afternoon he'd been frantic to report more progress to Washington, but today he seemed calmer.

Hopeful, Steven asked, "Has there been a break in the case?"

"You know the drill. We have strict limits on sharing intelligence information with you scientists. It assures us your technical interpretations won't be biased."

Exasperated, Steven exhaled noisily. "You can't blame me for being anxious, given what we're dealing with."

John pursed his lips. "Okay, the Director already told you about the one van driver. Five other Transportes Grupo vans passed through the Laredo port of entry prior to the one we intercepted. We assume each of them carried other HEU parts. We investigated the drivers of the vehicles that preceded and followed each van, and eventually eliminated all but eight as suspects. We combed the Laredo area and discovered six suspects returned rental cars yesterday. Turns out all six used fake IDs."

Steven said, "That means there are at least five HEU parts already in the U.S." He did a quick mental calculation. "I wouldn't be surprised if they still have enough HEU for a workable device. Though it depends upon the details of their design."

Sarcastically, John said, "More encouraging news from Steven." He bit his lip. "We've pulled out all stops on finding the suspects, and in short order we got pictures and names for all six. We put out an APB, but so far, not a trace. They've just disappeared."

Steven sighed. The pressure on the nuclear forensics team would lessen when the FBI made better progress.

At that moment, Alan walked in.

"Okay, we can get started now," John said. "I was on a telecon this morning that included several federal departments. State Department is pressuring the Russian government to help. But they insist none of their HEU matches the description we've given them."

"What a surprise!" Steven said sarcastically.

"State had much the same response and believes the Russians are stonewalling. We've alerted our intelligence assets to look for evidence that the Russians are investigating any of their nuclear facilities, especially fuel fabrication sites."

Alan asked, "Has State been able to talk with any Russian technical people?"

"Ah, a perceptive question. No." The corner of John's mouth turned up slightly. "Which brings me to the reason for our meeting."

Steven wondered where this was heading. "How can we help?"

John looked pleased. "Since we aren't getting anywhere on identifying the source of the HEU, I made a proposal. We should try communicating scientist to scientist. Steven, your leadership in the ITWG puts you in the best position. Everybody agreed."

Steven was flattered, but anticipated roadblocks. "If the Russian scientists suspect I'm working on a high-profile case, they'll clam up. To have any chance, I'll need a decent cover story."

John said, "We figured you could come up with one."

"Do you think an email or phone call will get us the kind of information we need?"

"We don't think so. You need to go in person. It's a risk, but given the circumstances, one that's warranted. As long as you agree, of course."

Steven sat back, shocked. John was a by-the-book kind of guy. This smacked of an operational intelligence role, which was strictly prohibited for Lab scientists. He'd already breached that boundary in Moldova, but apparently the FBI never got wind of it. Now they were asking him to do it.

Steven put his hands behind his head and gazed at the ceiling. Going on a rush visit to Russia would raise suspicions. He'd likely be followed. And given the State Department's request for help, Russian scientists might be warned against cooperating with him.

Steven said, "How about an indirect approach. I'll first go to Kazakhstan. Their scientists have extensive knowledge of Russian reactor fuels, and they're more likely to be forthcoming. If all goes well, perhaps I can get them to refer me to their Russian colleagues without raising alarms in Moscow."

Alan piped up. "That's a better idea. I've collaborated with some Kazakh scientists on reactor modeling."

John looked at Alan with an amused expression. "You know more about reactors than Steven, so you should go too."

Consternation crossed Alan's face, followed by a hint of excitement.

Steven asked, "What do you say, Alan?"

Alan squinted, his head tilted. Then his eyebrows shot up. "I'm game if you're game."

John closed the deal. "Good, it's settled. You have a plane to catch out of San Francisco tonight."

...

Steven startled Carissa when he came home in the middle of the afternoon. She asked, "Why home so early? Is everything okay?"

The only thing Carissa knew about the Laredo case was that the government had called upon Steven as their nuclear forensics expert in a national emergency. Before he went overseas on a quasi-operation, she deserved to know more. He could work around the classified aspects.

After he summarized the underlying strategy for his trip, Carissa's surprise turned to alarm. She was no dummy and had become adept at reading between his lines. She asked, "Are you putting yourself at risk?"

"I'll have a legal attaché from the American embassy along as my interpreter and he'll double as my bodyguard."

"Isn't it more important for you to stay at the Lab during this extremely important case?" She began to twirl her hair. "Couldn't somebody else go?"

"Alan's going with me, and Michelle is well-suited to lead the team while I'm gone." Steven had met with Michelle to finalize plans for the next several days. When she told him Sven had found interesting variations in copper abundances at the ten-micron scale, his antennae went up. They agreed to add more people to Sven's team to expand the investigation of chemical variations.

"What are the odds your trip will give you what you need?" Carissa's twirling threatened to snarl her hair into a knot.

"My chances are no better than 50%. But at this point, it's our best bet." He smiled and hugged her. "Don't worry. The U.S. government will look out for me."

She mumbled into his shoulder, "I still don't like it. But if this is what you need to do..." She stopped and a small sob escaped. In a husky voice, she continued, "I'll trust your judgment."

He hugged her and then stepped back. Tears glistened as they trickled down her face. This was so unlike her. Her fear for their son's future seemed to have wrapped itself around her like a bad dream she couldn't shake.

He asked, "Did Jacob go to a drug counselor today?"

She shook her head.

"Dammit, he promised the judge at his detention hearing. If he hasn't gone by the time I get back, I'll take him myself."

A flicker of hope appeared in her eyes. "Even if he goes just once before his next court appearance, it might help him with the judge."

"I'll be back as soon as I can."

CHAPTER 46

Astana, Kazakhstan (June 20)

Steven had met several Kazakh scientists the previous year at an International Atomic Energy Agency consultancy meeting in Vienna. The meeting opened with the IAEA highlighting the importance of every country developing their own nuclear forensics library. During a coffee break, Steven talked to the Kazakh participants about the approach the U.S. was taking.

Two days ago, when he contacted Kazatomprom in Astana, he seized upon this previous interaction to propose a visit by Alan and him. His offer to collaborate on developing Kazakhstan's version of such a library was met with enthusiasm. They were less enthused about hosting on such short notice, but Steven concocted a story about an urgent need to submit a proposal in order to secure funding for their part of the collaboration. That gained their approval.

When they arrived in Astana, they met with Dan Davis, the resident FBI legal attaché at the American embassy, to refine their strategy for the next day. In deference to their jet lag, they returned to their hotel for an early dinner. Before Steven crawled into bed, he texted Carissa and ended with, *"Love you always!"* He tossed and turned for only half an hour before he drifted off to sleep.

Later, he awoke, looked at the clock, and groaned. Only 2:15 am. Darn jet lag. Turning over, he stopped when he heard a scrabbling sound at his door. The scrabbling continued, more softly. It was probably just a drunk trying to enter the wrong room.

Then a click. He froze.

An instant later, the door opened and a light blinded him.

"What the ..." Steven yelled when a gritty hand closed over his mouth. A second flashlight clicked on and Steven realized two men had entered his room.

"No more words," a heavily accented voice said. "You come with us." The man spoke in a calm but authoritative manner. *This can't be happening!* But the hand on his mouth argued otherwise.

"I take hand off your mouth," the man said, "but you yell, I taser you. Understand?"

He nodded mutely. *Who the hell is this? What do they want?*

"Get dressed," the first man said.

Steven's shaking hands made it difficult to button his shirt. When he fumbled tying his shoes, the man muttered, "Come on, come on."

Once dressed, the man said, "You say a word, we taser you and carry you." A hard object jammed into his side. "Anybody look suspicious, we say you too drunk to walk. Nobody give it second thought."

Desperate, Steven tried to stall. Maybe Alan next door would hear. Loudly, he said, "I'm an American citizen. You can't do this."

"Shut up!"

"Where are you taking me?"

The answer came in the form of a slap to the face. The force would have sent him sprawling, except that the other man kept him propped up. Steven's outrage melted into fear. The taste of blood suggested shutting up might be the better part of wisdom.

After they shoved him into the backseat of a beat-up car, they handed him a sleep mask. "Put on. For own good." The mask blocked his vision completely. As the car weaved through the streets of Astana, he remembered the fear on Carissa's face and his assurance not to worry. She'd said, "I trust your judgment." If Carissa saw him now, she'd take that back.

The car stopped after a short ride. They pulled him out and gravel crunched under their feet as they pushed him forward. After they stepped inside a building, his mask was ripped off.

Steven guessed he was in an upper-class Kazakh living room. A well-dressed man was seated in an overstuffed chair, one leg crossed over the other and holding a glass of clear liquid. A tall, white, oddly curved bottle sat on a small table next to his chair.

"Welcome, Dr. Carter. My apologies for interrupting your sleep, but we need to talk. May I offer you a glass of Mamont, my favorite vodka?" The man's English was exceptional. He must have spent years in an English-speaking country.

Under the circumstances, it struck Steven as prudent to decline. He shook his head. The first man pushed him toward the chair across from the well-dressed man, who took a sip of his vodka and flicked his hand. Steven's two abductors whisked out of the room.

"You'd be wise," the well-dressed man said, "to answer my questions truthfully. If I'm not satisfied, you won't see your family for a long time."

Despite the man's urbane manner, Steven had little doubt about his willingness to follow through on his threat. Beads of sweat trickled down his sides, even though the room was cold.

"Tell me why you're visiting Kazatomprom tomorrow." His interrogator jabbed a finger at him. "I want the *real* reason, not what you told them." The man took another sip of his vodka, keeping his eyes on Steven.

Steven wondered if the man could hear his heart pounding. He suspected his interrogator was from the Russian Foreign Intelligence Service, successor to the KGB. He replied, "My government is collaborating with a number of countries on developing nuclear forensics libraries. But as you suspect, we have a more important and urgent reason for this visit." He paused to consider how to phrase his next words. The man motioned for him to continue. "We interdicted part of a nuclear weapon as it crossed over our Mexican border. The U.S. asked the Russian government for help in identifying the source of the highly enriched uranium. But you already know that, don't you?"

The only response his interrogator offered was a slightly raised eyebrow.

Taking a deep breath, Steven said, "The Russian government denied that the uranium matches any of their HEU." No saliva was left in his mouth, but he swallowed nonetheless. "The U.S. believes they are stonewalling."

The suggestion of a sneer tugged at the corner of the man's mouth.

Steven's voice cracked as he continued. "My government sent me here to see if Kazakh scientists can help us determine the source of the HEU. We didn't want to put them on the spot by asking directly, so we'll pose it as a test of the structure of their nuclear forensics library."

Deliberately, the man set down his drink. He pulled a revolver from behind a cushion and set it next to the glass. Panic shot through Steven.

With a growl, the man waved his hand dismissively. "That's a nice little story. I don't believe it's the entire story."

"That's the whole truth." Sweat poured down Steven's face.

"Let me pose a hypothetical. Let's say you find a Russian material that comes close to matching. You won't, but let's say you do. What will you do then?"

Steven's hands gripped the arms of his chair. *What's this guy want from me? I'm just a scientist!* In a frantic voice, he replied, "All my government cares about is stopping the terrorists from setting off their nuclear bomb. Knowing the source of the HEU could lead us to the terrorists."

His interrogator leaned forward, as if Steven had just said something particularly significant. Steven replayed his answer in his head. *Being blamed, that's what the Russians are worried about.*

"I assure you," Steven added, "I came here with the sole purpose of stopping the terrorist plot against the U.S. We have no intention of blaming the Russian government. Just the opposite, we want your help."

The man drained his glass of vodka. "That's what *you* say. But *you're* just a scientist. Can *you* speak for your government?"

Sagging in his chair, Steven said, "Not officially. But I work very closely with the FBI, and the U.S. government sent me here. I believe they'll listen to me."

His interrogator pulled out his phone and hit one button. "Let me test your story, Dr. Carter." He switched to a language Steven guessed was Russian. After a brief conversation, the man hung up.

"We also interviewed your friend Dr. Yang. Your stories are consistent."

"What else do you want from me?"

"Good question, Dr. Carter. I'm inclined to believe you're telling the truth. My revolver often proves to be convincing. I still have a choice to make. I could detain you as an insurance policy. If your government blames us for the HEU, we'll accuse you and your friend of espionage. We could point to your visit here as part of an attempt to frame us."

Steven gulped. Horror stories of Russian prisons popped into his mind. "But I think you know that's not true."

The man rolled his eyes. "Or I could allow you to leave as a show of good faith. In return, you tell your government we're telling the truth. This HEU is not from Russia."

Steven fought to quell his fear. He didn't want to return home empty-handed. "My government will find your assurances more convincing if you let me talk directly to scientists. Not only here in Kazakhstan, but also to Russian scientists in Moscow."

The presumed Russian agent paused, prompting Steven to infer—*The Russians aren't sure!* Perhaps they didn't know of any match to the Laredo HEU, but they weren't confident they could rule out a Russian origin. After all, their records from the Cold War era were notably incomplete.

The Russian agent's eyes narrowed. "I'll let you go on one condition. After you're done here at Kazatomprom, you go to Moscow to meet with Russian scientists. But before you leave Moscow, you must convince your government that Russia isn't hiding anything."

"And Dr. Yang can go with me?"

"Of course. You know, Dr. Carter, when I was a boy, my grandmother took me to the Orthodox Church. I remember the priest once said that the truth will set you free. That struck me as ridiculous. It certainly hasn't been my experience growing up in Russia, or in my line of work. But tonight, well, tonight it was true for you."

Steven wasn't sure what the Russian priest meant by his statement, but he hoped the Russian agent wasn't lying about letting him go.

"Oh, one more thing," the Russian agent said in a menacing tone. "Don't disappoint me. I have colleagues throughout the world. When people disappoint me, it doesn't go well for them. Or their families."

CHAPTER 47

Astana (June 21)

After they dropped Steven back at his hotel, he knocked on Alan's door. In a trembling voice, Alan shared his night of terror. When Steven heard his friend's story, he became even more distraught. "I'm so sorry I dragged you into this mess."

Alan waved away any regrets. "I never imagined a night like tonight. But one day it'll make for a good story."

Steven called the embassy, and they patched him through to Dan Davis. When Steven said he'd been kidnapped and repeated his interrogator's final warning, Davis said, "I'll recommend to headquarters that we cut your trip short."

A wave of relief swept through Steven. "Not sure I can argue with that."

The agent said, "We'll talk more in the morning. Now, get some sleep."

Easier said than done. He couldn't stop replaying the events of the night after he returned to his room. Should he really go back home? The question sparked a one-man debate. Who could blame him if he followed the advice of the FBI? He'd already done so much. And what was the likelihood of success if he went to Moscow? Even if he became convinced the Russians were clueless, could he convince the U.S. government? The parting words of the Russian agent echoed in his mind. *When people disappoint me, it doesn't go well for them, or their families.*

He put his hands to his head and squeezed. An old memory surfaced. In high school, he became the quarterback of the football team when the starter was injured. In his second game, he called an audible that changed the play the coach had called. It led to a disastrous loss. His furious coach ruled out future audibles. For the rest of the season, his team went undefeated and advanced to the regional playoffs. In the final minute of the game, his team was behind and facing a do-or-die fourth down. The coach sent in his favorite play. When Steven came up to the line, the defense switched into an unusual formation, which spelled doom for the coach's play. He was tempted to audible to a different play, but if he took the risk and failed, everyone would point a finger at him. Recalling the angry voice of his coach, he opted to play it safe. He ran the coach's play, and it failed spectacularly. But no one blamed him. For years, he replayed the end of that game and became more convinced his audible would have won the game.

He lifted his head and looked up at the ceiling, hoping for inspiration. He'd staked his scientific career on proving the value of nuclear forensics. Now his country faced the imminent threat of a nuclear detonation in one of its cities. Though he'd given his all to stop it, all his efforts could be for naught. He buried his head in his hands once more, rocking back and forth.

Suddenly, he stopped moving. His decision became clear, though he wasn't sure how he came to it. He'd do whatever might help save his country from a nuclear catastrophe, even if that meant calling an audible.

After an hour-and-a-half of sleep and a quick breakfast, Dan Davis picked them up. "The FBI Director just called me. He agrees. When you're done here in Astana, you go back home."

Steven cleared his throat. "I've thought about it more. I can't live with myself unless I do everything I can. If there's no breakthrough in the next couple days, I should go to Moscow."

Dan looked at him for a full three seconds. His hands tightened on the wheel. "You sure about that?"

"Frankly, no. But it's what I'm going to do."

Alan spoke up from the backseat. "He won't be going alone. I'll go too."

"You know, we could probably get your Lab to order you back home."

Steven said, "Probably, but if we're willing, why not let us?"

Dan muttered something incomprehensible about foolish scientists. "I'll let the Director know."

Steven followed his original plan to ensure the Kazakh scientists at Kazatomprom would engage fully. For the entire morning, they discussed database structures for a nuclear forensics library. Steven saved his crucial question until after lunch. "I'd like to propose a test of your preferred database structure. Here's data for a sample we analyzed a year ago. What can you tell us about it, based on your nuclear forensics library?" The data he gave them was for the Laredo HEU.

Almost immediately, the Kazakh scientists suggested it looked like fuel for some type of Russian research reactor. They dug into the details for the rest of the afternoon. For the most part, Steven became a silent observer, while the reactor experts considered various possibilities. Despite the eagerness of their Kazakh colleagues to impress, they couldn't pinpoint a specific reactor that fit all the data.

When they left Kazatomprom that evening, Dan didn't start the car after they climbed inside. Instead, he turned to Steven and said, "Washington decided to support you in your decision."

"Good. What's Washington's view on the Russian agent's claim?"

"They're skeptical."

Steven stroked his beard and squinted. "I get that, but I keep asking myself why we're having so much trouble finding a match."

Dan's phone beeped. He glanced at the text, grunted, and typed a short response. "Washington wants an update immediately."

Steven groaned. "I'd be more cogent after an hour nap. But if Washington insists, let's get it over with."

When he took the secure phone Dan handed him in the embassy, he was relieved to hear John Kittrick's voice. "I hope you've got progress to report, because the pressure here is getting unbearable."

John sounded as exhausted as Steven felt. "Believe me, I'm feeling it too. We did get new information on Russian research reactors. That'll help us in the future, but so far, no good match."

John's tone turned sarcastic. "I can't wait to communicate this update."

"I'm beginning to wonder whether the Russians are telling the truth. Or maybe it's theirs, but they don't recognize it."

"Well, where else might it be from?"

"That's part of our problem. There aren't any other good candidates." Steven shifted gears. "How's Michelle doing?"

"Michelle's good. Everybody's working to their limit. Every day your guys produce mounds of new data, but it just doesn't seem to be leading anywhere."

"When we need a straightforward case, we get a curveball thrown our way."

"We can't afford to strike out," John said.

Steven's gut was tugging to get his attention. "I'd like to hear what Sven is finding on the chemical variations."

"If we discover something important, I'll call you."

Steven felt like he was on a treadmill, running fast but going nowhere. He summoned up his last bit of positivity. "Somehow, somewhere, someone needs to have a breakthrough. Something like a home run."

CHAPTER 48

Astana (June 22)

Exhausted from the past two days, Steven fell asleep again after his alarm went off. He woke up half an hour later and scolded himself. He hated being late.

When he rounded the corner to the breakfast room, he spotted Alan taking a big bite of a croissant. He made a beeline for the table and never saw the server coming out of the kitchen. Until he ran into her.

"Excuse me! Are you okay?" he said.

The woman nodded as she straightened the items on her tray. As Steven backed away, he felt a flush creeping up his neck and onto his cheeks.

He plunked his briefcase under Alan's table. "Sorry I'm late."

After Alan finished chewing, he said good-naturedly, "you made quite a grand entrance. I'll get your coffee while you get some food. I recommend the croissant."

By the time Steven returned to the table, his coffee was waiting. He took a tentative sip, smacked his lips, and took a bigger swallow. "Thanks, buddy. Doctored just the way I like it."

Alan yawned. "I kept waking up last night, listening for a sound at the door."

"Sorry to hear that. I was so bushed, I woke up only once."

Steven cut open his croissant and spread a liberal amount of jam on it. As he lifted it to his mouth, his phone rang. "Are you kidding me?"

He pulled out his phone. "Hmm," he said. "Michelle, do you ever go home?"

"Steven!"

His heart thudded at the urgency in her voice.

She asked, "Can you talk privately?"

Angst shot through him. "Is my family okay?"

"They're fine. Or at least nothing has changed with them. I'm calling about the case."

"Okay, hold on a minute." In response to Alan's questioning look, he jerked his head toward the patio. "I need to take this call outside."

"Don't take too long. Dan should be here soon."

The morning air was brisk, and the sun had not yet reached the patio. Except for two men smoking cigarettes, it was deserted. Steven headed away from them and onto the lawn.

"Okay, I can talk now."

"I'll start with the bottom line. The sample, and you know what sample I'm talking about, is a mixture of two components!"

Jolted by the news, he stumbled. Then he spurted forward, like a racehorse responding to the whip. Breathless, he managed to ask, "Are you sure?"

"Last night, Sven began looking at the uranium-235 to uranium-238 ratio on the ion probe. After a while, he noticed it seemed to vary from spot to spot, as much as half a percent. At first, he suspected a molecular interference was the problem. After he ruled that out, he did many more analyses. The spread in the ratio was still there." The triumphant note in her voice suggested she had no doubt.

"But that's pushing the limit on the precision of the ion microprobe. Are you certain?" The moment he asked the question, for the second time no less, he realized it was stupid. This was Michelle he was talking to.

She didn't seem annoyed. "Today we put all our resources into verifying Sven's finding. We extracted very small samples from across the entire slab so David and his crew could analyze them on the multi-collector. By keeping them to a microgram or so, we hoped to enhance our chances of seeing isotopic variability. I just got the results."

Steven found himself holding his breath. "What did you find?"

"Six of the seven samples defined a total range of 0.4%."

He let out a war whoop. A variation of 0.4% was forty times larger than the precisions on David's measurements. All his doubt vanished. "This changes everything."

"It gets even better. The seventh sample was an outlier. It's 235 to 238 ratio was about half a percent higher than the next highest ratio." She paused. With a note of pride and exultation, she added, "That seals the deal. Two different sources of uranium were mixed together to make this sample."

He realized he'd stopped walking. The sun was warm on his back. "No wonder we weren't making progress in identifying a specific source!"

"Exactly!"

Steven shielded his eyes from the sun. In his euphoria, he began to devise the next set of experiments. "Here's what I think we should do next—"

She interrupted him. "John wants you to come back immediately. He's desperate to determine the nature of the two sources. Just text me your ideas."

"Do the isotopic correlation diagrams indicate some plausible sources?" he asked.

She hesitated. "Let's discuss that in person. Just get back here ASAP."

Steven took her response as a tantalizing hint that the new data suggested some candidates. "Okay, hopefully I can book a flight that'll get me back tomorrow. Oh, by the way, Michelle, great job! I knew I was leaving the team in good hands."

"Thanks. But I'll feel better once you're back here."

Steven stood still, basking in the moment. The birds were in full chorus, though he hadn't noticed before. The brightening sun brought the scene before him into sharp relief. Stately trees towered overhead, providing shade to the path below. Flowers planted around the patio popped into brilliant color. He took a deep breath, drawing in new hope and expelling the fog of confusion. This moment, the scene before him and the feeling of hope and excitement, would remain etched forever in his memory.

Almost on the verge of running, he hurried under the trees. He noticed his shoes were soaked from the heavy dew on the grass. Increasingly aware of the discomfort in his feet, unbidden, another feeling swam to the surface of his consciousness. The cold wet blanket of regret emerged and dampened his euphoria. Why hadn't he considered a mixture? He should have thought of that!

Lately, it seemed he'd been wrong more often than right. His family was a mess. Ben left for Los Alamos because of him. The FBI had been ready to throw him overboard.

But looking on the bright side, his team came through. He'd put this elite team together. And his gut feeling to expand Sven's exploration of micro-scale variations led to this breakthrough.

Alan was scrolling through his phone when he returned.

Steven said, "Let's go to my room." He grabbed his coffee and croissant. Alan caught up right before the elevator door closed.

While Alan sat on the bed, Steven recounted the entire phone conversation. Halfway through, Alan began to bounce up and down. His friend's excitement brought back Steven's earlier euphoria. He finished his story by saying, "I think Michelle has an idea for the isotopic composition of at least one source."

Alan jumped into the air, his eyes shining. "Eureka!"

Alan held up his palm, and Steven, carried away by their shared excitement, slapped it for a high-five. Then he caught his breath. "Time to get to work. I want to send Michelle suggestions about what to do next."

Alan left and Steven sat down with his pad of paper. He began to sketch out some possibilities. His eyes glowed and he pumped his fist. They were on the right trail now. And they would nail down the two sources if it was the last thing he did.

CHAPTER 49

The Lab (June 23)

Steven wasn't fully awake until he got out of his car at the Lab and walked to his office. Last night, fighting jet lag, he managed to sleep only five hours. As his mind emerged from its morning fog, he figured he must have driven to work on autopilot. Thankfully, Kittrick had scheduled this meeting for 10:00 am to give him more time to recover from his hurried trip back home.

When he walked into John's temporary office, the agent was eying the last bite of a donut. "Welcome back," he said.

Michelle choked out a hello with her mouth full of chocolate cruller.

"Glad to be back," Steven said as he surveyed the four donuts on a plate next to the Keurig. Seeing a maple old-fashioned, he grabbed it and sat down with a thump. "Did you bring these, Michelle?"

"Guilty."

"I'm not sure whether I should hate you or thank you."

It was an old joke between them, but nonetheless, she smiled. "The way you snatched that donut I'll take as a thank you."

John finished brewing a cup of coffee and placed it in front of Steven. "How're you feeling?"

"Tired, but more coffee will help." Steven bit into his donut, chewed it with relish, and washed it down with coffee. "How did

Washington take the news that the Laredo HEU is actually a mixture of two sources?"

"I called the FBI Director first, rather than spring it during a multi-agency telecon. Glad I did, because I got an earful of colorful language."

Steven peered at John. Small bags had formed beneath the agent's increasingly red eyes. "I understand the frustration. But does the Director understand this is a huge step forward?"

"Eventually he got to that point. But—and this is a very big but— he then asked how long it would take to identify the two components."

"What did you say?"

"That I have no idea."

"How did he respond to that?"

John offered a rueful grin. "More colorful language. And an emphatic order to figure it out. Fast!"

"So, let's get to it!"

John shoved a paper over to Steven and bent over his copy of the same document. "Here's the plan we've developed to find places in the HEU that are enriched in either one of the components. If we get lucky, we'll find places that have only one of the components."

Michelle jumped in. "I told John we've never done a controlled experiment where we mixed two sources while casting uranium metal. So it's purely a guess on where to look."

John tapped his paper and looked at Steven. "First, David and his team are taking microgram samples from across the slabs we cut out of the disk. By taking such small samples, we might find places with a higher proportion of one of the original sources."

Steven nodded.

"Second, the ion probe guys stopped doing chemical maps and are only measuring the uranium-235 to uranium-238 ratio. They'll first do low-resolution scans, and when they see a noticeable change in the ratio, they'll examine that area more closely."

"Sounds smart," offered Steven.

"Third, in your text from Kazakhstan, you suggested we look at inclusions. The SEM team prepared many more specimens, and they'll catalogue all the inclusions they find. Then we'll decide which inclusions to analyze isotopically."

Steven rubbed his hands together. "What kind of inclusions have they found so far?"

Michelle chimed in. "A lot of carbides. But occasionally we find some other types. When we're done here, let's go down to the SEM lab."

"Any other suggestions?" John asked.

Expecting this question, Steven had come up with another idea on the plane ride home. "I still think the inclusions are our best bet. But I have one more suggestion. The last material to solidify would be along grain boundaries. Maybe there's a mechanism in the casting process that caused one source to solidify later than the other. But don't ask me what the mechanism might be."

John jotted a note on his paper. "Interesting."

Steven was itching to see pictures of the inclusions. "Shall we go to the SEM lab now?"

"One more thing. I was surprised by one of your texts from Kazakhstan. You suggested we cut off another slab and send it to Ben at Los Alamos. I thought he left here on bad terms with you?"

"And with me," added Michelle.

Steven shrugged and held out his hands, palms up. "We're looking for a needle in a haystack. I'm not happy with Ben, but that doesn't change the fact that he's a hell of a good scientist. Does it really matter who finds the needle? Let's get the Los Alamos team working on the problem too."

John looked pleased. "The new slab arrived at Los Alamos several hours ago."

Steven gave a thumbs-up. "I'm glad you approved, despite the fact that the FBI usually doesn't want more than one lab to perform the same measurement. Did you get special permission from the Director?"

"In a time like this, it was an easy sell."

Michelle grabbed another donut. "Steven, there's one more maple old-fashioned for you. Let's go look at those inclusions."

"I've got some work to do here," John said, "so go ahead without me."

On the way to the SEM lab, Michelle handed Steven a diagram. "I wanted to give this to you when John wasn't around."

Steven slowed to look at it. She had plotted all the Laredo data on an isotope correlation diagram. He said, "The data define a pretty good mixing line. But the uncertainties on the line are quite large when you extrapolate beyond the data."

"Yes," Michelle said, and her eyes brightened as she handed him a second diagram. "Look at this."

It was the same diagram, except she'd added one data point with a Sharpie. His heart fluttered. "Wow, the Moldova HEU point you added lies close to the Laredo mixing line. Surprisingly close, considering the size of the error envelope for the line at that point."

"That's why I haven't told John yet, because I didn't want him passing it up the line until we confirm our suspicion."

"Good call. But if we get new data that better defines the line, and the Moldova point still lies close to it, then the Moldova case is relevant after all."

CHAPTER 50

Danville (June 24)

The next morning, Steven awoke, startled and disoriented. His dreams, though chaotic, had been so vivid. A searing flash of light followed by a mushroom cloud. An interrogation while in chains. Holding the dead body of his son Jacob. Fear coursed through his body while he struggled to consciousness. A ringing sound penetrated his confused mind. Oh, he was home again.

He reached for his phone and knocked it off his bedside table. Carissa stirred as he retrieved it from the floor. Kittrick? It was 5:25 in the morning!

Groggily, he whispered, "Hey, John. What's up?"

"News that couldn't wait!" John boomed. "We found an inclusion that's seventy-seven percent enriched."

Involuntarily, Steven let out a whoop. "Seventy-seven percent!" Carissa groaned and turned over. "Sorry," he whispered as he crept out of the bedroom.

By the time he reached the family room, his mind was buzzing. "That's a lot lower than the bulk sample. That'll really help define the mixing line. What kind of inclusion is it?"

"Sven called me an hour ago. He stayed up all night analyzing inclusions. The first dozen were isotopically the same as the bulk. Then came lucky number thirteen."

"You're killing me. Tell me about the inclusion."

"It's a silicon-rich inclusion. Probably some form of uranium silicide. It's fairly round and about fifteen microns in diameter." John sounded like he was relishing his rare opportunity to inform Steven of technical progress.

"I'll be there in half an hour."

"By the way, Sven said you made a point of analyzing this inclusion at some point during the night. Why?"

"Just a gut feeling. When I left last night, Sven had analyzed two carbide inclusions, and they had the same isotopic composition as the bulk. If that pattern continued, I figured one of the less common inclusions might be where we'd find a different isotopic composition."

With a hint of admiration, John said, "I guess in the future I should pay better attention to your gut feelings."

When Steven got to the Lab, he first spoke to Sven. Then he rushed to his office to plot the new data. He pumped his fist when he saw the result. They could take this to the FBI Director.

He was tempted to tell John right away, but then reversed course. Without Michelle's leadership, they wouldn't have gotten to this point so quickly. She deserved to hear the news at the same time as John. He called Michelle and told her to meet them at Denica's Real Food for breakfast at 7:15.

When they arrived at the restaurant, Michelle had already placed her order at the front counter and was sitting at a table in the back. She walked over to Steven and held out her hand. "I'll look at the correlation diagrams while you guys order."

Steven and John placed their orders, filled their cups at the coffee urn, and made their way to Michelle's table. Her food had already been delivered, but she'd pushed it to the side, uneaten.

She looked up at them when they sat down. "This sure confirms our suspicion, doesn't it, Steven?"

"What suspicion?" John asked.

Steven nodded at Michelle, inviting her to answer. She pushed a diagram toward John and said, "Look at how close this Si-rich inclusion point lies to the mixing line defined by our previous data. I have to confess, when the mass-spec guys tell me their precision is better than 0.01%, as a radiochemist, I tend to doubt them. But time and again, they're able to back up their claim. This result is yet another example."

John looked puzzled and a bit annoyed. "So what about your suspicion?"

Michelle's eyes gleamed. "I'm getting to it." She looked around to make sure no one was paying attention to them. No one was. It wasn't that unusual in Livermore to see scientists at a restaurant engaged in deep discussion. "See this point far to the left. It's not from this case, yet it lies quite close to the mixing line defined by all the data in this case, including this Si-rich inclusion."

John bent forward to get a closer look. "Holy crap!" His voice cracked in shock. "Is that what I think it is?"

Steven could no longer restrain himself. "Yep, that data point is from the HEU we analyzed six months ago. This previous material is very likely one of the sources in our current case." Leaning back in satisfaction, Steven thought back to his fierce objection to shutting down the Moldova investigation. "Of course, I could be accused of bias in drawing that conclusion."

Michelle was chewing the first bite of her sausage scramble. "I agree," she said. When Steven raised an eyebrow, she added, "Not about your bias. With your interpretation."

"Just how certain are you?" John said.

Steven put down his fork as he marshaled his thoughts. "Maybe as much as 90%. Because it's such an important conclusion, we should aim for even more certainty. I think we can extract enough of the Si-rich inclusion to measure the uranium isotopes with the thermal-ionization mass spec. Just a few nanograms should be enough to reduce the error bars substantially."

"That sounds risky," John said. "If we end up using most of the inclusion for that one measurement, we lose the ability to do other analyses."

"That's true," Michelle said. "But I think it's the most important data. If the improved precision defines a line that goes right through the Mol—" She stopped herself. "If the line goes through the data point we measured six months ago, that will pretty much nail it down as one of the sources. We could aim to extract only half of the inclusion."

"Sounds reasonable," John said. "How long will it take?"

Steven, as the mass-spec expert, weighed in. "We'll first do more in situ characterization and then remove the material this afternoon. The mass-spec analyses should be completed by tomorrow morning."

John looked at his untouched omelet. "Let's box up our food and get back to the Lab."

As they walked back to Steven's car, John was pensive. Steven kept quiet as well. After Steven merged onto the freeway, John finally spoke. "So... the Moldova case is back on the table."

Steven tried to suppress his urge for vindication. And failed. "In hindsight, it wasn't a coincidence that the Moldovan HEU interdiction happened only a few months before the Laredo interdiction."

John grunted but didn't expand upon Steven's point. Instead, he asked, "Why do you think this silicate-rich inclusion has more of the Moldova material?"

"Your question just gave me an idea. We found a large silicate grain in the Moldova powder. Maybe a large dust grain served as a nucleation site for the Moldova HEU during the casting operation."

"That at least seems plausible." John squinted. "I don't think I should wait until tomorrow to tell the Director."

"For what it's worth, I think that's a good call." The double meaning didn't occur to Steven until the words were out of his mouth.

"He'll be happy to hear about this latest breakthrough. He won't be so happy with the specifics. After all, he shut down the Moldova case." John ran his hand through his hair. "And I want you on the call with me. You can explain the isotope correlation diagrams."

Steven said, "You think that will be challenging, huh?"

John grinned. "You have no idea how much of what you tell people in Washington goes way over their heads."

Within minutes of John notifying the Director that he had an important update, John's phone rang. Without preamble, the Director said, "I hope you have good news."

"Very good news, sir. We believe we've identified one of the sources of the HEU. Steven Carter is here next to me and I'd like him to explain how we came to our conclusion."

"Go right ahead."

Steven cleared his throat. "Good morning, Director. The diagrams that Special Agent Kittrick sent you are what we call isotope correlation diagrams. Look at the one labeled as a model diagram. Any sample that's a mixture of two components will define a line on this type of plot. We labelled the two components A and B. Any measurement of this model sample will fall along the line and every point will lie between points A and B. Any questions so far, sir?"

The Director said, "If the sample is perfectly mixed, then all the points will plot on top of one another. You won't get a line. Right?"

"That's right."

"Now look at Diagram 1 with our Laredo data. As you can see, the points fall along a single line. Do you see the point labelled I-13?"

After a pause, the Director said, "Yes, way to the left. It's a long ways away from all the other points."

"That's what got us so excited. That point helps us define the mixing line much better. It also tells us that the lower-enriched source has an enrichment of seventy-seven percent or less."

"Why are the error bars on this point so much larger than all the others?"

"It's the only point on this plot from an inclusion. We analyzed it using the ion probe, which has a much lower precision than the instrument we used for the other data points."

"Okay. Can you reduce the error?"

"We're working on that, but we have very little material to analyze." The moment had arrived. Steven's leg started jiggling and his heart rate picked up. "Look at Diagram 2 now," Steven said. "It's the same plot as Diagram 1, with the same mixing line. The only difference is we added the point labelled M."

The Director said, "It's even further to the left and lies very close to the mixing line."

Steven waited to give the Director time to come to his own conclusion. After a long pause, he heard the Director sputtering. Then he yelled, "Shit! Don't tell me it's from the Moldova case!"

Steven pursed his lips. "You got it, sir."

The Director gave a long and loud sigh. "I'll brief the Attorney General right away. He'll be happy with the progress, not so happy with me. He knows I shut down the Moldova investigation."

They waited in silence until the Director spoke again. "John, do you have any idea what the other source might be?"

John and Steven looked at one another and Steven placed his forefinger on his lips. John said, "Sir, I called you right away with this latest result. We need more data to narrow the possibilities for the second source."

"Let me know ASAP of any further developments. Also, later this afternoon, I want the two of you to brief the interagency." Drily, he added, "Better you than me trying to explain these isotope correlation diagrams."

CHAPTER 51

The Lab (4:40 pm, June 24)

In twenty minutes, the interagency telecon from the National Counterterrorism Center would begin. Despite a very early start to what was already a long day, Steven expected to spend a few more hours at the Lab after the telecon. He should give Carissa a quick call, since they'd had so little time to talk after he returned from Kazakhstan.

"Hi, dear," he said. "How's everything at home?"

"Unfortunately, about the same." The forlorn tone of her voice had become familiar since Jacob's arrest. "You never call during the day. Is everything okay?"

"We had another breakthrough. In a few minutes, John and I are briefing the interagency."

"Will you be coming home after that?"

Steven sighed. She knew him too well. "That's why I called. I'll probably be here at least three more hours. So don't hold up dinner for me."

Her tone became more urgent. "Do you remember what we talked about just before we went to bed last night?"

"Don't worry, I'll talk to Jacob tonight and make sure he goes to that drug counselor."

"Good. I realize you're in a crisis, but our son has a court appearance in three days. Lots of people must be working on this national emergency, but I have only you to help me deal with Jacob."

A spurt of regret shot through him. Her plea reminded him of the haunted look that appeared on her face the past month when they spoke of Jacob. "I wish I could come home right now, hold you and talk with you."

"I appreciate the thought." She paused for several moments. In a brighter tone, she added, "I'm glad you've had a breakthrough in the case."

He was glad she'd changed the subject. "It's going to make a tremendous difference."

"I understand... kind of," she said, compassion entering her voice. "Work is your top priority right now. I hope, though, that in addition to getting Jacob to that counselor, you'll make it to his court appearance."

Her effort to lessen the pressure on him touched a deep part of him. "Oh, Carissa, I'm truly sorry I haven't been there for you more. Of course I'll do that."

Her voice warmed. "Just hearing you say that encourages me. Now, get ready for your telecon."

"I love you, dear."

"Love you too."

He hung up and dashed off to the classified video telecon. Before it started, John reviewed key details with him. The Director of National Intelligence appeared on the screen, and he introduced the participants, including Carolyn as the representative from the CIA. Steven nodded at her in happy surprise.

The DNI said, "I've convened this telecon at this late hour because the FBI has a significant new finding to report."

The FBI Director took his cue. "We previously reported that the Laredo HEU is actually a mixture of two sources. That means that up to this time we've been searching for the wrong HEU. But I'm happy to report that we've identified one of the sources. Special Agent John Kittrick, our nuclear forensics investigator, will present the evidence."

John worked through the same slides Steven had used earlier with the FBI Director, explaining them in a similar manner. With increasing confidence, John reached the climax of his brief. "Our expert opinion is that the evidence strongly supports the conclusion that the HEU interdicted last December in Moldova is one source for the Laredo HEU."

The DNI leaned forward. "How confident are you?"

Before John could reply, the FBI Director spoke up. "We are highly confident. Dr. Carter assigned a 90% confidence to this finding." John nodded to indicate his agreement. At the same time, Carolyn pushed away from the table and walked offscreen. Steven wondered what caused her abrupt departure.

"Special Agent Kittrick," the DNI said, "can you increase your level of certainty?"

John was well-prepared for this question. "Today we extracted about half of the silicon-rich inclusion, and by tomorrow morning we expect to have a more precise measurement of its isotopic composition. We will continue to analyze other areas of the HEU at both Los Alamos and here at Livermore. We hope to produce even more spread in the isotopic ratios and define the mixing line more accurately."

The DNI nodded in a way that suggested he completely understood the logic of this strategy. If Steven were taking a bet, he'd wager nobody on the call had fully grasped John's discussion of the isotope correlation diagrams, nor the reasons for their next steps. But if Steven tried to explain further, he'd likely confuse them even more.

The DNI looked around the NCTC conference table. "Any other questions?"

The representative from Homeland Security raised his hand. "I'd like to ask Dr. Carter two questions. First, why did it take you so long to discover that there were two sources?"

Steven's stomach tightened. "That's a good question, and—"

John cut in. "I lead the nuclear forensics investigation, and I take responsibility for it taking this long. I would add a caveat, however. It took a tremendous amount of data and a clever scientist to point us in this direction."

"That's true," Steven said, "and I want to make it clear that the clever scientist is one of my colleagues. I should have considered this possibility sooner, especially after we didn't make any progress identifying the source."

"Okay," said the DHS rep, in a tone showing it was not really okay. "Here's my second question. My understanding is that you previously developed evidence that the smugglers in the Moldova case had enough HEU for a bomb. So why did the terrorists in our current case use two sources of HEU?"

Though tempted to bring up the missed opportunity to stop this terrorist plot earlier, Steven dismissed it as counterproductive. No need to highlight the Director's earlier decision.

He turned his attention to the question posed. "At this point, I can only offer a guess. Most likely the terrorists wanted to hide what sources they used for their device. After all, if the weapon detonated, it would be impossible to detect from the debris that the HEU was in fact a mixture of two sources."

"Can you think of any other reasons?"

"Two, actually. One is that the terrorists couldn't get enough of the Moldova HEU, so they were forced to look for an additional source. The last possibility is the most disconcerting. Besides covering their tracks, the terrorists drew upon two sources so they could make more than one device."

Steven thought he heard groans coming through the telecon feed. Nobody spoke for a few moments. The DNI sighed. "Well, at least we've got a new lead to follow." He looked in Carolyn's direction and said, "I'd like to hear from Carolyn now—" and stopped when he saw she wasn't there.

"Where is she? A couple months ago, Carolyn opened an investigation into the Moldova HEU and suddenly that's very much relevant."

As if on cue, Carolyn bustled into the room. She seemed unfazed by everyone staring at her. The DNI said, "Good timing. I'd like you to brief us on the Moldova case."

"I'll be happy to do that, sir. But first I want to tell you what I just learned. When I heard the Moldova HEU was in play, I had an idea. After the Laredo interdiction, the FBI used surveillance footage at the port of entry and at Laredo rental car agencies to identify six suspects who brought parts of the bomb into the U.S. By the time they identified them, all six of them had gone off the grid. I left to double-check if any of these six suspects surfaced in our Moldova investigation." She paused.

Steven noticed that every person around the NCTC table was leaning forward. Carolyn let the tension build and then announced, "We got a hit. One of the FBI's suspects is Cyrus Safar. This same Cyrus Safar rented a car in Romania in January of this year and used it to kill the smuggler who was arrested in the Moldova case. In my opinion, that corroborates the scientists' conclusion that the Moldova and Laredo cases are linked."

"Excellent!" the DNI said. "What do we know about this Cyrus Safar?"

The FBI Director intervened. "We've found no record of such a person. Most likely it's a false identity."

The DNI looked back at Carolyn. "Okay, Carolyn, update us on everything you learned in the Moldova investigation." He turned to look directly into the camera. "Thank you, Agent Kittrick and Dr. Carter, for your hard work and excellent progress. Now I'll let you get back to it. When you identify the second source, call me directly."

Before John or Steven could reply, the video screen went black.

CHAPTER 52

Danville (June 25)

Thanks to extreme exhaustion, Steven got his first decent night of sleep in a week. After he woke up, he stayed in bed a few minutes, dreading the start of his day. When he got home last night, Jacob had disappeared. Steven queried Josh, who said his little brother had refused to tell him where he was going, claiming it was nobody's business. Steven tried to stay awake until Jacob came home, but after falling asleep several times in his armchair, he finally went to bed at midnight.

He had to talk to Jacob before he left this morning. After breakfast, he shook Jacob awake and ordered him to get dressed and come to the family room. His son looked more sullen than ever when he entered the room.

"Why'd you wake me up?" The anger in Jacob's voice didn't bode well.

Steven stifled the rise of his own anger. "You knew I wanted to talk to you last night."

Jacob waved his hand dismissively. "I'm sorry my schedule doesn't fit with yours."

"Your adjudication hearing is in two days."

"Really?" his son said, dripping with sarcasm. "Thanks for the reminder."

Steven took a deep breath. His son's attitude had gotten worse since his last serious talk with him. "Have you started going to drug counseling?"

"I'm not an addict. What's the point?"

"You promised the judge at your detention hearing."

Jacob shrugged.

Steven bit his tongue to keep from lashing out. When had Jacob become such a hard ass? In a voice that brooked no dissent, Steven said, "As soon as the counseling office opens this morning, call and get an appointment."

Jacob smirked. "I've already got an appointment for this afternoon."

"Why didn't you say that in the first place?"

"Can I go back to bed now?"

"You have stayed off drugs, haven't you?"

"You worry too much."

Steven searched for a way to end on a more positive note. "Hey, assuming all goes well at your hearing, how about us three guys go camping later this summer?"

"Maybe."

Steven wasn't sure, but the hardness in Jacob's face may have softened slightly. He said, "Talk to your brother about where you'd like to go."

Jacob waved his hand. "You and Josh can decide."

A year ago, a guys' outing would have thrilled Jacob. Steven stood up and put his hand on his son's shoulder. Jacob twitched, as if trying to rid himself of a pesky fly. Removing his hand, Steven made one last try. "We had so much fun on our guys' trip last year."

"It was two years ago."

Crap, he was right. "That's way too long, and I'm sorry about that."

Jacob looked at him with disdain, then shuffled back to his bedroom.

On the drive to the Lab, Steven replayed the conversation, which made him feel even worse. Nearing the Lab, he forced himself to put his family problems aside. He wondered, for the umpteenth time, what the terrorists were doing at that moment. Were they close to detonating?

Since nobody had called him during the night, it didn't surprise him when Michelle said there hadn't been any more progress on defining the second source. Then he made the rounds of everyone on his team, got the details on their latest results, and brainstormed where they might find a higher proportion of the second source.

While he was eating lunch, Michelle bustled into his office. Her first words were, "It occurred to me there's one place we haven't looked yet."

He put down his sandwich. "I'm all ears."

Her ponytail swished from side to side as her head bobbed in excitement. "When we dissolved gram-sized samples of the uranium, we always had some residue left. I called Ben at Los Alamos to see if he'd found that too. So far, he's dissolved only one large sample, and he also had residue."

Catching her enthusiasm, Steven sat up straighter. "Good move to check in with Ben."

"Both of us tried harsher treatments to dissolve the residue, but we always had some material remaining. While we talked, it hit me. I haven't characterized these residues yet. They may contain unusual phases. It's a reach, but maybe some rare phase will be enriched in the second source."

He felt a thump in his chest. "Good idea." He stroked his beard as his mind raced. "While you're looking at your existing residues, let's dissolve a huge sample. That'll increase our odds."

With mounting enthusiasm, Michelle said, "Let's make it a thousand times bigger. That would still leave most of the HEU part intact."

He stood up and moved toward the door. "Let's get John's approval so you can start right away."

She followed close behind him to John's office, where she explained their idea. John tapped his desk with his pen. "A kilogram of the HEU? On a hunch? That's crazy!"

Steven grinned. "Maybe crazy enough to be the right move. Besides, with so little time left, I can't think of anything better to do with that kilogram."

The agent's lips tightened. "Okay, go for it."

Michelle gave John a little salute. "By this evening, we'll be analyzing the new residue."

John said, "Tomorrow morning I have a scheduled call with the Director. Even if we don't have another breakthrough by then, I won't be able to hold back any longer from sharing our suspicion about the second source."

"We need more evidence," Steven said, "because when Washington hears it, all hell will break loose."

CHAPTER 53

The Lab (June 26)

The day promised to be hot, but the early morning air was delightfully cool as Steven entered the Nuclear Chemistry Building. Michelle had texted him: *Good progress on acid residues.* He was eager to hear the details from her, and when he spotted John waiting for him at his office door, his pace quickened.

"Carolyn called," John said. "She wants to consult with us, and we need to use Alan's high security phone."

Darn! Most days, Steven would be thrilled to hear from Carolyn. Today he wanted to confer with Michelle before the call. But John was already headed toward Alan's office, so he dropped his briefcase in his office, closed the door, and trotted to catch up with John.

On schedule, Carolyn called and got right down to business. "Suddenly, I have unlimited resources to investigate the Moldova case." She said it so matter-of-factly that her sarcasm barely registered with Steven. "Here's what we've learned in the past couple days. We initially focused on the hit-and-run in Romania. After an exhaustive search, we didn't find a Cyrus Safar who registered at a Constanta hotel during the three days prior to the hit-and-run. We did find, however, three Omars who checked in. We'll investigate all three, but my bet is on the Omar with links to Azerbaijan."

John tapped his notepad. "Sounds like a long-shot."

In an even tone of voice, Carolyn said, "Maybe. But right now, it's one of our best leads. Our assets are interviewing staff at the three hotels where these Omars stayed, hoping they'll remember something about them."

"Anything else new?"

"We found a third instance in which Cyrus Safar showed up. He checked out of a Nuevo Laredo hotel the morning of the interdiction. The hotel still had surveillance recordings, and we've obtained a better picture of Safar. The manager describes him as short, about five and a half feet tall, with a slender build."

John said, "Good progress. Any more hits on his phone?"

"No. He probably ditched it after the interdiction." Carolyn paused. "Okay, what do you have for me?"

"Our metallurgist concluded the terrorists used a vacuum induction furnace to melt and cast the HEU part. Steven suggested we look at recent deliveries of this type of furnace. Unfortunately, many companies around the world sell that type of equipment."

Carolyn snorted. "Another long-shot clue?"

"True enough." The agent chuckled. "Nevertheless, a week ago, the FBI mounted an all-out campaign to pursue that lead. We doubted the terrorists would buy from a U.S. company, and we also assumed they would find it difficult to connect with Chinese manufacturers, so we focused on European companies. Even after we narrowed down the field, we had about forty companies to look at."

"And...?"

"We investigated deliveries of lab-scale equipment, rather than the larger industrial scale units. And confined our search to purchases in the past year. Based on the Moldova connection, we prioritized deliveries made in Moldova, Romania, and neighboring countries. That still left us with twenty-six deliveries by a dozen companies. Then yesterday Steven had another suggestion."

John motioned for Steven to speak. Steven rubbed his hands together and said, "As you probably recall, the HEU part was wrapped in plastic. After we cut it away, we collected everything adhering to the interior of the plastic and the exterior of the HEU. Yesterday we examined dust particles from that material on the SEM. Their mineralogy indicates an arid climate. We'll continue to analyze this dust and hope to eventually identify a specific geographical area."

Carolyn said, "Just knowing the part was made in an arid environment should help, right?"

"Yes!" John said. "We prioritized the twenty-six furnace deliveries according to the climate of their location. The three with the driest climates are at the top of our list. One is in Sofia, Bulgaria. Given the previous suggested connection of Bulgaria with the Moldovan HEU, we consider that our top candidate. Another is Thessaloniki, Greece. The third location is in a small town near Ankara, Turkey. That region is considerably drier than most of the Balkans."

"Send me the names and addresses of all three companies ASAP. We'll investigate each of them today."

"Consider it done." John tapped his notepad with his pen. "And while you're at it, tell your agents to collect soil when they visit those companies."

"Good idea. Anything else from your end?"

Steven wondered if John would offer their tentative identification of the second source. John said, "Nothing more at this point."

Steven breathed a sigh of relief. After John hung up, Steven said, "Let's go find Michelle. I think she found something in the acid residues. Hopefully, it will either confirm or rule out our suspicion about the second source."

CHAPTER 54

CIA Headquarters (June 26)

Carolyn sent out orders to immediately investigate the companies at the top of the FBI's list of vacuum furnace deliveries. Then her shoulders hunched and a tingle ran down her spine. Experience had taught her to pay attention to this signal from her body.

She called Bill Yount, but he didn't pick up. She left a message to call her back.

She pulled out the day's New York Times crossword puzzle. This habit mystified her colleagues, but she had learned when she gave her mind a break, new insights often bubbled up.

When her crossword was half completed, her phone rang.

"Anything new, Bill?"

"I can't say for sure that Omar Hasanov is your man. He's a salesman with an engineering background. He left his old job in Baku six months ago, without giving notice or a reason. We haven't been able to identify a new employer."

"Curious. He quit his job about the same time he showed up in Constanta. Which was also when the smuggler was killed. Seems a stretch to be only a coincidence."

"My thought too."

She doodled along the edges of her crossword, repeatedly writing *Omar Hasanov*. "Have you located him yet?"

"I went to his last known address, but nobody answered the door. One of his neighbors was willing to talk to me. She confirmed he lives there, but travels a lot. He's been home only once during the past several months."

"That's consistent with him being part of the terrorist team."

"Consistent, yes. But proof, no."

"Did she give you any idea where he's been lately?"

"When I asked her, she thought for a minute and then looked surprised. She told me Omar usually tells her stories about the places he visits on his business trips, but this last time he was tight-lipped."

"Did you get any actionable leads from her?"

"Not really. I told her I had a business package for him, but she was unable, or maybe unwilling, to identify any of his business associates. She seemed to get suspicious when I kept asking questions."

Carolyn wracked her brain. "Anything else? A name? Or a place?"

Silence for a few moments. Then Bill said, "The last time Omar was home, she noticed he had a nasty cough. When she mentioned it to him, he said something about dirty Turks."

Carolyn's shoulders shot up. A shiver ran down her spine. The furnace delivery in Turkey—that could be the place they were looking for! "Try to determine whether Hasanov has been doing business near Ankara."

"Okay. We're also tracking down Hasanov's family and friends."

"Call me with anything new."

After Carolyn hung up, she put her fingertips together as she tapped her mouth. A few minutes later, she sent a dispatch to the agents who were interviewing people in Constanta, telling them to focus their search on Omar Hasanov. She queried the agents investigating the other two Omars. So far, they looked clean, which strengthened her suspicion of Hasanov.

Suddenly, it hit her like a half-ton of bricks. What about Cyrus Safar? Could he be Omar? Though Safar was a fictitious name, she now had acquired a good photo and a partial description. She logged onto her computer again and sent Safar's info to every CIA station working the Omar leads. She sat back and ruminated. Then she sent Safar's information to the stations working the vacuum furnace angle.

...

Jeff Lake, CIA station chief at the U.S. embassy in Ankara, picked up the cable from headquarters. It was a directive from Carolyn to investigate the legitimacy of a small business in a nearby town. He'd only met Carolyn once, but his initial impression validated her reputation as one of the Agency's best. For context, the cable referenced the search for information related to the nuclear terrorist threat. The emphasis on a recently purchased vacuum furnace further intrigued him. Even more surprising, he should immediately call Carolyn with his findings. Given the level of urgency and importance, he took the unusual step of doing the investigation himself. On the way out of the embassy, he grabbed a secure cell phone.

After an hour drive, he parked in front of the farm equipment shop. It looked deserted. He approached the front door and read the small sign attached to it. *Closed until July 15.*

It was way too early for a Turkish summer vacation. It was even stranger for a shop that catered to farmers. He peered into the large front window. The various farm items seemed reasonable for this type of business. In the evening's fading sunlight, he could barely make out two pieces of equipment in the back of the room. One resembled his photo of a vacuum furnace reactor.

He paced off the distance from the front of the shop to the back. Hmm, the shop must have a back room. The back of the shop was windowless and the back door was locked. He was tempted to break in, but decided to first talk to the neighbors. Later, he would return under the cover of darkness to check out the back room.

Only one nearby business was still open. Jeff talked to the owner about the farm equipment shop, telling him he wanted to talk to the shop about a business opportunity. The owner said the workers at the farming shop were friendly, and often waved as they passed by, but they otherwise kept to themselves.

Jeff expanded his search to nearby restaurants. At the fourth one, the owner smiled when Jeff mentioned the metal shop. Jeff's command of Turkish was sufficient to discern that the shop employees frequently ate at this establishment. The owner seemed eager to help with a potential business deal. But he hadn't seen any of the workers since the shop closed three weeks ago.

Jeff hid his growing excitement. Three weeks ago! Very weird to shut down for six weeks. Casually, in his passable Turkish, he asked, "Do you remember any names?"

The owner's face screwed up in concentration. Jeff put a twenty-dollar bill on the table next to the owner. The owner's face cleared. "Oh yes," he said, "I remember now. One of them is called Omar."

Jeff restrained his urge to kick his feet in the air. Pay dirt! Carolyn was looking for an Omar. Putting down another twenty-dollar bill, he asked, "Do you remember his last name?"

Sadly, the owner shook his head.

"Maybe I could contact him at his home."

The owner shook his head again.

Jeff drove down the street and parked his car. This couldn't wait. He called Langley, and the operator connected him to Carolyn.

"What do you have for me?" she asked.

"This could well be the place you're looking for." He explained by telling his story, beginning with the shop. When he came to the part about putting down the twenty-dollar bill, she interrupted.

"Come on, the suspense is killing me."

Jeff's eyes gleamed. "The money jogged his memory. One of the men is called Omar."

With a note of triumph, Carolyn said, "It must be Hasanov!"

"If you say so. The owner only knows him by his first name."

She was silent for a moment. "Did you get the information I sent the embassy about a Cyrus Safar?"

"No," Jeff said. "It must have come after I left."

"Give me your cell number and I'll text you his picture."

Jeff hurried back to the restaurant. He held up two twenties and showed the owner the picture of Safar.

The owner nodded vigorously. "Yes, that is the shop owner. Ahmad's Metal Works is named after him."

"Do you know Ahmad's last name?"

The owner took the two twenties. Then he said, "No, but you can find it at city hall when it opens tomorrow."

Jeff called Carolyn back as soon as he got into his car. When she heard the news, she yelled, "Fantastic! Cyrus Safar's real first name must be Ahmad. He and this Omar made the bomb in Ahmad's Metal Works."

He softly pounded his steering wheel in delight. "I'll get a team from the embassy to search the shop tonight."

She said, "I'll send instructions on what to collect."

"And I'll make sure the local authorities don't get involved."

"Great job, Jeff." Her voice conveyed relief as well as excitement. "We're on their trail now."

CHAPTER 55

The Lab (1:00 pm, June 26)

With a spring in his step, Steven led John and Michelle through the Z-Division maze to Alan's office. Along the way, Steven said, "Hey, John, you ready to set off fireworks?"

John cocked his head and grunted. "When this news lands in Washington, it'll be more like a bombshell."

Michelle said, "I'm glad we waited until we confirmed our suspicion."

When they reached Alan's office, all three of them stood in the hallway, waiting for someone else to go in first. Alan grinned. "I could make room by moving my desk into the hallway."

Steven smiled back at his friend. "Nah, I can just sit on top your desk."

Rolling his eyes, Alan looked at Steven and said, "The two of us can stand, and..." he gestured toward the two chairs by the phone, "John and Michelle can sit."

John sat, rubbed his shoulders, and let out a deep breath. To ease the tension, Steven said in a rather irreverent voice, "John, remember how upset the Director got when you told him the HEU was a mixture of two sources? When he hears this news, I bet he'll grab his wastebasket and throw up."

Alan chuckled, while Michelle gave Steven a dirty look, as if to say, "*I can't believe you just said that*." John was slower to respond. Then he deadpanned, "Too bad it's not a video call."

They erupted in laughter.

Smiling, John said, "Okay, let's get on with it."

Alan dialed the number and put the phone in secure mode.

"Good afternoon, sir," John said. "We've had another breakthrough."

"John," the Director boomed. "Give me the bottom line."

John sucked in his cheeks. "Our latest measurements strongly suggest that the second source of uranium is from the U.S."

The phone was silent for a moment, then the Director yelled, "What the hell?! Are you sure?"

"I doubt we're wrong."

"Two weeks ago, I assured the White House the Laredo HEU was not U.S. weapons uranium. That's not the second source, is it?"

John's lips pinched together. "Our previous conclusion was based on the assumption that the Laredo HEU was from a single source. We believe this second source is most likely U.S. uranium, probably enriched to more than 90%."

The Director groaned. In a somber tone, he asked, "How did you figure this out?"

"Did you see my email with the isotope correlation diagram?"

The Director groaned again. "Not yet." More silence. "Any bright ideas on how a terrorist got his hands on U.S. HEU?"

"Dr. Alan Yang will give you some background." John stood up and Alan slid into his place.

Alan cleared his throat. "Beginning in the 50s, the U.S. developed a class of reactors they called TRIGA reactors. These reactors were built around the world, and they used 93% enriched uranium produced by the U.S."

"That doesn't sound like such a bright idea," the Director said.

"The goal of the TRIGA program was to develop a safe reactor for research and training purposes. Edward Teller, who was part of the original design team, said it should be safe enough that it could be given to a bunch of high school children to play with, with no fear they would get hurt."

"How many of these TRIGA reactors are there?"

"Sixty-nine in total. In twenty-three different countries. Over the past couple decades, many have been converted to a lower-enriched fuel, but not all of them."

"Any idea which reactor is associated with this second source?"

"Not yet."

Steven gave Alan a thumbs-up on his succinct but clear description.

John tapped Alan's shoulder and slid back in front of the phone. "Do you have the isotope correlation diagram yet?"

"Yes, my secretary just put it on my desk."

John ran his hand through his hair as he slid a copy of the diagram between him and Michelle. "This is the same diagram we used to make the connection with the Moldova HEU. It includes all the data we showed you before. Because we're now sure that the Moldova HEU is one of the two sources, its isotopic composition anchors one end of our best-fit line. Last night, thanks to Dr. Michelle Johnson, we had another breakthrough. I'll let her explain."

Michelle slid her chair closer to the phone. "Good afternoon, Director. I'm sorry to meet in this circumstance."

The Director grunted.

Speaking calmly and with assurance, Michelle continued. "When we discovered the Laredo HEU is a mixture of two sources, our analytical strategy changed. That led to our previous discovery that the Moldova HEU is one of the sources. Yesterday, we dissolved a large hunk of the Laredo metal in acid and examined the residue. We found an unusual yttrium-rich particle, which we analyzed this morning.

The point labelled Y on the diagram represents its uranium isotopic composition."

The Director broke in. "It has a much higher level of enrichment than any other data point."

"Exactly," Michelle said. "It's 87% enriched. That gives us a much better constraint on the composition of this second source. Notice that our new best-fit line falls close to the point labelled U.S. That point represents 93% enriched TRIGA fuel."

"What's the point labelled R?"

"That's the uranium Russia uses in its nuclear weapons. You can see it lies significantly off our best-fit line."

"Got it. I'm getting the hang of these isotope correlation diagrams. Do you have any idea which TRIGA reactor is associated with the Laredo uranium?"

John said, "We just got started on answering that question."

Michelle looked at Steven and he smiled at her. He was proud of her. She was content to take a back seat to him, but given the opportunity to shine, she came through every time.

The Director cleared his throat. "I have my own surprise for you."

John raised his hands to signal he had no idea what was coming next.

With an air of excitement, the Director said, "We found the site where the terrorists built their weapon."

Steven jerked back in his chair and sucked in his breath.

The Director continued, "Turns out, the key was your suggestion to investigate induction furnaces delivered in arid environments."

A warm glow of satisfaction spread through Steven. John pumped his fist, and Michelle softly clapped her hands.

The Director said, "The Agency will enter the site soon. When I have more information, I'll give you a call."

John glanced around the small office and asked, "Anyone have anything to add?"

Steven wanted to ask more about finding the site, but realized it wasn't relevant at this juncture. He shook his head, and Michelle and Alan followed suit.

After a few moments of silence, the Director sighed. "Time for me to stir up a hornet's nest at the White House. I expect a lot of blowback."

Steven ventured to offer the Director a lifeline. "Once we determined the Laredo HEU was a mixture of two sources, we didn't explicitly say the possibility of a U.S source was back on the table. Truth be told, when our data pointed to U.S. weapons uranium, it shocked me."

"Shock! That's an understatement," the Director said. "People are going to get very upset, and they'll probably point their fingers at me."

Steven couldn't help but feel the Director deserved fingers pointing his way. After all, the Director shut down the original Moldova investigation. But he also couldn't help but feel sympathy for him as the messenger bearing bad news.

John ended the call by saying, "Well, sir, we'll get to work on identifying the TRIGA reactor."

CHAPTER 56

Somewhere in the U.S. (June 27)

Ahmad's trip across the U.S. to the assembly site was uneventful, thanks to the new identities provided by Raushan. Ahmad also made sure everyone on his team carefully followed all the precautions laid out by Uncle. After they unloaded the HEU parts and Ahmad said goodbye to his five comrades, he had little to do. The only highlight of the first week was the delivery of the crates with the structural parts of the bomb. After he unpacked the crates, he verified all the parts had arrived in good condition. Per Uncle's instruction, he found the high explosive buried in one of the crates. Then he waited, leaving the shop only twice to purchase food.

Time passed slowly. Making matters worse, the portable air conditioner worked sporadically. With no shower, he relied upon the sink in the small bathroom to cool himself. Yesterday, the delivery of a new part temporarily relieved his boredom. It was the steel jacket for Uncle's redesign. Ahmad couldn't fathom how it would make up for the missing HEU part.

While he was dozing on his cot, he was awakened by a knock. What if it wasn't Uncle? He jumped up and crept toward the front door. Peering out the front window, he gave a little wave and breathed normally again. He opened the door and smiled as he said, "Welcome, Uncle."

Uncle did not return the smile. In a clipped voice, he said, "Hello, Nephew."

Uncle nodded approvingly as he surveyed the structural pieces Ahmad had laid out on the shop floor, but he stopped in front of the high explosive. Uncle's brow furrowed. "You started shaping the high explosive. I told you to wait until I got here before you started assembling the pieces."

"With my training at the terrorist camp, I figured that's the one thing I could do ahead of time."

Sternly, Uncle said, "I do the figuring. You do the obeying."

Ahmad gritted his teeth, but let the reprimand pass. "Can we start the final assembly now?"

"I need to wait for one more delivery."

"How is the new design going to work?"

Uncle pulled a pen out of his pocket and began to sketch on a piece of cardboard. Ahmad kept bobbing his head as he followed Uncle's explanation.

"That's so clever," Ahmad said when Uncle finished. It wasn't flattery; Uncle was a genius. The redesigned bomb might actually work better than the original, even with less HEU.

Uncle said, "Almost as clever as mixing the two sources of uranium. It wasn't easy to get the TRIGA fuel to your shop, but now I'm glad I managed to do it. Even though the Americans intercepted one part, they'll never figure out where the HEU came from."

"How long until we detonate?"

Uncle grinned. "Tomorrow we'll assemble the pieces to make sure everything fits. If all goes well, two days after we receive the last shipment."

Ahmad's heart thumped. "When will that be?"

"Raushan is working on it. Should be any day now."

CHAPTER 57

Walnut Creek (June 27)

Midway through Jacob's adjudication hearing in a sterile, nearly empty room, Carissa whispered to Steven, "He's an excellent judge. Stern but fair."

Steven noticed the judge glancing in their direction. Mutely, he texted her. *Seems prosecutor has a strong case. Agree?*

Grimly, she nodded.

When the prosecutor sat down, Jacob's lawyer shoved back her chair with a screech and began her defense argument. At that moment, Steven got a text from John. *When will you be here?*

He texted back. *Not sure. Two hours soonest.*

The defense attorney did a masterful job, but she had little to work with. Even a hopeful parent like Steven had to acknowledge the evidence overwhelmingly proved his son had possessed a large amount of marijuana and some cocaine. Countering the drug trafficking charge, where the evidence was circumstantial, the attorney made some headway. However, she was unable to explain the rapid growth in Jacob's banking account. When the defense attorney sat down, Steven had little doubt of the judge's decision. The grief on Carissa's face confirmed his fears.

The judge asked Jacob to stand. Jacob glanced back at his parents and his brother, Josh. Steven nodded to show his support, and Josh gave a hopeful thumbs-up. The judge said, "Jacob Carter, I find the allegation of drug possession to be true."

Steven held his breath and waited for the judge's next decision.

"Furthermore, I find the allegation of drug trafficking to be true."

Jacob's shoulders slumped, Josh buried his head in his hands, and Steven's heart dropped. Carissa's face turned ashen, and she grabbed Steven's hand.

The judge continued. "In one week, you will appear in this court for your disposition hearing. Then I will decide on the penalties. Do you understand?"

Jacob nodded.

"Please answer verbally."

"Yes."

"Yes, Your Honor, is the appropriate response," the judge said. "These are serious crimes. I now have to decide whether to hold you in custody in the juvenile detention center."

Steven jerked upright. He had given a very low probability to that outcome.

In a brusque voice, the judge asked, "At your previous disposition hearing, you promised to go to drug counseling. Have you done so?"

"Yes, Your Honor."

"How many times?"

"Once."

The judge glared at Jacob.

Jacob added, "Your Honor."

"The bare minimum." The judge rubbed his chin as his eyes bored into Jacob. "Have you used any illegal drugs since your arrest?"

In a strained voice, Jacob replied, "No, Your Honor."

"At this point in your life, you don't strike me as a trustworthy young man. Accordingly, I'm ordering a drug test for you immediately after this hearing."

Jacob turned to his attorney and whispered something Steven couldn't hear. For the first time since the arrest, Steven spotted fear on his son's face. His sullen bravado was cracking.

Jacob faced the judge again. "Your Honor, I misspoke. Once in the past two months, I smoked a little weed."

Carissa squeezed Steven's hand. He squeezed back and looked at her. Tears spilled down her cheeks.

For the first time, the judge looked angry. "And when did this happen?"

Jacob shuffled his feet and looked up at the ceiling.

Steven's phone vibrated, but he ignored it.

In a forlorn voice, his son answered. "Three days ago."

Steven shook his head in angry disbelief. When he had asked Jacob the same question two days earlier, Jacob basically lied to him with his evasive response.

"Finally," the judge said, "the truth." The judge stared at Jacob. "I'm this close to remanding you to juvenile detention until your hearing next week." The judge held up his hand, showing about a millimeter between his thumb and index finger. "However, you have no previous offenses. Therefore, I'm placing you back in the custody of your parents. You shall be confined to your home, except for the purpose of attending drug counseling. Do you understand?"

"Yes, Your Honor," Jacob said, with a note of relief.

"But this time," the judge continued, "I'm ordering electronic monitoring. Any attempt to remove the ankle bracelet will have serious consequences." The judge pressed his lips together. "You're headed down a dangerous path." A note of fatherly concern entered the judge's voice. "Time to start making better choices. I expect you to meet with your drug counselor twice a week."

When the hearing was over, Steven rushed up to his son. He caught his eye and was pleased to see the hardness fading. Then Jacob looked away. Steven reached out to embrace him, but it turned awkward when Jacob stiffened and then moved toward his mother and brother.

While Carissa hugged Jacob, Steven glanced at his phone. John had texted. *Another big development. I need you back here ASAP.*

He texted back. *In two hours, maybe.*

After they escorted Jacob from the hearing room, Steven put his hand on Carissa's shoulder. "Kittrick wants me back at the Lab as soon as possible. I'll stay with you until they release Jacob. Then all of us can go back home together. But I need to go to the Lab this afternoon."

Her tear-stained face registered disappointment, followed by resignation. "I was hoping you could take the whole day off."

"I wish I could," he said, with genuine regret.

While they waited for Jacob to reappear, they agreed to give him space before they engaged him in a serious talk. After he had time to reflect on the morning's events, maybe he'd even initiate a conversation. After an hour, Jacob appeared, looking chastened.

On the drive home, Steven didn't comment on the hearing, other than to say he was glad Jacob was coming home with them. His son replied with, "Me too."

When they walked into the house, Steven said with an air of forced positivity, "Let's all have lunch together."

Jacob said, "Sorry, I'm not hungry," and he made a beeline to his room.

Josh's eyes followed his brother, and then he looked at his parents. "I think I should be with him."

Carissa waved for him to follow his brother.

"I guess it's just you and me," Steven said.

"Maybe that's best. I'll make us some sandwiches."

Before she finished, John called. "I realize you have a family emergency, but we're in the middle of a national emergency. When are you going to get here?"

Carissa must have overheard, because she waved for Steven to go.

Steven mouthed, "You sure?"

In reply, she handed the first sandwich to him.

Steven said to John, "I'll be there in thirty minutes."

Thirty-two minutes later, the agent was waiting for Steven when he rounded the corner and headed toward his office. John followed him in, shut the door, and launched into his update. "Last night, a CIA team searched Ahmad's Metal Works in a small town outside Ankara, Turkey. They confirmed it's where the weapon was fabricated. They didn't find any bulk samples of uranium, but they collected a lot of trace evidence. The samples should arrive any minute." The agent pointed at Steven. "You'll help me prioritize them."

"Do we know anything about the technical background of the terrorists?"

"We've identified two of them. One is Omar Hasanov. Apparently, he's an engineer by training, but he's worked mostly in sales. The second terrorist is Cyrus Safar. He was the man Carolyn connected with the Laredo interdiction. We suspected from the outset that Safar was a false identity. The CIA has learned that Safar is the man who owns the metal shop. His real name is Ahmad Abbasova."

"That's hutzpah, putting his real name on the shop."

"Abbasova has a degree in chemistry from Baku University. After he graduated, he seems to have disappeared."

John's phone buzzed, and he checked his text messages. "The samples are here."

On the way to the car, Steven asked, "How did the samples get here so fast?"

"The CIA used military planes. Two of our agents picked them up at Travis Air Force Base in Fairfield."

John spotted the FBI agents in the parking lot of the Lab Badge Office and drove next to their car. After the agent in the passenger's seat verified John's credentials, he handed John a diplomatic pouch.

When they got back to the Nuclear Chemistry Building, they brought the pouch into the sample receival lab and placed it on the clean-room work bench to guard against cross-contamination. John extracted a large, sealed bag from the pouch. It was stuffed with many smaller baggies. After cleaning the outside of the bag, he poured out the contents. Steven estimated they had more than a hundred baggies, and each one probably contained thousands of particles. It would take days to thoroughly examine the swipes in just one baggie.

Steven gestured at the pile. "We certainly need to prioritize. Let's bring in the team to help."

Within minutes, everyone arrived, eyeing the piles of baggies with anticipation.

Steven said, "Our hope is that among all these particles we'll find some that are close to pure samples of the TRIGA fuel. That will help to characterize the second source and identify its origin. We also hope to confirm our finding that the Moldova HEU is the other source."

John emphasized the time crunch they were working under. He segmented the baggies into a dozen smaller piles, and next to each one he placed a description of how those samples were collected and photographs that showed the sample locations within the production site.

John looked around the table. "Together, we'll select which ten samples to analyze first."

The debate became heated at times, although Danny, with his metallurgist's insights, provided particularly helpful suggestions of which samples to analyze first. When they settled on their top ten, Steven turned to Sven. "This will be a 24/7 analysis campaign. Everyone at the Lab with the suitable skills and instrumentation needs to be brought on board."

Michelle said, "Sven, give me your list of candidates, and I'll make the calls. We need you back on the ion probe."

John said, "By tomorrow morning, I expect a summary of your initial findings." He clapped his hands. "Good luck. And don't let me down."

CHAPTER 58

The Lab (June 28)

Steven drove into the Lab parking lot as the sun peeked above the eastern hills. He recalled his interaction with Jacob the previous evening with a sense of hope. Jacob had joined his mother and brother for dinner, and two hours later, the three of them were watching TV when Steven got home. He ate the leftovers while he watched the rest of the show with them. When Jacob got up to go back to his room, Steven walked back with him.

"How are you doing?" Steven asked, hoping to start a serious conversation.

"This monitoring device is driving me nuts."

"Maybe it's a good reminder of the difficult situation you are in. Like an albatross around your ankle."

His son looked puzzled, and Steven surmised he hadn't yet read the *The Rime of the Ancient Mariner*. Jacob said, "I know you want to talk, but can't it wait just one more day?"

"Okay, but tomorrow evening we talk, right?"

His son muttered "Okay" as he walked into his room, then said "Good night" as he shut the door.

Steven had hoped for more, but he was encouraged. Now he had to give his full attention to the Laredo case.

First, he sought out Michelle and found her pounding away at her computer. She paused and said, "I'll have a summary of all the results in a quarter of an hour. Then Sven and I will meet you in John's office."

His first impulse was to offer his help. Then he figured he'd just slow her down. Instead, he made a cup of coffee and headed to John's office.

When Sven shuffled into the office, with Michelle close behind, Steven was alarmed by Sven's bleary eyes. The way the man collapsed into a chair reminded him that the nuclear forensics team had worked twelve-hour days every day for two weeks. No wonder everyone showed signs of exhaustion.

Sven handed Steven and John a three-page document. "Here's our summary for the first five samples. We would've had more data by now, but one of my ion probes broke down. It took six hours to get it running again."

Steven groaned in commiseration and said, "Murphy's law."

John scanned the first page. "Okay, take us through your report."

Sven didn't bother to look at his copy that lay on the table in front of him. "The first sample was collected from the induction furnace. It had the most uranium particles, but so far, each one has the same uranium isotopic composition as the Laredo HEU."

Steven said, "Not too surprising, is it?"

Sven nodded. "Almost half of the particles in sample two are uranium rich. We have decent uranium isotopics for several particles and most of them are a clear match with the Moldovan HEU."

"Remind me," Steven said, "where was this sample collected?"

John said, "From a piece of plastic they found between a workbench and the wall. My guess is that the Moldovan HEU was wrapped in plastic, and this piece got lost."

"That makes sense."

At that moment, Alan appeared in the doorway. He looked triumphant despite the early hour. John looked over at him. "Join us, Alan. Sven is taking us through the early results from yesterday's samples."

"Okay, but I've made an important connection."

John was firm. "After Sven is done."

Sven took them through the results for samples three and four. Most matched bulk Laredo, though a few showed small but significant differences. Basically, nothing new.

Sven took a swallow of the coffee Michelle had placed before him. With a hint of a smile, he said, "Turn to the last page with the data for sample five. We started analyzing this sample only a couple hours ago." He became more animated. "We found twenty-three uranium-rich particles in this sample. Two of them isotopically match U.S. weapons grade uranium."

John spread out his hands. "Fantastic! You've already confirmed both sources. The Director will be very pleased."

Steven pumped his fist. "And where was this sample collected?"

"Along the edge of the floor," John said.

Michelle broke in. "Steven, you argued for that sample, didn't you?"

"I wasn't the only one. In a production facility, the corners are often missed when they sweep the floor."

"Great job, everybody," John said. "Sven, pass along my congratulations to Mark and all your team."

Michelle said, "I asked Mark to make chemical maps of these two particles."

"Good idea," Steven said.

John leaned back in his chair. A huge smile had chased away the frown he'd worn most of the past couple weeks. "Sven, keep your cast of characters at it until the first ten samples are thoroughly examined. If we're going to have any more surprises, let's discover them sooner rather than later."

Sven gathered his report and stood up. "Will do." Without another word, he left.

Alan had started to pace a few minutes earlier, occasionally glancing at his notes. Now he looked expectantly at John.

"Okay, Alan, what's got you excited?" John asked.

"For the past year, I've worked on a nuclear forensics library for TRIGA reactors around the world. The record keeping is usually pretty poor. The U.S. hasn't required countries to report regularly on their inventories. In a recent effort to reconcile inventories, some countries combined all their facility-specific input into one report, so we don't have data for each nuclear facility within the country."

John said, "The point you're making, I think, is that it wouldn't be terribly surprising if someone diverted TRIGA fuel without the U.S. finding out about it."

"That's right. Now, TRIGA fuel contains much more zirconium than uranium. To make a bomb from TRIGA fuel elements, you need to dissolve the fuel and chemically extract the uranium."

The light dawned for Steven. "That's why zirconium was high. It wasn't from a zirconia coating on a mold. It was residual zirconium from processing the TRIGA fuel."

Michelle tilted her head. "Then Mark should find a high level of zirconium in the ninety-three percent HEU particles."

John was tapping his notepad with his pen. Distractedly, he said to Michelle, "Okay, pass that along to Mark." John turned to Steven. "Do you think Abbasova processed the TRIGA fuel elements at his shop?"

Alan answered before Steven could respond. "Based on the pictures, I don't think the shop could handle such a complex chemical process."

Like a tag team, Michelle piped up again. "It would make more sense to do the chemical processing at a nuclear facility. Of course, you'd need to give a reason for doing it."

Steven said, "That gives me another idea. My sense is that Abbasova isn't the technical leader of this plot."

John interrupted before Steven could continue. "I'm beginning to respect your gut feelings, but explain your reasoning."

Steven smiled. "I'm often not sure why I sense something. It's kind of subconscious." He stroked his beard as he pondered. "None of the reasons that come to mind are compelling on their own, but taken together, they make a strong case that somebody else is the mastermind. First, Abbasova's a chemist. A physicist or nuclear engineer is better equipped to design a nuclear weapon. Second, as Danny pointed out, the quality of the metal part suggests someone had the insight to keep porosity low and the R&D skills to figure out how to do it. I doubt Abbasova did that on his own. Third, since he doesn't appear to have done anything with his chemistry skills after he graduated, would he have the kind of connections that could give him access to TRIGA fuel? I don't think so. Fourth—"

John interrupted again. "And since we know Abbasova was able to gain access to TRIGA fuel, the simplest explanation is that the mastermind works at a TRIGA facility. This supposed mastermind would have a higher level of scientific skills, and he'd also be in an excellent position to divert the material."

"Bingo!" said Steven.

Michelle said, "What's the matter, Alan?"

In a rather peeved voice, Alan said, "Are you guys interested in hearing what else I've discovered?"

Steven's pulse sped up. Alan had something big up his sleeve.

John said, "Sure, go ahead."

"This is where it gets really interesting. I began to look at the entire nuclear complex where each TRIGA reactor is located. One institute drew my attention—the Romania & Moldova Joint Nuclear Institute. Initially, the Moldova connection caught my eye, but that alone wasn't enough."

Steven frowned. Tariq Nazari was the director at this institute.

John asked, "Isn't a joint institute between two countries unusual?"

"Yeah. Romania has invested a lot in nuclear energy, but Moldova is a poorer country and hasn't had the resources to develop nuclear energy. Such an institute would be a boon for Moldova, but I'm not sure how it benefits Romania."

Now Steven was getting impatient. "So what else stood out about the institute?"

"Well, the TRIGA reactor is its primary focus. Several years ago, they replaced the 93% enriched HEU with 19.9% low-enriched uranium. At the same time, though, the institute started to develop a smaller reactor that uses 93% HEU. It's an aqueous homogeneous reactor they hope to use for molybdenum-99 production."

Steven asked, "What kind of reactor?" at about the same time John asked, "Why molybdenum-99?"

Alan replied, "One question at a time, please. Not surprised you haven't heard of this type of reactor. The first one was built at Los Alamos shortly after World War II. Oak Ridge published a tome on it in 1958, but it didn't catch on. Lately there's been renewed interest in using it for isotope production. A year ago, this institute commissioned their aqueous homogeneous reactor, and it was only the sixth one ever built."

"What's important about molybdenum-99?" John asked.

"It's the parent for technetium-99m. It's the radioactive isotope used most often by the medical community. For example, in the U.S., every day about 40,000 people receive technetium-99m. Developing a new way of producing this short-lived isotope would give their countries an economic boost."

Though Steven was curious about this unusual reactor, it was time to get past irrelevant details. "But how does this relate to our case?"

Alan rubbed his hands. "One of the problems with this type of reactor is that hydrogen and oxygen gases form. The pressure builds, and if it's not checked in some way, the reactor explodes. This institute addressed the problem by adding a reductant. They added copper sulfate."

Alan sat back, looking very pleased with himself.

For a moment, Steven was puzzled. Then the inference hit him. He pounded the table. "That's it!"

John looked puzzled. "What?"

Steven gave Alan a high-five and turned back to John. "That's why we saw the high level of copper!"

"To use your technical word, *bingo!*" Alan said.

Eyes flashing, Michelle said, "And the institute had to chemically process the TRIGA fuel rods in order to use the HEU in the aqueous reactor. They probably have a stockpile of aqueous HEU to refuel the reactor. That would make it much easier for the bad guy to divert some of it, and then convert it to metal at Ahmad's Metal Works."

John looked a bit stunned by their rapid traverse of a serpentine trail of evidence. "Are you sure this institute is the place?"

Steven had gotten so caught up in Alan's narrative, he momentarily forgot it might implicate Nazari. His mind reeled. Nazari was such a dedicated scientist. The man had never seemed the least bit political.

He held up his hands and looked square at John. "You might recall that Tariq Nazari is the director of this institute. You met him at the ITWG meeting a month ago. He's always struck me as such a nice guy."

John looked skeptical. "As the old saying goes, appearances can be deceiving. Wouldn't the institute's director be in the best position to covertly divert some HEU?"

"Yes," Steven said, and then he shook his head. "I just find it difficult to believe it could be him. He was so helpful when I talked to him about the Moldova case."

John wrote down Nazari's name and circled it. "Well, we need to find out fast whether it's him or someone else at his institute."

"How're you going to do that?" Steven asked. "I imagine Washington doesn't want word to leak out about this nuclear threat. Wouldn't it be risky to work directly with Romanian authorities?"

Looking steadily at Steven, John thought for a few moments. "You're right. I may have a quicker and better approach. We can draw upon your leadership in the ITWG and the fact that you know Nazari."

Uh-oh, thought Steven. *What does John have in mind this time?*

CHAPTER 59

Danville (6:45 pm, June 28)

Steven parked his car in the driveway and spotted Carissa through the living room window. Moments later, she opened the front door. She usually walked with a bounce in her step, exuding an unaware confidence that Steven found sexy. Today she had no bounce, which wasn't surprising, but she looked even more dejected than he'd expected.

While she buckled up, he asked, "How did your day go?"

"Let's wait until we get to the restaurant." She sounded and looked deflated.

He drove to their favorite Mexican restaurant, where the noise provided an effective cone of silence around their preferred table. After they ordered, he sipped his wine and cleared his throat. "I'm guessing things didn't go well with Jacob today."

Carissa sighed. "After he ate breakfast, I mentioned to him that the conversation tonight might be difficult for him, but we need to address things straightforwardly for his own good. I then stressed that he needed to be honest with us. Then he started to get defensive."

"Well, he did lie to me the night before the hearing, and then lied to the judge."

"I pointed that out to him, which only made him more upset. I assured him we don't view him as a liar, as it's so uncharacteristic of him. I suggested he was changing due to the influence of the alcohol and drugs."

"How did he take that?"

"He stopped talking all together and wouldn't even look at me."

Steven closed his eyes to block out the pain on Carissa's face. "I was more optimistic after yesterday. I don't get it."

"He's probably afraid he can't live without the alcohol and drugs. And his fear comes out as anger."

"That makes sense." He took another sip of wine. "Anything else?"

Her face contorted with despair. "I caught him trying to take off his monitoring device this afternoon. I got upset and told him that would only make matters worse. Then he said, 'Mom, stop being such a bitch.'"

Anger flared in Steven. "Good thing I wasn't there, or I would've..." He stopped short. Getting angry wouldn't help. "I can't believe he said that. To you, of all people."

A tear trickled down her cheek. Her lips pinched together, but she couldn't hold back a sob. "I don't feel like eating." Abruptly, she stood up and ran for the door.

Shocked, he ran after her. He caught up with her on the sidewalk by their car.

In a pleading tone, she said, "Can we just go home?"

"Please, Carissa, don't push me away. Is there something more you're not telling me?"

She dabbed her eyes. "You've got so much on your mind already. I don't know if I should tell you."

A spasm of fear shot through him. He waited for her to continue.

"It's like something broke in me after we returned from Oregon." She looked up into the night sky. "At first I was encouraged, but then things with Jacob deteriorated again. Last night I had more hope. Only to have it dashed again."

Her anguish cut deep into his soul. He put his arms around her.

"I don't understand my life anymore." Her face contorted with grief. "And I feel so alone."

He was stunned once again. When it came to life outside of his work, he depended upon her to hold everything together. She always seemed fully capable of doing so, but now he wasn't so sure.

"Please come back inside with me. While we eat, we'll map out what to say to Jacob tonight. And I'll take the lead in talking to him. Okay?"

She let him escort her back. The waiter was standing at their table holding their enchilada plates, looking puzzled. Steven smiled and assured him everything was okay.

While they picked at their food, they developed the key points to make with Jacob. By the time they finished, Carissa didn't seem quite so hopeless. After they ordered coffee, Steven said, "I need to update you about my case. The good news is we've had a breakthrough. The bad news is tomorrow morning I'm flying out of the country again."

Carissa winced. "Not again!" She closed her eyes and asked, "Why?"

He glanced around to make sure no one was in earshot. "We're zeroing in on the mastermind. We know where the person works, but we're not sure who it is. Kittrick asked me to go investigate with him."

"Why you?"

Steven thought back to John's reasoning. If Nazari was the mastermind, they wanted to flush him out quickly. If he wasn't the mastermind, they wanted Nazari's help finding the culprit. To avoid prematurely alerting Nazari, Steven sent him an email asking to visit his institute in two days. In the message, he explained that after the ITWG meeting, he'd taken a much-needed vacation, punctuated by visits to several European labs. Before he returned home, he hoped to explore a collaboration with Nazari.

He answered Carissa's question by simply saying, "Kittrick believes I can help with the interviews."

He fiddled with the saltshaker. "There's something I've been meaning to tell you. You won't like it, but you should know before I leave."

In an assuring tone, he told her about his kidnapping in Astana, minimizing his own fear during that terrible night.

Her lips quivered as she said, "You should have told me sooner." With a note of disbelief, she added, "And you just spring it on me now? Right before you leave the country again?"

He reached across the table and placed his hand on top of hers. She looked back at him, her face twisted with fear. Startled by the intensity of her angst, he said, "John will be with me this time." He squeezed her hand. "For us, the timing is terrible. I hate that, but if I can help, I need to go."

"You're right about the terrible timing." She heaved a deep sigh. "But if it's as serious a threat as you say, you should go." She drank more of her coffee. "This coffee is terrible. Let's leave now."

As soon as they got home, Carissa headed toward the shower. Realizing she needed time to compose herself before they talked to Jacob, Steven closed the door to his home office and checked his email. *Yes!* Nazari had replied.

Nervously, he clicked on the email, and read: *"Hi, Dr. Carter, What a pleasant surprise to hear from you. I'm honored to learn of your interest in our research on aqueous homogeneous reactors. I wish I'd known earlier of your potential interest so that we might have arranged a visit on another date. Unfortunately, we will miss each other. I'm in California, at the INMM Conference. Will you still be in Europe when I return late next week? Warm regards, Tariq Nazari."*

As soon as he finished reading, Steven looked up the dates of the Institute of Nuclear Materials Management meeting. Tomorrow would be the last full day. He called John and breathed a sigh of relief when he answered.

"Change of plans," Steven announced. He read the email verbatim to John. When he finished, he added, "Nazari's response seems plausible."

Steven heard John's harrumph. "It strikes me as too much of a coincidence. We'll fly to L.A. tomorrow instead of Bucharest."

CHAPTER 60

Palm Desert, CA (June 29)

During the flight to Los Angeles, Steven reviewed last night's conversation with Jacob. It didn't go great, but it wasn't too bad either. Jacob had silently listened to their new ground rules, including going to drug counseling twice a week, no more complaining about confinement at home, and treating his parents with respect. When Steven demanded a response, Jacob pouted and then said, "Okay."

Then Steven emphasized that one of their family's highest values was honesty. And given Jacob's situation, it was even more important that Jacob was honest from this point forward. Steven didn't specify a consequence if they caught Jacob in another lie, but he intimated it would bring severe consequences. Jacob scowled in response but held his tongue.

On the drive from the Los Angeles airport to Palm Desert, John offered a warning to Steven. "Some government officials are questioning how much longer we should continue the nuclear forensics. They acknowledge your work was the key to uncovering the plot, and then it led us to Abbasova and Hasanov. But after we identify the mastermind, they argue more nuclear forensics won't help us find any of them."

"You don't agree with stopping, do you?"

"Of course not."

When Steven stepped out of the car at the International Nuclear Materials Management Meeting, the summer heat hit him like a punch to the solar plexus. He sucked in his breath. It was only 8:30 in the morning, but he guessed the temperature was well past ninety degrees, on its way toward a predicted high of a hundred and eight. John and he joined the steady stream of scientists and engineers winding their way to the main building.

They found the registration table in a corner of the lobby, where a woman sat in lonely vigil on this last day of the conference. When she noticed them heading her way, she said, "May I help you, gentlemen?"

"We're not registered," Steven said. "We just need to talk to one of the meeting participants."

She looked disconcerted. "I can't let you into the meeting unless you register."

John brushed Steven aside as he stepped forward. "Perhaps this will help." He pulled out a wallet and flashed his FBI credential.

The woman turned red. She stuttered, "How may I help you?"

John closed his wallet. "Can you verify that Dr. Tariq Nazari is here?"

"I'll check." As she scrolled through her computer, she asked with a mixture of alarm and excitement, "You aren't here to arrest him, are you?"

"We're here just to talk."

"I see that Dr. Nazari registered."

Steven asked, "Did he actually show up?"

"Our records indicate he did."

"Are you positive?" John asked.

"I'll check the name tags that weren't picked up." She pulled a box from under the table and rummaged through it. "I don't see his name tag, so he must have picked it up."

"Okay," John said. "We'll look for him. Could you make up a registration badge for each of us." His voice communicated his request was a demand.

"Give me your names," the woman said without hesitation.

While they waited, Steven kept an eye on the people walking by. Maybe he'd get lucky and spot Tariq. Then he had a better idea. "Could you give me the conference program?"

He scanned the sessions for this morning and found one that focused on the future of TRIGA reactors, right up Nazari's alley. "Come on, John, let's head to meeting room four. That's where Nazari will go, and the first talk starts in five minutes."

"I'm right behind you."

Room four was about one-third full when Steven stepped inside. He surveyed the crowd, but didn't spot Tariq.

They returned to the lobby and positioned themselves midway between the two entrances to room four. As the crowd continued to file into the various meeting rooms, John said, "Isn't it possible Nazari left early?"

"Sure, but I doubt he'd leave before this session."

Just as the doors to the meeting room closed, Steven spotted a familiar face. "Joel," he yelled.

Joel jerked and spilled some coffee on his shirt. "Steven Carter, you S.O.B." He dabbed his shirt with a napkin.

"Sorry. This is my friend John Kittrick, and John, this is Joel Tannenbaum. He's a reactor engineer from Argonne National Lab."

Joel said, "I'm surprised I didn't notice you earlier this week."

"I came down only for today." With a sense of urgency, Steven said, "We're looking for Tariq Nazari. You know him, don't you?"

Joel looked perplexed. "Yes, but I don't recall seeing him this week." Joel screwed up his face in concentration. "But somebody mentioned him."

"Do you remember who?" Steven asked.

Joel snapped his fingers. "Marty talked to him."

"Is Marty here?"

Joel looked at the bank of coffee urns and then at the table with breakfast pastries. "There he is!" He marched over to accost Marty.

"Marty, this is Steven Carter from Lawrence Livermore. He's looking for Tariq Nazari. Didn't you talk to him earlier this week?"

A quizzical look appeared on Marty's face. "Funny you should ask. Monday morning Tariq sent me an email. He missed his plane connection in New York, and he asked me to pick up his registration materials. He said he'd get them from me in my hotel that same night. But he never showed up."

John's face darkened. "And then what?"

"When I didn't see him the next morning, I emailed him. He replied that he'd gotten sick and didn't know when he'd get to the meeting."

"And then?"

"That's the last I heard from him."

John's lips tightened. In a polite but clipped voice, he said, "Thank you very much. Nice to meet you, Joel and Marty."

Without waiting for a response, John turned on his heel and bolted from the room. Steven stood still, rooted to the spot. Dazed, he recalled Tariq's email to him yesterday. *"I'm in California at the INMM Conference."*

With faltering steps, Steven trailed after John. *Damnation all to hell! Nazari flat-out lied to me.*

CHAPTER 61

CIA Headquarters (June 30)

Carolyn drummed her fingers on her desk. Was Tariq Nazari really the mastermind? If the FBI wasn't able to find Nazari in New York City and interrogate him, it was up to her and the CIA to confirm their probable-cause case against the man. Her best bet was to interview Nazari's executive assistant. Right after Kittrick informed her of Nazari's deception, she had dispatched two agents to Isai, Romania, home of the Romania & Moldova Joint Nuclear Institute. She expected the agents to call any minute now.

An hour later, her phone rang and the lead agent launched into his report. "At first, Leila was very reluctant to talk. When we accused her of being Nazari's accomplice in a nuclear terrorism plot, she was stunned. We're convinced she didn't know."

"That means nothing if Nazari isn't our man," Carolyn said.

"We asked about Nazari's U.S. trip. She said that Tariq decided to attend only two weeks prior to the conference. Usually, he registers months ahead of time. And he always gives at least one talk, but not this time."

Her shoulders clenched. "He suddenly plans this U.S. trip about the same time we interdicted the part in Laredo. Interesting timing."

"When we told her he lied about going to the INMM meeting, she protested that Nazari is the most honest man she's ever known.

We showed her Nazari's two contradictory emails, the one to Carter and the other to this Marty at the conference."

"How'd she react?"

"She read each email twice. When she finished, she just sat there, looking rather distraught. Finally, she spoke, kind of to herself, about a trip Nazari took in March. Like this trip to the U.S., it came up with no warning. Even at the time, the reason he gave for the trip struck her as odd."

Her spine tingled. "Did she say where he went?"

"To Turkey. Ankara, Turkey."

She lifted her arms in the air, like a referee signaling touchdown. "That cinches it! Great job!"

As soon as Carolyn hung up, she called the Director of National Intelligence and communicated the latest finding. He asked, "Do you recommend taking Leila into custody?"

"I don't get the sense she's an accomplice. Let's leave her alone, and hope she tries to contact Nazari. That could lead us to him."

"Good idea. I'll call an emergency meeting at the National Counterterrorism Center. I want both you and Kittrick there to update the interagency."

"Yes, sir. I'll let Kittrick know."

"We need to expand the search for Nazari to an all-of-government effort. Since we know he entered the U.S. at JFK last weekend, we should be able to find him soon."

"Yes, sir," she said to the DNI, but when she hung up, she wondered, *Will it still be too late?*

PART 3. WHERE?

CHAPTER 62

National Counterterrorism Center (July 1)

The Director of National Intelligence rapped his knuckles on the conference room table. He glared at the FBI Director and the Secretary of Homeland Security, and said, "Stop squabbling!" His eyes swept around the dozen senior leaders seated at the table. "Stop Nazari! That's the goal. Our only goal."

The room became silent. The DNI said, "We're facing the most serious emergency of our generation. Now more than ever, we need interagency cooperation."

The DHS Secretary, who the DNI had interrupted, glared back at him. "Before we continue, I have a question. Why is a scientist from a national lab here?"

The FBI Director spoke up. "Because I invited him." He glanced at Steven sitting against the back wall.

Before the Secretary could respond, the DNI scowled like a pit bull and said, "And I approved it."

Steven swiveled in his chair so that his leg bumped against John. John gave him a thumbs-up, and Carolyn, who sat on John's other side, offered a hint of a smile. To Steven's surprise, John had argued strongly with the FBI Director that Steven should attend this meeting. It was an uphill battle, for the Director embraced the traditional view that scientists should keep to their scientific turf and stay out of government deliberations. But John insisted that Steven, as Nazari's fellow scientist, could better predict their adversary's thinking. John even made up a new title for Steven—scientist profiler.

The DHS Secretary loosened his tie and continued his brief. "Okay. As I was saying, after we verified that Tariq Nazari entered the U.S. through JFK on June 24th, we traced him to a hotel in Manhattan. Two days later, he checked out and then disappeared."

The DNI interrupted again. "Has anybody picked up any sign of Nazari after June 26th?"

Everyone shook their heads. The DNI asked, "What do you make of that?"

Several voices answered at the same time. "Let's hear from DHS first," the DNI said.

"Thank you. Since Abbasova used a false ID when he entered the U.S., we assume Nazari switched to a false identity after he checked out of his hotel. We've begun to canvas hotels in the New York area, showing Nazari's picture to hotel clerks."

"Seems reasonable," the DNI said. "What else?"

"In the remote possibility that Nazari left town, we asked airlines to search their records for an outgoing passenger with a passport bearing Nazari's photo. No hits. Which reinforces our supposition that Nazari plans to detonate in New York City. A nuclear weapon going off in Manhattan would make 9/11 seem like child's play. What a coup for a terrorist."

Steven looked around the table. The grim faces suggested visions of Manhattan after a nuclear attack. They were all terrified, as they should be, though he doubted they fully grasped the enormous differences between a nuclear and conventional bomb.

The FBI Director cleared his throat. "We have additional evidence that supports New York City as the target."

The DNI said, "Go ahead."

"The FBI previously identified six suspects who crossed the border in front of Transportes Grupo vans. One of them was Cyrus Safar, who we now know to be Ahmad Abbasova. We obtained pictures of all six men from the car rental agencies. When we couldn't pick up their trail in Laredo, we expanded our search and discovered two suspects used a second set of IDs to rent cars in San Antonio."

The DNI said, "Everything indicates this threat is well-planned and very well-resourced."

"We put out an all-points bulletin on both rental cars and the drivers," the FBI Director continued. "Nothing turned up," he paused, "until the two rental cars were returned in Brooklyn yesterday."

The DHS Secretary interjected. "It still puzzles me how all six suspects could evade your search for so many days."

The FBI Director shrugged. "My guess is they used cash for all their purchases. Or a credit card under yet another name." He scowled and added, "And is that really the most important thing right now?"

Steven wondered why the suspects turned in their cars before the bomb went off.

The DNI looked around the table. "We need all our assets focused on finding the bomb in the New York metropolitan area. Tariq Nazari is probably the key to locating it, but also keep looking for any of the other six suspects."

The DHS Secretary said, "We'll start using facial recognition software on surveillance recordings from the subways and key pedestrian areas in Manhattan."

Carolyn raised her hand. When the DNI acknowledged her, she said, "After we interrogated Nazari's executive assistant, she sent him an email. She really let him have it, saying she feels betrayed. The NSA is monitoring for Nazari's possible response."

"Good. Anything else?"

Two ideas had arisen in Steven's mind. His mouth suddenly dry, he raised his hand. At first the DNI looked taken aback, then he said, "Our scientist has something to say."

Steven said, "It'll be fairly complicated for the terrorists to put the device together. They'll need to assemble the entire gun barrel, install the high explosive in the firing chamber, and then add the ignition and communication system."

The DNI pursed his lips. Steven kept one eye on the FBI Director, who had seemed annoyed when Steven raised his hand. Now, the Director looked interested.

Steven plowed ahead. "I'm only speculating, but if I were planning the operation, I'd assemble the weapon in an industrial location. My guess is that they prefabricated the structural elements outside the country and then shipped them to the assembly site. No customs officer would recognize them as parts of a nuclear device."

The DNI said, "Could you give us a list of the structural parts, including an estimate of their size?"

"Sure. Then there's the issue of the high explosive. Nazari might include that with the structural elements. Or he may have decided it was less risky to purchase it from a U.S. supplier."

The DNI looked more hopeful. "This gives us some additional leads to pursue."

"One more thing," Steven said. "Why did Nazari come to the U.S. at this point in time? It doesn't seem like it was his original plan."

Around the table, heads snapped. John murmured, "I should've thought of that."

The DNI said, "Excellent question! What's your answer?"

The FBI Director said, "Dr. Carter, please come up to the table."

Steven wheeled his chair to sit between the Director and the DNI. "Off the top of my head," he said, "two plausible reasons come to mind. One possibility is that after the interdiction, Nazari lost confidence in Abbasova, so he came here to replace him." Steven paused and took a deep breath. "The second possibility is more disturbing. After the Laredo interdiction, Nazari may have been worried that his device didn't have enough HEU, so he came to the U.S. to install a modification."

"What kind of modification?" the Secretary of Energy said.

"The principle of a gun-assembly device has been described many times, with varying degrees of accuracy. In 1977, the Department of Defense and Department of Energy published a helpful resource on the effects of nuclear weapons. Glasstone says in the book, 'By surrounding the fissionable material with a suitable neutron "reflector," the loss of neutrons by escape can be reduced, and the critical mass can thus be decreased.'"

Steven looked up from the note he was reading and saw perplexed faces. "In other words, you don't need as much HEU if you add a neutron reflector."

The DNI looked intrigued and asked, "How do you make a neutron reflector?"

"There are a number of materials that effectively scatter neutrons. Glasstone goes on to say that if one uses a neutron reflector that has a high density, you also get the added benefit of a tamper that helps to hold the HEU together for a longer time during the fissioning process. That also increases the efficiency of the device. I wouldn't be surprised if Nazari plans to surround the HEU with lead, so he gets the double benefit of a neutron reflector and tamper."

The DNI asked, "Should we prioritize investigating industrial shops that recently received a shipment of lead?"

"That's what my gut is telling me." As Steven said it, he told his gut that if there ever was a time it couldn't afford to be wrong, it was now.

The men around the table began to devise plans that incorporated Steven's suggestions. The FBI Director motioned for Kittrick to join him at the table. A short time later, the CIA Director summoned Carolyn. After an hour, the DNI announced he was leaving and motioned for Steven to follow him. When they reached the hallway, the DNI said, "Your participation in this meeting made a huge difference. I'm glad the FBI convinced me you should attend."

"You have John Kittrick to thank for that."

The DNI extended his hand. "Report any new ideas to Carolyn. She'll keep me informed."

Steven gripped the DNI's hand and said, "Will do."

When Steven re-entered the conference room, John and Carolyn were waiting for him. John said, "You hit it out of the park, Steven. Which earns you a special assignment tomorrow."

Carolyn said, "Do you remember Nazari's girlfriend when he was at MIT?"

"I met her only a couple times. I don't remember her name."

"Does Sina Haddad ring a bell?"

"Sina! Yes, that was her name."

"Sina knows Nazari far better than anybody in the U.S.," Carolyn said. "We don't want to leave any stone unturned. Who knows, maybe he's even reached out to her recently."

John spoke up. "The usual procedure calls for the FBI to interview her. But we don't want to tip her off that we're pursuing Nazari as a criminal."

"What're you thinking?" Steven asked, though he suspected he knew the answer.

A small smile creased John's face. "Tomorrow morning, Carolyn and you will interview Sina in Boston. Since you know Nazari, she may be more willing to open up to you."

CHAPTER 63

Outside the NCTC (July 1)

Steven and John walked out of the NCTC and into the sauna that was Washington, DC in the summer. Steven dropped his briefcase to the pavement, took off his sport coat, and loosened his tie. "Whew," he said, "glad I don't live in this humidity."

John scoffed. "The high is only eighty-nine degrees today."

Bantering about the weather brought a sense of normalcy to their extraordinary circumstance. Steven replied, "Ninety-five percent humidity makes any summer day miserable." He flexed his shoulders to relieve his tension.

John started his car and put the air conditioner on full blast. Before he put the car into gear, he turned to Steven. "You know what hit me during that meeting? I took this nuclear forensics job to get out of the limelight, and here I am, in the middle of the biggest case ever." He shook his head. "I thought my days of taking big risks were over, but now I'm headed to New York to look for a nuclear bomb."

"Better you than me."

John turned pensive. "I want to ask you something. After you finish in Boston tomorrow, would you join me in New York City? I realize that'll put you in harm's way to a degree you never expected as a Lab scientist, so think about it before you answer."

Steven bit his lower lip and wondered what Carissa would think. "You're right. I never envisioned doing something like that."

John's mouth tightened as he looked into Steven's eyes. "Here's the thing. We're more likely to stop Nazari if my scientist profiler sticks with me."

Steven stared out the windshield without seeing anything. How could he say no?

"Here's the thing," he replied, deliberately mimicking John. "I dedicated my career to nuclear forensics because I believe it's an important element of our national security. If my sticking with you has any chance of helping, I'm all in." Upon making this commitment, he realized he should give Carissa a heads-up.

John put his hand on Steven's shoulder and gave it a squeeze. A hint of admiration crept into his eyes. "Thanks, my friend."

John turned the car into traffic, and the two of them began to share their impressions of the NCTC meeting. It was the highest-level meeting either of them had ever taken part in. John was thrilled with how well it'd gone. He pantomimed doffing his hat when he alluded to the moment Steven suggested the reason Nazari had come to the U.S. "None of us would have thought of a tamper. That was brilliant."

"We've got to find that assembly site," Steven replied. "And soon."

Another idea popped into Steven's mind. "Nazari must have made arrangements for the assembly site before his team entered the U.S., but I doubt he'd do it directly. Maybe there's a link between Transportes Grupo, the company that transported the device parts, and the company or person who rented an industrial shop in New York City."

John raked his hair again. "Maybe somebody in the FBI has already looked into that possibility, but I'll pass it along, just in case."

When they arrived at Steven's hotel, his friend looked over at him. "Something's bugging you, isn't it?"

"Yeah. I'm still wondering why the suspects dropped off their cars already."

CHAPTER 64

Boston (July 2)

On the elevator ride up to Sina Haddad's condo, Steven realized his neck muscles were tied into knots. His job was to put Sina at ease, but he was a bundle of nerves.

When Sina opened the door, she offered a smile, but her dark brown eyes crinkled with wariness. Steven recalled how impressed he'd been when he first met her at an MIT party. Afterward, on an afternoon run with Nazari, he teased him about his girlfriend who was way too good looking for him. Eight years later, Sina struck him as even more beautiful.

"Come on in," Sina said. Her voice was soft but assured.

"Thanks for agreeing to meet with us," Carolyn said. "As I explained on the phone, I'm from DARPA, a research agency in the Department of Defense. This is Dr. Steven Carter, a colleague of Tariq Nazari."

Steven shook the hand that Sina offered. Smiling, he said, "I got to know Tariq during my short sabbatical at MIT. I doubt you remember me, but Tariq sure talked a lot about you."

"I remember Tariq introducing me to a scientist from a national lab out in California, but not much else. Your voice does sound familiar though."

"My face has changed in the past eight years." He smiled good-naturedly. "And it's not been an improvement."

Sina turned back to Carolyn. "You said you wanted to talk about Tariq. What's the matter? Is he in trouble?"

"We're not sure. Has he been in touch with you lately?"

"I haven't seen Tariq since he graduated. We broke up six months before that."

"Has he communicated with you at all?"

"Not since he left Boston. Why are you asking?"

"He's collaborating with Steven on an important research project. Since the project includes another collaborator in New York City, they planned to meet there. But Tariq didn't show up. He seems to have vanished without warning. Because of the nature of the project, his disappearance may have national security implications."

Steven was impressed by the easy manner in which Carolyn spun her lie.

Sina looked puzzled. "Why do you think I can help?"

Carolyn said, "He hasn't shown up on any police reports. None of his co-workers in Romania have heard from him. Then Steven mentioned you were his old girlfriend."

Carolyn gave a slight nod to Steven, her prearranged signal. Steven said, "We're talking with anyone in the U.S. who had a prior relationship with Tariq, and your relationship with him was unique."

Sina frowned. "I thought we'd get married. It took me quite a while to get over Tariq, but he's become just a distant memory." She gestured toward a framed wedding photo on the wall. "I've been happily married for two years."

Smiling, Steven said, "I'm glad to hear you're doing so well. You were still with Tariq when I went back to California. Would you mind sharing why you broke up?"

Sadness filled Sina's eyes. "Tariq broke up with me. The end of our relationship began when his family was killed."

Taken aback, Steven said, "He's never mentioned that to me."

288

"It was terrible. An American military drone destroyed his family's house and killed all of his immediate family. It shattered him."

"That's horrible."

Sorrow overtook Sina's face and her voice became softer. "Every effort I made to comfort him seemed to make him angrier. In the space of a few weeks, he changed into a bitter man I hardly recognized. In a very real sense, the bomb that killed Tariq's family also killed the Tariq I'd known and loved."

"You said he broke up with you, rather than you with him."

"I still loved him. But the distance between us grew into a chasm. He kept trying to get me to hate the U.S. like he did. One day he screamed at me, 'You love the country I hate!' Several days later he ended our relationship."

Steven was moved by her story. "Must have been painful. For both of you." He paused to formulate his next question. "Was that the last time you saw or heard from him?"

"After he graduated, he invited me for coffee before he left to take a job in Europe. It was a very odd meeting. He treated me as though we'd never been anything more than casual friends. Malik was completely different from the last time I'd seen him."

Carolyn's eyebrows arched upward. "You said Malik."

"Oh, that was his original name. His father was on the U.S. terrorist watchlist, though Tariq never told me why. So he was worried the U.S. wouldn't approve his student visa, and he desperately wanted to get a PhD from MIT. His father had the connections to help Malik assume the identity of a boyhood friend who died a few years earlier and get a passport in his name. To my knowledge, Tariq didn't tell anybody else that Tariq Nazari was not his real name."

"How would you describe his emotional state when you met that last time?"

"That was the weirdest part. How should I put it? Affable, he seemed so affable. But it didn't strike me as genuine."

Carolyn questioned, "How so? What did you sense was going on underneath?"

Sina looked up as she pondered. "I'm not sure how to describe it. The word that comes to mind is 'hollowed out.' It was like he'd put on a shell of affability to hide his pain and bitterness."

Sina's memories cast Nazari in a new light. He'd become an expert in deception. He never showed an iota of his hatred for the U.S. And now, after years of bitterness, he was on the verge of unleashing unimaginable destruction upon his enemy.

CHAPTER 65

New York City (July 2)

Early in the morning, John Kittrick rounded a corner and spotted the tower of One World Trade Center rising into the sky. Its rebuilding testified to American resilience. The sight lifted his sagging spirits.

He entered the FBI field office in lower Manhattan and asked for directions to the team tasked with locating the weapon assembly site. With myriad possibilities, it was a daunting job. Would Nazari target the World Trade Center once again? Would he choose a location where he could detonate the bomb in place? If he did, he wouldn't need to transport it. They needed to focus the search.

Drawing upon Steven's suggestions, John explained his reasoning to the team he'd just joined. They agreed to first look at small industrial shops within a mile of the Trade Center. Any shop that had recently received a shipment of any heavy metal would be their initial priority. Because he was the only person in the room who knew anything about nuclear weapons, he described the details of a gun assembly device so they'd know what to look for.

By mid-morning, the team had a new list of places to investigate. Before John left to investigate the shops assigned to him, he heard a shout from an adjoining room. Curious, he ducked down the hallway. When he entered the room, he recognized one of the agents.

"Hey, Chris."

"Hi, John. I heard you were coming up today."

"What're you guys working on?"

"We've discovered that four of the suspects flew out of JFK last night."

Startled, John asked, "How did you manage that?" while he grappled with the implications for their search.

"We first concentrated on surveillance footage in the city, but this morning we checked the airports as well. The two drivers who dropped off their rental cars in Brooklyn showed up on a manifest for a flight to Paris. We compared the pictures of all six suspects to the surveillance footage from JFK. We just got hits on two others."

"Were they detained when they arrived in Paris?"

"It was too late. But the two additional identities may help us track their movements from Laredo to the assembly site."

"You said four of them flew out. That leaves two others."

"Ahmad Abbasova and Omar Hasanov were not on the plane. We assume they're still here to help Nazari with the final steps."

John's gut lurched. "They must be getting very close."

The search progressed slowly. Often John found a shop closed, not a surprise on a Saturday. When he tried to contact the business owner, many of them were out of town for the 4th of July weekend. Nonetheless, by the end of the afternoon, John along with the entire assembly-site search team had cleared, in one way or another, every shop but two on the initial list. No sign of the bomb.

On his way back to the field office, John wondered if Steven might be wrong about the tamper. When he entered the lobby, he was relieved to spot Steven waiting for him. A conversation with his scientist profiler might elicit further insights.

Without preamble, Steven asked, "Any progress?"

"Nothing yet. More people will get here soon from other FBI field offices and DHS, and that'll speed things up." The frightening urgency and massive scope of the search struck John anew. Yet, he was only human, and his rumbling stomach reminded him he was famished. "Let's grab dinner before we get back to work."

Steven moved toward the door. "My lunch was a bag of peanuts on the plane from Boston."

When they settled into a corner booth at a local diner, John asked, "How sure are you about the tamper idea?"

Steven rubbed his chin while he pondered. "If Nazari has more HEU, though I suspect he doesn't, he could try to quickly fabricate a replacement part. But if I were him, I wouldn't want to risk bringing it into the country when we are on alert."

That made sense to John. He prodded Steven further. "Nazari is a reactor expert. Would he come up with a sophisticated fix like a tamper?"

"He's an accomplished researcher, so yeah, I think it's likely. Besides, I can't think of other criteria to prioritize the search, can you?"

John shrugged. "The short answer, unfortunately, is no." He bit into his sandwich while he considered his next question. "Did you learn anything useful from Sina?"

Steven recounted the conversation with Sina, emphasizing her perception of Nazari's dramatic change after his family was killed.

John said, "Knowing his motive helps paint the picture."

"Just now, when I was telling you about Sina, my feeling that we're missing something got stronger. I think I just put my finger on it."

The glint in Steven's eyes gave John new hope. "Another gut feeling?"

"You could call it that." Steven leaned toward him. "Have we been too quick to conclude that New York City is Nazari's target?"

John tilted his head sideways. "I recall you wondered why they dropped off their rental cars here. They could've just abandoned them."

"And why have four of them flown out now?" Steven's volume rose. "It wouldn't surprise me if Nazari assumed the FBI would eventually make the connection by matching pictures from Laredo and JFK."

John sensed where Steven was heading. In a quiet voice, John said, "The trail of bread crumbs is a bit too obvious, isn't it?" He motioned for Steven to lower his voice.

In a softer tone, his scientist profiler continued. "Here's what just hit me about Sina's story. She specifically mentioned that a *military* drone killed Nazari's family. It's an odd phrase, and I doubt Sina would say it unless Nazari used those very words. Nazari wants to avenge his family. My guess is he's targeted the government who authorized the strike *and* the military that carried it out."

The emphasis Steven put on the "and" caught John's attention. "You're suggesting Washington, DC, aren't you?"

Somberly, Steven nodded.

John said, "Most people associate 9/11 with the terrible images of the World Trade Center collapse. But those terrorists also attacked the Pentagon, and we believe Flight 93 was also headed for DC."

Steven's lips tightened. "At the very least, we should also be searching in Washington, DC."

"I need to pass along this idea. I expect, though, it'll be a difficult sell. After all, it's only our intuition, and so far, all the tangible evidence points to New York."

They quickly finished their sandwiches and headed back to the field office. As they walked in silence, John reviewed their conversation. With every step he became more convinced they were on the right track. He turned to Steven. "We need to convince the Director to expand the search to DC. And that's where we should go."

Steven clapped him on the shoulder. "I couldn't agree more."

At that moment, Carolyn called. John darted into an alley they'd just passed and said, "Go ahead, and Steven's here too." He motioned for Steven to come closer.

"We've got a new electronic intercept. The DNI and FBI Director already know, but I wanted to contact you personally."

"What is it?"

"Nazari replied to the email Leila sent him."

Eagerly, John asked, "Where from?"

"From a hotel business center. A Hyatt in lower Manhattan."

Whipsawed, John leaned on a brick wall to steady himself. Steven looked shocked too.

John finished the conversation quickly and shoved his phone into his pocket. He reached up to run his fingers through his hair, but instead gave it a frustrated jerk. "Neither of us expected that answer."

Steven bit his lip. "Could we have been that wrong?"

Shaking his head, John said, "Wouldn't Nazari suspect we would intercept his email? This feels like one more bread crumb planted by him. But in order to convince the Director to expand the search, we'll have to prove it."

CHAPTER 66

New York City (11:00 pm, July 2)

Later that evening, after Steven checked into his hotel, he rehashed the events of the day. The device must be almost ready. Tomorrow could be the last day of his life. He reached for his phone.

"Hi, Carissa, my love."

"You're mushy tonight." Her surprise was layered with wariness.

"Sorry I haven't called the last couple days. You're often on my mind, but we're in a race against time."

"Are you in danger?" Her panic leaked through.

"I'd be lying if I said no. John invited me to leave, but he'd prefer that I stay."

In a quavering voice, she said, "That's not very reassuring."

"How's it going with Jacob?"

"Sullen. But he's following our new ground rules."

"I'd like to talk to him."

"I'll go find him." She sounded surprised and grateful.

Steven paced while he waited.

"You wanted to talk to me?" Jacob said. His surliness came through loud and clear.

"It's looking like I won't be able to get back home before your disposition hearing."

"Whatever."

"I want to be there for you. If it's at all possible, I will be."

Jacob didn't reply for several seconds. Then he said, "Okay."

Steven's sense, his hope, was that his son's *okay* wasn't accompanied with an eye roll.

"Have you talked to Josh about our guys' weekend trip?"

"Not yet. Why?"

"Let's plan to go two weekends from now. I believe your disposition hearing won't go too badly."

"Uh-huh."

This might be his last chance to talk to Jacob. "Your mother is struggling. Please don't push her away. She's only trying to help you." With a catch in his voice, he added, "It's breaking her heart."

"Is that why you asked to talk to me?"

"I owe you an apology, Jacob. I haven't always been the kind of father you need and deserve."

After several heartbeats, his son said, "What's happening back there, Dad? You're scaring me."

Tears gathered in Steven's eyes. Jacob hadn't called him *Dad* in a long time. "I love you, Jacob. I haven't told you that often enough, but it's true."

In an almost inaudible whisper, Jacob said, "Me too, Dad."

Tears streamed down Steven's face. "That's the main reason I wanted to talk to you. To tell you I love you."

"You're starting to creep me out."

"Deal with it," Steven said, in an attempt to lighten the mood. "Hey, is Josh around? I'd like to touch base with him too."

"I'll check."

Steven caught up with Josh, and then Josh passed the phone back to Carissa. She said, "Jacob's worried about you." In a bewildered tone, she asked, "What did you say to him?"

"That I loved him. I also apologized for not being a better father."

She was silent for a few moments. "Just how dangerous is your situation?"

Steven wanted to ease her concern, but she'd see through a dishonest answer. "Unlike anything I've ever experienced."

"Oh my God!" He heard her sob. "Be careful, my love. And call me tomorrow night, okay?"

Hoping to end the conversation on a lighter note, he recalled an old line from the days of their early romance. With a lilt in his voice, he said, "I love you little, I love you big, I love you like a little pig."

She offered a weak chuckle. "Good night, Steven."

"I really do love you. Good night, my dearest."

CHAPTER 67

Nazari's Assembly Shop (July 2)

Malik Karimov poured the last of the molten lead into the space he had created by attaching the steel jacket to the original exterior of the bomb. Sweat poured down his face as he switched off the turkey fryer he'd used to melt the lead. Turning to Ahmad Abbasova, he said, "Tomorrow, after the tamper cools, we'll check the alignment on the gun barrel."

"Is tomorrow *the* day?" Ahmad asked, his eyes gleaming at the prospect.

"That's my plan. Originally, I was going to detonate on the 4th, America's Independence Day. But I checked on their holiday celebrations, and the traffic will interfere with my plan."

Malik realized it was dangerous to underestimate one's enemies. It wouldn't surprise him if the Americans were closing in on him. "If the alignment is okay, we'll load the uranium pieces and the high explosive. If everything looks good, we'll set it off tomorrow evening."

Malik ducked into the shop's bathroom. By now, the room reeked of sweat, but the security of living in the shop was worth it. He stripped off his shirt and washed his upper body and face. When he emerged from the bathroom, Ahmad was sprawled across his cot.

"Wash up and I'll prepare dinner," Malik said.

Over their simple meal of curry and naan, Ahmad asked, "How many times have you met Raushan?"

"Still curious, huh?" Malik debated with himself and concluded that at this juncture, sharing more information with his protégé was warranted. "I've only met him in person several times, but I have a secure way to communicate with him."

"Does he own the company that delivered the structural parts and the high explosive?"

"Indirectly, through a shell company. It operates in the U.S. and sells construction supplies, and that gave us good cover. I used a different approach for the HEU parts to lower the risk."

Malik wiped up the last of the curry with his naan and said, "It's been a long day, and I need sleep. We must be at our best tomorrow."

When Ahmad lay down on his cot, Malik walked into the front room and pulled a packet of stationary out of the desk drawer. Though he was on the brink of the greatest accomplishment of his life, melancholy suffused his excitement. In the last email from Leila, she described the visit by the American officials and her outrage at learning he was a nuclear terrorist. His future at the institute had evaporated, along with his scientific career.

"Dear Leila," he wrote. His pen hovered over the paper while he considered several different opening lines. Frowning, he discarded each one. This would be his last communication with her.

He remembered Leila gazing at him with love and admiration. Suddenly, the picture changed. Disgust and horror now etched her face as she pushed him away. His melancholy gave way to a deeper reality. The bitterness he'd kept at bay during his years of careful planning now erupted and overwhelmed him. His life should have been so different. The Americans ruined him.

He fought to regain control of his emotions. He scratched out what he'd written so far. This needed to be more than a final letter to Leila. It would be his statement for posterity. He would keep it simple and to the point. Above all, he needed to convince her he was on a suicide mission.

He started again on a new sheet of paper. "*Dear Leila, By the time you read this, I will be dead. As I write, I feel strangely settled. I'd hoped that I could secretly avenge my family and then begin a new life with you. At first I cursed when your email alerted me that the Americans had discovered my plot. I agonized over your anger at what you perceive as my betrayal. I hope and pray that in time you will see my action from my perspective. When I succeed tomorrow, I will strike a blow for the freedom of our Muslim brothers and sisters. And my success will bring even greater honor upon my family. If ever you cared for me, do this for me. Tell the world that I willingly sacrificed my life to free my people from American shackles. Do not remember me as your closest friend, or as the one who betrayed your confidence. Remember me as your hero.*

He paused as he considered how to sign the letter. An expression of affection seemed out of place. Simply signing off as "Tariq" was too informal. He finally settled by signing off with "*Tariq Nazari.*"

With a small smile, he added, "*Allah's servant.*"

During the short walk to the mailbox, he encountered several people bustling through their busy little lives, pursuing their own happiness at the expense of the rest of the world. These self-righteous Americans didn't have a clue, nor did they care, about the misery they perpetuated upon the developing world. They all deserved to be hated and die.

As he passed each person, he wondered, *Tomorrow night, will you be dead, dying, or only deadly frightened?* When he deposited his letter, he expected to feel settled, a sense of satisfaction. Instead, a bigger wave of bitterness engulfed him. He searched beneath his bitterness for something more, but found nothing.

CHAPTER 68

New York City (5:30 am, July 3)

The ringing of Steven's phone startled him awake. A shot of adrenaline instantly cleared his mind. "Morning, John. What's happening?"

"Unfortunately, not much." John's voice was raspy. "Nobody at the hotel recalls seeing Nazari."

"How big is the hotel?"

"It's the typical big Hyatt. If someone didn't want to be noticed, the only person who might remember him is the clerk who checked him in."

"Were they able to question every desk clerk?"

"Yeah. The Director was *so sure* we were closing in on Nazari." John added, "Washington's going nuts."

"So what's our next step?"

"I'll meet you in your hotel lobby at six o'clock."

Steven's stomach rumbled in protest. "The Starbucks in the lobby opens at six. How about grabbing breakfast first?"

"Not going to argue with that."

When he got off the phone, he had twenty minutes to get ready. He took a three-minute shower, brushed his teeth, skipped shaving, and threw on clean clothes. He made it to the lobby with two minutes to spare. John was standing in front of the Starbucks stand, staring at the barista while she prepared to open.

The barista responded to the waves of impatience emanating from John and took their orders immediately. They sat in a quiet corner of the lobby, where John outlined his plan for determining whether Nazari deliberately misled them. When Steven was halfway through his breakfast sandwich, John stuffed the rest of his breakfast wrap back in its bag. "Grab your coffee. My buddy Chris from the field office will pick us up in two minutes."

On the short ride to the Hyatt, Steven asked, "Who else knows about your plan?"

John let out a disgruntled sigh. "Everyone's convinced Nazari is somewhere in New York, so I decided against broadcasting a contrary opinion. I told the Assistant Director at the field office what I needed, and he assigned four agents, including Chris, to help us this morning. That should be enough."

When they got to the hotel, John met with the manager. Yesterday, the FBI kept the manager in the dark about the reason for talking to his employees, so at first he objected to re-interviewing them. When John insisted they had a new lead, the manager grudgingly agreed they could use his office again.

John said to the manager, "Why don't I begin with you?"

"Okay, I'd appreciate that." The manager seemed mollified.

John put a picture of Nazari on the desk. "This first photo is the one we showed you yesterday. It's worth showing again. Do you recognize this man?"

The manager peered at the picture and said with assurance, "No."

John then pulled out the photo of Ahmad Abbasova, aka Cyrus Safar. "This is a new picture we didn't show you yesterday."

"He doesn't ring a bell either."

John laid the third photo on the desk. It was Omar Hasanov. "Any bells ringing on this one?"

"Sorry."

"Okay, I'd like to interview all the desk clerks and concierges who worked during the last twenty-four hours."

"The shift change takes place in half an hour, so I'll first send you the night-shift clerks, and after them, the morning staff."

"We can begin that way, but the people I most want to talk to are the clerks who were working around seven yesterday evening. When does their shift begin today?"

"Not until three o'clock."

"I can't afford to wait that long. Call them and ask them to come in early for an urgent FBI matter. If they can't do that, I'll send one of our agents to interview them."

The manager's eyebrows lifted. "It'll be faster if I make the calls from my office. You can use the employee break room."

An hour later, after John showed the final night clerk the three photos, he sighed. "Still no luck." He turned to Steven. "Could you check on where things stand with the evening-shift clerks? I'll start on the morning-shift people."

"If nobody recognizes any of the photos, what's your next move?" With every passing minute, Steven's suspicion grew stronger. They should be in DC, not here following another bread crumb.

"I'll cross that bridge if it comes to that."

Steven entered the lobby and saw one of the FBI agents scurry out the front entrance. He knocked on the hotel manager's door. When the door opened, he saw Chris was the only agent in the office.

"Kittrick wants an update on your progress."

Chris said, "About half the clerks are agreeing to come in this morning. The first one will be here shortly. We've already interviewed two people at their apartments. No hits."

"Will you be able to reach all of them by this afternoon?"

"It's looking likely."

"That's encouraging," he said. Though he didn't feel encouraged. It seemed they weren't making any headway.

By the time Steven got back to the employee break room, John had finished with the first morning-shift clerk. Nine clerks and one hour later, still nothing.

Morning-clerk number eleven entered the break room. A young petite Asian woman greeted them in excellent English, albeit with a slight accent.

John explained what he wanted from her, and then laid out the three photos. She put her finger on the first one, then pushed it back toward John. "I don't remember him."

Moving to the second picture, she looked for a moment longer, then pushed it toward John. "Not him either."

When she looked at the third picture, her forehead furrowed. She picked it up and looked more closely. "I remember this man."

John leaned in. "You're sure? When did you see him?"

"I checked him in yesterday morning."

"Any particular reason you remember him"

The woman looked offended. "I checked him in only a day ago, so of course I remember him."

The woman left little doubt. Steven was virtually certain: Nazari and the bomb were in DC.

John jumped up. "I need to know if he's still here."

The clerk looked curious but only said, "I'll check at the front desk."

Her heels clacked on the floor as she hurried toward the lobby, John trailing right behind her, and Steven behind him. After she logged back into her computer at the check-in desk, her rapid clicking on her mouse was interrupted only by the clacking of her keyboard.

"Ah," she said with satisfaction. "Here it is."

John peered at her monitor. "Nicholas Pappas. So that's his name now." Brusquely, he asked, "Is he still here?"

The hotel clerk glanced at John. "He's due to check out today, but he hasn't yet."

John wrote down Hasanov's room number. He moved closer to the clerk. In an urgent whisper, he said, "Get the manager and all the agents who are still with him."

Within seconds, the manager appeared, followed by Chris and another FBI agent. John issued his next set of orders.

To the second agent, John said, "You stay here and make sure Hasanov doesn't leave."

To the clerk he said, "Check the breakfast room to make sure he's not there."

To the hotel manager, he said, "Give me your master key."

To Chris and Steven, he said, "Come with me," as he moved toward the elevator.

As they entered the elevator, two hotel guests tried to scoot in behind them, but John cut them off and punched the third-floor button. He said, "Hasanov probably asked for a lower floor so he could use the stairs rather than the elevator. He's in room 338."

The doors opened, and John started down the hallway. Rounding a corner, they saw the end of the corridor ahead.

"Steven, you stay here." John instructed. "Don't let anybody get past you."

Without waiting for Steven's reply, John handed the master key to Chris and motioned for him to follow.

Steven glanced toward the elevator and confirmed the corridor was still empty. He turned to watch John and Chris, his heart pounding.

John pulled out his gun and Chris swiped the master keycard on the lock of Room 338.

When the lock tumbled, John jammed down the door handle and rushed into the room. Chris, his gun drawn, followed close behind.

Steven heard John's muffled shout. "Clear!"

Moments later, John emerged from the room, shoulders drooping. He looked at Steven and shook his head. "He's cleared out of his room.

Chris will search for evidence, though I doubt it'll help us locate either Hasanov or Nazari."

Grimly, Steven said, "There can't be much doubt. Hasanov sent the email to Leila on Nazari's behalf."

John ran his hand through his hair. "We were right after all. Nazari tricked us into looking in the wrong place. Washington, DC is his target."

"Time is running out!"

John pulled out his phone. "I'll update the Director."

"People in Washington are going to flip out."

"Going apeshit would be more accurate."

CHAPTER 69

Washington, DC (2:15 pm, July 3)

The Chief of Staff for the FBI Director picked up Steven and John at Reagan Airport. On the way to the White House, he explained that his boss and the DNI had requested Steven and John's presence in the Situation Room. The Chief also cautioned them to speak only when spoken to. When they approached the entrance to the West Wing, Steven spotted the President ducking into a limo.

Steven had never been in the Situation Room before, and its simple appearance and limited seating surprised him. A large conference table occupied the middle of the room, and monitors lined the walls, so multiple screens were visible from every vantage point. Many weighty proceedings had taken place in this room, and today ranked among the weightiest.

The room was half full when Steven and John arrived. The DNI nodded at them as the Chief escorted them to their seats along the wall. Steven recognized the Attorney General, who was conferring with the DNI. The Secretary of Energy scowled when he spotted Steven. Once again, he appeared unhappy that someone had invited a mere scientist from his own department to such a crucial high-level meeting. Moments later, the Secretary of Homeland Security entered, along with several other people Steven didn't recognize.

The Attorney General called the meeting to order. The room instantly became quiet, though it vibrated with tension. The strained faces around the conference table testified to the fear they were all trying to suppress.

The AG said, "We are on the precipice of a monumental disaster. We now believe New York City is not the target, and instead, at any moment, terrorists will detonate a nuclear weapon here. Our operational roles will remain the same as during the past two days in New York City. Before the President left this afternoon, he gave me marching orders for this group. We have one task and one task only. Find Nazari and stop him from detonating this weapon. The President and other Cabinet members are assembling outside of Washington. They'll handle all other aspects of this threat."

The DHS Secretary raised his hand. "I assume this information is highly classified. What should I tell people I put on the case?"

The AG said, "The highest priority is to stop the bomb. But the President insists we do that without letting it leak to the public. If the press catches wind of it, the pandemonium would make our task nearly impossible."

Steven saw heads nod around the room. The AG continued. "Now that we know the threat is directed here, I imagine many of you would like to warn your people. Don't do it."

The DHS Secretary's hand went up. "Are we sure DC is the target?"

Steven groaned to himself. What value did he add as an observer at this meeting? Wouldn't his time be better spent searching for the assembly site?

With a nod, the AG invited the FBI Director to respond. The Director said, "At this point, we're confident Tariq Nazari is the leader of this terrorist plot. All of our evidence pointed to New York City as the target, including the fact that Nazari sent an email from a New York hotel. This morning we discovered another terrorist, Omar Hasanov, sent that email, thanks to the excellent work of Special Agent John Kittrick and Dr. Steven Carter." He gestured in their direction.

The DOE Secretary said, "That seems highly suggestive, but it isn't actual proof. Especially when everything else points to New York."

The FBI Director tilted his head. "After this morning's discovery, we focused our surveillance efforts on June 25th, the day Nazari checked out of his New York hotel and disappeared. A couple hours ago we got our confirmation—a security camera at Pennsylvania Station caught Nazari boarding the Acela Express from New York City to DC. If Nazari is here, so is the bomb."

The Attorney General took the floor again. "Our strategy is two-pronged. First, locate the terrorists themselves. We're looking only for Tariq Nazari and Ahmad Abbasova, who also goes by the name of Cyrus Safar. We assume Nazari is also using a false identity. Omar Hasanov is no longer a target. After this morning's discovery, we continued to interview the hotel staff. A hotel concierge remembers that Hasanov took a cab yesterday evening. We've confirmed that a taxi took him to JFK, and then he boarded a flight to Frankfurt."

The meeting then turned to a discussion about departmental responsibilities and tactics in the search. Steven's mind drifted. Most likely the White House was ground zero. Right where he was sitting. The picture hanging in his office came to mind. He projected the awful devastation of Hiroshima onto downtown DC. For him, the carnage and mayhem was not unimaginable. He nudged John and whispered, "How long till we get out of here?"

John's face flashed a warning, and Steven realized everyone was looking at them. The AG said, "I was just saying that the second element of our strategy is to locate the assembly site. Agent Kittrick, would you explain the approach we developed for New York City."

John got up and stood next to the FBI Director. "We focused on small industrial shops. We cross-referenced with four other potential indicators, or attributes. First attribute, has the shop received any foreign shipment that might contain structural parts of the weapon? Second, have any conventional explosives been delivered? Third, has a substantial amount of lead or other heavy metal been delivered in the past couple weeks? Dr. Carter suggested such a material might be used to address the terrorists' loss of one of their HEU parts. And the fourth attribute—is there any connection between Transportes Grupo and the shop? For example, did the company lease that shop?"

The Attorney General added, "Use all of your resources that might possibly help. But coordinate with the FBI."

Steven cleared his throat to get John's attention. When John glanced at him, Steven mouthed the words "rental cars."

"Oh, one more thing," John said. "In looking at surveillance recordings, search for the rental cars the terrorists picked up in San Antonio."

The Director added, "If we get really lucky, we'll spot those rental cars at the assembly site."

Steven noticed the DNI staring at him. "Dr. Carter, could you tell us why you came to suspect New York City was a ruse?"

The AG and DOE Secretary looked annoyed. Steven was perplexed. Was that relevant now? The DNI's eyes were still fixed on him. When Steven remained silent, the DNI bobbed his head.

Steven stood up but stayed next to his chair against the wall. "Several threads came together, but the most significant was something Nazari's old girlfriend said when we interviewed her yesterday morning. When Nazari's family was killed by a drone strike in Yemen, his rage was specifically directed at the U.S government and the U.S. military. Later, it hit me. Wouldn't it make more sense for him to target the capital of our government rather than New York City?"

The DNI rubbed his chin. "So where do you think Nazari will detonate?"

The proverbial light bulb went on in Steven's head. "When people think of the U.S. government, they think of the White House and Capitol Hill. And when they think of the U.S. military, it's the Pentagon. Nazari probably would like to demolish all three, but he's also probably uncertain of the weapon's yield. My guess—he'll pick a spot where he's sure to destroy the White House and perhaps the Pentagon as well."

The room suddenly went deathly quiet. Steven guessed if they all made a bet on the likely target, the White House would be the "winner." By voicing that reality, he'd forced them to confront the likelihood they were at that very moment sitting in Nazari's crosshairs.

The AG asked, "Are you sure of that?"

"Of course not." Steven shrugged. "But it makes the most sense to me."

The DNI looked around the room. "Dr. Carter has as an advantage over most of us in trying to anticipate Nazari's moves. They're both scientists. Dr. Carter, given the targets you've suggested, where would you look for the assembly site?"

Steven hesitated and then took a deep breath. "If I were Nazari, I'd want to limit the distance between my assembly site and the detonation point. He probably assumes that the U.S. has radiation sensors deployed in DC. Though he may take measures to shield the device's radiation signature, he can't be sure we don't have the means of detecting it in transit." Steven's mind raced as he developed his logic in real time.

His mouth had become so dry that his voice cracked. "Nazari is showing an abundance of caution. That's why he tried to lead us down the wrong path. He may be worried that we'll set up emergency traffic controls, and bridges are obvious chokepoints. I think he'll want to avoid moving it across a bridge."

The Attorney General shifted in his chair. "So we should prioritize industrial sites in the downtown area, somewhere close to the White House. Right?"

"Yes, and the optimum location would be a place where he wouldn't even need to move the bomb. Just detonate it in place."

The DNI looked satisfied. "Thank you, Dr. Carter. That should help focus the search."

The AG stood up. "Any other questions or comments?"

Silence.

"Let's go find this son of a bitch!"

CHAPTER 70

Washington, DC (3:30 pm, July 3)

The FBI Director ordered Steven and John to ride with him back to FBI headquarters where they'd join the search for the assembly site. When they stepped outside the West Wing, Steven felt a drop on his neck. Looking up, he saw dark clouds gathering.

John noticed and looked up too. "Thunderstorms are predicted for this evening."

"That'll make the search even more difficult. It's already hard enough on the Sunday before the 4th." Steven's gut told him they were closing in on Nazari. But his gut also told him it could be too late. Nazari wouldn't expect his ruse to hold up for long. He'd detonate as soon as he could.

While the Chief of Staff drove, the Director said, "Steven, I'm going to incorporate your latest ideas into our search strategy. And I want you to join me in the Strategic Information and Operations Center. Feel free to roam the SIOC, and if you have any further ideas, report directly to me. John, you're on the coordination team that merges the inputs of all the teams."

"Yes, sir," they responded in near unison. Steven was glad the Director didn't relegate him to the sidelines, even though it meant he'd remain in the bomb's bullseye.

The Chief dropped them off, and the Director hustled Steven and John up to the fifth floor. The SIOC was full of agents, many on phones, others huddled in conversation, and still others on computers. Several agents noticed the Director the moment he entered, and the noise level dropped quickly, until only agents on phones could be heard.

The Director held up his hand. "I just came out of a meeting at the White House. We've agreed to concentrate on assembly sites where the weapon could be transported to the vicinity of the White House without crossing a bridge."

Steven felt a glimmer of satisfaction that he'd helped to narrow the search. Yet, it still left an awful lot of ground to cover.

"From this point forward," the Director continued, "I'll run this emergency search operation. This is one of the greatest crises our country has ever faced." The Director clenched his jaw, his face fierce. "But we will not fail."

He surveyed the room. "Who's leading each team?"

As the team leaders identified themselves, Steven's sense of chaos receded and the structure of the search became apparent. In addition to the coordination team, each search attribute had its own team.

The Director said, "Okay, I want a quick update from each team."

When they reached the leader of the team investigating specific shops, the Director interrupted. "If you can't get someone to open the shop for you, how do you clear it?"

The team leader replied, "We rely primarily on visual inspection from the exterior. The Hazardous Materials Response Unit also brings radiation detectors to look for a signal from the HEU."

The Director frowned. "Not good enough. If a location was leased recently, or it's received a heavy-metal delivery, that's an exigent circumstance that allows you to search the premises. If neither of those conditions applies, the HMRU will set up their radiation detectors. DOE will soon supply their search teams, who have more sensitive detectors. Any signal, *any signal at all*, is grounds for going in. Do you understand?"

The team leader nodded. "*Any* signal at all."

Despite the extraordinary danger, Steven smiled to himself. They would enter the shop even if the detectors only saw background noise.

The heavy-metal deliveries team drew Steven's closest attention. This team had already identified and contacted two major suppliers. One of these suppliers said they'd need a warrant. Agents were dispatched to *encourage* its CEO to cooperate, as the team leader put it. Steven took a seat where he could follow this team's progress.

Time passed slowly. He fought to keep his fear from bubbling up into his consciousness. He looked at the large map of DC someone had taped to the wall. Red pushpins marked the places that had been investigated and cleared. Every few minutes, another pin was punched into the map. By late afternoon, most of the shops near the White House had been cleared, and the Director expanded the search to the southeastern part of downtown, where the concentration of industrial shops was highest.

With little to do, extraneous thoughts kept intruding into Steven's whirling mind. If they failed in their mission, how would the history books portray the attempt to stop the threat? Would historians even know how close they'd come to succeeding?

He chided himself for speculating on failure. In his mind's eye, Steven drew a triangle on the wall map that was defined by the White House, the Capital building, and the Pentagon. Where in that triangle did Nazari set up shop?

A while later, Steven heard a commotion among the team assigned to investigate potential links to Transportes Grupo. He drifted over to their side of the room. An agent noticed him and gave a thumbs-up. Steven asked, "What did you find?"

"Earlier we traced Transportes Grupo back through a couple shell companies, and then hit a dead-end. When we got word the bomb was in DC, we began looking for a linkage to transport companies operating in the greater DC area. We traced a shipping company, one that does business in the Baltimore port, back through a chain of shell companies until the trail ended…at the same dead-end as Transportes Grupo."

"Fantastic. What's next?"

"Agents will soon arrive at the company and search their shipment records."

Steven wandered back to John. New information streamed in, but nothing other than the transport company seemed promising. DHS did find a recording of Nazari arriving on the train in Washington, DC on the 27th, but after that he seemed to have disappeared again. The tension in the room mounted and tempers began to fray. Team leaders pointed fingers at one another, betraying their own increasing frustration with the lack of progress. The air throbbed with fear, but no one openly acknowledged it.

For the rest of the afternoon, Steven periodically wandered around the room. Shop after shop with a heavy-metal delivery was cleared. When afternoon gave way to evening, he began to wonder if he'd been wrong about the tamper. Why all the dead ends? It was beginning to feel like New York City.

Steven's sense of impending doom grew stronger as the FBI agents toiled into the evening. The red push pins continued to bloom across the DC map, like a red-algae tide in the ocean. He kept his ear on field reports from the shops with recent heavy-metal deliveries, but every time it was "no evidence of terrorists."

It seemed like several days had passed since he and Carolyn talked with Sina Haddad in Boston, even though it'd been only yesterday morning. He recalled the emphatic way Sina described Nazari's response to his family tragedy. When she described how Nazari hated the U.S. military, her eyes had blazed as if she were channeling Nazari from years ago.

Once again Steven asked himself, *If I were Nazari, where would I choose to detonate?* Then a new idea began to form, but it stayed stubbornly lodged in his subconscious. He still thought Nazari would be worried about transporting the weapon to ground zero. And if he were Nazari, he'd worry that the Americans would position their most sensitive radiation detectors at choke points and put up emergency traffic controls.

His idea was taking shape and beginning to emerge. *The military. Transporting. Wait for it. Wait for it. Oh my!*

CHAPTER 71

Washington, DC (7:45 pm, July 3)

Steven rushed over to the Director and on his way tapped John's shoulder. The Director turned to Steven the instant he got off his phone.

"What's up?" the Director asked.

"I just had a Eureka moment. At least I hope it is."

"Just spit it out," the Director said.

"Nazari's best chance of destroying both the White House and the Pentagon is to put the device on a boat, then navigate on the Potomac to a point midway between those two places. If I were Nazari, I'd put my assembly site near the Potomac, not in the downtown area. That would minimize transport on surface streets. And no need to cross a bridge." As Steven concluded, he felt a surge of hope. *This is what I missed! This is it!*

John's eyes lit up. "He could transport it along the western side of the river, on the Memorial Parkway. From there, he could be sure of destroying the Pentagon and at the very least doing significant damage to the White House. If the winds are in the usual direction, the fallout on the Mall would be horrific."

"Here's another possibility," Steven said. "Rosslyn isn't too terribly far from either the White House or the Pentagon. If his assembly site was in Rosslyn, he could detonate it in place. I think this scenario is less likely than the river, but it would still inflict catastrophic damage and casualties at both places."

The Director's expression shifted from intense concentration to hopeful surprise. "All things considered, Steven, what's your best bet?"

"A boat on the river," Steven said, his emphatic tone conveying his growing conviction. "Not only is it the optimum location, the probability of being intercepted is lower than along the Parkway."

The Director turned to John. "Immediately broaden the search to include places along the Potomac River. From Rosslyn down to Mt. Vernon."

The noise in the SIOC grew to a fevered pitch as agents expanded the scope of the search. Not surprisingly, on the eve of the 4th and a Sunday to boot, requests for information were met with hostility. Extreme measures of cajoling often proved necessary.

Steven paced next to the heavy-metals delivery team. As time marched on, the map bloomed with more red pins, but still no hits. He wiped the sweat from his forehead. Would they ever get a break? The pen in his hand abruptly broke in half, splattering ink on his shirt.

Steven noticed John leaving the room. He guessed where John was headed and realized his own bladder was in need of relief. John looked back and smiled wanly when he saw Steven following him.

John said, "You look terrible."

"You don't look so great yourself."

"The Director seems to fully trust you now. Hope you're right about expanding the search area."

Steven grimaced. "So do I."

When they re-entered the SIOC, the air buzzed with excitement. A cluster of agents encircled the team investigating deliveries by the shipping company they'd linked to Transportes Grupo.

"What's happening?" John asked an agent on the perimeter of the crowd.

"They've found a shipment to a boat repair company in the southeast downtown area. The weight and dimensions on the manifest are consistent with the structural parts of the bomb. It's by no means certain, but it's the first good lead we've found."

Steven moved back to the heavy-metals team. Maybe they'd find a delivery to the same boat repair shop, even though it wasn't along the river. An agent answered the phone. A heavy-metals supplier was calling back with a list of deliveries in the expanded area. The agent wrote down three places. One was a welding company. In Alexandria.

Steven tapped on the shoulder of the agent. "What metal did they deliver to the Alexandria shop?"

"Lead," the agent replied.

In an instant, the pieces fell into place. Alexandria! Right next to the Potomac and just south of the Pentagon. Steven took in a deep quick breath. That's where John lived.

He scribbled down the address and ran over to John. He grabbed the agent's arm and shoved the note in his face. "Are you familiar with this part of Alexandria?"

"Doesn't ring a bell. Why?"

"It's a welding shop, and it had a recent delivery of lead."

John grabbed his phone and punched in the address. "That's in the Del Ray area. I'm not too familiar with that part of town. Did you get any other details?"

"No." Steven dashed back to the heavy-metals team, with John close behind.

In a few minutes, they determined that this welding shop had been vacant for some time before a new tenant took occupancy three months ago. Several hundred pounds of lead was delivered five days ago.

Adrenaline pumped through Steven, chasing away his exhaustion. "My gut tells me this is it, John."

"How sure are you?"

A surge of hope fueled Steven's optimism. "Over ninety percent."

"I can get there faster than anybody," John replied.

CHAPTER 72

Washington, DC (July 3, 8:55 pm)

John rushed over to the Director and told him he'd investigate the Alexandria welding shop. The Director replied that he'd redirect bomb experts in an HMRU team from the downtown area to Alexandria, and the unit would coordinate with John before they approached the shop. John barked at Rich, another agent, to come with him, and motioned for Steven to follow. The three of them sprinted out of the room.

They sped out of the underground parking lot, sirens blaring on their FBI car. John rode shotgun and navigated for Rich. Rich grunted as he turned on the windshield wipers. The predicted rain had begun as a light drizzle. Steven marveled at the way Rich zigged and zagged through traffic. Fortunately, it was late evening and the holiday weekend traffic was minimal.

John braced a hand against the windshield as they darted around a car that pulled in front of them on the 14th Street Bridge. John glanced at Rich and said, "Turn off the siren when we exit the freeway. We'll park a block away from the welding shop."

Steven peered between the seats at the map displayed on John's phone. John pointed at the map. "This welding shop isn't too far from Daingerfield Island. There's a marina there where they could launch a boat."

The excitement of the chase had momentarily chased away Steven's fear, but the idea of the nuclear device possibly underneath the bridge as they crossed it brought his fear surging back. His voice cracked as he asked, "Should we go there first?"

"First the welding shop," John replied. He turned around and handed Steven a radio unit. "Steven, you stay in the car. If things go bad, radio the SIOC. Otherwise, I'll let you know when it's clear for you to come in."

"How will I know if it goes bad?"

"I'll keep my radio channel open. You'll hear everything."

Steven experimented with the radio unit until he was sure he had the hang of it. They passed the exit to Reagan Airport and two exits later, Rich veered onto the off ramp and shut off the siren.

John's voice became clipped as he issued orders. "Next right." Two blocks later, "Next left."

Steven attempted to keep a sense of direction, and when John ordered Rich to park, he guessed they were heading south. So the river was to their left. They pulled to a stop in front of an auto body repair shop. Looking down the street, Steven saw signs for a Kelly Moore store, a masonry supply company, and then Vic's Welding.

John took the car keys from Rich and handed them to Steven. "Just in case."

Steven marveled at the calm in John's voice, even as he noticed sweat beading the agent's forehead and the artery in his neck pulsing at an alarming rate.

After John adjusted the gun in his shoulder harness, he opened the car door. "Steven, get in the driver's seat."

Steven watched the two FBI agents walk briskly down the empty street. If Nazari spotted them, he'd instantly be on alert. In this locale, even during daytime, they'd look out of place in their suit coats, but on a rainy Sunday evening, they'd raise anyone's eyebrows. Neither agent said anything during the walk to the front door of Vic's Welding, but their raspy breathing came through loud and clear on the radio.

Steven saw John peer into the window next to the door, while Rich plastered himself along the wall. Steven heard John whisper, "I don't see anybody inside."

Both men pulled out their guns. John dipped his head and Rich knocked out a pane in the door window with the heel of his gun. Rich reached in and pulled the door open, and John rushed inside.

Moments later, Steven heard "Clear." After a few seconds, he heard another "Clear."

John said to Rich, "Nobody's here. I checked the alleyway and nobody there either."

"Crap," said Rich.

John said, "Steven, come and take a look."

Steven ran down the sidewalk and stepped through the broken glass. The front part of the shop was an office. Its furniture was bleak: an old desk, a simple chair, and a beat-up metal filing cabinet. From the look of them, Steven guessed they were holdovers from the previous tenant. The only signs of recent occupancy were an open pack of stationary and a ten-speed bike leaning against the wall.

When Steven stepped into the main shop area, Rich handed him a pair of latex gloves. John stood by a cot in one corner, with a pair of jeans in his gloved hands. "These jeans would fit a small man like Abbasova."

Steven noticed a twin mattress on the ground in another corner. "Two people have been sleeping here."

Pieces of wood stacked against a wall drew his attention. They varied in size, with nails protruding from many of them. He surmised they were the remains of packing crates and started to sort through them, looking for markings. Finding nothing on the smaller pieces in front, he shoved them to the side.

Frantic, he pulled pieces of wood onto the floor. When he grabbed the second to the last, he yelped. A nail had taken a divot from his finger. He wiped his hand on his pants as he peered more closely at the very last piece. A faint logo was imprinted on one corner. It looked familiar. Was it the logo of the Baltimore shipping company the FBI had just discovered?

"John, come take a look," barked Steven.

When John didn't answer, Steven lifted his head. John stood next to a workbench, holding what looked like some kind of kitchen appliance. With rising excitement, John said, "No, you come here."

Steven rushed over and peered inside the appliance. "It looks like a deep fryer." A dark grey material coated the inside. He scratched at the coating with his fingernail and made a small groove. He took the appliance out of John's hands and jiggled it up and down. "It's heavy."

He rapidly sorted through possible explanations. "Nazari used this fryer to melt the lead."

John said, "That confirms it! Nazari assembled his bomb here."

In the next instant, their elation gave way to desperate fear. John took two quick steps to the middle of the shop and knelt down. "Look at these tire tracks. They're too narrow for a car or truck."

Steven looked above John and spotted an overhead hoist. "The entire assembly, including the lead tamper, must weigh at least five hundred pounds. They used this hoist to lift the device onto a boat. Those are trailer tracks."

John touched the track left by the boat trailer. "This mud is still damp," he said through clenched teeth. He pounded the floor. "Shit! We just missed them!"

CHAPTER 73

Alexandria (9:18 pm, July 3)

John yelled at Rich, "Call the Director."

He fixed his eyes on Steven. "Where will Nazari head on the river?"

"He'll go up the Potomac and probably detonate near the Memorial Bridge. But if he spots federal agents, I'm afraid he'll set it off immediately."

"I hope to head him off at Daingerfield Island. On the way there, I'll fill in the Director. He'll redirect all the HMRU and SWAT teams, and soon we'll have eyes on the entire river from here to the Memorial Bridge."

"Don't use helicopters. That'll warn Nazari."

"I'll pass that along."

The three of them sprinted out of the shop. At the front door, John skidded to a stop. He yelled at Rich, "Get the car and pick me up."

Steven stopped just short of running over John. "What's up?"

John turned to look at Steven. In a husky voice, John said, "You've done so much, but there's nothing more for you to do now." He pointed at the bike. "Save yourself and ride south on the Mount Vernon Trail."

Rather than an order, John's last statement came across as a plea. Steven bit his lip. He hated to quit now. His heart hammering, he said, "You may be right, but—"

Rich pulled up in the car. John said, "Bye, Steven," as he ran to the car.

Dazed, Steven watched the car speed away, its tires squealing as it rounded the next corner. He grabbed the ten-speed bike, swung it around, and winced as the bike hit the filing cabinet. Out of the corner of his eye, he spotted a sliver of white behind the cabinet. He poked at it and a folded up cardboard box came into view. "*Garmin GHP 10,*" Steven read. He pulled the box out further and muttered to himself, "Autopilot Compass Control."

Steven wheeled the ten-speed onto the sidewalk, tucked his pants' legs into his socks, and pedaled down the street. He'd biked on the Mt. Vernon Trail before, so he knew he'd reach it on the other side of Route 1. The rain was falling harder now.

An autopilot? Most likely that meant Nazari wasn't in the boat carrying the bomb. His mind churned, but he hadn't forgotten the lesson from his bike crash at the Lab, so he stayed vigilant for hazards on the road. He touched the brakes just before turning a corner and felt a twinge in his rear-brake hand. Glancing down, he realized he was bleeding. The nail had taken quite a divot from his finger.

Where was Nazari? Maybe the bomb was on a timer, and Nazari was already driving out of town. Or maybe Nazari was on the shore, keeping an eye on the boat in case he needed to detonate before it reached the optimal spot.

He keyed the radio he was still wearing. "Steven to John," he yelled. No answer.

Breathing hard, he pedaled under Route 1. Through the rain, he spotted a sign for the Mt Vernon Trail. He tried John again. Still no answer.

His heart pounded harder, not from physical exertion, but from the indecision that suddenly seized him. Maybe there was something more he could do after all.

An image of Carissa floated into his mind. Huddled with Jacob and Josh.

He reached the trail, paved and well-suited for a fast bike ride in the rain. If he headed south, he'd be far enough away in five minutes to most likely survive the nuclear blast. For a brief moment, he closed his eyes. His mind went back to that playoff football game. The roar of the crowd when everything was on the line. His frantic deliberation and then making the wrong decision.

He opened his eyes. *Time to call an audible.*

Softly, he said, "I'm sorry, Carissa."

He turned onto the trail. Left, not right. To the north, not south. Headed toward where the bomb would go off any minute.

The weather had dissuaded late evening walkers, which freed him to ride without dodging pedestrians. Blinking the rain away, he scanned the river for a sign of the boat. Nothing. The far bank of the Potomac was difficult to make out. His head swiveled back to check on the trail, and then he resumed scanning the river. He monitored the riverbank too, in case Nazari was following the boat from there.

His radio squawked, startling him. "Steven," he heard a second time.

He fumbled for his radio. "Yes, John."

"You called."

"When I grabbed the bike, I spotted a folded-up box for an auto-pilot. Nazari might not be on the boat."

"We found an empty boat trailer at the boat ramp. Unhitched. Now we're headed north on the George Washington Parkway."

"Me too"

"What?! Where are you?"

"Heading north on the Mt. Vernon Trail."

"What the hell, Steven!"

"Nazari might be on the shore, following the boat. On a bike, I have a better chance of spotting him."

"The Director has mobilized all our assets to find that boat."

"Right now, I'm by the airport, so I can't see the river, but soon I'll be past the airport. If I see anything, I'll call."

He turned off the radio and stood up on his pedals. He sprinted until the river came back into view. Rounding a bend, he spotted a boat. Gasping for air, he reached to call on his radio, but stopped when he realized the boat was headed in the wrong direction.

A couple minutes later, he came around a left-hand bend and passed under the 14th Street Bridge. His continual scanning netted nothing. The rain lessened to a drizzle, and for a brief moment, he could clearly see the other side of the Potomac. No boats. Nor anybody along the shore.

Maybe he'd missed the boat when the airport blocked his view. What should he do if he reached the Memorial Bridge without seeing anything? Had he risked his life, only to fail in the end?

From the time he'd hopped on the bike, adrenaline had fueled his desperate optimism. Doubt now loomed larger, followed by a creeping sense of despair.

Suddenly aware of a terrible thirst, without thinking, he reached for his water bottle. *Stupid! This isn't your bike.* Frustrated, he pounded on the handlebars.

Wait! Did someone move among those trees? He wiped his eyes and slowed his pace. He kept his gaze fixed on the spot ahead that had drawn his attention. An indistinct figure stepped from behind a tree and began jogging parallel to the shore. It struck Steven as somehow familiar.

The figure suddenly turned away from the river and broke into a run. Steven's memory flashed to his sabbatical at MIT, where once a week he'd run with Nazari at noon. Several years ago, during an evening run at an ITWG meeting, he'd been reminded of Nazari's distinctive way of running. The shadowy figure ahead ran just like him!

Steven sped up again, hoping to intercept Nazari before he could cross the path and head toward the Memorial Parkway. When Steven was twenty yards away, Nazari turned in his direction. Nazari slowed and brought his left hand in front of him. *Is he holding the detonator?*

He got up on his pedals again and sprinted toward Nazari.

Ten yards away, he saw Nazari sneer as his right hand began its descent.

Taking aim, Steven adjusted his bike so his shoulder would ram into Nazari's arm. An instant before impact, Nazari's finger made contact with the detonator.

Steven heard the crack of bone as he slammed into Nazari. Then his world went black.

CHAPTER 74

Lady Bird Johnson Park (9:34 pm, July 3)

Raindrops splashed on Steven's face and he heard groaning. *Is that me?*

He opened his eyes. *Where am I?*

Turning his head, he spied a muddied bike close by, its front wheel twisted. He tried to sit up, but a sharp pain shot through his right shoulder and forced him back down. *What happened?*

He heard another groan. This time, it came from behind. He rolled onto his good side. Nazari was sitting on the ground, holding his arm, bent at an unnatural angle. Steven's head snapped back as he suddenly remembered crashing into Nazari. *He hit the button! So what happened?*

Nazari saw him and drew back, his face contorted in pain. "Damn you!" he snarled.

Nazari shifted onto his knees, and as he did, Steven saw his face more clearly. Rage registered in those dark eyes, as well as something more. A hint of victory, perhaps.

Nazari struggled to his feet and limped toward the Memorial Parkway.

Steven shook his head and wondered if the bomb had fizzled. He recalled Nazari jogging along the riverbank and then sprinting away from it. Then the answer hit him.

Fear washed over him again, overtaking the pain in his shoulder.

He fumbled for his radio, but it was missing. Guessing it had gone in the same direction as the bike, he propped himself up on his good arm and gathered his legs under him. He tried to stand, but his leg buckled and he crumpled back to the ground.

Desperate, he dragged himself through the wet grass toward the bike. Waves of pain almost caused him to black out again.

He reached the bike, grabbed it by the stem, and flung it out of the way. He dried his eyes with his shirtsleeve, and then spotted the radio a few feet away.

He gathered himself for one desperate lunge and his fingers closed around the radio. He prayed it still worked.

He pressed the call button and heard a crackle. "John, come in, John!"

For what seemed an eternity, the radio was silent. Then John answered. "Steven, where—"

"Listen," Steven cut him off. "Nazari hit the detonator button, but it's a time delay. I'm in Lady Bird Park and the boat must be nearby. Blow it up!"

"Where's Nazari?"

"Headed toward the Parkway. Take out that boat with a missile if you've got one!"

The radio went silent again. Steven assumed, hoped, prayed that John wouldn't question his plea.

He rolled onto his back. All he could do now was wait.

His mind turned to his family. He recalled the morning he'd left home, only four days ago. The worried look on Carissa's face. The comfort of her parting embrace. And yesterday on the phone, the sound of her voice when she said, "Be careful, my love."

Steven's tears mingled with the rain running down his face. *I don't want my life with you to end. I don't want you to raise our boys alone.*

He thought of his last conversation with each of his sons. Thank goodness he took the opportunity to tell them how much he loved them. He smiled as he savored Jacob's response, *"Me too, Dad."*

An explosion from the direction of the river rocked him out of his reverie.

He drew in the deepest breath of his life. Slowly, he breathed out while a deep sense of fulfillment settled over him. He hadn't failed. The weapon was disabled.

He felt faint and his vision blurred. In the distance, he thought he heard people yelling. Then John's voice rang out. "Stop, Nazari! FBI!"

Seconds later, John yelled again. "Don't do it!'

Shots rang out.

Steven's world faded to black again.

CHAPTER 75

Department of Justice Headquarters (September 14)

The Attorney General rapped his knuckles on the conference room table. "Welcome to the second day of the Nazari case review."

The room quieted as people took their seats. To fortify himself, Steven grabbed another pastry and headed to his chair at the table. He appreciated the FBI Director's insistence that he and John move up to the table for this review, even though he missed sitting next to Michelle and Alan against the back wall.

When he settled in by John, his FBI friend whispered, "How's the shoulder feeling today?"

"Pretty good." A month ago, Steven had discarded his arm sling, but his shoulder had stiffened up yesterday because he wasn't doing his physical therapy exercises during this trip.

When the buzz in the room stopped, the AG said, "We begin this morning with Special Agent John Kittrick presenting his perspective on the final days that led to Nazari's capture."

While John walked to the front, Steven recalled with satisfaction yesterday's praise for the crucial role nuclear forensics played in the case. His own talk on the earlier Moldova case drew an appreciative response, albeit with a notable exception. Midway through his presentation, a spirited discussion erupted about the appropriateness of his decision to ignore the FBI's order to stop. To Steven's surprise, the FBI Director came to his defense. After his talk, Michelle gave an excellent presentation on the Laredo HEU analyses. Her clarity and poise validated Steven's insistence that she should present their team's work.

This morning, John began with their discovery that Nazari had lied about attending the INMM meeting. He then moved on to the search in New York City. When he described Steven's sense they were missing something, the Director of National Intelligence interrupted to ask Steven to explain his gut instinct.

"I can't fully explain it." Steven paused. "Part of it comes from my research experience, where I've learned the crucial importance of deciding which problems to address. Another aspect involves paying attention to what I call a nagging feeling. That's my signal to reflect on my assumptions and prior conclusions. So my gut instinct also involves critical thinking."

The DNI stroked his chin. "It's striking, the way you followed the scent of Nazari's trail." He grinned. "You're not only a nuclear scientist, you're a nuclear bloodhound."

Steven let the comment pass and avoided looking over at Alan, whose eyes no doubt were rolling. The AG turned back to John. "Please continue, Agent Kittrick."

John resumed by describing the search in Washington, DC. When he recalled the moment he informed the FBI Director that the bomb had just left Nazari's shop, the Director spoke up. "I immediately ordered all our resources to find Nazari's boat on the Potomac. My most difficult decision was what to do about Dr. Carter's concern that Nazari would immediately detonate if he thought we were about to stop him. We deployed Army helicopters, but I ordered them to keep above two thousand feet."

A short time later, John asked Steven to tell his part of the story after he left Vic's Welding. When Steven got to the part when he told John to destroy the boat, the Secretary of Homeland Security interrupted.

"That wasn't really your call, was it?" the DHS Secretary said. "Destroying the boat could itself have caused the bomb to go off."

"I knew it was a gun barrel design," Steven replied. "Hitting that type of device with a missile would cause the barrel to deform before the weapon's own high explosive could detonate. The disruption would prevent the two masses of HEU from smashing into each another."

John picked up his narrative again. "I relayed Steven's message to the Director. Turns out, the FBI had just spotted the boat."

John paused, and the FBI Director said, "When John contacted me, I realized we had to act fast. I gave the order to fire an air-to-surface missile from a helicopter. As Steven had expected, the weapon's conventional high explosive did detonate, but there was no nuclear yield."

The AG held up his hand. "It's imperative that the public never learns how close we came to nuclear catastrophe."

The FBI Director added, "As you might expect, an explosion on the Potomac attracted attention. We told local officials that the FBI thwarted a terrorist attempt to destroy the Memorial Bridge. We explained that they set off their bomb prematurely when we closed in on their boat."

The AG said, "We used this cover story to explain the recovery operation. Last week, we finished dredging the river to remove any evidence."

John cleared his throat. "Let's back up to when Steven first radioed me. After he told me about the autopilot on the boat, I drove north on the George Washington Memorial Parkway. For most of the way, it parallels the Mt. Vernon Trail. When I reached Rosslyn, Steven radioed with the urgent message to blow up the boat. I called the Director at SIOC as I headed back to Lady Bird Park. When I neared the park, I pulled off the road. That's when I heard an explosion on the river, which I assumed meant the bomb was disabled. Seconds later, I saw a man fifty yards ahead, limping toward the Parkway. I ran to cut him off."

Steven wished he could have watched this encounter. Prior to this case, he'd only interacted with John in laboratory settings, plus an occasional restaurant meal. The search for the bomb cast the agent in a new light. He was a man of action, ready and willing to risk his life.

John continued, his voice deepening. "It was Nazari. When I identified myself as FBI, he reached behind his back and pulled out a gun. I skidded to a stop and yelled, 'Don't do it!' Nazari raised his gun, and I dropped into a crouch. When he fired, I fired twice and he went down. When I reached his side, he was on the ground, moaning. One of my shots hit him in the stomach."

The DNI said, "A remarkably good shot when you were in the line of fire."

"It comes with the job," John replied matter-of-factly. "I asked Nazari, 'Where's Abbasova?' He just glared at me. I'll never forget that look. Hatred and hopelessness. Then he went unconscious and stopped breathing."

Steven recalled Nazari snarling at him with hateful yet deadened eyes. Evidently, Nazari's last words on this earth were, "Damn you!" *You got it wrong, Nazari. I'm alive and damn you!*

The AG nodded in approval. "Thank you, Agent Kittrick. The subsequent FBI investigation filled in more of the details. A security camera at a nearby parking lot recorded Abbasova in a pickup truck. We believe Nazari waited until the boat's autopilot brought it near to the optimal location, and then he made a beeline for Abbasova in the truck. He probably planned to trigger the time-delay detonator after they took off in the truck. Given the light evening traffic, the delay would be long enough to allow them to escape the critical zone. He intended to make it look like a suicide mission, and he used his letter to Leila to foster that impression, but in reality he planned to escape."

The DNI asked, "What's the latest on Abbasova?"

"When the boat blew up, he took off. He probably passed Nazari's body while John knelt beside him. We found the pickup abandoned in

Tyson's Corner. Abbasova has disappeared once again, and we suspect he switched to yet another identity. But we'll keep looking for him."

During the next couple hours, various agencies weighed in with details about Nazari's operation that they'd gained over the past ten weeks. After a lunch break, the DNI took the floor first.

"I appreciate the tenor of this review," the DNI said. "Rather than finger-pointing, we're listening and learning. Many of us in this room are political appointees..."

Steven quickly counted six people meeting that description.

"... and we often experience," the DNI continued, "politics getting in the way of truth. All too often, when our perspective doesn't match reality, we try to adjust reality. Politicians do it all the time."

The DNI looked at Steven. "One arena in our society stands out as utterly dedicated to seeking the truth. Science. Of course, politicking happens in the scientific community too, but this community insists that scientists willingly submit their perspectives to reality."

The AG took the floor. "Dr. Carter, you displayed this truth-seeking spirit throughout this case and notably at a key juncture. You didn't want to believe Nazari was the mastermind. Yet, at considerable risk to yourself, you followed the trail of evidence. How fortunate for all of us."

The DNI and AG began to applaud, and soon everyone joined in. Steven didn't know what to say, so he swiveled to look at Michelle and Alan. He gestured toward them and said, "I couldn't have done it without my team at the Lab."

He turned back to face John. "And how fortunate I was to work with you. Your trust in me enabled us to accomplish what neither of us could have done alone."

A slow flush climbed up John's neck. He smiled at Steven and then nodded to the AG. The AG took the hint and resumed the formal review.

The AG said, "This afternoon, we'll look at what would have been the aftermath if Nazari had succeeded. Dr. Alan Yang from Livermore will start us off."

Alan walked to the front of the room and squared his shoulders. "My presentation is based upon the assessment of weapon designers and engineers from Lawrence Livermore, Los Alamos, and Sandia National Laboratories. We conclude that Nazari's weapon would have successfully detonated with a yield of about thirteen kilotons. We have high confidence in this conclusion, in part because the FBI gained access to Nazari's computer and recovered his notes and drawings for the device."

The DHS Secretary asked, "How does that yield compare to Hiroshima?"

"It's slightly lower, but within the uncertainties, the yields are indistinguishable."

The room became very quiet. In a hushed voice, the DHS Secretary said, "Hiroshima, in the middle of DC. Unbelievable."

Then Alan described the probable casualties and radiation fall-out, in much the same manner as Steven's presentation many months ago to the class at Berkeley. As Alan neared the end, the DNI had a specific question. "What would've happened to the White House?"

"Very likely, the blast would have destroyed the White House."

Once again, the room became still. The DNI cleared his throat. "Here's the picture I'm getting. Tens of thousands of people would've died, including the President. Downtown Washington, DC would be uninhabitable for many years. Much of the government would need to move temporarily, if not permanently. Remediation would require workers to receive substantial doses of radiation."

"You've got the picture," Alan said.

Internally, Steven applauded his friend for getting across the magnitude of the disaster they'd barely averted. He recalled how close they'd come to missing vital clues at numerous junctures in the case. If they'd failed at any point, Alan's briefing would be horribly different. Instead of calculations and projections, they'd be looking at actual pictures of nuclear destruction at the center of the U.S. government. He shuddered as he imagined replacing the Hiroshima photo that hung in his office with a picture of a devastated Washington, DC.

CHAPTER 76

Tysons Corner, Virginia (8:00 pm, September 14)

Steven's eyes sparkled as he looked around the restaurant table, encircled with recent and long-time friends. Though the Nazari case review had one more day to finalize findings and recommendations, everyone at this table had completed their part. It was time to celebrate.

After the waiter took away their dinner plates, Steven said, "Given the occasion, let's have dessert too."

With a grin, John said, "Leave it to Steven to suggest dessert. But I'm game."

John's wife, Sue, nudged him. "Yeah, blame it on Steven."

During the past several days, a new friendship had blossomed between Carissa and Sue while their husbands participated in the review. This development delighted their husbands, who then suggested they should vacation together as couples.

Carolyn picked up her glass of wine. "I'd like to offer a toast. Working on this case has been the highlight of my career. I'm impressed by the expertise and dedication of each one of you, but we were successful because we collaborated so well. So let's drink to our collective success."

After everyone set down their glasses, Steven spoke. "I want to thank you, Carolyn, for listening carefully to a hard-headed scientist. And to Alan, my closest friend, for taking a risk by introducing me to Carolyn."

"Hear, hear," echoed the chorus around the table.

"I'm so happy that our collective success," he said, nodding toward Carolyn as he repeated her phrase, "has already garnered recognition for several of us. In case you didn't know, Alan was offered a group leader position in Z-Division. I had to twist his arm to get him to accept."

A sheepish smile spread across Alan's face. "At first I told my division leader that a management job was way out of my comfort zone, but he pointed out I'd already busted out of my old comfort zone. Finally, I realized that if I turned it down, I would never hear the end of it from Steven."

His confession elicited knowing nods and chuckles.

Steven next looked at John. "At the end of today's review, I overheard someone refer to the two of us as the dynamic duo. But let's not argue about which one of us is Batman. I believe John has some good news to share with us."

John fidgeted with his wineglass. "Well, Robin..."

John paused until people grasped his reference and laughed. "I wasn't going to bring this up, but the Director has awarded me the FBI Medal for Meritorious Achievement. If it hadn't been for the work of all of you, I would've never received such an honor. Steven, I especially want to thank you. You've taught me so much about nuclear forensics, and you've also taught me the value of trusting your gut and having the courage to go out on a limb."

Steven smiled and said, "We made a great team. And thank you for climbing trees with me."

Next, Steven turned to Michelle, his faithful lieutenant. She had so expertly guided the team, most notably when she stepped up in his absence. Yet, she never drew attention to herself. Over the past month, he'd pondered the ways their careers had intertwined and, after discussing it with Carissa, he had arrived at a decision.

As he looked at Michelle, a wave of gratitude and affection swept over him. She returned his gaze, but gradually a puzzled look replaced her smile.

"Michelle, the best decision I ever made in my career was to bring you onto my team and make you my co-leader. You've supported me through thick and thin. Your leadership has been vital to our success. As your supervisor and as your friend, I believe you have earned more responsibility. Accordingly, I will step out of my role so that you can become the new leader of our nuclear forensics team."

Michelle's eyes opened wide. "Are you sure? What about you?"

"Opportunities will come my way. And you're ready to step up to the plate."

"But the team won't be the same without you."

"True, and in time, that will make for a stronger team. You're so good at attracting new talent and fitting them in."

"Congratulations, Michelle," John said. "I've witnessed first-hand your leadership, and I'm confident you'll do great."

"I appreciate that."

John smiled and added, "Though I'll miss the arguments with Steven."

"Don't be fooled," Steven said. "Michelle has a backbone of steel. She's just a lot more graceful in the way she disagrees."

"Hear, hear," the chorus echoed again, prompting a wry grin from Steven.

"Well," Steven said, "in one way or another, things are changing for each of us. What about you, Carolyn?"

"I love what I'm doing."

At the end of the review meeting, Steven had noticed the DNI cornered Carolyn. "It appeared to me the DNI asked you to do something."

Carolyn said, "He wants me to serve on a new task force, something about developing better interagency cooperation." She grinned. "Could be an impossible task, so I'll probably say yes."

"Good for you," Steven said. "Okay, a last toast to all our new opportunities." He said it exuberantly, without a trace of irony, even though he had no inkling when his next opportunity would come along.

CHAPTER 77

Tysons Corner (8:45 pm, September 14)

When Steven and Carissa left the restaurant, they linked hands while they walked to their hotel. After a few steps, Carissa said, "How do you feel after making your announcement?"

"I'm not worried. New opportunities usually come one's way after a big win."

"Yes, usually. But not always."

"There's no need to be pessimistic. I just had the greatest success of my career."

"I used to believe there was a cause and effect between doing well and life going well."

"But not anymore?"

With a mysterious smile, she said, "No, and that's helped me a lot."

He was puzzled. In fact, Carissa had perplexed him for weeks. After the judge sentenced Jacob to two months in juvenile hall, Carissa's anxiety spiked through the roof. During those two months, though, her mood shifted. Her anxiety receded. She even seemed at peace. Jacob's ordeal in juvenile hall wasn't as bad as she'd feared, but that alone didn't seem to account for her change.

"I see a question on your face," she said.

"What's happening with you? You seem much less anxious."

"One day it hit me. Guilt was driving my anxiety. I'd been assuming if I was a *good person,*" she made air quotes to show her uneasiness with the term, "then life would go well for me. When I ran smack into our difficulties with Jacob, I realized this hidden belief of mine wasn't true at all. It simply doesn't align with reality."

"You felt guilty?" His face registered his surprise. "You've been a much better parent than me."

"That may be true, but I could have done better. My anxiety started to lift when I realized that even if I'd been a perfect parent, Jacob might still have had the same struggles. Remember when I told you I was learning more about forgiveness?"

Steven sucked in a breath. That night in Newport had marked a turning point for him. After she forgave him, he opened up more to her. He became more willing to face his shortcomings. And he realized more profoundly the ways in which he had hurt her and others close to him.

He gazed at her, puzzled once again. "What does forgiveness have to do with your anxiety?"

"I discovered the one person I couldn't forgive. Me. When I finally forgave myself for the ways I failed as a mother, it felt like a weight came off my shoulders. When I gave up the illusion that I could control my life through my performance, it was freeing."

He rubbed his chin. "Can you forgive me for my failings as a father? And as a husband?"

She smiled and reached out to touch his cheek. "I already have. And here's what really helped me. You've changed. That crystallized for me when you called from New York City in the middle of the biggest crisis of your life."

"Facing death has a way of re-ordering one's priorities."

"That's been apparent from the day you got back home. You're home for dinner almost every evening. And you spend more time with the boys. But the biggest difference is the way you relate to me. I feel so much closer to you."

"If only I had made these changes earlier." He sighed. "And I'm still worried about Jacob." *And will I ever be able to forgive myself for my failures as a father?*

Carissa spun around to face him. "I believe he's made a turn for the better."

"I see hopeful signs too. He seems to be taking his counseling seriously." He shook his head slightly. "But he still has a long way to go."

"You know what made the biggest difference?" She didn't wait for him to answer. "Your call from New York. Later, I told Jacob your life was in great danger when you called. He was stunned to learn that in your dire situation, he was the person you most wanted to talk to."

"I should have told him myself, but I'm glad you did."

Carissa put her hand on his arm. "Do you know what made the deepest impression on him?" This time she waited for him to answer.

"When I told him I loved him?" he guessed.

"That meant a lot to him, but that wasn't what impacted him most. It was your apology. Instead of feeling judged by you, he felt like you were with him in his struggle."

His simple apology had that much power? Amazing! Come to think of it, though, he rarely apologized. "I'll do everything I can to help him get his life back on track."

"He gets that now, at a deep-down level. That's why I'm confident he's going to make it."

He put his arms around her and whispered, "Yes, together, as a family, he'll make it. But no matter what happens, I'll always love him. Just like I'll always love you."

He leaned down to kiss her when the ringing of his phone stopped him short. "Wonder if it's one of the boys."

He pulled out his phone and grunted. "Hey, what's up John?"

"I just got a call from the Director. The President would like to meet with us tomorrow."

Steven wasn't sure he'd heard right. "Why does *the President* want to see us?"

Carissa's eyes widened.

"Don't know," John said.

"Who's the us?"

"Just you and me."

CHAPTER 78

The White House (September 15)

The President got up from behind his desk when Steven and John entered the Oval Office. "Welcome, Special Agent Kittrick and Dr. Carter." He gestured toward a couch as he sat on the opposite couch. "Please take a seat."

"Thank you, Mr. President," Steven and John replied in near unison. Steven steered around the prominent presidential seal in the center of the thick carpet. He rarely found himself awed, but he suddenly felt the need to sit down. The embodiment of American power was sitting across from him.

Smiling, the President opened his arms toward them. "I'm glad we could meet today. Even with all the global problems I've faced as president, I wasn't prepared, intellectually or emotionally, for the reality that terrorists came so close to unleashing a nuclear bomb on our country." He inclined his head toward them. "Stopping them involved many people, but I believe the two of you deserve much of the credit."

Steven was tempted to sneak a peek at John, but he kept his eyes fastened on the President.

"The main reason I asked to meet with you is to tell you, on behalf of our nation, thank you. Because of your perseverance, skill, and courage, a tragedy of almost incomprehensible dimensions was prevented. I'd like to honor you publicly, but as you know, I can't do that."

The President paused, then continued. "I can assure you, however, that I will include your role in my classified presidential records. One day, history will take note."

Steven said, "Thank you, Mr. President. Your words are more than honor enough."

John quickly echoed Steven's sentiment.

The President's tone became more informal. "One benefit of being the President is that I can have a conversation with just about anybody. As I understand it, Steven, without your early nuclear forensics work, this plot would've never been uncovered. Which means I probably wouldn't be alive today. So you have my very *personal* thanks as well."

The President looked directly at him. "The Director of National Intelligence has spoken with me about your scientific gut instinct. Could you tell me more about that? How you've developed it and how it played a role in this case?"

In the conversation that ensued, the President probed with many questions. After some time, there was a knock on the door. An assistant to the President stuck in her head to remind him he had to wrap up in five minutes.

The President became pensive. "On the subject of gut instincts, I have a gut feeling about you, Steven. You've already demonstrated the ability to go far beyond what any normal research scientist could do, but I believe you can do even more. That's why I'd like to invite you to join my National Security Council."

"I don't know what to say," Steven stammered. "I'm honored by your offer. But I'd like to talk it over with my wife first."

"Ah, a wise man."

"Do you have a specific role in mind?"

"Our country needs a more robust nuclear forensics capability, and we also need to convince the world that nuclear forensics should be a core component of nuclear security. I want you to develop a plan to accomplish both objectives. Beyond that, I'm sure we'll find other areas that would benefit from your scientific mind and ability to think outside the box."

"I assure you, I'll give this very serious consideration."

The President stood up. "I'm sure you will." He shook each of their hands as they said their goodbyes.

When they exited the West Wing, John turned to Steven. "You *are* going to accept his offer, aren't you?"

"We have some family issues to consider. But it'll be difficult to say no to the President."

John's eyes twinkled. "I'll keep my eye out for a place for you in Alexandria."

As Steven walked to the coffee shop where Carissa waited for him, his euphoria from the President's praise was tempered by the offer to join the NSC. He had his own doubts about such a drastic change in career, and it wouldn't surprise him if Carissa objected to a cross-country move at this delicate time in the life of their family.

When he stepped into the coffee shop, Carissa jumped to her feet. "What did the President have to say?" she asked when he reached her table.

He recounted the conversation and finished with the surprising offer to join the National Security Council. Startled, she asked tentatively, "Is that something you'd want to do?"

"Not sure. It's flattering for the President to ask, but it would mean I'd no longer be doing science. And we'd need to move to DC. On the other hand, I'll probably never have another opportunity like it. Let's take a couple days to consider it."

For a few moments, she silently gazed into his eyes. Her eyes softened as she reached across the table and grabbed both of his hands.

"Steven," she said. The way she said his name evoked the memory of their wedding day when she looked into his eyes and spoke her vows. "I'm so proud of you. I admire your perseverance, your courage, and all you've achieved." She squeezed his hands. "The President himself values your leadership and capabilities."

She tilted her head. "But right now, you know what I admire most about you? You've grown in humility. During this past year, when you persevered and reached the pinnacle of your career, you arrived as a more humble man. And kinder too. That's extraordinarily rare and I'm so thankful."

She saw him as more humble? He shook his head in amazement.

Humility had never been one of his goals, but today her words felt strangely affirming. Warmth radiated throughout his body as he absorbed her praise.

He reversed their grip, so he held her hands. He squeezed gently and said, "That's the most surprising compliment you've ever given me."

She jumped up and held out her arms. While they embraced, she said, "Let's get a taxi back to our hotel."

His heart full of joy, Steven ushered his wife outside, where a glorious sunny autumn day greeted them. They held hands as they waited for a taxi. *The longer I know you, Carissa, the more you're a mystery. You've been changing too, though I'm not sure how to describe it.*

"Carissa."

Her auburn hair swirled as she turned and said, "Yes?"

"Nothing is more important in my life than you."

Oh, I've got it. Grace. She's grown in grace.

Suddenly overcome with a profound sense of gratitude, he struggled to speak the words he wanted her to hear. "More than ever, I realize…" He paused in an effort to gain control of his emotions enough to finish. "You are a gift to me."

Her shining eyes spoke of her delight in his words, sparking a deeper joy in him. His lips trembled as he added, "A gift I don't deserve, but will treasure the rest of my life."

AUTHOR'S NOTE

When I started writing this book, I didn't aim to write a typical thriller. My goal was to create an engaging and entertaining story that illustrates the importance of nuclear forensics in combatting nuclear terrorism.

A secondary goal was to give readers an accurate picture of the science involved in a nuclear forensics investigation. But I hold a security clearance, so I had to respect the boundaries of classification. Moreover, I didn't want the book to serve as a how-to-do-it manual. To that end, I skipped lightly over many aspects of what's involved in making a nuclear bomb.

Although the story paints a reasonably accurate picture of how scientists work and think in this field, I also didn't want to risk massively disappointing the expectations of thriller readers. From writing experts, I often heard, "increase the level of conflict." That inspired me to cause Steven Carter to go rogue and circumvent the FBI order to stop the investigation. To the laymen, that might not seem like such an extraordinary move, but my beta readers who work at national laboratories objected. One wrote that perhaps several decades ago a national laboratory scientist might have taken such a drastic step, but no way would one do that in today's world.

Another expectation of a thriller reader is that the hero stays in the story until the very end, and of course she (or he) provides the resolution of the conflict that marks them as the hero. In today's world, the FBI would not use a scientist in the way John Kittrick uses Steven Carter. So, I invented the "scientist profiler." As I wrote the story, though, it seemed to me that it might be a good idea for the FBI to consider using scientists in this way. But I imagine the FBI wouldn't agree.

With regards to making the case for the importance of nuclear forensics, I co-wrote an *Arms Control Today* article in 2007 about the need to place greater importance on conducting nuclear forensics investigations of interdicted nuclear materials. Midway in writing the first draft of *Atomic Peril*, I realized I was making the same argument through the more compelling avenue of a thriller. In chapter 27, a quote is drawn directly from this article.

The International Technical Working Group (ITWG) is a real-world entity. In 1995, I chaired an International Conference on Nuclear Smuggling Forensic Analysis. At the end of this conference, we formed the ITWG. I co-chaired the ITWG for its first twelve years, giving it a culture and organizational structure that has served it well to this day. It's widely regarded as the international entity most responsible for global cooperation in the technical development of nuclear forensics.

Like the ITWG, most of the elements of the book related to nuclear forensics are drawn from the real-world. For example, the brief summary of the history and current status of TRIGA reactors is accurate. The nearly-forgotten aqueous homogeneous reactor was indeed explored during the Manhattan Project, and more recent research has proposed using it for medical isotope production. The most important exception is the Joint Romania-Moldova Nuclear Research Institute, which is purely a product of my imagination, for reasons that are obvious after you've read the book.

ACKNOWLEDGMENTS

Where do I start, with so many people to thank? My first reader comes to mind, my wife Debbie, who often after reading the first draft of a technical scene would say, "You need to dumb this down." Thanks for putting up with me spending much of the first four years of my retirement pounding away at my computer and enduring many nights when I couldn't sleep because I was trying to work out some aspect of the story.

Writing a thriller is quite different from writing a scientific article, and many people helped me learn the craft. Linda Clare was my first writing coach, who often wrote "RUE" in the margin, i.e., "resist the urge to explain." Jennifer Fisher was enormously helpful with her developmental edit of my second draft and a line edit of the third draft. I've learned much from the many faculty members at writers' conferences, especially the extensive fiction tracks taught by Bill Myers and James L. Rubart. A special thanks to my critique group, led by Debbie Jones Warren, and especially to Wendy Craig, who led our fiction sub-group and unfailingly provided the most helpful feedback.

I owe a great debt to my beta readers who provided valuable feedback at various junctures in my writing journey. In roughly the chronological order in which I received their input, thank you, Kathy Engel, Emily Greco, Colin Harthcock, Larry Niemeyer, Louis Tullo, Cassie MacDonald, Tom Jourdan, Stephen Hayes, Donna Beals, David Smith, Charlie Craft, Joe Ghiringhelli, William Daitch, and Amy Pendino. Special thanks to author Rick Acker, not only for his timely advice throughout this process, but when I didn't dare ask him to be a beta reader, he surprised me by volunteering.

Finally, my thanks to the global nuclear forensics community. Though I helped to foster this community early in its development, you have contributed so much to my own understanding. With far too many to thank individually, I'm grateful for Mike Kristo's support as my supervisor during my sixteen years as a part-time retiree, including his timely classification reviews.

SPECIAL THANKS TO MY LAUNCH TEAM

As I write this section, the work of my Launch Team lies in the future. But I'm thankful for each person who has volunteered to help spread the word about Atomic Peril. I'm confident this group will aid immeasurably in getting the book in the hands of readers who will enjoy and appreciate it. In anticipation of their efforts on my behalf, I offer my gratitude to: Rick Acker, Brenda Black, James Blankenship, Frank Burger, Noah Chiu, Barry Craner, William Daitch, Kathy Engel, Cheri Galt, Narek Gharibyan, Joe Ghiringhelli, Steve Glavan, Howard Hall, Randy Harman, Betsy Harrison, Colin Harthcock, Stephen Hayes, Tom Hutton, Thomas Jourdan, Ruth Kips, Kent Laws, Mark Lewis, Cassie MacDonald, Casey Millerick, Jennifer Mitchell, Debbie Niemeyer, Larry Niemeyer, Rick Pate, Amy Pendino, David Kenneth Smith, Carol Trebes, Jan Villott, Mark Wyse, and Rupert Young.

ABOUT THE AUTHOR

Why has Sidney Niemeyer been called a founding father of nuclear forensics? Among his scientific leadership roles at Lawrence Livermore National Laboratory (LLNL), he served as the Nuclear Chemistry Division Leader. In this role, he began to articulate the need to develop a nuclear forensics capability to address the new reality of a post-Cold-War world. In 1995 he chaired an international conference that led to the formation of the Nuclear Forensics International Technical Working Group (ITWG). He co-chaired the ITWG for its first twelve years, and to this day, it's recognized as the major international entity for the technical development of nuclear forensics.

When the Department of Homeland Security stood up, he convinced the transition team to include nuclear forensics in its counterterrorism research program. Soon after, he was asked to become a detailee to fill two roles: to lead the DHS research program for "RadNuc Forensics," and to work with the U.S. interagency to develop an integrated nuclear forensics capability. His work in this latter area reached fruition with the formation of the National Technical Nuclear Forensics Center (NTNFC). During the first year of the NTNFC, he was its scientific advisor, and he joined its Nuclear Forensics Science Panel when he retired from LLNL in 2007.

Over the years, he became painfully aware of how few people have even heard of this new field of nuclear forensics. Four years ago, he drew upon his love of science and thrillers to begin writing *Atomic Peril*. The aim of every thriller is to entertain, and while he believes his novel meets this mark, he hopes even more it will show the critical importance of this capability for deterring and responding to nuclear terrorism.

For more information about Sidney Niemeyer and his thriller writing, visit his website at sidneyniemeyer.com. To keep updated on his writing journey, subscribe to his newsletter by scrolling to the bottom of the home page.